PRAISE FOR

TOWN & COUNTRY

"Refreshingly thoughtful . . . clever . . . There's a poised elegance to Schaefer's prose in this confident debut novel, the sense of a writer who appreciates when to jab and when to comfort. *Town & Country* is never short of engaging."

—Ron Charles, *The Washington Post*

"*Town & Country* is so thoughtfully and beautifully written, I could read it over and over again. A rumination on who we think we are versus who we really are, on loyalties and betrayals, family and politics, and, above all, love. It is a book to bring us together. Bighearted and true, it will capture readers' hearts as it did mine."

—Andrew Sean Greer, Pulitzer Prize–winning author of *Less*

"Flush with gripping and sharply drawn characters . . . *Town & Country* is about contrasts: gay vs. straight, gentrifiers vs. the gentrified, marriage vs. divorce, rugged individualism vs. the public good. Schaefer explores the gray areas that complicate those binaries with a profound and admirable empathy."

—*The New York Times Book Review*

"In Schaefer's intelligent debut novel . . . contemporary American anxieties about belonging, change, and community are vividly explored. . . . Schaefer resists easy satire, instead plumbing the emotional terrain of six converging lives. . . . What emerges is a novel that is both keenly attuned to regional specificity and surprisingly universal in scope."

—*Chronogram*

"A thoroughly engaging and intelligent debut, brimming with insight and a sense of place."

—*Kirkus Reviews* (starred review)

"*Town & Country* uses a light and humorous touch to lure us to some profound and moving places. Brian Schaefer gets to the heart and soul of our current predicament: the suspicions, divisions, and other-izing that blinker us to all we have in common as humans whose greatest need is to connect."

—Geraldine Brooks, Pulitzer Prize–winning author of *March* and *Horse*

"An enchanting debut—a powerfully urgent story about communal and familial loyalty and the politics of place. With prose that's as propulsive as it is precise, Brian Schaefer announces himself as an author of unique sensitivity and depth, delivering sharp observances with elegance and wit. This is a heart-filled, generous, and unabashedly entertaining book. And it's a book we need right now, in town, in the country, and beyond."

—Colum McCann, National Book Award–winning author of *Let the Great World Spin*

"Engrossing . . . [Schaefer] has his finger on the pulse in this appealing story of a battleground district."

—*Publishers Weekly*

"Sparkling with wit, truth, and unforgettable characters, *Town & Country* is a dazzling debut. As necessary as it is fun, as heartbreaking as it is hopeful, this is the novel we all need."

—Cat Shook, author of *If We're Being Honest* and *Humor Me*

"Engaging, empathetic, and often heartbreakingly authentic . . . An auspicious debut."

—*Booklist*

TOWN & COUNTRY

A Novel

BRIAN SCHAEFER

ATRIA PAPERBACK

New York Amsterdam/Antwerp London
Toronto Sydney/Melbourne New Delhi

ATRIA
PAPERBACK
An Imprint of Simon & Schuster, LLC
1230 Avenue of the Americas
New York, NY 10020

This book is a work of fiction. Any references to historical events, real people, or real places are used fictitiously. Other names, characters, places, and events are products of the author's imagination, and any resemblance to actual events or places or persons, living or dead, is entirely coincidental.

First Atria Paperback edition July 2026

Interior design by Davina Mock-Maniscalco

Manufactured in the United States of America

1 3 5 7 9 10 8 6 4 2

Library of Congress Control Number: 2024058720

ISBN 978-1-6680-8689-6
ISBN 978-1-6680-8690-2 (pbk)
ISBN 978-1-6680-8691-9 (ebook)

For Mom & Dad,
and Stephen—
My two homes.

MEMORIAL DAY

BY TEN O'CLOCK ON Monday morning, there's a line out the door of every coffee shop on Granger Street. The sidewalks steam with the breath of a hundred lattes and bubble with the excitement of a preshow theater lobby. On each block, young families claim prime curbside seats, the unyoung assemble frayed folding chairs, tourists unknowingly plant themselves on corners soon to be in the sun's harsh spotlight, and local teens lean against storefronts, insisting with crossed arms that they're here ironically, not because this parade has signaled the start of summer since they were kids and missing it would feel somehow vaguely inauspicious. Definitely not.

In the staging area next to small, neglected Van Deventer Square, a municipal microcosm prepares for its annual display. Frazzled volunteers consult clipboards, count heads, and pass out silk-screened T-shirts that stamp each participant by whatever civic affiliation they've chosen for today. Children race around a dry fountain as their parents demand they *stop this instant* so sunscreen can be applied.

Nearby, on a patch of hopeful grass, a banner with a red-star rainbow proclaims Chip Riley for Congress. The bearded, brawny candidate, wearing his uniform of a thick plaid shirt tucked into dark blue jeans, studies his printed name with a glare of incredulity, as if unsure whether it really refers to him. Nearby, his wife, Diane, wearing a tasteful white sundress—new from the secondhand shop—reapplies lipstick. The campaign banner hangs indifferently between two reluctant recruits, Joe and Will, their sons, both lanky, freckled, and sullen-faced, each grasping one end of the wooden pole. The rest of the Riley contingent, a small unit of antsy staff and supporters, roam about chattering with friends and neighbors.

As per tradition, the Griffin Memorial Day Parade begins with a minute of silence in honor of fallen soldiers, followed by the wail of a fire engine. Just after ten, the vehicular beast rolls into position. Its long boxy red bulk and white trim set against this beaming sky—a blessing in blue—is almost a patriotic cliché, never mind the dozen American mini-flags flickering from its ladder, making the top of the truck dance like a candled birthday cake. The same can be said of Granger itself, lined with honey locusts and Old Glories fluttering from double-branched streetlamps that jog for a mile until they halt at the banks of the Munsee River.

The truck flashes its lights and begins to creep forward, its imposing size undermined by its comical slowness. Behind it, a marching band announces itself with a brassy blast reminiscent of a Friday night football game. Then comes the caravan of delegations, each little network representing some vital facet of Griffin's identity. Among them: a regiment of multi-generational veterans, a local dance studio, a social justice farming collective, and a flock of Girl Scouts leading a massive, slightly malevolent, inflated bald eagle on a dozen leashes. The quilt of an eclectic community, ready to take the asphalt stage.

Soon it's the Rileys' turn. At the signal of a parade coordinator, Diane and her family enter the gauntlet of Granger and are met with cheers. They proceed through the center of their hometown with the ease and authority of lifelong residents, the road unfurling before them as if it were their own driveway. This street contains Griffin's history, its storefronts testimony to the region's cycles of depression and reinvention. It contains Diane's own history as well: Nana's Diner on the next block, where Chip courted her a quarter century ago; and on the right, the Lucky Buck, the pub he has owned for the past fourteen years, now a member of the family that she tolerates like a rowdy brother-in-law.

Yet for all its intimate familiarity, Granger also confronts Diane with its fancy new boutiques and bakeries, reflecting the town's recent striking transformation. Walking down Granger's spine, she ponders how much the town has changed since her youth and how much it hasn't. It retains its inviting scale; it hasn't expanded or contracted or even seemed to age, really. It has simply transitioned from one expression of itself to another, with the old toy and candy stores eventually replaced by this gourmet tea shop and that high-end hair salon. During the last economic drought a decade ago, a smattering of boarded-up windows had broadcast Griffin's desperation, making Granger look like a sinister grin with missing teeth. Now the handful of empty windows with "For Lease" signs declares the town's newfound allure and the hungry churn of desirable space. None of those windows will stay empty for long.

Diane is so sure because Griffin's popularity has been a boon for her real estate practice. Which means she knows the Lucky Buck's current retail value and that its lease is up in a year. It is unclear whether Chip will be able to afford a new one. But the question may be moot, depending on the outcome of this race. If Chip wins, he'll have to give up the Buck anyway or temporarily entrust it to someone else. They've only briefly discussed these contingencies, but Diane wonders if he has fully considered the cost of winning and what he might lose in the process.

In the meantime, she watches him zigzag the street, as if sewing up Granger with a cross-stitch, shaking hands and waving to acquaintances. He looks invigorated, allowing his lopsided grin to peek through his mottled brown-gray beard. For the first time since he announced his candidacy, Diane is almost glad he's running. His genuine enjoyment, rarely so visible, gives her the pleasure of a seasonal flower's brief bloom.

In front of his mother, Will tugs down the bill of his baseball cap and readjusts his hold on the campaign banner. He stares at the street, tracking the dashes of yellow paint that bisect it, childishly imagining that if he doesn't look up, he won't be seen. Why do public appearances with his family at nineteen inspire the same mortifying indignity as when he was in middle school? Maybe because then, as now, it signaled a failure of independence, even though he just completed his first year at college—only the state school an hour away, but still. He should be on campus right now, where he'd intended to stay this summer, staffing the athletic center by day, stumbling drunk between dorms at night, perhaps into the bed of the husky baseball player with the Cheshire grin, all while pretending his hometown is farther away than it is.

But then his father decided to run for national office, his brother's best friend OD'd, and his mother, in an uncharacteristically wobbly voice, asked him to come home.

So now he's carrying this unwieldy sign—supposedly an honor, but it feels more like punishment—and now he'll spend another summer behind the bar of the Lucky Buck, where he has worked for his father for the past three years. He glimpses the pub's black awning on his right and its long narrow windows of unlit liquor logos. He pictures the dull scene behind that unassuming door: the cracked brown leather booths, battered billiards table, mounted stag heads, and chunky TVs protruding from wood-paneled walls like malignant moles. A stage set as well known to him as his childhood bedroom. The daring side of him, still stubbornly submerged, had considered defying his family and taking a job at one of the swanky spots on Granger instead, aligning himself with the new, attractive, unaffordable Griffin. It would have been a kind of protest after the friction of last year, after they so profoundly failed him. But Will Riley remains unclear on his current status in the family, so he is here, marching beside them. Because while he may be hurt and resentful, he is not, by nature, rebellious.

He walks on, obedient as ever, past the pizza parlor with its checkered tablecloths where he celebrated many a birthday, the deli with its proud foot-longs, and the new gourmet grocery store with its inexplicable lavender yogurts and blueberry beers. His end of the pole now hangs at his waist, giving the banner a severe slant. Will looks to his older, taller brother in a futile attempt to commiserate and correct the sign's imbalance. But Joe is looking straight ahead, committed to his stoicism, holding the pole high.

As they approach the chrome curves and vintage signage of Nana's Diner, Joe lowers his head, allowing his limp chin-length hair to fall around his face. He shuts his eyes and tries again to swallow the stone that's been stuck in his throat for almost a month. He continues forward in this waking sleepwalk, consoled and unnerved by his momentary blindness. After several long, dark steps, he opens his eyes, but his hair continues to act as blinders, blocking Nana's from his peripheral vision, erasing the place that figures so prominently in Riley family lore and in his own happy bygone summers. Here's where his parents met and here's where he used to gather with his rambunctious friends, cramming eight to a red vinyl booth, scouring the seemingly limitless menu they'd already memorized, no meal complete without one of Nana's famous milkshakes, that frothy vanilla heirloom passed from generation to generation.

And no visit worthwhile without Matt's bark of a laugh, his wide arms splayed across the booth's back, spanning its width, embracing them all. Matt, three weeks gone. Joe is here at the parade because his parents insisted, because he couldn't form the words to resist, because it's safer than being alone. He takes a step, then another, drifting in a stupor of grief and other substances, trying to remember how a Nana's milkshake tastes.

FARTHER DOWN GRANGER, the marching band attempts a jazzy orchestration of a pop song while a flatbed carrying the social justice farmers hiccups over a speed bump, sending a bale of hay somersaulting off the back, shedding hair like a golden retriever. The bale comes to a rest in the center of the street, becoming a prickly, imminent hazard for the approaching dance studio, causing a buzz of concern among the spectators.

The commotion reaches Eric Larimer, a new part-time Griffin resident who stands in a cluster of effervescent men in bright shirts, short shorts, and designer sunglasses—among them his husband, Alex, wearing the brightest of shirts and shortest of shorts. The men have been circled up conspiratorially for much of the parade, passing around a surreptitious bottle of rosé, frequently erupting in hot spurts of laughter and self-satisfaction as they await the arrival of a black convertible carrying their friends. Now they turn to the street, tickled by the amateur circus passing by. Phones emerge to document the scene, later to be cleverly captioned. Like Eric, most of these men have homes here—second homes, to be clear—and most washed into town with the recent wave of migrants from the city, drawn to Griffin's trumpeted mix of trendy and quaint.

Eric is still surprised to find himself with a mailbox and mortgage here. Alex, the more aspirational of them, dreamed for years of a second home as a symbol of social ascendence. Eric dismissed the idea as extravagant, unnecessary, and financially unfeasible. But when he began to tire of the overstuffed urban life they've shared for more than a decade, and started to fret that their relationship was quietly rusting into complacency, he agreed that a place to escape might do them good. It was Alex who chose Griffin for its confluence of prestige and relative affordability, given its increasingly upscale town center and ample surrounding land. Sensing Eric's lingering skepticism of their big purchase, Alex suggested that Eric spend the summer here to better acquaint himself with the area, and Eric accepted the challenge, a perk of being a freelance graphic designer. This parade is the kickoff to his experiment in rural residency.

On Granger, the approaching tiny dancers spot the runaway hay and break formation to shriek at the obstacle, save for an oblivious child who stumbles right into and over it. Spectators gasp, stifle laughter, touch their throats with worry. When it's clear the little one is rattled but fine, his teacher prompts him to take a bow, which is rewarded with a wild ovation that turns his stunned, quivering frown into a toothless grin. Right behind him come the veterans in their starched uniforms and noble expressions, stepping expertly around the bale, though one former soldier hesitates as if considering defensive action until the swift current of the parade sweeps her along. A few feet later, she looks back with a flat expression of resigned acceptance.

Eric's clique is enraptured by this minor drama, fully invested in the parade now that it holds a hint of innocuous danger, now that it has provided them with an anecdote to bring back to the city.

From the opposite curb, Leon Rogers ignores the street spectacle and instead observes those spirited short-shorted men with irritation and envy. He, too, has recently moved to Griffin, albeit under unfortunate circumstances that make it feel more like an exile. He seeks a fresh start but knows no one in this town and has had few social interactions in the months since his arrival, other than polite conversations with various shopkeepers and baristas. He rents a small apartment above a pottery shop in one of Granger's old brick buildings and heard the clamor of the parade from his kitchen window this morning. He stubbornly ignored the crowds until he was hit with a furious urge to join them. At street level, a stranger smiled at him. It was a small, automatic act, but it seemed to contain a kind of universal goodwill, and suddenly Leon felt embraced by the town in a way he hadn't yet felt, as if the theater of the parade also included a performance of communal generosity. The proximity of all this humanity had a revitalizing effect until those men showed up, flaunting their fellowship, illustrating what he still lacks. They remind Leon of what he was forced to leave behind in the city, what he is determined to regain here: the reassurance of a social circle to drown out the loneliness and self-doubt.

A shadow drenches the sidewalk. Leon looks up into the bulging black eyes of a massive bald eagle. A predator ten yards long with an austere white head, enormous yellow beak, and matching talons, wrapped in a skin of taut, glistening plastic, breathing helium. A frightening vision of liberty but adorable, too, as led by an army of green-vested Girl Scouts.

Then a piercing squeal. Encountering the hay, one of the Scouts has released her string, sending the troop into a tizzy. Other strings are relinquished, the bird's hardware gets knocked about in the chaos, and swiftly begins to hiss and descend as if diving for prey. One squeal becomes many, accompanied by a fair amount of scrambling. The parade stutters to a halt in front of Eric and Leon. But up ahead, it continues to bounce blithely along as the band strikes up a Sousa march.

Several onlookers rush to assist, ushering the children away from the great collapsing bird. After a hectic minute of examination, one of the first responders diagnoses a loose valve and calls for air. A woman in a large sun hat suggests the sporting goods shop one block away, and a chubby dad in gray sweats hands off his kid to sprint in that direction. Then nothing. After the burst of thrilling activity, boredom settles over the crowd as they wait for the parade to resume. Within a few minutes, the chubby dad is back with an air pump, and soon the raptor is revived. No longer flying high on gas but inflated enough for half a dozen adult volunteers to carry the rest of the way.

A great cheer erupts for the quick-thinking heroes, which Eric contributes to, though his cup of rosé makes awkward his applause. A little crest of wine breaches the rim, blotches the sidewalk, and splatters a man nearby, who looks down and laughs, unbothered. But the mishap, however minor, embarrasses Eric. It seems to indict him and his friends for their brash gaiety and immobility in the face of the rogue eagle. None of them had made a move to help; none of them had thought to. And that passive indifference now feels to Eric very unneighborly.

HALF A MILE back, the parade's few remaining participants look around absently, wondering why the procession has stopped. Stan Banks fidgets in the back of a black convertible with large door magnets announcing Paul Banks, his husband, for Congress as Paul sits beside him with a nervous, expectant, unconvincing grin. The engine is off, and they are exhausted, having been kept awake last night by a shrill cricket that was eventually flushed silent. They've been here for almost two hours, as per their call time, despite being among the last in the lineup. Stan smells a conspiracy, given that Paul's opponent, Chip Riley, is the town supervisor. The Bankses, in contrast, are new to Griffin, residents only a year and resented for that fact, as made clear by the surprising number of articles, blog posts, social media rants, and even a *Griffin Gazette* editorial harping on the apparent insult of their recent inhabitancy.

As they wait, the sun laughs at Stan's outfit. He insisted they wear suits, arguing that it would make Paul look older than his thirty-two years and thus project a more serious image of someone ready to represent the citizens of the Twenty-sixth District. But the day is warming quickly. Sweaters are being discarded, and no one else appears fool enough to mistake this event for a board meeting. As sweat trickles down his back, Stan curses his miscalculation.

Finally, the local 4H chapter ahead of them stirs, stretches, and begins to saunter down Granger. The convertible shudders to life and crawls after them along the blacktop tributary, now littered with confetti and assorted debris. Stan narrows his gaze and adopts an expression just friendly enough not to be off-putting. He doesn't know how to enjoy a parade. The last time he participated in a similar procession was decades ago, but that was an angry march, a crusade, a requiem for all those devoured by AIDS. His chest reflexively locks, his shoulders rise, his jaw clenches. The physical memory of protest. His guard is up, and so is his chin.

Next to him and nearly a quarter century younger, Paul has none of Stan's trauma, but he is clearly uneasy. His wave, for example, is stiffly regal. Noticing this, Stan experiences a jolt of self-disgust. What must they look like—in these suits, in this car, with that mechanical gesture—to those lawn-chair spectators in sports apparel? Foreigners, he answers himself. Outsiders. Carpetbaggers chasing the region's political potential for personal ambition. Not entirely inaccurate but an impression Paul will have to combat by November, or at least mitigate enough to earn their trust and their vote. Stan's stomach plummets at the immensity, the near impossibility, of that task and how little time they have to accomplish it.

But here comes a tsunami of enthusiastic hoots to their left. Stan sees the little all-male pep section made up of their friends, eyes shielded in their fashionable shades, arms raised and flapping, legs exposed to midthigh like a squad of high school cheerleaders. An absurd picture, but a comforting one, and a reminder that he and Paul do have a small community here, and that beyond their insular network is an existing and growing constituency in the region amenable to their perspective and possible representation. With the district's deep purple nature and rapidly shifting demographics, Paul might actually have a long shot if he plays it smart.

That little surge of encouragement gives way to a tugging undertow of humility. They cannot forget that they are here to make a difference, that their constituents are their top priority, that any residual career upside for Paul is just frosting, not to be publicly discussed. Or so their campaign consultants repeatedly remind them.

Stan sees that the sounds of support and the sight of affable faces have thawed Paul's rigidity, spurring him to remove his coat, roll up his sleeves, and begin to wave vigorously at his friends with the freedom of his entire torso. Watching Paul loosen up inspires in Stan a flash of awe toward his young husband—*husband!* a most remarkable, once unimaginable thing—who is seeking a position of power on behalf of all these people, many so unlike them. Stan assumes that, given the district's political promiscuity—the seat has flipped twice in the past three cycles, every race a toss-up—at least half of this crowd is predisposed against Paul. But if so, they have been smiling and waving back anyway, like this old man with a shar-pei face who lifts a hand to Stan in a kind of salute. He's not exactly smiling, but the tacit acknowledgment dents Stan's skepticism and inspires him to remove his own coat. He rolls up his sleeves and discovers a breeze that brushes his forearms, bringing with it a new benevolence toward this town and a rush of optimism for the race ahead.

Then it's over. They've arrived at the end of Granger, where the street meets the Munsee. The river is at its widest here—imposing, majestic, sweeping south with its own parade of tiny whitecaps, floating leaves, and the glinting backs of trout, bass, sturgeon, and pike. The previously distinct parade groups blend into a contaminated puddle. Musicians mingle with politicians, farmers mix with Girl Scouts still giddy from their ordeal, bystanders reunite with participants, and everyone helps themselves to bags of popcorn. The Riley family turns around and begins walking back to Chip's pub, where he'll host an afternoon meet-and-greet, while the Bankses keep driving, their convertible headed to another Memorial Day event in the next town over.

By noon, the crowds have dispersed, Griffin's busiest tourist season has officially begun, and the election is less than six months away.

JUNE

CHAPTER 1

ON A SUNNY SUNDAY morning after the parade, Diane Riley's heels sink into damp grass. Why does she insist on wearing such shoes, given the requirements of her job to traverse lawns, meadows, and fields? Because, she answers herself with proud impatience, the kinds of houses she now sells require her to project refinement. Her city clients—like these two eager men following her across the front yard of a splendid eighteenth-century farmhouse—expect polish. Her former attire of sneakers, boots, and fleece zip-ups just won't do. It's also why she had purchased this silk blouse, on clearance at All4Less but never mind, and splurged on the blond streaks that brighten her short tawny hair. (For local clients, the fleece and boots return. Can't appear too fussy.)

It's all projection, she knows. No one has ever commented on, or even seemed to register, her appearance. But it's about how she presents herself, about embodying confidence and believing her locally grown tastes are credible to this burgeoning category of clientele who seek not to swap their urban life but to supplement it.

The Duffels, they're called by her friends and neighbors, by cashiers and mechanics, by her chatty hairdresser and the cheerful but caustic women at the DMV. She can't recall when or where she first heard the term. Perhaps whispered at church, or dismissively dropped in a social media post, or angrily slung about in the comments section of *The Griffin Gazette* articles about rising rental costs and another new microbrewery. In any case, about five years ago, the phrase seemed to surface in half her conversations. After some confusion, she learned that the nicknamesake referred to the small satchels carried by weekenders as they disembark from trains and cars, the only bag necessary since, whether they're antiquing or apple picking, staying at a hotel or in a second home, attending outdoor performances or extravagant rustic nuptials, they won't be sticking around past Monday.

When their numbers began to swell, many locals spoke of the Duffels with both mild irritation and grave concern, unsure whether these stylish aliens had landed with benign or malicious intent. Diane, who considered herself a staunch champion of her hometown, initially shared in the collective disdain and was among the more vocal of the Duffels' early detractors.

But by this point she was also selling homes. And quite unexpectedly, Duffels began calling with interest in her most expensive listings, regularly paying over asking, offering cash. Diane started to wonder what good it did to resist their arrival. If they were coming anyway, why not benefit from welcoming them?

Her evolution on the matter, illustrated by new ads placed in identifiably Duffel territory on Granger Street, earned her a few awkward encounters at church and a slew of nasty remarks online. Her entrepreneurial pivot was ungenerously interpreted, even by close friends, as crass capitalizing on Griffin's newfound popularity. But they misunderstood her. She is still a staunch champion of Griffin, just now as its promoter rather than its guard. Perhaps she is ambitious, yes. But she is ambitious on behalf of her town, wanting for it the same prosperity she wants for her family.

Her ambition—like Griffin's, like most ambition—was born from desperation and a feeling of being undervalued. When the Rileys were struggling, her return to work kept them afloat. She worked so Will could go to college, she worked to keep Joe stable, she worked so Chip could serve this community as essentially a glorified volunteer. She works with the Duffels to prove that success can be homegrown in Griffin—and because if she doesn't, enterprising Duffels will cater to their own.

So now, out of a genuine if convenient shift in perspective, she has come to consider the Duffels largely harmless, like the field mice, wolf spiders, milk snakes, and brown marmorated stink bugs that infest the area. More annoyance than danger; a self-isolating species. And, as evidenced by these two eager men behind her, a lucrative wellspring of prospective buyers.

She rushes up the front steps to the wraparound porch and turns to them, smiling. Even if they don't notice her aesthetic efforts, she notices theirs: the same contrived version of "rural" she has come to expect. The tall, skinny one with the mustache wears pastel plaid. The short, stocky one with the neat beard also wears plaid, but in a more vivid palette. Each shirt is tucked into complementary-colored shorts that land well above the knee, all carrying the sheen of affluence. It's as if they're testing a country wardrobe, or its elevated approximation, to match their imagined country house. Diane finds this pastoral cosplay endearing, if a tad ridiculous.

She pauses before opening the front door, building anticipation. She warns them that this house has stayed in one family for over half a century, spanning three generations, which makes it special but a tad shabby, in need of sophisticated stewards.

"This home has been loved deeply," she tells them. "But it could use some attention and a bold vision. I think you'll know exactly what to do with it."

She ushers them inside the small foyer, covered in fading floral wallpaper. She lets them take in the space, adjust to its pearly light, turn a slow circle to orient themselves to the snug living room, the dining room with a pendant chandelier over fresh-cut flowers, a glimpse of the charmingly retro kitchen. She watches their eyes scan dark wood floors, colorful rugs, antique fixtures, and furniture scuffed by the affection of family. She sees a dozen such homes each month, but she knows the effect of these scenes on those more accustomed to cold metal finishes and frosty marble. She senses that they're smitten, that this might be just what they've been looking for.

She waits a moment, then breaks the spell, proposing renovation projects small and large, firing up their imagination, flattering their style.

She knows a great contractor, not to jump the gun. As their minds swirl with plans to host dinner parties and family holidays, she nudges them upstairs, first to the smaller bedrooms and finally to the largest, which features two walls of windows overlooking a petit pond and undulating hills in the distance.

Pastel plaid draws breath and places a hand on the back of vivid plaid, who reciprocates.

Diane notices the matching rings, but she didn't need confirmation. Of course they're married, because God has a sly sense of humor and a knack for imaginative punishment. These men have been sent to her, she is sure, in response to her self-serving embrace of the Duffels, her struggle with her son, and as payback for her efforts eight years ago when she co-chaired a church group fighting a same-sex-marriage bill.

Back then she filled her home with strategy sessions, letter-writing campaigns, and the buttery smell of fresh-baked oatmeal raisin cookies she served to her fellow devotees and to her sons. In the end, of course, marriage rights were granted. Her campaign was a political failure and, she would learn abruptly a few years later, a familial one as well. She hadn't once considered that the issue she so passionately opposed would one day be so personally relevant. Ironically, though, her defeat has turned out to be an unexpected professional blessing. For the sake of her clients, she has arrived at a stiff forbearance on the matter, accepting God's test with tempered grace and a three-quarter smile.

She still can't believe there are so many of them—husbands, impossibly plural—and that somehow they have all found their way to her. Well, it's not a mystery. It's called referrals, it's how her business works, and it's why business has never been better: because the types of homes these husbands seek (sizable, secluded, possessing some elusive quality they call "character") are several tiers above the homes she sells to locals (unassuming, practical, proximate to schools and neighbors), and because these husbands and their fellow Duffels have little sense of the rural market, little appetite to learn, and come with an urgency that translates into quick deals. In any event, she shoulders her fate and the accompanying discomfort. She has become adept at performing acceptance.

Discomfort, however, makes her gossipy, and just as she's about to share some dishy intel about the affair and impending divorce that has forced the sale of this property, she catches herself. Instead she asks, "Did you see the latest issue of *National Holiday*?"

Of course they have, they are its target subscribers. That glossy travel and lifestyle magazine's recent cover story on Griffin—"The Best Big Small Town in America"—and its so-called renaissance is responsible for the tidal wave of real estate inquiries this summer. But it's worth reminding her clients that they're investing in a verified hot spot. She quotes the article's breathless descriptions of restaurants, popular outdoor excursions, and the cultural abundance of the broader Munsee River Region, with its robust schedule of summer festivals currently under way. The men smile at each other, reassured of their discernment.

Diane hates promoting such slobbering profiles, but she knows that she, too, is selling a story, one that promises a bucolic, ostensibly simpler life with all the same perks and comforts as the city. Serene, but with a side of creative energy, and matcha. Which isn't to say the article is a fabrication. It's just curated, as it's allowed to be. And she can't deny her surprise, even a spark of pride, at seeing her hometown suddenly deemed so desirable.

But it's not the Griffin she knows. Not the modest, middling Griffin of her childhood nor the Griffin she inhabits, which extends well beyond the tiny, shiny stretch of Granger Street so lavishly depicted in *National Holiday*'s pages. Her Griffin comprises the big box stores on Kinghill Road, the industrial mile where she bought this blouse; the modest church where she began this day in worship; the linoleum-floored supermarket where she'll shop later for frozen dinners, with coupons; the hardware store where her elder son works—a godsend that she prays will help him through these dark days. And, of course, there are Nana's Diner and the Lucky Buck.

The latter two are also on Granger but were excluded from the article. An old-time eatery and a local dive don't fit *National Holiday*'s revival narrative. Nor, she imagines, would such establishments appeal to these plaid partners, who look at her with an expression she knows well: They have fallen in love with this house. As usual, the realization delivers a sweet dose of relief and accomplishment, as well as the familiar tart aftertaste of making a deal with the Duffels. She used to call that flavor remorse, when she was more self-conscious and defensive about participating in Griffin's burgeoning second-home market. But that's too burdensome a term to apply to a job she loves. Now she calls it defiance.

A FEW MILES away, Stan Banks weaves through the rows of folding tables at the Griffin farmers market, a seasonal weekly bazaar in the shell of an old barn at a small municipal park. The space features vendors displaying their glistening early-summer produce—asparagus, beets, rhubarb, squash—as well as those hawking baked goods, jarred sauces and jams, lotions and potions made of floral oils, and a variety of homemade crafts from pottery to jewelry to little knit hats with animal ears intended for some unfortunate child. And one table peddles a politician, his husband.

Stan watches as Paul attempts to hand a flyer to a short, plump woman with long gray hair carrying a basket of curly lettuces. Paul smiles widely but succeeds only in scaring her off. Stan looks at his watch. It is eleven. He hasn't been here long and won't stay much longer. He appreciates local food as much as anyone, but he's wearing leather loafers and prefers not to shop on dirt. Besides, the morning has been largely uneventful. Only four people have paused at Paul's table in the past hour, and two were surprised to learn there is a congressional race this fall. As someone who follows off-year elections the way others closely follow off-season sports, Stan finds it confounding that most of his fellow Americans are largely ignorant of, and indifferent to, the political cycle. Sometimes he envies their unawareness.

However, one person at the market saw Paul at the Memorial Day parade and has signed up for a phone-banking shift on Tuesday, an exercise in proactive political engagement that intrigues Stan because his own involvement, while substantial, is far more detached. He'll host events for those in his various influential circles and write big, meaningful checks.

But those are easy, impersonal acts compared to cold-calling strangers to vouch for another stranger. Stan finds such courage impressive, if a bit suspect in its blind trust.

In the absence of politically curious shoppers, Paul chats with the vendor to his left, a dairy producer surrounded by ice-packed coolers of raw milk, butter, and cheese. Paul will probably end up buying some of each—as well as meat from the meat woman and eggs from the egg guy—just to ingratiate himself, most of which will go to waste because Stan and Paul don't cook. Neither of them has the passion nor the patience. In the city, they only ever ate out or ordered in, and they've imported that habit with them to Griffin. In the year they've lived here, they've become regulars at the town's good restaurants and fans of the prepared foods at Poppy's Pantry, Griffin's upscale grocery store. These days Paul sometimes eats on the road as he crosses the district, subjecting himself to breaded chicken strips, all manner of chowders, and all-day omelets for the sake of connecting with "regular folks." Stan never joins him. There are limits to his spousal support.

Has it really been just over a year since they embarked on this improbable odyssey? To Stan, it feels like a lifetime. But it was indeed only last spring when Stan's old friend Serge mentioned that his congresswoman was not seeking reelection. Serge and his husband, Luke, had bought a house in Griffin a few years ago, when Serge became the director of a prestigious theater festival nearby. Though they kept an apartment in the city, they changed their voter registration to the sprawling farmland of the Twenty-sixth District because, they boasted, "our vote actually matters there." Upon further examination, Stan agreed that the region's ideological range, its commonplace economic issues, and its nationwide obscurity meant it could be precisely the kind of low-profile springboard he sought to launch Paul's legislative career. And after a few terms representing the Twenty-sixth, steadily building national name recognition, who knows where Paul could go from here? Stan accepts that this may make them look like political opportunists, but isn't everyone? It doesn't mean Paul will be any less committed to his constituents.

The decision to move to Griffin and enter this race was also one of impatience. Stan has long been looking for the opportunity to make this strategic move. Decades ago, at a personal crossroads, he could have committed to advocacy, dedicated himself to nonprofits, taken a vow of activism. But he was worn out, empty from fighting, and afraid that he would spend his life professionally angry. So he chose a path that has granted him the means to replace emotional dedication with financial and thus political clout. His ongoing doubt about this tradeoff ensures that he always gives generously, and Paul is now part of that project, a beneficiary of Stan's deep pockets and deeper guilt. If Paul succeeds—if this young gay man enters Congress—Stan can imagine no greater fulfillment of his promise to his community, nor a more emphatic justification of his bargain with himself.

So with that unspoken understanding, they made a soggy visit to Griffin last spring, then a Rothko-esque landscape of blurred browns and grays that did not persuade them of the area's homesteading appeal. But a flurry of research by a pair of pricey consultants (Stan's first big check) confirmed the district's political viability, and soon the Bankses were visiting regularly, imitating residents while based out of Serge and Luke's guest room, attending county barbecues, and meeting small business owners across the district while introducing themselves as philanthropic investors. Stan had an idea to launch the Griffin Investment Group (his second, bigger check) to disperse loans with attractive rates as a way to build quick, fruitful relationships in the community. Among the beneficiaries: a craft brewing company, a husband-and-wife florist shop, and a gluten-free bakery, all of which are represented here today at the farmers market.

That expensive initiative was well received. Celia Rhodes, the bespectacled junior reporter for *The Griffin Gazette,* even wrote a small, friendly profile on the group last fall, which gave the operation—and the Bankses, by extension—a nice gloss of legitimacy. This spring, when she informed them that she'd be covering the congressional campaign for the paper, Stan was pleased. He assumed a young Black woman would be politically predisposed to Paul's platform, and while naturally he expected complete objectivity and dispassion from her, he hoped Celia might prove to be a tad more amenable to Paul's campaign than to Chip's. But that illusion burst after she reported the embarrassing fact that Paul had filed to run in the Twenty-sixth District before escrow on their new home had closed, before he'd even registered to vote here. An unfortunate oversight and one that Stan felt really didn't need to be broadcast to the entire town. He'd argued this to her, but Celia had published anyway.

The Bankses ultimately found their home through the same real estate agent who had helped Serge and Luke find their lovely nineteenth-century Colonial. She was amusingly gaudy—clothes too serious, highlights too blond, jewelry too big—but shrewd and straightforward and delightfully gossipy. Stan enjoyed her sharp, chatty company and imagined that when he and Paul were settled, they would invite her and her husband out for dinner. After they closed on their house—an angular structure perched on a hill, invisible to the road—they sent her a gift basket with a note: "Thank you, Diane. We're glad to be your neighbors."

Well, now neighbors and adversaries. Not long afterward, they learned that her husband, Chip, had entered the congressional primaries of the opposing party, and just a few weeks ago, voters decided that Chip would be Paul's opponent in the general. Last Monday, Stan laughed out loud when he spied Chip and Diane preparing to walk in the Memorial Day Parade. At first because of the unlikelihood, then because it struck him as a perfect small-town coincidence.

Now he sweeps his gaze across the market, looking for Chip's campaign table, wondering if Diane might be here as well. It would be fantastically awkward to see her. What could they possibly say to each other?

But he finds no other political pop-up, just bakers and butchers, competing brands of local honey, and the Griffin Distillery. If Paul does come home with bags of useless provisions, perhaps Carly the caterer can make use of them at the fundraiser they're hosting next weekend at their home. Locally sourced hors d'oeuvres sounds appropriate, and local bourbon would complement it well. Stan stops by the distillery's table on his way out to purchase a bottle. The Bankses may have little use for perishables, but a liter of liquor always comes in handy.

LATER THAT MORNING at Delphi's Hardware on Kinghill Road, Joe Riley catalogs inventory, unboxes merchandise, restocks shelves, and welcomes customers with a vacant upward nod. Contractors chatter for a bit then grab the items they need for the day's work while casual shoppers slowly collect ingredients for a DIY home-improvement project. The regulars, many of whom have known Joe since he was a kid, greet him with a brusque slap to the shoulder, ask about his parents, and share some small, celebratory or sad news about their own lives.

These easy, intimate interactions can make Delphi's feel less like a business to Joe and more like a kind of social hub. There's even a domestic feel to the vast square space, enhanced by the sections of the store that mimic a house—the model kitchens and stretches of patio decking, the patch of plastic green turf with a carefully angled chaise longue next to a grill, the span of picket fence, and the Design Center, with its crown molding and faux fireplace, where advisers will help you imagine a better version of home, or second home, tailored to your budget, big or small. When Joe completes his morning checklist before opening, he likes to lie on the chaise and imagine a domestic space of his own, one that's clean and uncluttered. In other words, the physical manifestation of the inverse of his mind. These quiet minutes of visualization used to be a highlight of his day, when his days had highlights.

Still, he'd rather be on this stamp of artificial yard than on the real grass behind his own house, under the scrutiny of his mom, the indifference of his dad, the judgment of his brother. Unlike everywhere else, at Delphi's he's useful.

Shortly after noon, a Duffel wanders in and looks around as if unsure of the meaning of this place. His ginger beard is trimmed, his slacks snug, his polo pink, his face flummoxed. Joe can identify the Duffels by the fit of their clothes, the style of their hair, the way their brows lift in angst. They're easy to make fun of, which his coworkers do, which he's not above, because the Duffels *can* be entitled. And rude and dismissive and patronizing. But Joe learned from his father to take people at face value and so has formed his opinion of the Duffels based on the evidence of his interactions. For the most part, he finds them innocuous, polite, and grateful, if generally clueless.

"Can I help you?" he says to the pink polo.

The man blinks behind rectangular tortoiseshell frames and describes a faucet he's seeking. Joe guides him to a wall where dozens of ball, disc, cartridge, and compression faucets are on display. He gives a brief overview of their differences and hands the man a pair—one brass with a flamingo-like neck, the other brushed nickel with winged handles like a duck in flight. The man weighs them in his hands as if their heaviness will determine his choice, and asks, "Is this a thing where you can get away with going, um, less expensive?"

The question surprises Joe, especially from a Duffel, but he appreciates it. Most Duffels reach for the priciest item as if that compensates for their lack of knowledge, while most locals grab the cheapest object and announce, "It's all markup." A customer who asks is a conscientious customer and one who respects Joe's expertise.

Joe pulls a third faucet from the shelf, a single-handled, low-arc spout in polished chrome. "Best bet is something in this range," he says, then remembers to add, "Whether that meets your aesthetic needs, sir, is up to you."

He learned to include this last bit after an unpleasant encounter with a Duffel last summer. An impatient woman with a streak of gray in her short black bangs had stomped around with fabric swatches in the paint section. After he'd shown her numerous samples, she'd scoffed, "Are you serious? They're all so ugly." Joe hadn't known what to do or say. He became suddenly self-conscious about his taste, or lack thereof, which hadn't been a requirement for employment, nor a skill he'd ever considered acquiring, even if he had any idea how to acquire it.

His boss, Amir, laughed when Joe shared this. "You're not a goddamn interior designer, Joey," Amir said. "God knows there's plenty of those hucksters up here nowadays. Not our job to give customers everything they want, just help 'em find what they need. If we don't have it, oh well! The Duffel designers can order it custom."

Pink polo quietly examines the chrome faucet while glancing at the more expensive nickel, like it's taunting him. Ultimately he chooses the nickel. "To be safe," he says, almost to himself.

At the counter, Joe rings up the item. "Got an account with us?"

"I don't know, actually. We've gotten a few things from here recently, so perhaps?"

"Name?"

"My name?"

"Yes, sir."

"Eric Larimer."

"Don't see Larimer here. Another name, maybe?"

The possibility seems to make the man nervous. His gaze slides away before rebounding with resolve. "Well, my husband might have opened an account," he says loudly, like a challenge, like he's daring Joe to look uncomfortable or disapproving.

Joe stifles a smile. He's used to the preemptive defensiveness of those who assume that the kid at the local hardware store would have a problem with that. When he first began interacting with clearly gay customers, it's true, Joe didn't know what to make of them or how to handle the overtly flirty ones. His face may have betrayed his bafflement. But then he largely forgot to distinguish them from all the other needy Duffels. Now he just tries to understand how his younger brother fits in with them, but doing so only renders Will even blurrier.

"What's your husband's name?" Joe asks.

The repetition of that word puts Eric at ease. "Liu. Alex Liu."

Joe knows who he's referring to, because Alex Liu had worn a tight striped T-shirt, shorts that barely bothered to cover his crotch, and sunglasses that he flipped to his head as he inspected bathroom tiles. And because he was probably the only Asian person Joe has seen in the store in the past month. And because he was the flirty kind, winking at Joe when he created his account, asking for a "new neighbor" discount.

"Got it," Joe says. "I'll add your name."

Eric's expression relaxes as he gathers his faucet. He departs with an appreciative smile, and Joe experiences the glimmer of contentment that comes with helping a customer.

For a moment, he can see the possibility of a manageable summer ahead, here among the widgets and tools and in the company of Callie, whose presence has made him lightheaded ever since she arrived at Griffin High sophomore year, instantly improving his attendance record with the promise of her daily presence. She's back from college on break, back at the ice cream parlor where she's worked the past two summers. Last Friday after her shift, she delivered a half-full, half-melted pint that Joe ate on the spot, allowing his old goofiness to reemerge just long enough for the ice cream to dribble down his chin, eliciting her deliciously deep laugh, which sent pleasant shivers through his stomach and pacified him like a painkiller.

After he finished the pint, she suggested they join their old crew for sunset at Rainbow Rock. At first the invitation galvanized him with the suggestion that the past whisper of romance between them still lingered. But then his mind clouded and his chest clenched as he thought of that outlook on Griffin's highest hill. During high school and in the years since, gatherings there defined summers, along with flailing backflips off the Swintons' rickety dock, late-night fries at Nana's Diner, and heady hours at the Lab. All fueled by Matt Swinton. But Matt won't be at Rainbow Rock, or anywhere, and Joe doesn't know how to do all this without him.

Callie understood when he went silent at her suggestion. "Maybe in a few weeks?" she said, and put a hand on his arm. Her touch made him feel that in a few weeks, maybe he could.

Now a farmer asks Joe for steel siding to repair a barn. Another anxious Duffel inquires after Delphi's millwork specialists, assesses Joe's chin-length hair, and asks for referrals. A contractor places a big order for stone and tells Joe, at great length and with great cheer, about his grandson's shotgun wedding. And in between, all the other people seeking little fixes in their lives. They depart with nails, screws, tape, glue, gum, and other adhesives meant to mend.

In the late afternoon, the automatic doors wheeze open, and a gust of hot, heavy outdoor air reaches Joe. He senses someone walking toward him. The oxygen flees his body when he sees that it's Julie Swinton. She's on her phone as she approaches the counter, rummaging through her purse with her other hand, which emerges with an incandescent bulb blackened from having blown. She ends her call and begins to ask a question before she looks up.

She's two years younger than her brother, with Matt's same wide nose and thin, mischievous eyes, albeit in different proportions and framed by long blond wisps. Looking at her, Joe sees the ghost of his best friend's face. Julie and Joe stare at each other for what feels like many frozen minutes, his agony mirroring hers, their pain transferring back and forth like electric currents. Her eyes moisten, his head throbs.

But he is at work. Joe forces himself out of his trance. He gives her a weak smile, which, rather than comforting her, makes her eyes spill. She places the blown bulb on the counter and rushes from the store. As the doors close behind her, the bulb rolls off the counter and shatters.

Joe remains in place, stunned, until his coworker Troy jogs up, drawn by the sound of splintering glass. "What . . . You okay, Joey?"

"Yeah. Sorry. I got it."

"Actually, I got it. Customer has questions about decking, Aisle Eight. Your turf."

Joe drifts toward decking, feeling a storm gathering within, one he'll have to mollify soon. If he'd told Troy that Julie came in, Troy would have understood. But then Joe would be right back there, looking into her eyes, and therefore into Matt's, and he's not sure he'd be able to crawl back out into daylight.

CHAPTER 2

AFTER HIS VISIT TO Delphi's, Eric continues with his other prescribed errands, as per Alex's orders: the garden store for topsoil and plant saucers; the general store for dish soap, candles, and a Crock-Pot; the home goods store for bath mats and hand towels. Hungry and fatigued, he pauses for a gourmet sandwich at Poppy's Pantry, then wearily proceeds to his final stop, as dictated by *National Holiday*. The magazine's story on Griffin mentioned a small farm celebrated for its raw milk and exquisite eggs, describing them with the awe of luxury items. Alex insisted that they get some, though they never drank milk and rarely ate eggs; he argued that it was their "duty" to support local producers. But Eric suspects it's simply so Alex can perform his savoir faire at the next dinner party.

Eric heads south on Route 12, realizes he needed to go north, and turns clumsily around at the next gas station. Decades of public transit has deteriorated his driving, and he is not yet familiar with these roads, many of which are numbered rather than named, which makes them less personal and therefore harder to befriend. That and the fact that there are three possible routes to every destination in the Munsee region, all roughly the same length, so none become habit. You can be off course yet ultimately find your way, or on the right path yet feel completely lost, which can be comforting or disorienting, depending on the day.

Eventually he pulls onto the small patch of dirt and weeds that constitutes the parking lot of Cherry Hill Farm. He parks in front of a rust-colored barn, next to a faded blue van with the farm's logo stenciled on its side. Signs at the entrance advertise various meats—pork shoulders, beef ribs, whole chickens—as well as homemade butter, seasonal jams, and the now-famous milk and eggs. He enters the cold, damp space and faces half a dozen frosted refrigerators, each crowded with stacks of vacuum-sealed flesh swimming in blood. He scans the room for dairy items and notices a man behind the counter.

Late twenties and massive. Easily six-three, possibly taller, with shoulders extending far beyond the straps of his overalls. Eric takes in the face—a marvel. Odd at first glance, but with quick, subtle inspection, Eric decides that it's uniquely beautiful. Big mouth, thin lips, smashed nose, a prominent brow bone hanging over swampy brown eyes, casting them in shadow. The forehead creases, the eyes squint, and Eric realizes he's been staring. He raises a hand awkwardly in greeting and says, "Milk?"

The young man scans Eric's shirt and snug slacks with what can only be described as disdain. His bony forehead nods to another bank of refrigerators filled with glass bottles and blue cartons. Eric selects a quart of raw milk, a dozen eggs, and a container of butter, then visits the meat shelves and adds a bag of ground beef to his pile. As he moves through the store, he senses the scrutiny of those swampy eyes. The attention is intimidating, its coldness unnerving, especially compared to the reassuring nonchalance of the kid at Delphi's. Eric is once again on guard, attuned to every possible slight, reminded of the homophobia he presumes present this far from the city, and of the need for discretion, if discretion is ever possible in a pink polo.

He places his purchases on the counter and finds himself at eye level with the young farmer's name tag. Dalton. He risks another look at that oddly pretty face, steeling himself for more disdain. It's still there, but with it, something else in the murkiness. A trace of curiosity? Possibly a dash of desire? Eric wouldn't have thought it if the man hadn't looked away first, as if now he were the one caught staring. Dalton rings up the items and shoves them toward Eric, who silently pays and bags them himself. He chances a look back in case Dalton is tracking him, but Dalton has already turned away.

Heading home, Eric turns off Route 17 onto a small dirt road that curves through dense woods alongside a creek, one of the Munsee River's many capillaries, ending at a small cottage with a steeply pitched roof and a front porch flanked by planters of cascading geraniums, the first cosmetic improvement he and Alex have made to their modest new house.

As Eric ascends the porch steps, Alex flings open the front door. "What took so long? I need the car. Stan is insisting on finishing the living room before next weekend's gathering and wants to meet on Granger at four. What's that?"

"This is beef."

"Beef? We don't need beef. Where's the soap? Where's the faucet?"

Eric extends the bag in his other hand that contains the home goods, and says, "I thought I'd make a Bolognese tonight."

"That's sweet, but I can't. Stan and I are getting a bite after to go over lighting and fabric."

Alex snatches the keys and flies down the stairs with the buoyancy of vindication. He chose Griffin for their weekend escape in part because of its proximity to an up-and-coming, design-minded town with a growing network of wealthy potential clients, and that instinct quickly paid off when he was introduced to, and hired by, Stan and Paul Banks to furbish their new home.

As Alex drives off, Eric puts away the food and hardware, annoyed at his now-empty evening. He stands uncertainly in the stillness. Then, with the tiniest of hunches and a bit of hope, he checks an app and finds a message from a twenty-seven-year-old headless hairy torso named FarmFreshMeat: *Got milk?*

Eric smiles and writes: *Aren't you a little young for that ad?*

Do you know how often someone says that to me?

The conversation quickly becomes suggestive. Eric requests a headshot to confirm that this wide chest is attached to the same singular face that just sold him provisions at Cherry Hill Farm.

FarmFreshMeat replies: *I don't do face pics.*

OK. What's your name, then?

Why?

So you feel like more of a person.

What if I don't want to feel like a person?

Dalton, right?

After a minute, FarmFreshMeat writes: *Not to you.*

But he agrees to come over after closing the store, and an hour later, Eric watches from behind sheer curtains as the dented, faded blue van with the farm's decal pulls up to his house. Dalton, still in overalls, remains behind the wheel, staring ahead as if in a trance, as if he's waging, and losing, some internal battle. Eventually he jolts himself out of his daze, raps on the wheel as if sentencing himself for a crime, stomps up the steps, and bangs on the door.

Dalton is even taller than Eric remembered. There is no longer disdain in those murky eyes, only desire and desperation, which gives Eric a small thrill and a strange feeling of responsibility. He senses that words could be dangerous, that even the simplest greeting might scare away this timid, ravenous animal, so he turns and walks to the bedroom and, after a moment, hears heavy steps follow.

Eric pulls back the bedsheets and looks up to find Dalton watching him from the opposite side of the bed, preferring to keep the expanse of a mattress safely between them for now. Then, with a few perfunctory moves, Dalton removes his boots and overalls and stands military-straight in baggy blue boxers, his gaze focused above Eric's head. Taking this cue, Eric removes his own clothes and lies on his half of the bed, silently inviting Dalton to meet him halfway, granting him one last off-ramp should he need it. Several seconds pass, then the mattress sinks under Dalton's weight.

Once he's in bed, hunger overrides his hesitation, and Dalton rolls toward Eric. He is rough and clumsy with inexperience, the way a puppy playfully nips before he learns restraint. He smells of stables, dank hay, and livestock. Though he is clean save for the crud under his nails, the earthy scent gives Eric the impression that this man has been molded from soil, and tumbling around in bed with him is like rolling through a grassy field. Dalton is in some ways more deferential than Alex, yet in others more violent. His teeth frequently scrape Eric's lips and ears. It's an intoxicating combination of passivity and aggression.

Dalton refuses a shower after, steps naked into his overalls, and heads to the front door with his T-shirt and boxers crushed in his fist. Eric follows, unbothered by the abrupt exit, intending only to lock the door behind him. But Dalton turns back and says, "Thank you."

And Eric says, "Any time."

Dalton nods. Then he's back in the blue van, churning up the gravel as Eric watches, his lips lightly throbbing from Dalton's bite.

THAT SAME AFTERNOON, behind the scuffed bar of the Lucky Buck, Will Riley daydreams of flickering wicks from last night's tented Duffel wedding and the cluster of handsome, laughing men there whose crackling energy was its own flame. A snapshot of their easy intimacy and animated joy periodically flashes in his mind, and he indulges the fantasy by inserting a spiffier, more sophisticated and sociable version of himself among them. In reality, he spent the evening silently refilling their champagne, delivering their entrées, clearing their dishes, drawn to their light. In contrast, it seems especially dark and lonely here at the Buck, his other job, which the many neon signs contribute to rather than combat.

As he swims through these illusive images, his right hand mechanically wipes the counter like it has since high school when his father began paying him under the table to replace a barback who'd overdosed out by the dumpster. An enviable job for a sophomore, a big social-status boost until Will's peers realized it didn't get them any closer to the booze. Any other teen—one more reckless or desperate for popularity—would've taken advantage of the liquid currency at his fingertips, but Will was content to be largely unnoticed at school and wouldn't risk jeopardizing whatever sign of approval his father might grant him. His one rebellious act was sharing an occasional secret beer with his brother on the black spill mat behind the bar, their own private happy hour, back when Joe was more easygoing and they weren't such strangers to each other.

The door jangles, extinguishing Will's restless thoughts. He fills a pint as Gerald McAfee takes a seat in front of him.

"One of those when you get a chance," Gerry says, removing a trucker hat to free a tangle of thinning gray hair. Will hands him the brimming glass, and Gerry studies it from beneath the snowdrifts of his eyebrows. "You're a good kid, Willy," he says, touched by the anticipation. "Wanna swap with mine?"

Gerry says such things whenever his own son, eight years older than Will, gets into trouble, which he has recently, another DUI. Will knows this is particularly inconvenient because Gerry lost his own license for the same reason.

"Hope your dad appreciates you," Gerry says, lifting his pint in thanks and turning to the golf tournament on TV. "Tell him I said hey and that he shouldn't be such a stranger in his own place."

Will nods and slides away to take inventory. At a safe distance, he starts softly singing along to the country music station that serves as the Buck's soundtrack, accompanying Patsy: "'He called me baby, baby, all night long.'"

A fluffy crimson cloud floats behind him and says, "We doing karaoke now?"

Maren, the Buck's manager, delivers a crate of freshly washed barware, giving her heavily inked arms a muscular flex. Her artificially coppery curls settle around her aggressively tanned face and land on her customary black T-shirt. Will blushes as though caught at something lurid.

"Don't stop singing just 'cause I said something."

He smiles and begins to unload the crate.

"What? Not even talking today?"

Before Will can respond, Gerry calls out from down the bar, "I'll talk to you, darling."

"I don't want to talk to you," Maren shouts in the exasperated tone she reserves for him.

"But today's my birthday! I get a free drink on my birthday, don't I?"

"You sure do. Now let me see your driver's license."

"Ah, don't mess with me, Mare. You know I don't have one."

"Policy is I have to verify your birthday, just like I had to verify it when your birthday was a few months ago."

Gerry instantly relents, grinning like a naughty child, then becomes distracted by the TV, which has cut to a commercial. Paul Banks fills the screen with his stiff flaxen hair, shiny black eyes, and a face of archetypal soap opera handsomeness, a face Will dutifully despises even as he finds it very attractive.

The TV is muted, but they've seen the commercial so many times, it's as if they can hear it. With extravagant vitality, Paul introduces himself with a little wave, then, suddenly somber, proceeds to enumerate the region's many problems: the decline of family farms, the lack of affordable housing, the resulting exodus of youth. Then the nation's: health care, special interests, gridlock in Washington, etc. A checklist so standard they could sing along, if they did do karaoke here. Paul vaguely explains how he'll make everything better, before the ad concludes with a quick montage of him touring factories, waving to seniors, high-fiving a Black man.

"Fancy faggot," Gerry mutters when it's over.

The words hang above Will like icicles, cold and sharp, threatening to pierce him.

"Hey!" Maren barks.

"Hey yourself!" Gerry turns to Will. "You know I got nothing against you, right, Willy?"

Will is paralyzed by this casual reference to his sexuality, which he guarded fiercely until nine months ago, when he blurted it out to his mother, unplanned and clearly unwelcome, in a sort of lucid daze just before he left for college. He has never formally come out to Gerry or Maren or anyone other than his parents and brother. But given the Buck's affectionately intrusive intimacy, he's unsurprised to find it common knowledge here. Still, Gerry's overt reference rattles him. He reaches for a retort, but gumption evades his grasp. Instead, he dries a glass that doesn't need drying to keep from hurling it.

"How about you forget that word, then?" Maren says on his behalf, her bluntness exacerbating the shame of his silence.

"'Cause it's effective!" Gerry grins again as if her anger is his goal.

"That word's not welcome here," she snaps.

Will is grateful for her protection yet embarrassed to require it.

"Yeah, well, neither is that kid." Gerry jabs at the TV, which now shows a golfer visualizing his putt. "He and his . . . *homosexual* husband moving to this district five minutes ago, touching down like a tornado, then thinking he's got a right to represent us just 'cause he bought a big fucking house on the county line? No, ma'am. Bet you ten bucks a whole committee of Duffels convinced him to do it so they could flip the seat and impose gay marriage on us."

"Don't bet money you don't have," Maren says. "Especially on stupid wagers. Gay marriage is already legal."

"Welp!" Gerry says, throwing his hands up as if she's proved his point. He drains his beer, then slides it over to exchange for another. "So here's my question. You already got your gay marriage, why hide your gay husband? I'll tell you. 'Cause he thinks we're all a bunch of bigots."

Maren arches a brow. "Well."

Gerry chuckles, accepting the implied accusation. "You gotta admit, though, the kid's as much a bigot as me, even if the suit covers it up. I'd like to hear some of the names he and his kind have for me and the other folks around here, all their snobby ways of dismissing us. Right, Willy?"

Maren snaps a towel at Gerry. "Leave him alone."

Will rolls his eyes, a default defense he has learned to deploy against the offensive jokes, incendiary assertions, and grab-bag grievances that Gerry delivers with fatherly affection and a wink, like verbal noogies. He is hot with cowardice, feeling conned and complicit, as usual. He's known Gerry all his life. He should be less deferential by now, able to stand up for himself, toss back a barbed word, or at least brush him off with a cavalier quip. But Will's general tendency toward acquiescence and a childish deference to his father's best friend muzzles him.

"Whatever," is all he can manage, a pathetic period to end the conversation. With the sting of defeat, he relocates to the far end of the bar, grabs a knife, stabs a cucumber, and slices it into discs. Then he rips basil and mint leaves off their stems and begins bashing them.

He's attempting to re-create last night's signature wedding cocktail, as if it's a potion that might conjure that electric evening and that cluster of radiant men. In a sense, it works. The zesty freshness of crushed leaves cuts through the Buck's blend of malt and manure, with notes of bigotry. But even this fresh scent can't offset the fact that he's still standing behind this bar, listening to Gerry's bluster. He tilts back his head and closes his eyes.

When he opens them, he meets the marble gazes of the two stoical deer heads mounted above the bar. "The Brothers," they're called, because they were shot in the same hunting season a decade ago by Gerry and his father. Will recalls a moment at last night's wedding when the guests spied a snacking doe and everyone clamored to photograph her. Sensing an audience, she looked up, posing for the paparazzi, and Will could briefly appreciate her brazen innocence and delicate beauty.

But the sibling stags remind him of the animal's filth and menace. It is universally accepted throughout the region that deer are a scourge, vastly overpopulated in recent decades on account of a decline in predators—wolves, coyotes, foxes, bobcats, bears. Humans used to be a reliable check as well until, according to Will's father, *Bambi* made a generation of sentimental Americans sympathize with the white-tailed vermin. Will understands that, to the Duffels, deer are mere set dressing, props for a rural portrait. They don't understand that deer are actually embezzlers of crops and smugglers of ticks, bioterrorists feeding a plague of Lyme that threatens the hunter, the gardener, the meadow-frolicking children alike. And they don't get that deer are also the region's primary traffic hazard. But just wait until that adorable doe from the wedding bolts in front of their cars. They and their SUVs will learn.

The glassy-eyed Brothers now seem to chastise Will for his uncharitable contempt. He abandons his amateur cocktail to greet the Buck regulars who arrive just as the summer sun starts to mellow. There's soft-spoken, dimpled Pastor Reggie of First Presbyterian, sipping diet soda with Celia Rhodes of the *Gazette,* whose offices are across the parking lot. No one makes Celia laugh like Reggie, and when she does, her tightly coiled hair bounces around her full-moon face like jostled wisteria. The Buck used to host monthly *Gazette* happy hours until half the newspaper staff was let go. But Celia still comes by, and Will's glad she does. He's fond of her lively giggle and intimidating stare, the little sounds of affirmation she makes when listening to someone share something personal, the way her skin turns dark cherry when she gets worked up about an issue, which is often.

Rounding out the regulars, there are the stout blond sisters with matching hummingbird tattoos playing billiards with the owner of the nail salon around the corner and the brusque but benign lesbian with an inverted bowl of silver hair who runs the liquor store on Kinghill Road—plus half a dozen others who slip onto their regular stools and back into conversations that have been paused since their last visit, ongoing for years.

There's always an unfamiliar face during tourist season, and today it's a hefty, unshaven man, mid-fifties maybe, curled over the counter like a breaking wave. A lost Duffel, probably, though a bit ungroomed for that label. The man stares at Will with a fleshy, pockmarked face. His jaw hangs open slightly, giving his expression an earnest, almost innocent quality that's enhanced by dark erratic eyebrows, which he lifts to get Will's attention.

Will approaches. "Hey there, what can I get you?" He modulates his voice to one of chipper hospitality, a tone reserved for new customers, an imitation of his father.

"Oh, hello!" The man appears surprised by the quick and amiable service. "Well, let's see. That green mess you were just making. A very unexpected oasis among all this brown beer and bourbon. How about one of those?"

Will is unsure at first what the man is referring to, then realizes that the first order of his new cocktail has just been placed. He retrieves the abandoned tumbler, drowns the crushed herbs in liquor, and floats a sprig of mint on top.

The man sips. "Mmm. Much less sweet than I feared. Well done! What's your name, young man?"

Will suppresses a smile. "I'm Will."

"I'm Leon. Pleasure. Now, tell me—"

Will's phone judders his pocket. It's Carly, his other boss. "Sorry, just gotta . . ." He moves a few feet away. Carly's catering events, like last night's wedding, supplement his meager Buck income. Or that's how he justifies the work to his parents. The real, undisclosed appeal is the access her gigs grant him to the hidden world of the Duffels, who comprise a significant portion of her clientele. If Will is to be consigned to Griffin this summer, he needs a form of refuge, some means of temporary escape, both from the monotony of this routine and from the inhibited version of himself that's stuck behind this bar.

Carly skips the greeting. "It's only because Sam's out of town and no one but Aimee is available. Otherwise I'd never ask."

"Why not?"

She's quiet. "It's a fundraiser for the Paul Banks guy on Saturday morning."

"Oh." Will sees Leon watching him and moves farther down the bar.

"Right. So . . . I know it might be awkward . . ."

He finds himself nearly whispering. "Carly, you know I can't. If my dad found out—"

"Will, you're not supporting Banks, you're supporting me. It's your job."

"But if anyone saw me—"

"No one knows who you are!" It's meant to be reassuring; instead, it's bruising. Will looks around for Maren and Gerry, paranoid that they might discern his dilemma from the nervous strain of his face. But they're preoccupied by an empty keg and a car commercial, respectively.

How would he explain this to his parents? He finds no acceptable answer and is about to insist to Carly that it's impossible. But when he looks up in vexation, he again catches the polished black eyes of the Brothers, who now appear to simultaneously pity him his stolen summer, mock him, and challenge him. He is being offered an opportunity, albeit a small one, within the confines of his commitments, to steal a few hours of independence and assert his own wants over his parents'.

"What time?" he asks.

AFTER HIS VERDANT cocktail at the Lucky Buck, Leon Rogers visits an antiques store a few blocks farther down Granger Street. In the two months since he moved to Griffin, he has come into this store half a dozen times, drawn especially to a Louis XVI mahogany console table with white marble top. At first the store's proprietor—a gummy bear of a man in sweater vests and red wire-frame glasses—was chatty and attentive, reciting a mini-biography of the console and any other piece that Leon happened to glance at. But after learning on the third visit that Leon was only renting a small apartment nearby, he became noticeably less gushing.

"I'm on the lookout for the right property," Leon kept reminding him. "You can't rush these things, you know. And there's no harm in creating a furniture wish list, right?"

The proprietor nodded politely and excused himself to attend to other customers. Now he remains behind his elaborately carved desk, offering a small smile to indicate that while Leon is welcome, he no longer merits such individualized attention.

Never mind, Leon still enjoys browsing this crowded repository of relics, and much prefers it to the sleek and sober spaces elsewhere on Granger selling the latest in Scandinavian design. The clean lines and handsome, neutral tones of that modern decor remind him too much of the apartment he fled in the city and the life he was forced to abandon when Peter, his romantic and business partner of fifteen years, left him for their twentysomething assistant—also a piece of sleek, smooth Scandinavian design. In contrast, these eclectic, centuries-old items before him, which have survived so much, speak to the dignity of age and endurance.

Leon checks the price of the console to see if it has changed. It has not, and why should it? It is not subject to sales and seasonal whims; its value doesn't fluctuate with the latest fads. It is old, proudly so, carved with care, confident of its worth. He has a sudden, dangerous impulse to buy it right now as a kind of statement of intent. He *will* one day own a home that deserves it. He *will* one day rebuild his self-worth and net worth. In the meantime, this ornate table can lord over the flimsy IKEA items in his small, fully furnished rental, reminding those cheap Swedish pieces what real craftsmanship looks like.

Leon approaches the proprietor with a triumphant smile. "I may have finally found the perfect house for that console," he says.

This is partly true. He has identified a stately Federal Colonial circa 1840 with an entry vestibule that would contain it nicely. Except he has viewed the listing only online, and it is out of his price range by six figures.

The financial package he received from his ex to formally sever ties was criminally inadequate—barely enough to buy a tiny studio in one of the city's peripheral neighborhoods or a fixer-upper far beyond the city limits. On the radius of affordability, the town of Griffin suddenly reappeared on Leon's map and in his mind. He and Peter had visited here years ago on a brisk fall weekend when their relationship also felt full of color. On a cool evening in a warm restaurant, they noticed a table of four men around their age and of their kind, as evidenced by their trendy haircuts, fitted shirts, and other such stereotypical indicators, and confirmed by the looks they stole at Leon and Peter with a welcoming curiosity that seemed to ask, "Why don't we know you?"

This dance of glances prompted Peter to wonder aloud about a second home in the area. Dinner then became a playful negotiation between them about which amenities to prioritize. Land or proximity to town? Pool or vista? It was the happiest meal of Leon's life. The next day, strolling down Granger, they paused at every real estate office window to examine listings, which were quite affordable. That they might return to the city having made an offer seemed wildly possible.

But they didn't, and in fact never returned to Griffin together. Talk of a second home dwindled to an occasional passing comment, which Leon only later understood signaled Peter's dwindling commitment. So when Leon, newly discarded, reencountered Griffin in his search and in *National Holiday*, he felt an almost oppressive impulse to reclaim the home that he felt had been taken from him. He could do it without Peter, and he trusted that the clique of curious men at that restaurant, or their equivalent, would still be here to welcome him.

But when he scouted home prices recently, he found them fantastically inflated. He is still coming to terms with the fact that he is no longer a person of means, no longer someone for whom this console in that Federal Colonial would be easily plausible.

The proprietor examines Leon between his thin red frames and either believes him or chooses to play along. "Wonderful! I know your affection for that piece. I've been hoping that the stars would align for you. Where is the place? Perhaps I know it. Have you made an offer?"

Thankfully the front door chimes, and a tall, bald man in tailored slacks and a pressed oxford shirt strides stiffly over. The proprietor turns eagerly away from Leon. "Mr. Banks, always a pleasure! I'll be with you in just a moment."

"No urgency, I'm waiting for Alex. I believe he called ahead."

"Yes, he said you wanted to see the credenza again."

"But don't let me interrupt. I'll just be over here."

Stan nods to the proprietor and then to Leon, quickly appraising him as if he too were an item for sale. He then folds himself into a thronelike rococo chair swathed in light teal silk and busies himself with his phone.

Before the proprietor can return to Leon, the door chimes again, and a hunky Asian man in snug jeans and a cleavage-revealing button-down hurries toward Stan, muscles fighting against fabric. "Sorry to keep you waiting."

The new arrival, who must be Alex, then addresses the proprietor. "We spoke about the midcentury walnut buffet."

"Yes, I . . ." The proprietor glances at Leon, makes a calculation, and says to him apologetically, "Excuse me, it'll just be a minute. I hope you don't mind."

"I do, actually." It's not usually in his nature to be insistent, but Leon is tired of being dismissed.

The proprietor freezes. Alex opens his mouth but hesitates. Somewhere, an old clock ticks off three seconds before Stan rises.

"The gentleman's right," he says in the tone of a judge sustaining an objection. He nods to Leon as if to say that he would have done the same. "You were here first. What item are you interested in, if I may ask?"

With pride and slight discomfort, Leon indicates the console.

Stan nods approvingly. "Exquisite. You have a home in the area?"

Leon eyes the proprietor. "Closing in on one. I've only been here a few months."

"I'm a relatively new resident myself. Stan Banks." He extends a hand. "My husband and I moved here about a year ago. Still getting settled."

"Leon Rogers." They shake. "I left my husband in the city. So still getting single."

Stan chuckles. "A big transition, then. Do you know many people here?"

"I don't, really."

"In that case, come for dinner Friday. We're having a small gathering of friends."

The invitation is quick and unexpected, as is the intensity of the gratitude flooding Leon's throat, which he must swallow before he can gravely say, "I'd be delighted."

Another half-smile from Stan. "Of course. Now, please don't let me delay you any longer. You were in the middle of a transaction."

Leon straightens. "I think we're just about done here." He ponders the beautiful old steadfast table and turns to the proprietor. "Yes, I'll take it."

CHAPTER

3

A FEW DAYS LATER, Diane bounces down Martindale Road, a buckling squiggle of hard earth off Route 9, until she reaches a small gravel driveway. She's greeted by a colorful new planting of Chip Riley signs that lately rebuke her for her lack of involvement with the campaign. But all this recent attention on Griffin means she's busier than ever, which supports her family and thus ultimately benefits the race. She shakes her head at the signs, refusing their reproach.

When she pulls up to the one-story blue clapboard bungalow where she and Chip have lived for over twenty years, she's surprised to find his battered white pickup truck out front. She eyes it suspiciously as she ascends the small front porch where an American flag offers her its daily salute. In the dim entryway, she flicks off mud-caked heels and finds Chip crouched in the kitchen before the oven. He's a dot of denim against faux wood laminate flooring, sunflower-stamped wallpaper, and white cabinets made of medium-density fiberboard—the consequence of a two-year-old remodel, Diane's gift to herself when her real estate practice became profitable. It was the first time that the Rileys had altered their home for purely aesthetic reasons, and it had been a thrilling, terrifying, extravagantly indulgent experience. It still feels frivolous, but Diane loves it. She understands why the Duffels are so addicted to decorative cosmetic surgery; she now appreciates all the ways a space can be made new again.

"I didn't expect you home tonight," she says.

Chip spins toward her, then crosses the kitchen to deliver a kiss. He's wearing the pink "Because I'm the Mom" apron that their sons gave her one Mother's Day before they understood the only person in the family who needed such an item was Dad.

"I was at AJ's," he says. "Figured I'd grab some veggies and whip up a quick meal before tonight's phone banking." When he can, Chip spends a few hours handing out campaign flyers in front of Griffin's largest supermarket, a long gray rectangle on Kinghill Road where fluorescent tubes buzz above canned soups, boxed cereals, bagged chips, and cleaning supplies.

"I must have just missed you." She stuffs the frozen dinners into the freezer for another day, then hides the lavender jelly and local salami log she picked up from the Duffel-owned Poppy's Pantry on Granger. Her neighbors refer to it, snickering, as "the Pansy," and Chip has called its prices a form of theft, yet after shopping her entire life with coupons in the garish glare of AJ's, Diane has been seduced lately by the artful display of specialty items in incandescence. Besides, it's the kind of place where she's likely to run into clients, or potential clients. Another splurge for the sake of her business, or at least a convenient way to justify it. She takes pride in demonstrating, to whoever may notice, that despite the period of near poverty in her past, she has remade herself into a businesswoman willing and able to overspend on imported cheese. But she doesn't want to flaunt this need to her family. "Pick up any votes?" she asks.

"Think I may have bagged a few."

"I could've made dinner."

"That's all right, Di. I didn't want to burden you."

His smile is triumphant and expectant, like that of a kid who knows he's done good and anticipates praise. She puts on an appreciative look for him, happy to be spared the cooking but irritated that he thinks it a burden for her to make a simple dinner, though he's not wrong.

Chip sets a timer and pivots to a bouquet of broccoli on a chopping board. As he prunes it into bite-sized florets, she marvels at his energy. If he's depleted from hours of knocking on doors and calling "Hey there!" to skeptical shoppers, he doesn't show it. Politics fuels him in ways she never expected. After years of seeing him weighed down by running the

Lucky Buck, by fatherhood, by losing a mother to a heart attack and then, a few years later, a sister to cancer, Diane was pleased when Chip decided to join the Griffin Business Alliance, which led to the school board, then to the town council. She doesn't visit the Buck often—she doesn't like dark spaces, or the smell of beer, or half the people who hang there, and she certainly doesn't like sitting around doing nothing—so she hadn't considered a connection between pub and policy. But it makes sense that Chip's innate interest in people would be required of bar owners and lawmakers alike.

He dumps the broccoli carcass into the trash and begins dicing carrots. He's adequate if graceless with the knife, which also could describe his early administrative style: sharp and stiff, with the occasional outburst that once led a fellow school board member to deem him "Bud Light Riley" because, when misunderstood or backed into a corner, he could explode, albeit mostly harmlessly.

But over the past decade, culminating in his election as Griffin's supervisor, she has watched him learn to lower the temperature, and Diane has come to understand leadership as essentially climate control. Now his undramatic directness, quiet humility, and openness to compromise are respected by council members of both parties. Because in a town of this size, partisan politics is as useful as a snowplow in summer. Or, as Chip likes to say, "Ideology doesn't repair streetlights."

As a result, she has observed the regeneration of his sense of self. In their years of scarcity, she watched helplessly as he wilted before her, shrinking in shame from his inability to support his family. Local government proved an unexpected source of confidence. As he rose in the town ranks, that confidence took on the flavor of ego and expressed itself in a more youthful strut, dusted off from high school, as if he were once again the star running back. All of which Diane welcomed. She saw how the respect he earned as supervisor aerated him, puffing him back up to his former healthy pride.

In the beginning, though, she worried about the impact of his civic involvement on her burgeoning business, especially when it increasingly consisted of Duffels. She assumed, based on their bumper stickers and disparaging offhand comments about certain national figures, that they didn't share Chip's politics or his party, which were also her own. If she were to be found guilty by association, she feared the steady flow of referrals would run dry. But she never mentioned these concerns to Chip. Doing so might be misinterpreted as lack of support in his endeavors while revealing her to be ashamed of her ideals, which she is not. She is simply careful to maintain a clear separation between state and real estate.

She was reassured to quickly realize that none of her city clients paid attention to local politics, other than to inquire about property taxes. So she dropped her silent objection to Chip's municipal involvement and assumed that town supervisor was as high as you could go on the political ladder here.

She never imagined: Congress!

In the month before Chip confessed his desire to run, he wouldn't look her in the eye. She was sure he was cheating on her and was building the courage to confront him when he broke down one night and revealed his intentions.

She laughed in disbelief. At first she was relieved. Then she wished it *had* been an affair. Because it would have been in the past, and she could forgive him, and they could begin to heal together. But running for Congress was like telling her he planned to start cheating on her with a hundred thousand mistresses spread over roughly a hundred square miles and that she was supposed to be excited about it. She tried to convince him that she was, but when he fell asleep, she cried into her pillow. Not because she felt a threat from his new goal or dreaded the long absences should he win, and not even because the increased visibility of a congressional race would make it that much harder for her to maintain the appearance of ideological independence among her Duffel clients.

She cried because he had surprised her with his ambition, because he'd hidden his dreams from her the way she hid Poppy provisions from him. The ego she welcomed back had continued growing without her awareness. And egos are ravenous organisms of the soul, prone to metastasize when fed. She should have known better.

Now that he has won the primary, she is forced to accept the cruel fact: Her husband is a professional politician. Meaning an ego-driven being—though one of noble purpose, she firmly believes. And, thankfully, an enthusiastic and competent cook. She leaves him to the carrots and retreats to the small room at the end of the hallway that she uses as an office, bringing a glass of merlot for company.

WILL PARKS HIS gray hatchback (borrowed for the summer) behind his father's dirty pickup and his mother's gleaming red sedan. ("A goddamn parking lot," his father grumbles whenever he sees the three cars lined up.) Will trips over his mother's shoes in the entryway and hears her on the phone.

". . . the old brick factory two blocks from Granger . . . yes, a hotel and spa. I'm telling you, it's going to be the new heart of Griffin, your value will double in three years . . . That's right, a new sewer system . . . town council's been discussing it since January and approved plans just last week . . . No, final vote is in August, but I assure you, it will pass. I have it on good authority from an inside source . . . But there are other interested buyers, so I advise acting fast. You may have to go over asking."

Will is glad to find his father hovering over the stove, if only because it means a respite from frozen dinners. "What're you doing home?"

Chip doesn't look up. "Reminding you boys what a home-cooked meal tastes like." He checks the oven temperature, and Will is about to walk away when Chip looks up. "So, uh, what's new downtown?" he says, meaning the Buck.

Will hesitates. "People still drinking, people still drunk. Gerry says hey, says you should come by more."

"Hey to him." A pause. "I'll try."

It's something of a script they cowrote when Will started working at the Buck—what's new downtown, people still drinking, so-and-so says hey—a foundation they've built and can return to if they don't know where to start, which, these days, they don't.

Chip has never been an outwardly affectionate father, always more at ease with his patrons than with his sons, but Will has felt a new chill in their interactions since he left for college last fall. A reluctance to meet eyes, a note of trepidation behind innocuous questions, exchanges that quickly hit dead ends. Stemming from either embarrassment or disappointment, Will suspects, or a scoop of each. But since Chip initiated their script, Will continues with his lines.

"What's the chicken wearing?" He knows they'll be eating chicken because that's what Chip makes, what he's been making for his family since his own father died when he was sixteen. He can competently flip burgers, but chicken is his comfort food.

"Stilettos and a mini," Chip says, his moment to improvise.

"Cool," Will mumbles, as though it were a perfectly reasonable response. Sometimes the chicken "wears" a top hat, sometimes combat boots, sometimes a bikini, each outfit absurdly indicating whether said chicken would be barbecued or baked, prepared with certain spices or sauces, paired with a pasta or grain, or rolled in a tortilla.

The chicken began donning these fanciful outfits fourteen years ago, after Chip took over the Buck, when Will and Joe were in elementary school. At the time, Will didn't grasp the significance of the fact that the chicken was purchased at AJ's with a card screaming "Benefit" in large letters, that clothes arrived in bags with the same logo as the orange donation bin next to his school, that eggs were grabbed quickly from a standalone cabinet next to Town Hall marked "Community Pantry," that canned food was dropped off weekly by a friendly woman who asked "How you holding up?," and that later, Will would feed those empty cans into a big mechanical monster outside AJ's that burped money in return with a rude indifference that gave Will a shiver of discomfort.

But he did comprehend the constant strain on his parents' faces back then, his mother's muffled tears at night, the desperation in her grace when she thanked God for the "generosity of Your church and the angels among us" and added a prayer "for a return to self-sufficiency." Will hated the sadness that hung over family meals, hated more the forced cheer of his parents' performance of normalcy, and hated most the wormlike feeling of disgust in his stomach that he only later recognized as deeply burrowed shame.

Around this time, his mother started working temp jobs, embarking on a long, exhausting path from one shaky stepping stone to the next over many years, which eventually led her to stumble upon the gold rush of realty in their newly desirable town. The sudden impact of that work was profound. Within a few years, his parents resurfaced, blinking and bewildered, from the dark cave of debt into the bright clearing of solvency. His mother's blooming self-assurance was particularly striking as she adopted her formal new look and a glaze of professionalism that made her seem almost regal yet more remote.

In the kitchen, Chip has nothing more to say, so Will leaves his father to style the chicken and retreats to his bedroom, which looks just as it did in high school. The walls are covered in movie and music posters of cowboys, surfers, rock stars, and other muscular men which, at the time, he thought confirmed his masculinity but now make a rather obvious declaration. The shelves are still stacked with old schoolbooks, a few track-and-field trophies, and family photos smuggled in by his mother that he doesn't dare discard.

He falls back onto his bed, roused and jittery, and studies the glow-in-the-dark sticker solar system above that Joe helped him make in middle school, which has since lost all its luminance. In the past week, the universe of this room, this house, this town has shrunk with the discovery of that twinkling new constellation of men at the fancy hilltop Duffel wedding. Each night since, Will has returned to the event in his mind, in particular to a moment when he realized one of the men was staring at him with open interest, as if he saw something desirable in Will that Will has yet to see in himself. The man smiled slightly and lifted a brow in a way that felt like an invitation. Will stared back until his courage dissipated and he hastily resumed the catering task at hand.

Under these faded plastic stars, he has imagined all the ways he might have accepted that silent invitation and parlayed the man's attention into a conversation, or more. For the past week, he's been rewriting the moment as if it were a key that could unlock a portal back to the mysterious galaxy of the Duffels, which feels distant yet suddenly within reach. He hopes that Paul Banks's campaign event may be that portal.

HALF AN HOUR later, Joe is dropped off by a Delphi's coworker and the air swampens, becoming muggy and electric, as though a storm has developed inside the house. Will tenses, ready for anything. He was startled, when he came home two weeks ago, to find Joe both depleted—his face pale, his eyes dull—and as dicey as a live wire. At family meals, they regard each other with the surprised realization that they understand each other less than they did before, a kind of reverse knowing. When they accidentally come face-to-face, after opening a door or turning a corner, Joe's expression either tells Will to fuck off or pleads for connection. Or it's blank, lost in a private fog.

Now Will's in the hallway when the unpredictable weather system that is his brother blows past, sending him into a third-grade photo, which falls to the floor, saved by the carpet. After Joe's bedroom door thunders shut, Will bursts into his mother's office.

"You didn't say he'd gone psycho!"

She's at her desk, leaning back, wineglass in hand, reading *National Holiday*, the magazine that just proclaimed Griffin's new golden age. "'Psycho' is a bit much, don't you think? I said he was struggling."

"He just shoved me."

"So?"

"So that's okay?"

"Obviously not. But be generous. He's still dealing with . . . He's *coping*."

"With what substances?"

"William!" She springs forward, knocking the desk, rattling a mug of pens, and creating a small tempest in her wineglass. "After what happened to Matt, he knows the consequences." She watches the red sea settle and speaks to the swells. "That phase is over now, thank Jesus. Though of course we all wish it hadn't ended the way it did." She reclines again.

"He's a zombie. He looks like shit."

"I don't care how much college has expanded your vocabulary, William, there is still no swearing in this house." She takes a sip of wine.

"He looks *better*. You haven't been here to see the improvement. Delphi's been a blessing."

"Has it? They have a tool to fix him? On Aisle Seven?"

"Don't be snide. The routine's good for him."

"So everything's fine?"

She looks at her reflection in the glass as if an answer might appear. "No. But now you're here, so . . ." She twirls her wine, upsetting it until a whirlpool forms. "Anyway, your father and I are glad you're home."

Will's eyes widen and his mouth parts in ready rebuttal. He's not home of his own accord; he was coerced by guilt to return and would like some acknowledgment of this sacrifice, especially in light of the way they left him last fall. But his mother has already returned to her magazine and now looks up with a closed-lipped approximation of a smile to signify the conversation's end.

After Will leaves, Diane considers again the liabilities that are her children. Their respective predicaments have flummoxed her and Chip, becoming more fraught with the campaign. With Will, it's a matter of his . . . preferences. Luckily, he's been away at college, far from idle chatter. (Though were it someone else's son rumored to be of that persuasion, such chatter might well have come from her.) Surely Will is aware of the need for discretion now that he's back home and his father has embarked on such a high-profile endeavor.

With Joe, it's a matter of his unpredictability, building for years but increased alarmingly since Matt's overdose. A string of "sick days," his manager calling twice to say he hadn't shown for shifts, all-night disappearances, spates of shouting, and worse, days of silence.

When Chip was working on his campaign website this winter ahead of his official announcement, he'd drafted a platform that simply but forcefully described his commitment to addressing the region's drug crisis and his careful hedging on same-sex marriage that acknowledged both its legality as well as the validity of faith-based objection. He'd also written a biography that included his sons' names, ages, and current pursuits, a profile filled with familial pride.

But Diane was uncomfortable and overly cautious. "Don't you think

Will might appreciate some privacy? I imagine he's still getting used to, you know, being . . ." She twirled a finger.

"Out?"

"Yes, that."

"Or maybe *you're* still getting used to it."

She rolled her eyes, and the website went up mostly intact. But after Matt's recent passing, Diane suggested that Joe "maybe doesn't need that kind of attention right now. And since Will is coming home for the summer, perhaps he doesn't need a spotlight, either."

"So, what? I can't even mention my own sons, for Chrissakes?"

"Charles, language."

"Sorry. But they're our children. I'm not ashamed of them. In fact, I consider them among my best achievements."

"Oh, please. I'm not ashamed of our sons. But they're both in a fragile place. There's scrutiny that comes with being a candidate's kid. Maybe best to keep things vague? And maybe safer not to call so much attention to the . . . *issues* they're both dealing with. Focus on farming, taxes, whatever the current cultural flash point is."

"Cultural alarmism's not really my thing, Di."

"My point is, we don't want our sons to become policy symbols, do we? For their sake."

But they knew she meant for Chip's sake and her sake. So he reordered his priorities, neutralized his words, and wrote that he "lived with his wife, a real estate broker, and two children in Griffin." No names, ages, or genders, no need to invite any probing into the family. For protection, they reasoned, not evasion. Besides, there was nothing to evade. Will was still adjusting; Joe was just coping.

NOW THE RILEYS face one another under a dusty brass chandelier like poker players. Diane closes her eyes and holds out her palms. The family clasps hands. Will and Joe feel the scratch of their mother's nails and the imprint of her rings.

"Lord, thank you for the meal we are about to eat, for the abundance before us, for the sustenance of food, and for this family. This complete family." She squeezes their hands. "Through Jesus Christ, our Lord. Amen."

Chip and Will respond, "Amen." Joe says nothing.

They pass around a floral-patterned platter of rosemary chicken and a bowl of steamed vegetables. Chip's cooking is a treat, but it reminds Diane that she'll have to deal with dinner for the remainder of the campaign, and longer, should he win. Who knows how many terms he'll serve? Some of these politicians sit pretty for decades. The thought makes her choke. She coughs violently and reaches for her wine. Her only consolation is that the Twenty-sixth District isn't a place where representatives relax, it's a bright purple pendulum. A swing district, they call it, but that sounds too pleasant. Given how politics works these days, Diane thinks a seesaw is more apt, crashing down hard one way and then the other in a vicious effort to fling the opposing side off.

"I think I'm close to a sale, God willing," she says, changing the subject that only she was dwelling on. "That old house by Creskey Pond, the big white one with the red barn. Another, um, couple from the city."

She glances at Will as she says this, and he turns pink, which makes her turn pink, as if embarrassment were contagious. Whenever Diane stumbles on a couple and doesn't elaborate, they know whom she's referring to. Otherwise, she'd say something like, "He's a painter and she's a therapist." Once she tried to be neutral—"He's a doctor and he's a . . ."—but then she snorted, looked away, and said, "Anyway, they're very nice." She intended this as a corrective, but Will heard it as doubly dismissive.

"Hope you finally sell that place," Chip says, sounding more impatient than supportive.

He *is* supportive of her work, always has been, especially as it became the bulk of the family income. But he doesn't love that most of her sales are now second homes, even as he appreciates the boost to Griffin's tax revenue. For Chip, it's a philosophical question: If you're always shuttling between two homes, are you ever really rooted? Or, as he once said to her, "Can anyone love two sets of neighbors as thyself? Most people can't even do one, so which are you most responsible for?" He shares the wariness of many Griffin locals about the rapid upgrading of the town, this rural renovation none of them asked for. Diane knows her neighbors blame her in part, but she's unsure whether Chip does as well. She's afraid to ask.

"Did they make an offer?" he adds.

"Not yet. But they called today and want to come again this weekend with an architect." She is intent on sawing her chicken. "The thing is, they can only do Sundays. Same time, unfortunately." Which means she'll miss another day of canvassing. She searches for something to fill the subsequent silence. "I shouldn't share this, but the reason they can't come earlier is because one of them has a dermatology *procedure* on Wednesday that requires three days' rest. He said this to warn me that he might look a little puffy when I see him next. Of course, I know a few women who have gone in for a bit of freshening, but never a man. I guess it's a . . ." She glances again at Will. "A city thing."

They all look at her blankly. She redirects. "So, Joey, did you finish that deck? Whose was it, by the way? Do we know them?"

Joe takes a second to respond. "Some place on the lake."

"Our porch could use a few new boards and a fresh coat," she says. "Maybe you boys could spruce it up this weekend?"

"I'm working for Carly on Saturday," Will says.

"What's the occasion?" his father asks.

Will fills his mouth to delay answering. He decides to tell the truth, but what comes out is: "A birthday party. Some woman's sixtieth." He's impressed, and appalled, by the quickness of his lie.

"How lovely," Diane says. "And what's new at the Buck?"

Well, Maren still smokes behind the bar in front of the "No Smoking" sign. Gerry essentially called him a faggot again, and earlier this week Will found more discarded needles in the bathroom, where, a few months ago, a patron was barely revived. But he won't share all this with his mother, who tends to go sullen whenever drugs infiltrate a conversation, especially when Joe is present.

"Nothing," Will says, though her question reminds him that he forgot to pick up more naloxone. He'll stop by the pharmacy tomorrow.

"Nothing?"

He has to give her something. "I made a new cocktail today."

Will sees his father wince. According to Chip, the Lucky Buck is not a place for cocktails. Country music has many an ode to whiskey and beer and the occasional margarita but nothing to say about concoctions with more than two ingredients.

"How creative," Diane says.

Does he catch a whiff of condescension? He hesitates, his gaze volleying between his parents. "Well, it's summer, right? So I thought, like, a 'Griffin G and T,' with cucumber and basil and—"

"That's so gay," Joe mutters.

"Joseph!" Diane gasps.

Will's head goes staticky. First Gerry, then his mother, now Joe, all reminding him of his unwelcome difference. He thought, when he went to college, that such hostility would evaporate in his absence. Instead, it has been patiently awaiting his return.

"Fuck you!" he shouts, eyes wild and wounded.

"William!"

"Enough, goddammit!" Chip smacks the table.

For several moments, the Rileys sit in battered silence. Diane looks as if she's been hit, Will masks his hurt with a scowl, Joe smirks at his plate.

Chip takes a breath, resetting his face and tone. "We don't attack each other in this family," he says, rattled but practicing his politician's calm. "Now, who wants ice cream?"

CHAPTER 4

ON SATURDAY MORNING, THE sky is a highway of speeding clouds as Will drives through metal gates landscaped with "Paul Banks for Congress" signs. He heads stealthily up a long driveway, tingling with anticipation and the hope of some consequential encounter while also feeling like a spy on a self-deployed mission with unclear objectives.

The Banks home comes into view. It's an imposing study of horizontal lines and intersecting angles rendered in cold gray concrete, wrapped in glass, like cellophane around a gift basket that both projects and protects its contents. As Will approaches, the windows oscillate between reflections of a white birch grove and glimpses of the carefully arranged diorama of living within.

A frantic Carly greets him at the austere entrance in front of a puzzling wall of bamboo, an affront to the surrounding native flora. "Marsden Farms came up short on the lamb, so we're doing beef sliders instead," she says as she ushers him through the house. Other substitutions have been made, but Will is lost, floating through the extravagant emptiness, marveling at the few magnificent items allowed inside.

She deposits him at a pop-up prep station next to the garage with Aimee, a former cheerleader in his brother's grade and known for her exceedingly thick eyeliner, a trademark she maintains. They tweeze salmon and dill onto crackers as she gabs about former classmates he barely remembers. Will had been worried that Aimee, gossip that she is, might exploit the fact that he's working a fundraiser for his father's opponent, but she appears to have no idea the purpose of this event.

As she chatters, Will observes the arriving guests, who meet each other with easy hugs and greetings of surprise and boredom, as if they can't believe they're already doing this again. He studies the way they stand like mannequins on display, the way they hold a wineglass as if they've forgotten it's there, the way their sunglasses perfectly fit their respective faces. One woman seems to epitomize this attitude. She keeps flicking long black bangs with a bold gray streak off her face in a way that suggests they are not so much an inconvenience as a marker of self-importance.

A sudden clamor causes him to turn. A small herd of dapper men have appeared with animated purpose. They head toward him, seeming to form a prism that catches the sun, shooting him through with vibrant color. He braces as they rush past in search of a bar. As if by some gravitational pull, he turns to follow, but a tap on his shoulder brings him back.

Paul Banks stands before him, hair lighter and eyes darker than they appeared on TV, two black beads on a smooth, smirking white face. Paul clinks his wedding ring impatiently on a tall glass and says, "Can you help me out with this?"

"Water?"

Paul laughs as if Will is teasing him. "I was thinking something stronger."

"Red, white, or beer?"

Paul's face puckers like a disappointed child's. "We didn't get a full bar? Hmm. I guess we'll have to dip into the personal stash, then. Vodka's in the kitchen freezer. On ice, squeeze of lime."

He hands Will the glass, pats his shoulder paternally, and walks off, leaving Will annoyed, smitten, and with palms so damp that he fears the glass will slide right through.

On the back porch, he tries several doors before one grants him entry to a bright living room. He looks for signs of the kitchen but is distracted by the theatrical set he has stumbled into: white couches, white-brick fireplace prepped with white birch, two framed photos on an elegant antique credenza. In one, Stan and Paul wear tuxedos and raise clasped hands with the blissfully baffled smiles of newlyweds. In the second, they are shirtless and surrounded by other bare torsos on the bow of a boat against a sapphire sea. Will is startled to catch Paul in a state of undress, but it's the first photo that feels somehow more illicit in its intimacy.

He turns toward a glass coffee table stacked with design and travel magazines, including the latest *National Holiday,* and a tome titled *Customs of the Country: Instructions for Living Off the Land.* He looks around for signs of surveillance before putting down Paul's glass and flipping to the table of contents: "How to Build a Chicken Coop," "How to Keep Bees," "How to Make Butter." The spine is uncracked. It's a peculiar prop, since it seems to bring further attention to its owner's outsider status, a kind of self-deprecating admission of incompetence in rural environs. Will picks it up and sees that it also served to cover up an artful catalog of male nudes.

At the sound of distant footsteps, he replaces the book and scurries through a dining room with an elaborately set table and an air of newness and neglect, then into a spotless black-and-white kitchen with a large, veiny marble island. He opens the stainless-steel refrigerator, empty save for oat milk, eggs, and yogurt. In the freezer he finds an array of vodkas and gins and begins pouring.

"May I help you?"

Vodka splashes the counter. A tall, bald man in a trim linen suit stands rigidly in the doorway.

"Sorry, I was just getting a drink for Mr. Banks."

"*I'm* Mr. Banks. Stanley Banks."

It takes a moment for the declaration to make sense, for Will to understand that this severe older man is, in Gerry's words, the "homosexual husband" who remains suspiciously invisible and undisclosed in Paul's campaign ads.

"Oh. I meant the other Mr. Banks."

Stan frowns. "Paul asked for this?"

"Yes, sir."

Stan sighs. "Maybe I should be the one to deliver it, then."

Will hands over the drink like a piece of contraband.

"Were there any other instructions?"

"A squeeze of lime," Will says.

"A squeeze of lime," Stan repeats. He blinks at Will as if just seeing him, then exits.

AN HOUR LATER, the backyard swarms with stylish loafers, cream-colored trousers, and crisp button-down shirts in pinks, blues, and yellows, as well as a sprinkling of summer dresses, flowing and floral. As Stan weaves through the crowd, determined to deflect conversation and avoid the numbing small talk, he notes that, with only a few exceptions, the guests also wear chardonnay-colored skin, some more buttery, some more pearly, but all a variation on blanc, largely reflecting the region's demographics as well as the monochromatism of their social network.

A microphone squeals, and everyone turns toward the porch, where Paul's campaign manager, Jeremy—a near facsimile of Paul, albeit with sharper features, lighter eyes, and curlier hair—beckons the crowd closer and introduces Paul in terms befitting a lifetime achievement award rather than the inaugural campaign of a political novice. Stan maneuvers to the back of the crowd to ensure that Paul won't be tempted to call him up.

Paul bounds to the mic. "Hi folks, nice to see you, *thank you* for being here, and *welcome* to our home. If this is your first time visiting Griffin or the Munsee region, it is a *true* joy to introduce you to this place that has captured our hearts, which I would be *honored* to represent and which I *intend* to represent!"

Stan crosses his arms. Paul's delivery is too emphatic. And he shouldn't say "folks" when an event is held at a multimillion-dollar home, especially when that home is their own.

The applause dies quickly, which Paul seems unprepared for. He smiles into the silence, blinking with minor panic, then stumbles back into his speech.

Such moments, however small, remind Stan how easy it is for zeal to come across as amateur, how much rehearsal it takes to be spontaneous, how hard it is to sound sincere. In other words: how very young and unseasoned his husband is, how much of a learning curve this campaign will be, and what a leap of faith this journey has been since they met seven years ago, at the annual gala of the city's largest AIDS service organization.

Stan was, and still is, on the board. That year, his hedge fund was honored for leading the capital campaign of a new youth center. Receiving the award, Stan spoke, as he had many times before, about Asher and the others he'd lost to the disease. From the lectern, he saw ghosts in every empty chair and in the troubled eyes—both calcified and still screaming—of the attendees his age who never stopped seeing them, either. Among the guests that night were his friends Serge, Luke, and Nate, who are also here today in Griffin.

At the gala, Paul had been seated at Stan's table, invited through a program for promising future leaders whose secondary purpose was to brighten the hall with youth like the sprays of spirea in the centerpieces. Stan felt adrift after speaking about Asher, in no mood for vapid conversation, but Paul had nipped away at his armor.

Stan was forty-six then and slowly resigning himself to solitude. Paul was twenty-five and in possession of bubbling confidence, grand but vague political plans, and an appetite for the stuffed social schedule that Stan had tired of. They each provided what the other sought: Paul became something of an adopted puppy who forced Stan out of the house, while Stan became something of a mentor and manager, steering Paul toward experience and connections. A year later, Paul moved in.

They began hosting fundraisers to build strategic relationships among political, financial, and cultural leaders, and it wasn't long before Stan was overcome with a profound new feeling toward his frisky young boyfriend. Pride. He already felt adoration and desire, frustration, and fear—could such a young, luminous man really love a bald investor more than twenty years his senior; how long could it last?—but watching Paul swim among the opinion shapers and power brokers, Stan had the sense of potential embraced, of a match struck. And it was all the more terrifying because it was accompanied by that sickening insecurity Stan had felt only twice before and had learned to recognize as the onset of love.

Two years later, they wed in the ballroom of one of the city's storied hotels, and Paul took Stan's surname. (To hell with Paul's parents, who didn't attend.)

As soon as they were hitched, the Bankses became "power gays," which was an official designation from a snooty but popular magazine in an article profiling rich homosexuals who exerted influence in media and politics. Though Stan hated the phrase, he recognized that its inverse, gay power, was precisely what he had worked for his entire life, after watching Asher die in an indifferent world. Stamped with that crude but correct label, the Bankses quietly sought political opportunities for Paul, who had become an accomplice and soon-to-be agent of Stan's crusade. So now here they are, as Paul continues:

". . . for those of you who live in the city and feel you have no way to register your frustrations with what's happening in this country. This race is a piece of the national puzzle, and if you support me, you *will* be heard. Let me represent your values! Let me be your voice of discontent!"

Stan nods along as Paul finds his rhythm and his voice. Just look at him up there. To be a viable congressional candidate with a husband? In a rural district? Until recently, that was unthinkable. If Asher could have seen . . .

Stan buries the thought to stave off tears. Thinking about Asher in public places, in this way, is never advisable, nor productive. He clears his throat, furrows his brow, and refocuses on the daunting logistics. A long-shot race requires a substantial up-front investment, and Stan has already committed a quarter million dollars of his money. ("Our money," Stan generously insisted to Paul.) He doesn't mind. This is exactly how he intended to use his wealth: to support a generation of innocent and historically ignorant gay leaders less traumatized than he. That's purchasing power, Stan thinks. The purchasing of power. He's still surprised to find himself in a position to buy it. And equally surprised to discover how quickly his money is being spent.

AFTER THE SPEECH, Eric, Alex, Serge, Luke, and Nate gather on the back lawn to debrief. Hovering nearby is Leon, whom they met last night at the dinner Stan hosted, and who had failed to impress them by loudly inserting himself into conversations, boldly criticizing Serge's curatorial choices at the theater festival, and sharply dismissing a designer that Alex admired. Serge later said that he found Leon "astringent." But Stan was amused and charmed by Leon's desperate performance, intrigued by some of his aesthetic arguments, and still felt a charitable pity toward him for his unfortunate marital situation.

Stan told Serge, "Actually, I find him refreshing."

At the dinner, Leon sensed a confusing mix of superficial welcome and barely concealed resistance toward him, and he feels it again today. In retrospect, he knows he tried too hard. He wanted only to engage and be engaging, to demonstrate that he could converse in their cultural language, to contribute in a lively way. But his humor, or attempts at it, burst instantly like a soap bubble when met with the cold shell of their skepticism, and he left the meal with the feeling of having failed an interview for a job he wasn't sure he wanted but still needed because of the security it offered.

Now he is determined to correct that impression. He offers a generous, if disingenuous, assessment of Paul's speech. "He's well-spoken and seems to have a good grasp of this place."

"You didn't think he would?" Serge says with a tinge of rebuke.

"Oh, I just meant . . . Well, he's a bit *untested*. And only here a year. I mean, he wouldn't even qualify for in-state tuition! Mhah!" Leon's laugh is a blend of chuckle and guffaw.

Nobody smiles.

"Paul went to a private university," Alex says with such pompous gravity that Leon almost laughs again.

"I found Paul to be very articulate," Serge says. "He's smart, charismatic—"

Leon jumps in. "Yes, exactly, that's what I—"

Serge continues. "And most importantly, he's a friend of our community, obviously, and will vote all the right ways, nationally speaking."

Eric finds this a vague and weak endorsement, which is also what he thought of Paul's speech. It had been too calibrated to the nonresidents from the city, more an advertisement for the Twenty-sixth District than a prescription for its improvement. At times it sounded like Paul was inviting them to move here or invest in the Munsee region by way of investing in him, as if he were its fiscal sponsor. And he had presented himself as a soldier-for-hire in the nation's ideological civil war, in which, no matter where you live, you are also responsible for influencing the votes of your fellow citizens in the next district, the neighboring state, or anywhere in the country threatened by hostile takeover. The underlying pitch was "Paul Banks, political mercenary." But that seemed to be all that Serge, and others, wanted from him. Eric bites into a mini lemon tart and refrains from sharing this assessment.

"Anyway, you're all registered here, right?" Nate asks, not for the first time.

Everyone nods except Alex, who throws up his hands to shield his face from Nate's glare. "Jesus! I know!"

Serge beckons to a passing waiter, the cute one they've been ogling all afternoon with the triangular frame, freckled cheeks, and light brown hair swept across minty-brown eyes.

Will approaches the men. His face colors under the intensity of their collective gaze, and Leon's mouth parts when he recognizes the Lucky Buck bartender who made him that green drink.

"Can I get you guys anything?" Will's voice wavers and his eyes flit around the circle, squinting at Leon, widening slightly, then moving on until they land and remain on Serge's stiff silver hair, sunset skin, and Errol Flynn face.

Alex calls Will back to attention. "What are you offering, handsome?"

Will looks like a startled lamb, so Eric jumps in. "Forgive my crude husband," he says, which earns a chuckle from the others, as though it's a known punch line.

Will bashfully scratches his neck. "Red, white, or beer?" he asks.

"Surprise me," Alex says with a wink.

The others place their orders and Will scurries away. Leon is intrigued to realize that the young barman seemed more flattered than discomfited by the interaction.

"I, for one, intend to drink the entire value of my donation today," Alex says, playfully bumping into Eric, acting the clown, as he sometimes does.

"Well, I'd rather my non-tax-deductible dollars go directly to overpaid campaign consultants than overpriced booze," Nate says with a trace of scolding.

"No, of course. I was kidding. I just meant since we're here." Alex deflates and looks to Eric with the defeated expression he wears when he feels dismissed, which is often. It reflects Alex's social sensitivity, the result of his broader insecurity for having grown up poor and as one of the few nonwhite people in their friend group, even if the offending comment refers to neither fact. Despite what looks like a solid social position, especially now that they have a home in Griffin, Eric knows that Alex still evaluates every comment like the twist of a screw that either strengthens or loosens his standing.

Eric touches Alex's back to soothe him. "Cigarette, babe?"

Alex scowls. "I'll wait for my free drink."

"I'll join you," Serge says to Eric, oblivious to the tension.

They make their way to the back side of the garage, near the catering station. After they've lit up, Eric says, "So, Paul's opponent. What do we know about him?"

"Town supervisor. Pub owner, too, I think. Which is cute."

"What's he like?"

"No idea. Probably a nut."

"A nut?"

"You know . . ." Serge exhales and looks to the plume as if it might reveal an answer. "Like, extreme. I mean, he must be, to some degree, if he's one of *them*."

"Maybe he's a decent guy," Eric says.

"Well, sure. Everyone's supposedly decent in these types of places." Serge exhales a fresh cloud. "My mother used to say, 'The city corrupts, the country corrects.' I think it's how she made peace with where she ended up. For me, it was the opposite. More like, 'The country suffocates, the city . . .' I don't know. Something."

"Seduces?"

"Ha! Well, yes. But I was going to say something like 'rescues.' The city saved me from all the isolation and harassment I endured growing up in a very pretty little town like this one. Same with Paul, from what I understand of his childhood."

"I think *Stan* saved Paul," Eric says. The comment slips out with the smoke, and Eric glances sideways to gauge whether Serge considers it seditious. He changes the subject. "Maybe all this farmland will correct for me as well. I'm spending the whole summer up here, you know. Figured I can design websites and marketing material anywhere, might as well do it in tranquil environs, get to know the area better." Eric thinks of Dalton. They've spoken twice since their unexpected tango last week and have tentative plans to meet again after Alex returns to the city.

"Wonderful. But correct for what? Everything okay?"

"Oh, sure." Eric pauses, deciding whether to share more. "I guess I've been wondering lately if I still need all the chaos of the city as much as I once did. I have a feeling the country will be good for me. The space, the quiet . . ."

"Nature! Fresh eggs! All the clichés."

Eric laughs and pictures Dalton's dirty overalls crumpled on his floor. "Basically."

"What about Alex?"

"He has a lot of projects in the city this summer. He'll be here most weekends, though. Stan is keeping him busy on the house."

"Still?"

"They've been more focused on the campaign. Understandably."

"Sure. But the real question is whether they'll make it another year here."

"What do you mean?"

"If Paul loses. I imagine they'll just buy a house in another district and try again."

"You think? But Alex says they're investing quite a bit in this one. And they have friends here. You guys, Nate, the others."

"I think they'd rather have constituents than friends. But who knows? If Stan—I mean, Paul—plays his cards right, maybe they'll get both."

Something metallic clatters nearby. Eric and Serge turn to see Will stumbling toward them, struggling to maintain his grip on a large coffee urn whose lid is spinning on the ground. Black liquid sloshes over the rim and stains the pavement. Will's freckled face burns as if it, and not the driveway, has been scalded.

Eric and Serge rush over. Eric retrieves the fallen lid while Serge grabs the urn's handles, cupping Will's hands.

"Got it," Serge says, cigarette bouncing in his mouth, the ashy tip inches from Will's face. Now sharing the urn's burden, they shuffle to the dessert table. Eric follows.

When the urn is in place, Will wipes sweat from his upper lip. "Thank you, um . . ."

"Serge." He extends a hand. Will hesitates, then clasps it like he's attaching to jumper cables. "And this is Eric." Serge retracts his hand so he can grip both of their shoulders as if facilitating a peace treaty. "What was your name again?"

"I'm Will."

"Nice to meet you, Will. You're from around here?"

"I am."

"Well, maybe when you're off . . ." Serge stops abruptly and squints across the lawn to where Luke is calling attention to his cigarette.

"Oops!" Serge quickly removes it and stubs it out. Now Luke is waving them over. "Sorry, gotta go, but hope to see you again, Will."

AFTER MOST OF the guests have departed, Will gathers dirty dishes from abandoned tables. He's still intoxicated from taking drink orders from those men and from that eventful coffee encounter but feels deflated by a sense of missed opportunity. He'd acutely felt how the men locked on to him and how, later, silver Serge seemed on the verge of proposing some future plan before being cruelly called away. Will drops the plates in a bin and hears one break.

"Shit!" he shouts, and spins around, coming face-to-face with onyx eyes.

"So, do I have your vote?" Paul asks.

Will forces the only possible response. "Of course."

"Good." Paul's smile tilts off-balance. "And thank you again for sending Stan with my *water*. It put me at ease, and he was only a little upset."

"Sure."

Silence dances between them, then Paul says, "My friends enjoyed meeting you."

"They're very nice."

Paul laughs. "Yes, around certain people, when they want to be. You took good care of them."

"It's my job." That sounds impolite, so Will starts again. "But I enjoyed it, too." No, too effusive. He tries another path. "It was my pleasure. And if you ever need . . ." He stops, unsure of what he means to add, but the words rush out anyway: "If you need help at another event."

"Then I'll be sure to call Carly and request you." Paul peers at Will for a moment, then smiles. "Unless you meant I should contact you directly?"

Will's body prickles with sweat. He cannot bring himself to verbally confirm this intention, so for the sake of plausible deniability, he responds with a floppy shrug like a child unwilling to admit a secret but also unable to deny it.

"I see," Paul says. "Well, we're having a little gathering here in a few weeks for the Fourth of July. Not like this." He gestures about. "Very casual, much more unbuttoned. A barbecue potluck. So, not sure what kind of help we'd need. But maybe you can keep an eye on drinks and assist with the cleanup?"

"Sure!" The answer is too quick, too eager.

Paul chuckles. "Of course, you're welcome to enjoy yourself as well. That is, if my friends aren't too . . . objectionable?" He spins the question with a zesty little curve.

Will is aware of the moisture accumulating on his nose and upper lip. He understands the real intent of the query. "No, not objectionable." He fights to maintain contact with Paul's lively eyes.

"Then I suppose you'd better give me your number." Paul takes out his phone. "Remind me your name?"

"Will."

"Okay. But Will *what*? I'm sure you don't want to be 'Will Catering.'"

Naturally, Will didn't plan for this. In a slice of a second, he decides he cannot reveal his identity, and therefore cannot use his actual last name, and therefore needs another one, and needs it immediately, because you cannot be suspected of not knowing your own last name.

"Martindale," he says. The street where he lives, where he has always lived. "Will Martindale."

He is proud of his quick thinking, but later, the shame will set in. All those years lying about one aspect of his identity, all the energy expended in hiding. And just when he thought he finally freed himself from one closet, he willingly stepped into another.

CHAPTER 5

THE FOLLOWING SUNDAY FINDS Diane at First Presbyterian, a small white church with a bright red door and an intersectional architectural identity featuring Colonial columns, a broad Grecian gable, and a Gothic steeple pointed to the sky like an antenna aimed at heaven. It occupies an otherwise empty crossroads a few miles from Granger Street with a marquee out front that today reads, "Come as you are, you can change inside."

Diane sits near the front, as usual, in a demure lilac midi dress, and smiles at Pastor Reggie, who flashes his dimples back. She waves to nearly everyone who enters, but when Raina and Derek Swinton approach, she dives into her purse for lip balm. It's the first time they've come to Sunday worship since Matt's death, over a month ago, and Diane cannot bear to face their grief. As she shamefully moistens her mouth, she tells herself that she will speak to Raina after the service.

Reggie begins with Matthew 11:28–29: "'Come to me, all who are weary and burdened, and I will give you rest.'"

Diane nods along. It has been a particularly wearying week. An inspection went poorly, an escrow fell through, and a seller signed with her nemesis, Emma, a button-nosed blonde who recently opened a satellite office in Griffin for one of the city's big real estate agencies.

First Presbyterian is usually Diane's sanctuary in every sense, but today, sitting on this hard wooden pew with ample space on either side of her, she feels unmoored and out of place here in a way she hasn't felt in years.

She didn't grow up in the faith, so this church was not a character in the Griffin of her childhood, which was an unspectacular town with few hints of the popular destination it would become. It was an unconstrained upbringing: her mother overly permissive and her father only mildly vigilant, so indulgence defined the household. By the time Diane was in high school, her mother discussed drugs frankly. When one of Diane's classmates was suspended for pot possession, her mother railed at the school's overreaction. "It's so silly!" she exclaimed. "Drugs can be an important tool in getting to know yourself."

"How?" Diane, then fifteen, asked.

"They show you places inside your mind where you'd never have thought to look or might be afraid to." Her mother leaned on the kitchen counter and offered Diane a cigarette, which she accepted so her mother wouldn't think her boring. "I know it's not conventional wisdom, but it's what my life taught me, and it wouldn't be fair to keep it from you." She paused and squinted at Diane. "But some drugs *are* bad, mind you. Just do the good ones, sweetie."

The same unorthodoxy applied to sex.

"*Preparing* yourself for marriage is more important than *saving* yourself for marriage," her mother said after tossing out a flyer about abstinence that Diane brought home her junior year. "It served your father and me well."

"How?" Diane, then sixteen, asked.

"We knew what we were in for, and we learned to talk about it. I can't tell you how many of my girlfriends still, to this day, treat sex as some secret shame. With their own husbands! Mind you, I'm not saying you *should* give it a go so early, sweetie." She sipped her chardonnay. "But I'm not saying you can't."

And because Diane's adolescence was filled with parentally sanctioned experimentation, it was hardly a crisis when she got pregnant the summer before her senior year.

"It's nothing to be ashamed of," her mother said, petting her head.

"It happens," said her father, not quite masking his disappointment.

"But what do I do?" Diane, then seventeen, cried. Mixed in with the panic and embarrassment was a sliver of resentment toward her mother for the negligence that had led to this predicament.

"I'll make an appointment, honey," her mother said.

In fact, she made two appointments. They also got manicures.

At her parents' urging, Diane went to a big university in a big city where she studied education, looked inside her own mind just as her mother had encouraged, and saw that she was deeply unhappy, still scarred from the callousness with which her aborted pregnancy had been treated.

Homesick and adrift, she returned to Griffin frequently. During a visit in her second year, she went to Nana's Diner for a milkshake. There she noticed the brawny, bearded waiter with floppy hair studying her from behind the chrome counter. She recognized him from the Griffin High football team, a few grades above her. Then he was beside her with a lopsided smile somewhere between cocky and shy, holding Nana's famously large laminated menu with its overwhelming selection of dishes.

When she reached for it, he yanked it away and shook her hand. "Chip," he said. She held on in shock and refused to let go, even when she returned to school.

Chip was not one for letters, nor much of a conversationalist by phone, but he sent a small package every week. A jar of jam, a scarf knit by his mother, one of his well-washed plaid shirts with a note that said, "I hope it fits." He visited once a month, making the eight-hour round trip on his one day off. They spent their brief time together at various parks, which they agreed were the city's only virtues. Despite her earlier ill-advised lapse into promiscuity, his chaste patience made her feel unstained. They rarely spoke in between visits, but Diane never had doubts. Chip always showed up.

By the end of the following summer, she was sure. She left college, moved home, and married Chip six months later, despite her parents' disapproval. Shortly after, she began accompanying his family to First Presbyterian. There, with them, she found a serenity she didn't know she lacked, a structure she didn't know she wanted, and a salve for the self-inflicted wound she'd suffered as a teenager, which hadn't yet healed. Here, through the words of Christ, as shared by gentle Pastor George, she finally found permission to choose restraint and vowed that her own children would be spared the confusion and inevitable pain of poor choices born of excessive permissiveness.

And for a happy decade, Sunday mornings here were an inviolate appointment for the Rileys, when the boys would swing their legs between Chip and Diane, when she felt all of God's love and forgiveness in that familial sandwich.

Today Chip is busy with the campaign, embarking on another long canvassing marathon which she will again miss. But he stopped coming to church with any regularity years ago, after he found politics and took more interest in demographics than doctrine. Democracy has become his new dogma and policy, his prayer.

As for Will, she hoped he would join her here this summer, at least occasionally, like he used to until just before he left for college. He'd loved church as a child, loved brushing his hair flat, wearing a collared shirt, singing psalms while staring out the vaulted windows and squinting at the maples that guard the graveyard at the church's side.

"Why do the trees interest you so much?" she asked one fall when he was nine.

Will became bashful. "Because I'm trying to catch God."

"What do you mean, sweetie?"

"I'm trying to catch God at work."

"At work?"

"How they change color, but you can't tell until after they do."

Weeks later, she saw him delight at the brittle leaves letting go, blanketing the graves in a crunchy multicolored quilt. And in winter, she watched him ponder brown twigs twitching against gray skies, the trees' skeletons communing with the ones underground. From this, Diane knew that her younger son was an observer, sensitive to small changes, capable of awe.

Will would take such pleasure in the fullness of the maples today, which paint the sky with a thousand fluttering green dabs. But she suspects she knows why he's not here: that yearlong period when she and her fellow devotees coordinated with other church groups to oppose the state sanctioning of same-sex marriage. She had never been so filled with purpose, so invigorated by political participation, so sure she was modeling righteous conviction for her sons. She had such an abundance of energy then that she even found herself baking for the meetings she hosted in her home, which was how she discovered an aptitude for simple oatmeal raisin cookies, her one competence in the kitchen. Only in retrospect did she recall Will's reluctance to eat them, his hesitant small bites, the rest tossed in the trash. He was twelve.

At family dinners, in front of her sons, she would report on the committee's progress and plead with Chip to be more proactive on the issue. His vexing response, which she chalked up to a cowardly political caution, was always "Why would I want to step in front of that train?"

As she saw it, that train was a runaway. She was just trying to get it back on track. How could she see it otherwise? When the church said being gay was a choice that could be overcome, especially because Pastor George said it with such kindness, she accepted it and believed him because she, too, had made poor choices in her youth and had been invited to make a better one in accepting Christ, who consoled and redeemed her. Others could do the same, especially those engaged in regular, unrepentant sin. It wasn't discrimination, she reasoned, merely the protection of a sacred religious rite. She had nothing against *them*, other than the ostentatious impiety of their lifestyle.

But a few years later, the Presbyterian Church voted to sanction same-sex marriage anyway, and it made Diane dizzy. Hadn't her efforts been a manifestation of the church's teachings? Now those efforts were in opposition to the church's formal position. It was very inconvenient when you thought you were doing God's work and then God, through the general assembly, upon the vote of a majority of presbyteries in the United States, changed His mind. At first she felt betrayed, thrown under the spiritual bus. Then she felt abandoned, left on the side of the road as many in her congregation accepted or even welcomed the new edict and sped past her to a place they called "inclusivity." But she'd never intended to be exclusive, only ever consistent in her faith, a defender of the truth as she was told and believed it.

And instead of Pastor George standing steadfast behind the pulpit as he had for decades, there was Reggie, newly arrived, a shockingly young and nervous thirty-six-year-old recent seminary graduate. Diane distrusted him immediately. No one that fresh-looking, with his neat auburn hair, comically blue eyes, and dimples—what religious leader has dimples?—could offer valuable insight into the human soul.

She looks at Pastor Reggie now, consumed by his black robe, framed by a shiny green stole. His face is thinner, his eyes sharper but still sweet. She has grown fond of him, won over by his sincerity, despite his mouthiness on politics. At the beginning, she bristled at his sermons, which he tried to make relevant with references to social issues and current events. After the church's reversal on marriage, he spoke boldly in favor of it, which upset her with its implication that she had somehow acted in bad faith. She didn't need her spiritual leader impersonating a pundit. Pastor George, averse to the day's headlines, would have found solace in Scripture and would have consoled them with timeless words of grace.

Then, last summer, Will came out the week before he started college. He and Diane were driving home from All4Less with dorm supplies when a song came on the country radio station in which the singer shrugged at the prospect of two girls kissing, suggesting it was as valid a choice as any other.

"Well, that's just wrong," Diane said, a reflexive habit from when she'd been so vocal on the matter. She wondered why she still felt the need to comment out loud.

"That's me," Will said, somewhat breathlessly, as if the words had taken him by surprise.

Diane was quiet for several anxious seconds. She knew exactly what he meant but wanted to delay this moment for as long as possible. "The girl part?" she eventually said.

"The gay part." He said it with a firmness that startled her. Behind those three words was a person she hadn't known had been part of her family, living in her house all along.

She squeezed the steering wheel and continued to look forward. Her head filled with a haze that blotted out the son sitting beside her, obscured her thoughts and blocked all potential responses. She was silent the rest of the ride home and, on this matter, she has been silent with Will since.

They found Chip in the kitchen, wearing his pink apron and dressing the chicken in drag.

"Will has something to tell you," she said, then went to her room.

When Will did, Chip looked down and scratched behind his ear. "Well, shit," he said.

Then Chip, clearly at a loss, made Will tell Joe so he wouldn't hear it as gossip. Joe looked to his father for guidance but received only a resigned and flummoxed shrug, so he finally mumbled, "If it makes you happy?" as if challenging Will's confession. Will felt all his family's dismay in the question.

That Saturday, Chip and Diane took Will to his dorm. Diane hesitated, then hugged him the way she always hugged her sons once they'd grown taller than she was, with hands on their shoulder blades, head against their chest. Usually Will rested his head on hers, but that day there was only muggy August air above her. His rejection of her overture stung. And she detected a haughty defiance in the way he quickly turned away without looking back. She had the sudden impression that he had planned it this way, that he'd waited to pull the pin on this grenade until he was leaving, then tossed it to his family on his way out. It felt as abrupt and unjust a bomb as the moment she'd learned of her teenage pregnancy a quarter century ago.

"It's just so rude!" she complained to Chip on the car ride back. "And selfish."

"He can't help it, Di," Chip responded. A curt, inelegant appraisal, but she later envied him, and still does, his easy acceptance. She has often wished she could simply adopt this casual tolerance, just accept her son's truth and the church's convenient affirmation of it. But if this particular tenet revealed itself to have been so mutable all along, what would that mean for every other element of her hard-earned faith?

The next morning at church, she glared at Reggie and his dimples, as if he'd been an accomplice to the crime. But buried beneath the betrayal was a fuzzy, as yet unacknowledged gratitude to the young pastor, and the church, for preapproving her son when she wasn't yet able to. And now that, in business, she finds herself courted by so many, um, couples, she is also grateful for the professional cover this theological about-face has offered.

Reggie invites the congregation to join in corporate confession. Diane stares at the words for a few moments as the chorus of voices rise around her, before she's ready to add her own:

Merciful God, we confess that we have sinned against you
in thought, word, and deed,
by what we have done,
and by what we have left undone.
We have not loved you with our whole heart and soul
and mind and strength.
We have not loved our neighbors as ourselves.

At the last line, she looks again at Raina and Derek Swinton leaning against each other. In her discomfort, Diane scrutinizes Raina's prim navy cardigan set, the kind found in catalogs in solid conventional colors. Diane has gossiped unkindly of them to others in the past, which she isn't proud of. But now the outfits have a strange way of allowing Diane to locate Raina in her memories. Raina wore plum the day she was announced as the new clerk of session; she wore mustard when she sang a solo at the last Christmas concert.

And she wore merlot one cold Sunday morning late last fall when she pulled Diane aside after worship. Her son, Matt, had been Joe's best friend since sixth grade. Diane liked him. He had the same cocky but friendly openness as her son, unlike Raina, whom Diane found a tad dim. Raina had placed a hand tentatively on Diane's forearm and nervously sucked air before launching into what must have been a prepared speech.

"I felt I've got to tell you," she began. "It started a few months ago, but I wasn't sure . . . And of course I didn't suspect him right away. Lord, no! Wouldn't want you to think that, Diane. But I felt you ought to know."

She shifted side to side, saw Diane's confusion, and began again. "You remember the surgery I had over the summer? After my accident? The doctor prescribed me oxy. Two months' worth, more than I needed. The pain wasn't as bad as I expected, thank Jesus, and frankly, I like to avoid medication if I can. Especially given . . ." She gestured around, indicating either the church or the entire world. "Well, you know."

"Raina. I don't."

But Diane did. Several families in the congregation had been visited by that demon in recent years—"the whirlpool," she called it—and she'd watched them get sucked under. Reggie conducted funerals for overdose victims: young mothers, star students, respected community elders. He preached about the plight of drugs in Griffin, inviting compassion for those who'd lost their way, suggesting that addiction was not their fault. Diane pitied and prayed for them, of course, but she prayed for them to lead holier lives, to resist temptation, to choose better, as she had. So she knew what Raina meant and knew that her feigned ignorance was offensive.

Raina got to the point in a huff. "Well, now my pills are gone, and I think Joe's the one who's taken them."

Diane laughed, loud enough to cause a few congregants to swivel around. "Excuse me?"

"Look, I know—"

Diane's voice plunged so low it became hoarse, and the patient, virtuous face she wore to church, as much a part of her outfit as her rhinestone cross necklace, fell away. "No, you are mistaken. How dare—"

"Let's step outside." Raina steered Diane through the red door and around the corner to the edge of the graveyard. The air warned of winter.

Diane composed herself. "Why do you think Joe took your pills?"

"As I said, I didn't use many after my surgery. I had a near-full bottle. Then a few months ago, I knocked it over and noticed it was half empty. I got suspicious. I asked Derek, and he didn't have a clue, so I asked Matt and Julie, and they said they didn't know what I was talking about, either."

"Of course they'd say that."

Raina ignored her. "Then last month, when Joe was over, I saw him coming out of our bathroom. He doesn't ever use that one. Not that he can't, it's just . . . Anyway, it was strange. When I went into my bathroom after, the medicine cabinet was open and the oxy bottle tipped over, so I straightened it out. It felt so light. I checked, and there were only four pills left."

Diane looked up and saw God at work on the three maples, which were splattered with leaves the same color as the church door. She folded her arms across her chest for warmth.

"He was over last night," Raina said, more gently now. "I checked this morning. The bottle was gone."

"Could've been Matt," Diane said. She hated the denial in her voice.

"Sure," Raina said slowly, a concession meant to ease the blow. "It's just, they never disappeared in between, you know? Just after Joe was over."

Wind rattled the fragile leaves and the two mothers. Neither had brought a sufficient coat. Diane hugged herself and firmly shook her head. "Raina, whatever issues you're having with Matt, please keep Joe out of them." Then she returned to the warm safety of the church.

Diane hasn't seen the Swintons since Matt's funeral, where Raina wore black.

Now Reggie begins his sermon and Diane sits upright, caressing the bumps of her rhinestone cross, feeling a trinity of guilt, gratitude, and apprehension. She tries to follow Reggie's message but after a few minutes allows her gaze to drift to the trees. With the sun shimmering behind them, the leaves sparkle like emeralds. She prays for Matt's soul and asks God to watch over Joe, to keep him far from the whirlpool and to warn her if he ever gets too close.

After a few announcements, the service concludes. Diane sees Raina and Derek stand and scoot through the pew. She should intercept and comfort them. But worship went long, and she has a house showing, so she slips down the aisle and out the red door.

AS DIANE FLEES First Presbyterian, Will arrives at his father's campaign headquarters, a three-room suite in a strip of storefronts on Kinghill Road, previously home to a travel agency, as evidenced by an abandoned poster of Acapulco. It's Will's second volunteer session, and he arrives with a renewed sense of self-serving purpose. Working at the Buck taught him that pleasing his parents pays dividends. As baffled as they were by his coming out, he suspects that the delicate détente they've established since is possible in part because of his years of service behind the bar. So after working Paul's fundraiser, and especially after offering himself up for the Fourth of July pool party, he thought it best to begin banking his parents' favor again.

Chip's campaign manager, Gabrielle, is sorting stacks of paper for the other volunteers expected shortly. Her wide frame swings between the printer and her desk with the brisk determination of someone intent on proving herself. This is only her second political campaign, after a state assembly race last year for which she served on the field staff but proved a "shrewd workhorse," according to her letter of recommendation from the candidate, who lost. She also happens to be a recent alum of Will's college, which he resents because of the implied expectations it places on him.

"Didn't expect you," she says by way of greeting. "Can you make coffee and cut up muffins?" She points to a kitchenette in the corner. When he has, she informs him, "Lawn signs are low."

"That's good, right?"

"Not for the budget. I'll have to reallocate funds."

It was this no-nonsense efficiency that prompted Chip to hire her five months ago. That and the fact that her untested talent was a perfect match for his limited resources. Will is still adjusting to seeing his father so deferential to someone barely older than Joe.

Will and Gabrielle are silently compiling welcome packets when the globular figure of Terry enters. "Shabbat shalom, *Greenblatt,*" he says, emphasizing her surname in the uneasy way he does. "Will," he says with a dismissive nod. Will shoots Gabrielle an indignant look, but she just shrugs and explains to Terry that Shabbat was yesterday.

Terry was one of Chip's rivals in the primary, a sputtering blowhard who punctuated his hyperbolic rants with a fat jabbing finger. Now he's Chip's treasurer—Gabrielle's idea—an attempt to procure and placate Terry's rowdy followers. But his fevered and unfiltered presence has already proved a liability, as when he leaves his guns and ammo magazines around headquarters, or when he called Paul a "carpetbugger" in an interview with the *Gazette* last week, a derogatory amalgamated allusion to Paul's residency status and sexuality.

"You can't say that," Gabrielle had hissed at Terry after convincing Celia Rhodes not to use the quote. He stood before her in the office like a ripe strawberry with prominent sweat stains. Chip leaned against the open door, arms crossed, as Will watched from the main room while stacking chairs after his first volunteer session.

"The fuck I can't," Terry said, mustache quivering. "You should be thanking me for throwing punches so Bud Light Riley here doesn't have to." He jabbed at Chip. "It was damn clever, too. Everyone's said so." He seemed more upset that his wordplay wasn't appreciated.

"You're part of *Chip's* campaign now." Gabrielle was calm but firm, and Will wondered how a twenty-five-year-old could retain her composure while a blubbering sixty-year-old could not. "We don't take cheap shots," she said.

Terry spun toward Chip. "You think that was a cheap shot, Riley?"

Chip pushed off the door and faced Terry. "Look, Banks is a rich opportunist. Call him a carpetbagger, I don't care. But don't muddy it with a slur that'll just get him easy sympathy and potentially put us in the national spotlight for the wrong reasons."

Terry cocked his head to the main room. "This isn't 'cause your son's a bugger, too, right?"

Chip whipped his head to Will, who quickly resumed stacking. The door clicked shut and a loud exchange ensued. A minute later, Terry stormed out. Neither Chip nor Gabrielle brought up the incident afterward, and Will was too shaken to mention it. But he had assumed that Terry was fired, so his swaggering reappearance now boils Will's brain.

Terry grabs a quarter muffin and pops it into his big red mouth, then retreats into the office, leaving Will to stew on the fact that this noxious man remains on his father's team.

Volunteers begin to trickle in, and soon the main space is full of nervous, energetic helpers. Chip usually kicks off the canvassing sessions, but this morning he's at a volunteer firefighter event in Clarksdale, a town on the other side of the district, so Gabrielle fills in.

"Think of what made you show up today," she tells the volunteers, using the earnest, encouraging voice she makes available only to them. "Put that into your own words. Don't underestimate the power of a face-to-face conversation with a neighbor. It's rare and powerful. And don't forget to rank afterward. 'One' for likely voter, 'four' for unlikely. That'll help us refine our lists."

She runs through the script, answers questions, hands out assignments. She thrusts a folder at Will containing printed addresses and a map of East Vernon and South Griffin. Cell service is spotty, and soon he won't be able to consult GPS. The orientation takes fifteen minutes and utterly fails to prepare him to knock on unfamiliar doors and talk about his father.

The first address on his list brings him to a small brown house with peeling white shutters, a decrepit shed in the back, and a rusted car with a flat tire, asleep in the driveway. It's the kind of house his mother would accuse of intentional neglect, leaving the exterior in disrepair to avoid a higher property tax assessment, though Will can't imagine justification for such self-inflicted ugliness. He rings the doorbell; a dog barks inside. He waits a minute, fondly poking a pair of mosquito bites on his neck, souvenirs from the Paul Banks event, and leaves a flyer in the doorframe.

"Chip Riley is Proud to Represent YOU," it says over a smiling portrait that mocks Will because that smile is so rarely directed at him.

Back in the car, he works himself up. Suddenly the idea of handing out his father's pride to strangers feels profoundly unfair when Chip can't even defend his own son in the face of Terry's cheap, demeaning boneheadedness. Will considers heading home, but the idea of quitting feels equally intolerable. He shares his father's burden of commitment, though he often wishes he had more of his mother's self-prioritization or his brother's ease with bailing at whim. Plus, he still feels guilty about Paul's fundraiser. He smacks the wheel and starts the engine.

The next house sits in a clearing at the end of a very long dirt driveway, as long as Stan and Paul's, though theirs was paved and thus had an air of permanence. A rickety swing set, scattered toys, and an inflatable pool litter the front yard. A truck guards the home, tattooed with bumper stickers that reveal the owner to be a supporter of the police, a navy vet, a devotee of national parks.

A young woman answers the door in wide, worn jeans and a large white T-shirt that stretches over ample arms and stomach, her hair in a messy ponytail. Behind her, Will hears a clatter and a child's shriek. The woman looks frazzled and impatient but allows him to make his pitch, which he delivers like a middle school student reciting a memorized poem. When he finishes, she folds her arms across her stomach and waits. More sounds of demolition come from within the house. She looks back and seems ready to end the visit when Will remembers Gabrielle telling the volunteers to ask a question if they get stuck.

"So, um," he stammers. "What are your biggest concerns?"

She squints at him. "You mean what I'm dealing with? You wanna know my problems?"

"No . . . Well, I want . . . My dad just wants to make life a little easier for his neighbors."

As he says it, he realizes it's true. He thinks of his father listening to the woes of Buck patrons, coming home late from town council meetings, bringing Will to events for the farming association, the historical society, the Boys & Girls Clubs. Chip's endless effort of showing up for this town. "He's involved in a million things, always trying to help people. I've seen it my whole life."

This new note of respect appears to thaw her. Her hands migrate to the back pockets of her jeans, an opening up. She eyes him for a moment, then says, "We don't have Internet here. I have to go to the library to look for jobs."

Will nods.

"I work part-time at the All4Less."

"Sure."

"I want to work full-time, but they won't give me the hours. So no health insurance. My husband works at a garage. Well, two. Each part-time, so no insurance there, either. We got two kids."

"How old?"

"Four and three." More shrieks, the children confirming this.

Will smiles. Her face briefly relaxes, then hardens again. "Some woman came by last week asking if we wanted to sell the house. Said we could get an ungodly amount for it. But where would we go? Not around here, not at these prices. And too risky to start somewhere new. So, can't afford to move, can't afford to stay." She laughs. "Your dad's gonna fix that?"

"He'll try." But Will also considers that the real estate agent easily could have been his mother.

"They all try." She sighs with a kind of cosmic exhaustion. "But they can't or won't change a thing." She laughs with a note of melancholy. "Politics is just like the weather, completely out of your control. Just a bunch of storms to hunker down and get through, hoping they don't hit you directly." A volcano of tears erupts from inside the house. She turns warily to assess the severity of the outburst. "All right. Looks like that's all the time we've been given." She says it with a trace of reluctance that reminds Will of the Buck patrons who find brief solace in unloading themselves to him until they must return to their lives. "Give me one of those flyers. If I decide to vote, I'll consider your dad."

Will hands her his father's face. "Nice smile," she says.

The other houses Will visits are spaced generously apart, some separated by vast fields, others by thick woods. His mother is forever blessing and cursing the land. It's what her clients want: sprawling acreage at prices he considers a fortune but they consider a steal. Land to just look at, to build on, to do wacky things with. A yoga retreat, a sculpture zoo for bizarre metal animals, an ATV course etched onto a hilltop. The region is a blank canvas for those who can afford to paint on it. The flip side, his mother complains, is that properties don't move when land is so abundant. Or, he now thinks, when the owners can't afford to move and can't afford to stay.

As he drives from door to unassuming door, at one point stuck on a single-lane road behind an obscenely slow truck, Will thinks of the fancy homes he's recently been granted access to on account of Carly's events. Big, hidden dwellings, a whole mystical world nestled within the one he thought he knew. He contemplates their expensive emptiness, the bland tranquility of their indistinct palettes, the many beautiful, useless objects within that have no apparent meaning to their owners. Objects that reflect the personality of the residence rather than the residents. As enchanted as he was by Stan and Paul's house, as eager as he is to return, he also felt its coldness. He's suspicious of their home and homes of its kind—shrines to style and status—but enamored of them, too, for the same reason. Despite his ambivalence, he would like to think himself worthy of such places.

More homes, more unanswered knocks. Between every doorbell and (possible) appearance of a person, Will's body swells with the adrenaline of anticipation. The ebb and flow of that chemical, like an ocean tide within him, feels like a physical erosion. Then: a frail man with a cane looks skeptical but takes a flyer, followed by a big woman with a young face and old eyes who says, "Ain't got time," and closes the sentence with her door, followed by a bulldog of a man with loose white jowls that jiggle when he shouts, "Don't come around again, got me?"

Next Will approaches a tiny blue cottage trimmed in white and decorated with lush plantings like ripples of frosting. At his knock, an elderly woman in curlers appears with a smile, as if expecting him. When she hears of the reason for his visit, she gets excited, tells him to wait right there, shuffles away, and returns with a plate of cookies she just baked for her grandkids.

"I know of your father," she says. "Lucky Buck guy, right? He's done good by this town. Lived here most my life, but I'm starting not to recognize it. Haven't shopped on Granger in years, can't afford to. And even if I could, don't need no Duffels proclaiming their politics every time I walk in their stores, understand? All those rainbow flags and 'No Hate' signs. They call it inclusion, but really it's *exclusion,* understand? Like they're saying if I don't see the world their way, then I'm not good enough for their coffee!"

Will concentrates on the cookie. Oatmeal cranberry, reminding him of his mother's mediocre baking, as well as the unsavory circumstances that prompted it, and making him wonder again how someone can display such hospitality while espousing such inhospitable opinions.

The woman continues. "'Course, the prices make clear that us regular Griffiners aren't welcome anyhow. Instead of a rainbow flag, just put up a dollar sign. That'll keep us out just the same!"

Will, still chewing, lifts a corner of his mouth in tepid acknowledgment.

"Funny way to move into a town, don't you think? Flying your own flags, drawing lines as to who your store's for. Why not an American flag? That includes everyone! Bet your daddy agrees."

Will swallows. "I bet he does."

She gives him twenty dollars as a donation and promises to come in for a phone bank. As she shuts the door with a fluttering farewell wave, he's forced to face yet again that while his father may ostensibly accept him, the campaign's success depends on people like this woman, like Terry, who do not. He experiences a hot flush of complicity in his own degradation and must remind himself that his father is not like them. At least he hopes not.

IT'S BEEN ALMOST a month since Dalton first came to Eric's cottage, anxious and nearly mute. Now he bounds up the front steps with clumsy exuberance. After sex, he's giddy and goofy, as though he has released not just semen but all of his seriousness. He tickles Eric, splashes him with water, does a naked jig in the kitchen. In short, he becomes a twenty-seven-year-old. He also uses Eric's deodorant, grabs books from the shelves to take home, and ransacks the house for food, finishing off a loaf of bread and a block of cheese. He drinks nearly an entire bottle of milk that Eric just bought from him, a ritual so routine that Eric has started buying two bottles and wonders if it's a sales strategy.

"You sure like this milk," Alex said last weekend after drinking from the same bottle that Dalton guzzled from hours earlier. "But I don't think you're supposed to drink unpasteurized."

Eric took the bottle from Alex and washed down his daily fixed-dose combo pill. "It's fine."

But this little act of defiance only made Alex more skeptical. Later, he held up his copy of *Howards End*, which Dalton had left on the coffee table. "Since when do you read novels?" he asked.

"Since always."

Alex laughed, amused and unthreatened. If he suspected anything, he didn't care. He was the one who had proposed opening up their relationship this summer, since they'd be spending so much time apart. The only rule was tact. Alex asked that Eric not fool around with anyone in their social circle; he didn't want them to be seen as one of *those* couples. So Eric evaded his husband's questions without guilt and explained away the evidence, pouring himself another glass of raw milk in a silly show of denial.

On an earlier visit, Eric learned that Dalton drinks so much milk in part because he doesn't drink alcohol, or rather, he's trying to stop. When Eric asked why, Dalton answered with a silent shrug. But that small confession was the first cautious drop in what has become a steady trickle of intimate details that has started to render Dalton in abstract relief. Just today he brought up his parents' divorce and shared, unprompted, his resentment toward his mother for leaving a decade ago and his anger at his father for prompting her departure.

But later, naked in bed, when Eric called Dalton's dad an "asshole," repeating Dalton's own word, he was reprimanded. "I'm the only one who gets to call him that," Dalton said. "I've earned the right, and I know the other things he is, some of which aren't so bad." With that, he went to take a shower.

Despite this growing intimacy, Dalton still feels to Eric like a lark. And while larks are now allowed in his marriage, Dalton is a fuzzy new zone. Not adulterous, Eric reasons, because the attraction is not emotional. Though it occurs to him that just as an untended garlic clove will eventually sprout green shoots from the mere mingling of moisture, heat, and time, so, too, have those same ingredients led Eric to sprout affection for Dalton.

He contemplates all this as he listens to the shower's wet white noise. Through the din, he thinks he hears the doorbell, probably a delivery, something he couldn't find at Delphi's and had ordered online. He slips on a pair of sweats and finds, to his astonishment, the freckled catering kid from Paul's fundraiser, the one with the troublesome coffeepot, standing on the front porch.

And when Eric appears in the doorframe behind a mesh screen, Will is equally amazed and confused, speechless for many moments. "Mr. Richardson?" he eventually says.

Eric steps out onto the porch as a flyer that had been stuck in the screen door flutters to the floor. He stoops to retrieve it.

"No, I'm not," Eric says. He becomes aware that he is shirtless. He crosses his arms over his chest as if impatient, though really the pose stems from self-consciousness. His wedding ring catches a spear of light. "And you are?"

"I'm Will." He swallows. "Martindale. I think we met at—"

"Right." Eric ejects the word abruptly, like a warning, an approaching cliff. "Can I ask what you're doing here, Will?"

"Actually . . ." Will stops. He coughs. It sounds forced, like he's trying to buy time, which he is. He looks down at a clipboard. "Sorry . . . I must have the wrong house. It says Lyle Richardson lives here."

"He's the previous owner."

"And what was your name again?" Will asks.

Eric hesitates. Then he sees Will's eyes focus on something behind him and widen. Eric turns as Dalton's tall, broad silhouette passes by, wrapped in a towel. Will's face now wears a confused expression, and Eric recalls that Will met Alex at the fundraiser, that Eric explicitly referred to Alex as his husband, and that the nearly naked man behind him is most certainly not Alex. Eric realizes he is in a delicate situation and pivots to politeness; engagement seems the most prudent way to secure privacy. He steps forward and shuts the screen behind him.

"Eric," he says, to answer Will's lingering question. "Eric Larimer. Nice to see you again, Will," though it does not sound sincere. "Now, how can I help you?" As Eric says this, he looks at the flyer in his hand. "Wait, is this Paul's opponent? Did you bring this?"

Will thinks quickly. "My parents know him. I'm . . . It's a favor. To my dad." Eric's silence makes him barrel on. "I don't really know the guy, and I didn't know what that fundraiser was for until I got there. Honest."

"I see," Eric says. "Unfortunately, I'm not registered to vote here." But this is not true. He, unlike Alex, has already changed his registration, given the Twenty-sixth District's national value. He hopes the lie will conclude this encounter, but Will ignores the off-ramp.

"You're not?" He didn't mean to sound so accusatory.

"No, I'm not," Eric says sharply, then remembers the strategic need for civility. "I'm just living here for the summer."

"Oh."

They go silent again, each considering what the other now thinks or suspects, worrying what he might do with his newly gleaned intel. But it's hard for Eric to see a threat in the awkward young man fidgeting on his porch, and he has no reason not to believe Will's explanation.

A bee flies between them, causing Will to dodge it adorably, which causes Eric to smile and Will to reciprocate. In this little dance, they seem to reach an understanding of mutual discretion. Eric reaches out a hand and Will shakes it.

"It's not really a good time, Will. But thanks for stopping by."

JULY

CHAPTER 6

ON THE EVE OF the Fourth of July, Leon passes the big glass window of Bramble & Berry, the most popular of Griffin's new restaurants (as decreed by *National Holiday*), and observes an artfully framed party of five. Toulouse-Lautrec revelry within a Hopper exterior. He then realizes that these are the same men he met recently through Stan Banks, first at dinner, then at Paul's fundraiser. With a hiccup of hope, he sees that their table accommodates six. He could pretend to pop in for a bite at the bar and maybe score an invitation to join them.

But a server appears with appetizers. The meal is already under way, which is probably for the best. He fears his scheme might have been met with poorly disguised reluctance or no invitation at all. So, hunched further, Leon crosses the street and enters his original destination, the Lucky Buck, where it is acceptable, even expected, to drink alone in the company of others.

He takes a seat at the bar. After a too-long wait, Maren, the bartender in black with the wild red hair, stands in front of him with a sour expression. When she asks what he wants, he says, "The young man with the drowned shrubs, please."

She glares at him, then walks away, either to honor his request or to deny him service altogether. In the meantime, Leon surveys the scene and notes with some satisfaction that he recognizes a few of the regulars: the blond sisters with matching hummingbird tattoos, the nail salon owner, and the liquor store lesbian with the silver bowl cut who's being consoled by them.

"But where am I going to find another brilliant, beautiful dyke like Debbie?" she's saying. She drains her beer and tips it over like a checkmated king. "Everyone talks about Griffin as this queer mecca. But it's all just pretty boys." She grunts. "Pretty boys cruising for local bourbon and aged mezcals and brut reserve, which, I've got all that shit at my store, too . . ."

"But you don't light it like modern art," says one hummingbird sister. "I get it. At least you're not alone. You've got a son that actually likes you, which is something! Just think, you could be in Gerry's shit-covered shoes."

Leon sees the comment reach the other end of the bar where a man with bushy white eyebrows under a trucker hat yells back, "Whadya say 'bout me?" His face remains fixed on a baseball game.

The sister yells back: "That your son's a fuckup and he hates you!"

"Yup, that's about right," the man mutters.

Will appears behind the bar, and Leon thinks he detects a flash of disappointment on the young man's face, as if Will's freckles briefly rearranged to imply it. Leon suppresses his paranoia. He is determined to be amiable.

"Oh, hello!" he says brightly. "I was hoping you'd be here."

For Will, the reappearance of this pockmarked face and these prying gray eyes is an unexpected and unwelcome bridge between the Buck and Paul's event. He counted on the two never intersecting. "I've been here," he says cautiously.

Leon chuckles. "Well, sure, except when you're at Banks's—"

"Right." Will severs the sentence and keeps his face blank. "So, what can I get you?"

"Leon. Leon Rogers. And you're Will, yes? If I recall correctly. Will what?"

"Huh?"

"Your last name! A person isn't complete without a last name."

Will is about to answer honestly but stops himself. He is on home turf, and Leon is an ambassador from the world of Paul Banks and Eric

Larimer, where "Riley" is a liability, and where he has already adopted an alias.

"Martindale," he stammers softly. He looks down at the polished wood of the bar and sees the reflection of the antlered Brothers mounted above him.

"Sorry?" Leon leans forward.

The Brothers remind Will where he is. To deny himself a Riley here would be a mad and audacious act of self-disinheritance.

"Will Martindale," he says, barely louder.

Leon laughs. "Martindale? That's marvelous! And just Will? Not William?"

"Only when my mom's mad."

"Of course! Only an angry parent has the patience for a full name. You don't mind if I call you William, though, do you? It's more distinguished."

"But I've always been Will."

"And I've always been Leon. Short for nothing, unfortunately. I would have preferred something like William, with more versatility. Easier to reinvent yourself, no?" He grins.

Will shivers, and a chill enters his voice. "What're you having?"

"Right. Well, William, how about your excellent little green drink? I've been craving it."

Will is too on edge to object to the name or to be flattered by the request. He begins pulping leafage with a shaky hand. Meanwhile, Leon looks around.

"Cozy place," he says. "Reminds me of my old haunt in the city. In spirit, at least. That rare sense of . . . how to describe it? Impartiality." Will hands him the cocktail with a frown. "Now, don't look so skeptical, William, it's a compliment. All I mean is that it's an escape from the judgment I feel elsewhere in this town." Leon sips his drink. "Though I suppose no place is immune from judgment as long as there are people in it." He laughs. "But it feels more real here, you know?" He looks around again: the man with the bushy white brows is blankly fixed on the TV, and a hummingbird sister continues to comfort the lovelorn lesbian while the other sets up a billiards game. "Real people living real lives," he says wistfully. Then his tone hardens. "Not the pageant of happiness you find elsewhere, like that pretentious glass cage across the street."

Will raises a brow. "Sure. Only real people with real problems here. No happy robots allowed."

"Don't get me wrong, William. I just mean I like it here. I've only been in town a few months, and this is the first place I've felt comfortable." Leon stirs the flecks of green floating like lily pads on his alcoholic pond. "Unlike that fundraiser a few weeks back, with Griffin's rich and famous. Such stuffy people!"

"Aren't they your friends?"

"True, true." Leon taps his fingers on the counter as if deliberating. "Well, to be honest, William, they're somewhat newish friends. Stan Banks was one of the first people I met, and he was generous enough to take an old faggot like me under his wing, even if it was only out of pity. Not that he said so, of course, but you can tell these things. I appreciate it, though. The transition hasn't been easy."

Will snags on that epithet. Still sounds like an insult, but casually self-assigned, unlike how Gerry spits it at others. There's even a note of dignity in the self-deprecation, which makes Will curious. "What brought you to Griffin, anyway?"

Leon is about to brush away the question with an evasive riposte but reconsiders. This young man has expressed interest, he sounds genuine. That combination is pleasant and rare. Take a risk, he tells himself. Share a little.

"That's kind of you to ask. I wish it were a happier story. Let's just say that I had fond memories of Griffin from a fall visit here a few years back, and when my life took an unfortunate turn recently, an article in some travel magazine reminded me of those happier times. So I returned, thinking maybe this is where I could start fresh."

Will deploys a go-to phrase he picked up from his father. "Sorry to hear." Just a standard defense against patron woes, but in that prepackaged morsel, Leon hears sympathy.

"Well, thank you. Together fifteen years, then the son of a bitch left me." Leon thinks he sees confusion in Will's eyes. "Yes, William, I was with a man. Faggot here, as I've already confessed. I'm sorry if this shocks you, but I assumed you'd guessed from my association with Banks and his crew." Will blushes, and Leon adopts a devilish smirk. "I'm sure you noticed they took quite a liking to you. You didn't seem to mind."

Will's face now reddens severely. "I didn't mind," he says, and is suddenly aware that he has come out or been outed, it's unclear which. This admission, both mundane and momentous, still feels to him part triumph, part defeat.

"As I suspected. But why so serious, William? You should be flattered! Let me buy you a drink, you look like you could use one. And so could I." He wiggles his tumbler. "Another, please."

Will pours himself a beer, swallows his discomfort, then gathers a fresh bouquet of herbs.

As Leon watches them being crushed, simmering in the memory of his own romantic betrayal, his tightly held hurt escapes. "He left me because it turns out he was a duplicitous cunt with a boy on the side."

Will looks up, startled. But he says nothing, which Leon takes as permission to proceed.

"Our perky little assistant, straight out of college, not much older than you, in fact. Very cliché, I know. Suddenly no husband, no home. And somehow *I* became the pariah in our world, cast out by so-called friends, who, it turns out, were really only ever his friends."

Leon pauses to gauge Will's reaction. His eyes seek compassion. But Will wears the stunned look of someone who has walked into a screen door. He didn't ask for such one-sided intimacy, but he must respond, it's part of his job. He borrows another line, this one from Maren, indicating neutral support: "That must be hard."

Leon shrugs. "Well, now here I am, adrift in Griffin, starting from scratch."

Will slides over the completed cocktail. "You like it here, though?"

The question seems to deflate Leon. His chest caves, his head drops. "What's not to like?"

"You've made friends."

"Just because you attend someone's fundraiser doesn't mean you're their friend."

"It doesn't?" Will thinks of tomorrow's pool party and wonders how many such gatherings one must be invited to before they can reasonably be cashed in for friendship.

"I don't know," Leon continues. "Maybe they needed to inflate the numbers. Don't get me wrong, I was happy to be there. They've been kind. Everyone's been very fucking kind. At least to my face. But I can tell they don't think I belong in their world, just as I see now that I never really belonged in Peter's. I don't flatter them, and I don't figure in their fantasies. Not like . . ." His gaze floats up to Will, hovers, then lands back on his nearly empty drink. "Never mind. They'll eventually tire of me, just as Peter did."

Will considers the implications of this confession. Leon isn't really part of Paul's crowd after all, just a lonely man hoping to gain a foothold there. Like Will. This rant has merely been a plea for sympathy and an invitation to enter an alliance against all the world's exclusionary forces: duplicitous exes, shallow new acquaintances, and pretentious restaurants across the street.

Will is unwilling to enlist. He won't preemptively taint tomorrow's pool party in faux solidarity with Leon's discontent. He deploys his most neutral preset response: "I guess."

Leon senses a cold new distance in Will's tone, a familiar withdrawing. His face darkens, his teeth clench. He had merely tried to be open and frank with the boy. He takes a long sip and savors the drink's botanic acidity, which rouses his own bitterness. He leans across the bar and says in a low, hoarse voice, "But they won't tire of a young, pretty thing like you. I saw how they ate you up and how much you liked it. I know those looks. Experience has taught me to recognize them."

"What?" Will's face begins to warm.

"Don't be coy, William Martindale. You think playing dumb reads as modesty, but really it just reads as cunning. You were all they could talk about at the fundraiser. The jock waiter with the innocent face and who would be the first to fuck him."

Will's eyes bulge and dart around the pub. His face twitches with fury. He feels like a lab specimen given a small dose of poison, then studied to determine its effects.

"Oh, I'm sorry!" Leon exclaims, though to Will the words drip with scorn. "There I've gone again, offending the one man kind enough to listen to my woes. Shame on me! Please accept my apologies." But even Leon is unclear as to his own sincerity.

Will imagines flinging Leon's drink at him. He'd like to watch the wilted greens glom on to that large cratered face. But the bartender reflex kicks in, and he becomes a stoic server. "Anything else I can get you?"

Leon shakes his head, which feels very heavy, flooded again with misery. His incorrigible rancor has again sabotaged his attempt at connection.

Will prints out a check, slaps it on the counter, and walks away. Leon stares at the soggy herbs in his glass and wonders why he took such pleasure in badgering the poor kid, why it felt so necessary in the moment and so vile the moment after.

A minute later, he senses someone next to him. It's the man with the trucker cap and fluffy brows. "You sure like those green things, don't you?" the man says, pointing to Leon's cocktail with the neck of his beer. "Only fellow I've seen order 'em."

"Why are you so fucking interested in what I drink?"

"Hey now! Meant no offense, buddy. What's got you so riled up?"

"It's just been a day."

"Tell me about it! Every day's a day." The man sticks out a hand and adopts a tone of exaggerated formality. "Gerald McAfee."

"Leon Rogers."

"I've seen you around." Gerald says it like a challenge.

Leon squares himself. "I've been around."

Gerald chuckles. "So why's it been a day?"

Leon spots Will conversing with the hummingbird sisters. "Let's just say I chose some regrettable words for someone who didn't deserve them."

"Ah, hell. That's just called a conversation! I'm sure it wasn't so bad."

"Don't be sure, Gerald."

"Musta been an accident, though, right? And call me Gerry."

"Yes. Or rather, no. It was very much intended, that's the regrettable part."

"Listen, whoever you hurt, I'm sure they'll forgive you eventually."

Leon dunks his fingers in his drink and extracts a slice of gin-soaked cucumber.

Gerald continues. "I had a shitty week, too. Shitty year, actually. Ten years. Hell, shitty life. Ha! Okay, not all of it. Trina was good to me until she was fed up with me. The kid started out okay. But it's the cows, man. The cows are what's killing me." He takes a drink. "Killer cows." He grins at the discovery of this new species. "Ever met a killer cow?"

Leon shakes his head.

"Know how they kill you? They bankrupt you! Follow me around one morning. You'd swear I was milking them, but truth is, they're milking *me.* Milking me dry. Every one of them creature's a one-ton hole in my savings, though I guess you can't call it 'savings' when there aren't any, right?" His grin pleads with Leon. "Not so different from my ex-wife, now that I think about it. The cows, I mean. Can't stop loving 'em even when they turn against you."

"I'm sorry, Gerald," Leon offers. "That sounds wretched."

"'Wretched.' That's a good word. Sounds nice when you say it. Sounds almost noble. Same with 'Gerald,' if you insist."

"Well, I didn't mean—"

"Ah, fucking Christ! Not this faggot again."

Leon follows Gerald's gaze to the television, where another Paul Banks ad has come on.

"Excuse me," Leon says. "I'm also a faggot."

"That so? Well, Leon, you're the most sympathetic faggot I ever met, and I appreciate you listening to my wallowing."

"Fine. But choose another word."

"How about 'asshole,' then?"

"I guess that's . . . better. If he deserves it."

"Well, they both do." Gerald tips his beer up to near vertical, drains it, then raises it overhead as if in victory, which is apparently a sign to Maren, who appears to swap bottles.

"Who's the other guy?" Leon asks.

"Seriously, pal? You're drinking his alcohol!"

"You mean Chip Riley is the owner of this pub?"

"This is news to you?"

"Why haven't I seen him?"

"Because of the goddamn campaign, man. Too busy for us these days, too important."

"You think he's an asshole? And you still patronize this place?"

"Welp, he's also my best friend. Ever since I've had pubic hair. But still an asshole sometimes. Best friends aren't supposed to steal your land, right?"

"He stole your land?"

"Trying to. I mean, it's the town that's doing it, but he runs the town and he's not stopping it, is he? And he prefers 'expropriating,' which is a word I know all too well now 'cause of all the damn lawyers. Twenty-five acres they're seizing under eminent domain for a sewage system. And that's twenty-five acres I don't want seized, so I say that's stealing."

"Won't you be compensated?"

"Doesn't matter! I'm losing money on this 'expropriation,' and I don't have money to lose, thanks to my killer cows. And what do I get for it? Diddly shit, man. New sewage won't do squat for my farm. Council says they're investing in 'economic growth,' says they're fixing Griffin's 'infrastructure inequality.'" Gerald hooks his fingers in the air.

"Sounds like the town needs it."

"Yeah, and Chippy needs the immigrant votes. The sewers will mostly service their crappy homes in South Griffin. Hardly any value added to the farms."

"So it'll help a lot of people?"

Gerald raises his chin at this challenge. "The real story is that they need the sewers to turn the old brick factory into a snazzy fucking spa. That's gonna raise the property values around it. And guess who's selling them properties? Chippy's wife. Now ain't that a coinkydink?"

"I see."

"Meanwhile, these immigrants, they're just an excuse. But are they paying taxes to support it? That's what I'm not so sure about. Griffin may *look* richer these days, but it's not *getting* richer, at least not for those of us who always lived here, you know what I mean?"

"Mmm."

"And meanwhile, Chippy gets hailed a first-rate supervisor and is gonna ride my stolen land to his political future." Gerald guzzles his beer and burps. "So, yeah. Asshole."

"Why do you come here, then? Someone screwed me, too, and I wanted to get as far away from him as I could. That's why I came to Griffin."

The anger recedes from Gerald's eyes. "But where would I go? And where else would I find a friend like Chip? You see those bucks up there?" He points to the stag heads mounted above them. "Those are the Brothers. That's me and Chip. Brothers. You can hate your brother sometimes, but you can't give up on him."

IT'S NEARLY SEVEN, and Will is expected home for dinner. He wipes the counter one last time, tosses his rag into the hamper, and taps Maren on the shoulder. She spins around, spooked.

"Jesus!"

"Sorry. I'm heading out. See you soon?"

She nods and waves him off, then returns to the crate she's unloading. She's aloof today, as she sometimes is, a quality many of the Buck's male patrons (and the liquor store lesbian) find alluring but that Will finds puzzling in contrast to her typical insouciance. He would ask if everything's okay, but he has learned that Maren doesn't respond well to questions in this state, seeing them not as expressions of care and concern but, rather, as distrust and intrusion.

As he leaves, she calls after him, "Tell Mom and Dad I'll be there by seven-thirty." She omits the "your," as usual, which is part laziness, part ownership, and a sign that she still values these meals as much as the Rileys do, that she considers them family as much as they do her.

Will exits through the Buck's back door into the small parking lot, where his borrowed, battered gray hatchback blends into the asphalt. The sky is marbled with purple and yellow streaks, which makes even the telephone poles and dumpsters look romantic in their slim and stocky silhouettes.

At home, he learns from Chip that the chicken will wear a ballgown and a tiara tonight. His father is spinning around the kitchen in his pink apron, singing along, decently, to Merle Haggard: "'When they're runnin' down our country, man, they're walkin' on the fightin' side of me.'"

A half hour later, the doorbell rings, and Will finds Maren on the front steps. The two porch lights bestow a sparkling ruby halo on her head and cast a double shadow behind her, like some ominous angel.

"Hey, bro," she says with a wily grin. She hands him a bottle of wine. "For Mom and Dad."

"From the new shipment?"

"Office perks. Let's make sure it's a good batch." She winks. Whatever cloud she was in before has dissipated. She's still in her black jeans and T-shirt, but she removes her acerbic shell when she comes over, as though her sarcasm is a coat she hangs in the entryway.

Joe waits for Maren in the hallway. He was a high school junior when the striking redhead first entered the Riley home. He had stared with adolescent lust at the then-thirty-five-year-old and began showing up at the Buck more regularly after soccer practice, pouring himself pints until his nerves settled and he could confide in her about the social dynamics of school, frustrations with his family, the merry-go-round of his budding romantic life. Maren indulged him, advised him with her typical candor, acted the big sister, but unknowingly fueled his incurable crush.

"Hey, Joey," she says now. He looks down with a sheepish smile.

At the table, the Rileys and their guest clasp hands. Diane says: "Lord, thank you for the food before us, for the people gathered around this table, and for the freedom we celebrate tomorrow. Protect this great nation and grant us the strength and opportunity to serve it the best way You see fit." Her eyes lift to Chip, whose beard rustles with humility. "Through Jesus Christ, our Lord. Amen."

"Amen."

The chicken is distributed in its evening-wear finery, accessorized by roasted baby potatoes and a spicy corn salad.

"How's the apartment working out, Mare?" Diane asks. Last month, Maren's rent rose suddenly and sharply—"to catch up to the market," her landlord said—and she needed to move immediately. Chip felt awful that her Buck paycheck couldn't cover her housing and promised to help. Diane had just sold three shoddy townhouses near the brick factory project to a developer, so they secured a temporary unit for Maren in one of them at a discounted rate while it awaited renovation.

"Got everything I need, thanks," Maren says.

"I'm glad to hear it," Diane says, though she recently learned that those townhouse renovations are imminent. She hasn't told Maren yet, but she's already looking for the next accommodation. "More wine?"

During the meal, Maren is an eager audience member. She nods along as Diane rails against a homeowners' association, and goads Chip into impersonating Buck patrons, particularly Gerry, whom he portrays as a drunken Charlie Chaplin. She casually mentions how popular Will's cocktail has become (he's not sure this is true, but he blushes in gratitude) and adds with a wink, "I think Will's become pretty popular himself."

She must be referring to Leon, which makes Will's stomach clench. His parents give confused semi-smiles. His father says, "Ah, well, that's good," and his mother remains quiet, unwilling to probe the comment further. Maren registers the awkwardness and pivots to Joe, hooking him into telling stories about clueless Duffels attempting their own home-improvement projects.

Maren's presence, especially when she's at her most intuitive and engaging, massages the family's knots. They loosen up for her, perform for her. Chip trots out his goofiness, rarely seen in public. Diane exaggerates her ruthlessness, playing a woman exasperated by all the incompetence around her. Even Joe reverts to a more vital version of himself, one that his parents and brother thought no longer existed. Maren has always had this effect on him.

Over dessert of mint chip ice cream, Chip asks, "You going to the picnic tomorrow, Mare?"

"Hadn't planned on it. Not really my vibe."

"But I like seeing friendly faces!"

"If it's friendly faces you're looking for, I'll be sure to stay away." She laughs and turns to Will and Joe. "You boys going?" A silence blows through the room. Maren interprets the silence correctly and directs her question to Joe. "You'll be there for your dad, right, Joey?"

His eyes swing to his father, then back to Maren. He beams at her, looking again like an enamored teenager. "Yeah, 'course I will."

Diane swallows a sob and thanks God for the bartender in black.

CHAPTER 7

EARLIER THIS MORNING, THE Griffin Independence Day Picnic commandeered the sports fields behind the town's unassuming youth center. The baseball diamond hosted face-painting stations and a petting zoo with a pair of alpacas whose fleece contributed to the socks and unseasonal scarves for sale at the nearby craft stalls. A team of excessively spirited volunteers at the soccer pitch facilitated an olympiad of contests and games, while the aging tennis court hosted a communal dining hall with rows of folding tables proffering all varietals of potato salad, richly sauced BBQ meats, and splendid displays of fruit-filled pies, artfully latticed and golden-crusted. Patriotic streamers, ribbons, tinseled garland, bows, and bunting covered every conceivable inch of decorative real estate.

Paul was in a sparkling mood because, after the picnic, he planned to take the rest of the day off from campaigning. The Fourth of July is his favorite holiday, because in addition to celebrating America's birth, it celebrates summer leisure, which is Paul's favorite pastime. Stan knows that a happy, refreshed candidate is an effective candidate and so granted Paul his pool party. In the meantime, they hobnobbed with attendees, visited the information booths of local organizations, cheered on a tug-of-war, and sampled greasy food with inflated enthusiasm. The air smelled of cut grass, burnt oil, and benign nationalism.

It was an uneventful morning until Celia Rhodes showed up. Just as they were making their way to the bandstand for a small ceremony, she jogged over, round cheeks taut from grinning. "Hello, gentlemen! Happy Fourth."

"Nice to see you, Celia," Stan said, and mostly meant it. He still hadn't quite forgiven her for that embarrassing story about Paul filing to run before he was registered to vote, but since then, her reporting on the campaign has helpfully portrayed Paul as gaining momentum, closing in on Riley's lead.

She was casually chatty this morning, telling them about a hike she'd just taken, recommending they try the ribs on the tennis court, asking whether they'd visited the big sculpture park an hour away, which they had not. Then, almost as an afterthought, she said, "Actually, mind if I ask you a few questions, Paul?"

Stan immediately tensed, but Paul was oblivious. "Sure!"

"It's about the Griffin Investment Group."

"Oh." Paul's smile wavered. He shot Stan an anxious look. "Well, we're just here to enjoy the picnic, so—"

"I haven't heard back from your people in several days," she interrupted. "So when I saw you here . . . Anyway, it'll be quick, just need to clarify something." She smiled sweetly and turned on her recorder. "So, one of the group's goals, as it says on the website, is to bring clean energy to the region."

"That's right."

"And you've invested in the science program at the state college to spur research in this area. Wind and solar and such."

Paul spoke cautiously. "We're very proud of the program."

"Sure. It's just that, I was scanning your recent financial disclosure and noticed you two have significant investments in the energy sector. Like, major oil and utility companies. Seems kind of inconsistent with your campaign position and the stated goals of your investment group."

A bullhorn screamed and Paul flinched. A three-legged race began, spurring shouts of gleeful competition. A playlist of eighties hits crackled through speakers spaced around the fields. And Paul wore the silly smirk he adopts when he doesn't know what to say. He laughed nervously. "Well . . . I . . . That doesn't sound right, does it, Stan?"

"No, it doesn't," Stan said crisply. "There's been some confusion. A misinterpretation of the filings. How about you follow up next week, Celia? After the holiday. We'll sort everything out."

"Okay, Mr. Banks. It's just that—"

"I'm sorry, we really need to get to the bandstand."

NOW BACK IN their unthreatening kitchen, Paul slouches against the marble island with a tumbler of vodka, still in his slacks and oxford shirt, fuming. He's recounting the episode to Jeremy, who has just arrived with a tacky American-flag cake from AJ's Supermarket, encased in plastic with a sticker in one corner that says "White," referring, presumably, to the batter. Paul requested the confection; he loves cheap cakes.

"It was a total ambush!" Paul makes a sudden gesture to evoke the alleged assault, sending a spray of vodka onto the floor, which he ignores. "She comes up, pretending to be all chummy, and wham! Blindsided by baseless accusations and—"

"She didn't accuse you of anything, Paul." Stan's sharp annoyance masks his lingering unease.

"But who does she think—"

"You thought she was your publicist?" Stan snaps, though he's also chastising himself.

"But what do we do?" Paul whimpers.

"We'll discuss that at the staff meeting," Jeremy counsels. "For now, enjoy your day off. And your cake."

Paul stares at his drink. "Bitch."

Just then Will walks in. Three sullen faces turn toward him. He freezes, a startled animal in black board shorts and a large, loose T-shirt. The audit reminds him of the last time he was in this kitchen, retrieving a secret drink for Paul, discovered by Stan. Now he's the one interrupting, but somehow he feels like he's been caught again.

"Hi, sorry. I wasn't sure . . ."

Paul's pout mutates into an exaggerated grin. "Will! Good to see you, glad you're here. This is Jeremy, my campaign manager. Did you meet? And you remember Stan? Can I get you a drink? Where have you been?"

"Sure." Pause. "With my family."

Paul fills a second tumbler, hands it to Will, then refreshes his own. "At the picnic?"

"Uh-huh," Will says, accepting the drink.

It would be easy to tell the truth, that he was at home with his brother, but the morning had unnerved him. Last night at dinner, Joe had looked the happiest Will had seen him all summer, thanks to Maren. But he was a wreck this morning. Angry, pallid face, flickering pupils caught in a web of red vessels, in no shape to be seen in public. Their father was furious, their mother devastated. They'd left Joe in Will's care so they could attend the picnic, and the brothers had passed the morning in silence and suspicion until they were suddenly shouting in the kitchen. Will accused Joe of sabotaging their father's campaign, and Joe, rattled with rage and withdrawal, told Will to fuck off back to college because they didn't need him here, after which Joe either accidentally or purposefully dropped a porcelain coffee mug, severing the handle.

"What a great tradition, the picnic," Paul says. "Do you go every year?"

"Um, most." Will fills his throat with vodka and savors the burn.

"I envy you, Will. Such a privilege to grow up in a small town with a family who takes you to stuff like that. Not my experience at all. Maybe that's why I moved here, because I was robbed of that small-town, happy-family stuff."

Stan and Jeremy blink. Will empties his glass.

"I'm just kidding!" Paul laughs. "But wow, that drink went quick! Another? Or maybe you should change first?"

"Um, I didn't bring a uniform," Will stammers. "I'm sorry, I thought—"

"Ha! No, no. I meant into your swimsuit."

"Oh. Actually, I'm already wearing it."

Paul eyes Will's shin-length shorts with a pained grimace, and Will instantly understands. Such a garment was the only acceptable swimwear among his high school peers, who had hunted for signs of nonconformity and flamboyance with the vigilance of prison guards.

Paul squints at him. "Maybe you'd like to borrow something more . . . appropriate?"

Paul takes Will's silence as affirmation. "We'll be back," he says to Stan and Jeremy, then steers Will up a flight of stairs and down a long hallway to a large, bright bedroom with a four-poster bed and a handsome credenza. Paul extracts a turquoise swim brief from a drawer full of them. "This is a good color for you."

He hands it to Will and stands expectantly. Will fingers the smooth scrap of fabric. He has never worn so little so publicly and feels utterly unprepared for the exposure. Paul gives a prodding cough and raises impatient brows, and Will realizes that Paul intends to watch him try it on. In a hectic second, he debates whether to seek privacy in the bathroom, but Paul looks restless, or greedy, and the vodka has dulled Will's restraint.

His body asserts control. Feet fling sandals, hands untie shorts, and waist bends forward so his large shirt becomes a cotton shield of modesty, as it was in the high school locker room. Will's shorts puddle at his feet, and cool air tickles his testicles as he quickly steps into the springy turquoise fabric. He stumbles, hops on one foot, surrenders to Paul's gaze, and pulls up the suit with such speed that, for a second, his brain sparkles whitely. The spandex sucks on his hips, and air-conditioning cools his thighs. He cannot decide how best to position his bulge. All options feel lewd.

And yet. The suit's snug skimpiness conjures an unexpected, buried naughtiness.

Paul's look is one of devious accomplishment. "I think those will do," he says. "Now I've got to get out of this fucking costume. Hold on."

He unbuttons his shirt, flings it on the bed. The slacks follow, and Paul stands unabashed in tight black underwear. He selects a tropical-print brief and casually strips.

Will concentrates on the concentric diamond pattern of an area rug while his body hums with unease and arousal. In the blur of his peripheral vision, he registers Paul's curved, tan back and smooth white tush.

This is not right, he thinks. I should not be seeing this. I should not have come.

But some brave and unsung urge nudges his eyes up as Paul's naked body comes into focus. Paul senses the attention and straightens, the bright flower print paused on its journey up. This time Will refuses to look away. Paul faces him with smug surprise, as though he didn't think Will would dare, as though aware of the battle he has instigated in Will's mind and aware, too, of his victory. He secures the swimsuit and approaches, placing a cool hand on Will's warm, available waist.

Will holds his breath. He wonders if his pulse can be detected near his stomach. If so, Paul will surely feel every mutinous beat of his desire.

"Shall we?" Paul says. Then he leaves the room.

OUTSIDE, THE BANKSES' pool reminds Eric of the safari photos he has scrolled through when imagining his dream vacation, a watering hole surrounded by sixteen exotic male creatures (and a sole female, Molly, the labradoodle) who scamper and sniff each other as they flaunt long necks, sharp beaks, big ears, hairy chests, smooth paunches, and voluptuous hinds in tones ranging from cream to copper to burnt umber to a rare sable. Nate calls for a photo, and this menagerie squeezes together. Documentation demands adjustments: stomachs cave, torsos turn discreetly to more flattering angles, pecs coyly flex. Vanity is a prominent muscle, even in repose.

As far as Eric can tell from the chatter, no one here attended Griffin's Independence Day Picnic earlier. These men have come from all over the region in little delegations representing towns across the river or the neighboring district—a confederation of rural homosexuals, half of whom Eric does not recognize. So everyone here has either driven a considerable distance, or their weekend guests slept in, or breakfast included mimosas, or body hair needed trimming. In any event, the morning passed them by, and the communal picnic slipped their minds. Or, in Alex's case, he just didn't want to attend.

"We went to the Memorial Day Parade, like, a month ago," he argued last night. "An hour looking for parking, an hour waiting for the damn thing to start, *another* hour waving at Girl Scouts, all to watch Paul pass by in seconds. I'd say we've done our civic duty for the summer, and for Paul."

"That was completely different," Eric insisted.

"Was it? Flags, cheap food, bad music. Sounds the same to me. And frankly, I'm not really interested in being stared at again like we're an invasive species."

"What are you talking about?"

"I saw the looks. The ones I always get around here. The ones that say, 'You don't belong.'"

"Maybe you're projecting."

"Maybe you're naive. They distrust my Asian face."

"They distrust your exceptionally short shorts."

"Either way. Besides, what's the fucking point?"

Eric didn't want to keep arguing, and they ultimately didn't go. But he knows the reason has something to do with spending time near your neighbors, even and especially if you don't really know them. Dalton has made him think differently about the value of that proximity, though that's not something he's ready to share with Alex. In any case, Eric is starting to consider these picnics and parades as rare chances to convene when everyone's in a generous mood. It's a missed opportunity, he thinks, that he and his friends did not attend, at the very least to signify their goodwill. What would it have cost? A slight delay in their revelry? A few fewer cocktails? On the lip of Paul's pool, second glass of rosé in hand, he looks down at his wobbly reflection in the wine and wonders: What *is* the point of watching a Girl Scout troop walk and wave? The point is to wave back.

His next sip reveals a familiar, acrid aftertaste: the arrogance of self-isolation, with complex notes of complacency, laziness, and inertia.

Eric senses the collective attention shift to the sliding back door, where Paul is leading Will onto the patio. He hears Paul say, "You can leave your clothes there," and sees him gesture to a chaise longue.

Will, still dazed, places his board shorts on the chair, knowing he will never wear them again. He slowly pulls off his shirt, feeling a dozen pairs of eyes on him. They are not unwelcome, but he cannot bear to meet all those looks. Paul hands him a glass of rosé and, once in the pool, formally introduces Will Martindale to a circle of men, among them Eric and Alex, Luke and Serge.

"What a pleasant surprise!" Alex says. He leans in and presses his cheek against Will's, which feels unearned in its intimacy but also feels wonderful.

"Nice to officially meet you," Eric says with intentional flatness. He extends a hand. The strength of their grasp and its meaningful duration acknowledges their recent meeting and reaffirms their silent agreement.

Serge, of the silver hair, smiles with the warmth of his sunset skin. "Good to see you again," he says, affectionately gripping Will's shoulder as he did at the fundraiser, delivering a prickly shiver.

"You, too!" Will says, a bit zealously.

Serge sweetly inquires how Will's been, as if he's an old friend, and asks expected introductory questions about family, school, and work. Will deceives only by omission.

"But do you enjoy the catering?" Serge then asks.

"It's okay for now."

"I'd imagine it's a good summer job," Serge says in a way that seems to question whether it is. "But I wonder what you ultimately *do* with it."

"True," Will says, though he has wondered no such thing. His paycheck contributes to his tuition and housing, that's what he does with it.

"You into *theater*?" Serge asks, imbuing the last word with ornate gravity—possibly ironically, possibly not.

"Yes!" Will says emphatically, although he can't recall ever seeing a professional production. But he could be. Here, as Will Martindale, he can be whoever he wants to be.

Serge rewards this with a long baroque description of his festival, currently running, and extends an invitation to attend. Will has heard of the festival from a Buck patron who complained that a ticket there cost nearly as much as a tank of gas.

Then Serge says, "And if you're not set on a future in catering, maybe next summer you can be one of my interns."

Suddenly Will Martindale has been handed future prospects that Will Riley never could have imagined. The party already feels consequential, a step toward some unknown yet promising new future. Surely that justifies his presence and lies?

Paul directs Will to another batch of men for another round of introductions. "Will is from here," Paul informs them, like an expat tour guide who has befriended a native and is eager to show him off. The men receive him with charitable smiles.

But it's Will who feels like he's a visitor in a foreign land, a small, wealthy nation inhabited by a single-sex populace. Having never been abroad, he doesn't know the nervous thrill of encountering a new culture, aside from college, though that felt less like a new culture than a heightened, inebriated version of the one he already knew. This place feels instantly distinct. He has had to reevaluate his sense of space, his relationship to touch, his assumptions about the proper fit of swimwear. Like many first-time international travelers, he is quickly enamored of this new country and indulges the tendency to deem it superior to his own: See how they appreciate beauty! Note their unapologetic embrace of leisure! Observe their uninhibited affection toward one another! His own cultural inheritance—his upbringing in Griffin—feels bland and lacking in comparison. He would discard it all in exchange for this sensual land.

Of course, the problem every smitten tourist soon encounters is one of bureaucracy. To extend your stay requires permission, and Will has been issued only a temporary visa for today. A work visa, technically. He will earn his attendance by picking up trash at the end of all this.

In the meantime, the men pelt him with questions that express curiosity, albeit dipped in condescension.

"So what was it like growing up here, before the renaissance?"

"I've heard that's one of the better state schools."

"Do you know anything about fences? A wild turkey ran into ours, and our landscape guy can't get to us until next month."

Each inquiry has the whiff of rendering him some rural cartoon. But

Will doesn't mind being a stereotype as long as it means they consider him interesting enough to be invited back. He realizes, belatedly and with a small implosion in his chest, that his performance today will determine the rest of his summer. Either they'll decide to adopt him, granting him eight more weeks of companionship in lavish settings, or he'll be relegated to shuttling back and forth between the Lucky Buck, campaign headquarters, and his childhood home. This new awareness of their power, which they don't even recognize, renders him painfully inarticulate.

"Fences? Um, no, sorry."

But then he thinks: Joe knows fences. Will would refer them to his brother, if they were on better terms, if he trusted Joe, if Joe hadn't scared him earlier with those spiteful words and that severed mug. Will flushes away the morning with more wine.

THE NEXT FEW hours stumble forward as if time, too, were buzzed. The sun slides through the sky, transitioning from white to lemon to saffron. Will scans the patio for ways to be useful. He collects empty bottles and abandoned beverages, lining them up on the outdoor bar like trophies. The guests cycle in and out of the pool, doze, awaken to reddened bodies, resubmerge. All with an endless glass of rosé in hand, any lull in conversation filled with a cry for more. Soothing liquid outside; soothing liquid inside until the brain is bubbly, until the men feel as toasted and airy as a soufflé.

Conversation bobs along as directionless as one of the pool's foam noodles, any topic of discussion as good as any other as long as the water's gentle rhythm carries it somewhere. At one point, they commiserate over attacks by the region's insurgents: wires chewed through by mice, wasp nests wedged into stone walls, a spider with a bumpy back that, when provoked, reveals those lumps to be dozens of babies, which go scurrying in all directions. The men shriek in terror and hilarity as if telling ghost stories around a fire.

From there, they segue to status reports on the land management of their respective properties—seasonal plantings, topographical cosmetic surgery—then on to house renovations, travel, TV, and gossip, all of which seem somehow thematically related. The mention of a resort in Singapore leads to a debate about a reality show, which reminds someone of something he heard about so-and-so, which inspires an anecdote about a harrowing bathroom remodel, which then swerves to the upcoming launch party for *Fodder*, a new local lifestyle magazine, which they'll all be attending next month.

Will already knows about the event because he'll be working it for Carly. At first this feels like a stroke of luck, the guarantee of being back in the company of these men. But quickly the fortuity generates a wave of nausea, stemming from the shame of having to serve them again after being allowed to laze among them. Well, technically he's at their service here, too, but it doesn't feel that way from inside this blue water and Speedo.

Then a slight disturbance in the air, and a large shadow stains the patio. Will looks up to determine its source and goes cold when he sees Leon standing unsmiling over him. Will had worried that Leon might appear, but with each passing hour and pink refill, the fear had faded.

Leon gives a curt little wave to mask his surprise at seeing Will. Don't be so shocked, Leon scolds himself, of course they'd invite the cute young waiter. But it strikes him now as an extraordinary coincidence that this local boy has managed to wedge himself between two congressional candidates—working for one while fraternizing with the other, seemingly at ease in these two vastly different spaces while Leon struggles to establish himself in either. He squats at the pool's edge, eager to probe Will on his social versatility. Then Stan approaches, and Leon rises to greet him.

"Glad you could make it," Stan says.

"Thank you for having me."

Leon had called Stan just this morning. "I'm sure your husband will be running around to numerous events this afternoon," he said. "If you need a reason to escape, perhaps a drink later?"

"Well, that's very thoughtful," Stan said. "As it turns out, we're having a few people over. Why don't you join us?"

It was the invitation Leon hoped for, an extension of the same generosity Stan had shown when they first met at the antique store, which led to the dinner party and fundraiser where Leon had met many of the men he sees around the pool now, though he still can't match face to name to partner to profession. They've all blended into an indistinguishable wad of white wealth. He does recognize Nate, the media executive (big, loud, and single), because they slept together shortly after the dinner party, because it is expected that two unattached men, especially those in their mid-fifties, should give each other a try. Leon enjoyed the encounter and proposed an encore, but Nate delayed and deflected. Now Leon sees him towering over a young, taut buck in designer sunglasses, and the message is clear.

Stan leads Leon over to the bar. "What's your poison?" he asks.

"Self-loathing," Leon replies. "But if you're out, I'll have a gin and tonic."

Stan chuckles, procures a beverage, then guides them to an unoccupied corner of the deck, glad for an excuse to extract himself from the frolicking fellows.

"That boy . . ." Leon says, looking back at Will.

Stan sighs. "Paul's idea."

"I remember him. But I've also seen . . ." He stops to consider that perhaps he shouldn't admit to patronizing the Lucky Buck, both because it's the establishment of Paul's opponent and because it might reflect poorly on Leon's social status. "Never mind."

At that moment, Molly trots over and tosses her front paws on Leon's legs, staring at him with hopeful panting.

"My apologies," Stan says, swiping at the dog.

"It's fine. Nice that *someone's* paying attention to me."

"But she wasn't invited."

Initially neither was I, thinks Leon, but says, "She fits in well, though. As frisky as all the other puppies here." He scans the pool area and mumbles, "So many puppies."

Stan swipes again at Molly, the Persistent. "I shouldn't be so uptight. I just can't stand the presumption. As if she were a child that can't be left alone, but even then I'd expect the courtesy of being asked first. Dogs and children are so inconsiderate, and powerful in their ability to hijack anything with their demands." The slobbering hijacker curls into a crescent at Leon's feet. "Reminds me of my husband sometimes."

Leon raises a brow, and Stan smiles with devious wonder, as if he has surprised himself. Since Luke first handed Stan a glass of wine, it's been topped off as much as anybody's. It makes such days tolerable, and he's not immune to alcohol's influence. It helps him shed his stiff civility and now incites a rare cheekiness.

From the pool, Will watches this conversation, terrified that Leon is informing on him, sure that this is the source of Stan's amusement. He becomes so focused on watching them that he doesn't notice he's been left alone in the shallow end. Flustered by his sudden solitude, he scrambles out of the water, wraps himself in a towel, and heads into the house in search of a bathroom. He hears voices in the hallway and heads toward them but stops when the conversation sharpens.

"The local kid?"

"Yeah. Who's he here with?"

"Came alone, I think."

"No. I mean, who's he fucking? Or did they find him on an app?"

"Picked him up at Paul's fundraiser, actually. Leftovers."

The voices, now laughing, get closer. Will rushes out of the house, body aflame. He's hurrying back to the pool when—

"Don't know how he got here."

He turns to find Paul leaning against the bar, gripping a near-empty bottle of rosé. Will isn't sure who he's talking about. In light of what he's just overheard, he fears for a moment it could be him. But then Paul cocks his head in Leon's direction.

"I sure as hell didn't invite the oaf. Hold on a sec." He dumps the remainder of the rosé into Will's glass, frees another bottle from the ice bucket, and, after a few missed stabs, liberates the cork along with a small wave of wine.

"Whoops!" Paul licks his fingers. He attempts to fill his glass and misses. "Shit. Sorry. Ha! Just haven't had a day off in months. I think

I've overcorrected. But it's been a very unfair morning. This campaigning shit is hard!"

"I know." Will swallows the wine to wash away what he overheard.

"You know? How the hell do you know?"

"I . . . I can imagine."

"No, you can't!" Paul juts his glass forward and sends another crest over the rim. "Fucking exhausting. I mean, the *hours* . . . You know how big this district is? How long it takes to drive to Vernon and back? How many events you can stuff into a day?" He sucks on his glass like a pacifier, goes quiet, then works himself up again. "And the *pressure*! From everywhere. From voters, your own staff, your own fucking *husband*. All so needy. I mean, not the voters. Well, *some* voters. And the journalists! Out to get you, for no good reason. Finding small stupid shit to make into big stupid shit. For their own goddamn glory."

"I get it."

"You don't! But that's okay. And y'know what, Will? I don't mind it. Don't mind it at all. It's exhausting, but I love it. They're all stupid, but I love them. I really do, y'know why? 'Cause they all *care* so damn much. Makes me care more, too. Really, really. Sounds bullshit, I know, but it's true! Just you and me here, Martindale. No campaigning, so you know I mean what I say. And I'm saying I love it, and I love them 'cause . . . you're gonna laugh, but I'll say it anyway: I love America."

Will is wide-eyed and silent, mesmerized by Paul's sloppy confession, if doubtful about its sincerity. Paul somehow senses this and leans forward, steadying himself on Will's shoulder, and insists, "No, really, Will. It's true. I could scream it." He does. "I love America!"

All heads turn, perplexed. He does it again. "I fucking love America!"

Several people whistle and hoot. Buoyed by this reaction, Paul raises his glass. A pink waterfall cascades down his arm as he shouts: "To America!"

The guests respond, in earnest or in jest: "To America!"

To Will, it sounds at once like a joke, a benediction, a warrior's roar.

But at the opposite end of the patio, Paul's strange, spontaneous salute provokes a deep sadness in Stan. Normally he could easily stanch its expression, but the wine has worn away his defenses, and he feels a terrifying wetness creep into his eyes. He excuses himself from Leon and slips away, following the grassy slope down to the thicket of trees at the river's edge.

SITTING ON A boulder, Stan tries to steady his breath. The river is a calm companion, gliding purposefully forward, giggling over a constellation of small rocks as if tickled by them. He wipes his eyes and thinks of Asher, and of the Ship, and of the many beautiful young men who flocked around its pool, and of the large American flag that dangled from the Ship's back balcony, as tacky and sweetly sincere as Paul's patriotic cake.

Not really a ship, of course, but an angular asymmetrical house with that moniker, built of faded gray wood with round windows and a rickety rear deck, all seeming to teeter on a dune on that blessed barrier island. Every weekend during that summer many decades ago had felt to Stan like a maiden voyage to an uncharted part of himself, with Asher as his guide.

Stan, the recent high school grad, and Asher, his flamboyantly free-spirited older brother. The two degenerate sons, according to their parents. Stan spent the summer before college in the city, immersed in Asher's chaotic world, which churned with adventurous art, artful adventure, and a cast of enchanting characters. He slept on Asher's tattered couch, spending weekdays waiting for weekends (while filing papers at an uncle's advertising agency), until their next visit to the Ship.

There, time stretched like warm taffy. Bodies baked on hot wooden slats, clothed and unclothed, the distinction suddenly arbitrary, though the brothers remained covered out of respect for each other's comfort. Stan saw how such exposure among the Shipmates encouraged a fraternal openness and intimacy that he'd never experienced or even imagined. After his lonely, tortured high school years, these ritualistic immersions into pool and sea cleansed Stan's shame and proposed new possibilities of self-love and friendship. It was a constant wonder to him—a miracle, even—that his own brother had been the one to show him this paradise, that he and Asher shared membership in this sacred tribe.

But they were granted only a single summer. In the fall, as Stan was swaddled in scarves on a Midwest campus, two Shipmates became inexplicably ill. Then two more. Soon Asher became consumed as their caretaker. The smile faded from his voice, replaced by anger and despair. He told Stan to stay away. "I don't want you here," he said. "Don't make yourself part of this." The numbers of the sick exponentially grew. The world ignored, then slowly woke to, their plight. A year later, Asher whispered, "It got me," and Stan shattered.

He took a semester off to become Asher's nurse, to attend rowdy meetings, to scream at clergy, to block intersections, to kneel at a hospital bed and hold his brother's thin damp hand. He attended half a dozen funerals, including, finally, Asher's.

He hasn't been back to the Ship, nor that blessed and cursed barrier island, since. For years, he couldn't tolerate a pool party for more than an hour. When he and Paul moved to Griffin, he focused fully on the campaign and intentionally avoided all the same-sex socializing, afraid to find Ship-like scenes that would continue to haunt him here.

But a year later, something has shifted. He feels his long-carried suffering beginning to lift, the ever present weight of his grief somehow lighter.

It helps that these pool parties are set in woods rather than on beaches, and it helps, too, that many of the men in his new Griffin circle are younger, unscarred by loss. Perhaps that's also why Paul's youth and promise were such strong ingredients in Stan's attraction to him. He believed that trauma-free Paul could help him fulfill a vow that Stan had made to himself after Asher's passing: Our community will not be powerless again. We will be represented. We will represent ourselves. And we will remake this country in the process. Perhaps because that process has now advanced substantially, he finds he can tolerate pool parties again.

Stan has spent his career earning the money to buy the influence to ensure they will never again be ignored, left to die undignified deaths. Paul's impromptu little toast back at the pool reminded Stan of a time when America had failed him, had failed Asher, had failed so many like them. But now Stan lives freely, with his husband, part of a community that has faced the cruelest of adversaries in stigma and science, and survived. In professing his love for America, Paul unknowingly declared a kind of victory. He demanded more. He promised to continue fighting for others. And without even understanding the significance, the men all shouted back: Amen!

Stan dips his hand in the water and wipes his eyes, the river's coolness soothing the heat of his tears. He heads up the lawn, back to the party.

LUNCH PREPARATIONS ARE underway. Will has taken the initiative to lay out the plastic utensils, paper plates, and containers of side dishes purchased from Poppy's Pantry. The meat is Stan's territory.

"Where have you been?" Paul scolds his husband when he reappears. "Everything's ready except the burgers."

Stan takes his position behind the grill, grateful for a purpose. Here he gets to be both alone and useful, one of those rare times when contributing to the social atmosphere allows for solitude. He turns on the gas and presses the ignition button, but nothing happens. The grill is temperamental, probably offended by its lack of use. He presses again. Just irritated clicks.

There's a squeal by the pool, and he turns to look. Someone has pushed someone in, and everyone applauds. Water spills over the pool's lip, and Stan feels like a proud papa watching his kids wrestle with the neighborhood boys, a show of strength and innocence. He turns back to the grill and gives the ignition button another forceful jab.

Suddenly a scream of flames. An angry, fiery orb brushes his face. In an instant, Stan is on the precipice of an inferno. In another instant, it is gone.

Cries of "Holy shit!" as the collective attention swerves to the fireball billowing upward until it dissolves into a wisp of black smoke. Molly whimpers. Paul rushes over. "Babe! What happened?"

Stan is fine, sweaty and humiliated, unaccustomed to public missteps or encounters with danger. He looks at Paul with surprise, feeling no longer the protective papa. He forces a chuckle and shakes his head as though the grill were just a rambunctious child playing tricks.

"That was wild!" Alex says.

"I missed it," Nate moans.

Paul gives his husband a comforting rub and, perhaps thinking to give Stan relief from the gawkers, turns to his guests with a ringmaster's grin and says, "How about a replay?"

He leads the men inside, drinks in hand. They twist through two hallways to an A/V closet featuring a humming console with blinking lights and digital displays that attest to its vigilance.

Paul pulls out a thin metal drawer and flips open a laptop. He clicks on an icon, and a grid of security camera footage appears, each with a tag identifying its area of observation: Front Gate, Main Entrance, Side Patio, Pool Deck, etc. Paul maximizes one of the small squares, and there's Stan on camera, flipping burgers. With another few clicks, Paul reverses through the recent footage to just before the incident. He presses play, and again flames send Stan stumbling backward.

Gasps and giggles.

"How frightful!" Leon says. "Poor man."

"Play it again!" Nate demands.

Paul obliges. He obliges three more times, each screening eliciting yelps of delight.

"I had no idea this place was under such surveillance," Serge says.

"I can only imagine what other fiery incidents this thing has captured," Alex says.

Paul grins, eyes half closed in his boozy stupor. "Wouldn't you like to see?"

The men shout their affirmation, and Will joins the cajoling.

Paul demurs, but the clamor grows until he holds his finger to his lips, as if to both quiet them and swear them to secrecy. He scrolls through files sorted by date, pauses to reflect on the calendar in his head, and selects one from a few weeks ago. He chooses Pool Deck and presses fast-forward.

It's a bright day. The deck is empty, then it's not. One figure, then another, then Paul appears, then two more men, five in total. They dart in and out of the frame, like cartoons, at enhanced speed. Minutes then hours tick by in seconds. Then one swimsuit is gone, then all are. Naked bodies scurry in and out of the pool until they're in a circle in the shallow end, then moving closer together, then seeming to combine into one big fleshy ball.

A suspended hush, then a blast of scandalized surprise. Will's lips part in disbelief. Paul blushes with pride or discomfort and abruptly shuts the laptop.

"That's your free preview," he announces to a chorus of boos. "The rest you have to pay for."

"How much?" Serge says.

"More than you can afford."

"How about a campaign donation?" Leon shouts. "Mhah!"

But this is met with thorny silence. Paul looks at him with wide, suddenly sober eyes, as if he forgot Leon was there.

Leon instantly realizes that mentioning the race at such a provocative moment has punctured the playfulness and reminded Paul of this material's potential liability. In the awkward seconds that follow, Leon berates himself and is about to backtrack with something self-deprecating and apologetic when Nate swoops in.

"Well, all that flesh is making my mouth water. Burgers, anyone?"

Paul joins the nervous laughter and shepherds everyone outdoors.

AFTER THE CAKE has been politely picked at and the leftovers brought inside, the men crawl back into the pool's cradle. The sun starts to melt into the horizon, and Will debates whether to commence cleanup duties. He also wonders if the increasingly inebriated Paul will remember to pay him. He hopes not. Payment would confirm his status as hired help. He would forgo compensation if it allowed him to maintain the illusion that he is simply another guest.

These thoughts fade when he finds himself back in the pool, in a circle in the shallow end, reminiscent of the scene he's just glimpsed on-screen. He can imagine how it continued but wonders how it began. Perhaps like this: Serge's foot bumps into his and lingers; Serge's hand brushes his thigh and stays. Later, the hand migrates to Will's lower back, then slips down to his upper glute. Will welcomes its journey, the natural progression of this lusty day.

Then someone says, "Fuck it," and a wet bathing suit slaps the patio stones. Other swimsuits follow. Initially the exposed bodies remain underwater, flesh rendered as squiggly lines, like the fast-forward footage they just watched. Then someone demands more rosé, and a naked body rises out of the pool, sauntering unabashed to the bar. With the bravery of one, others find courage. Soon half the group is naked and the other half not. There is no pressure to be in either state, so Will keeps his borrowed blue suit on.

With the shedding of clothes, though, Leon is relegated further to the energetic periphery of the party. He hasn't even taken off his shirt. It is simply too much to be an unfit man in his fifties among so many sprites. Worse, his contemporaries Serge and Nate are participating in the exhibitionism. Serge boasts an admirable physique, disciplined by the expectation of these recurring summer scenes to remain vigilant, to prioritize the gym, to decline the cake. Nate has taken a different approach, cultivating an insouciance that allows him to carry his hairy heft with admirable and likely hard-earned self-respect.

Leon has not made the effort in either direction, physical or psychological, and thus has never felt at ease in such settings, or in his body. He's happy to merely observe, but there's only so long you can sit on the sidelines watching. And Leon is the only one on land now. A whale out of water, he thinks. A much too neat illustration of the avoidance he's sensed since his reckless campaign comment or, frankly, since he moved to Griffin. He feels the familiar burn of rejection, as though the glistening bodies in the pool are redirecting the sun's last rays at him.

He decides it's time to go. He looks for Stan, but Stan has disappeared. (Stan has escaped upstairs to a current-affairs magazine.) He looks for Will and sees him in the shallow end, the recipient of Serge's flirtatious attention, which makes Leon burn further. Why is it that bland boys are so easily absorbed while mature men must mount a case for their inclusion? He knows the easy answer. Youth is the eternal siren song, as his ex-husband reminded him.

But the ease with which Will has slipped from behind the Lucky Buck bar and the catering tray into the Bankses' pool is especially maddening because Leon can't shake the feeling that Will is edging him out, that once again Leon's age and disposition have become liabilities. It's an unfair and unreasonable accusation, he knows. A social circle has no official limit; in theory, it can expand endlessly. Yet the reality is, a circle must close somewhere. It must exclude.

Leon fears he will be excluded from this one, just as he was from the previous, but he is determined to avoid that fate because he has identified no alternative in Griffin. He has succeeded in a similar feat before, ultimately winning over Peter's friends in the city, however temporary a coup that proved to be. But he learned that infiltrating a group is simply a matter of proving your worth, contributing something of use, whether a sharp wit or a beautiful face or a large bank account. He will find a way to add value to this one.

He informs Paul of his departure. Paul waves distractedly and turns back to the group with what looks like relief. As Leon gathers his bag, Molly dashes over and wags her tail, the only member of the party to bid him a proper farewell.

The sun extinguishes itself on the horizon. The colors drain overhead, and the air takes on a pleasant chill. Underwater lights turn the pool a spooky green and transform submerged bodies into tantalizing chevrons of skin. More swimsuits smack stone, then someone announces that he's cold. One by one, bodies rush to the hot tub a few yards away, their slippery, silvery skin like fish in the moonlight. They cram in, a dozen men confronting a tub intended for half that. The tub's nosy white light makes everyone look especially sinister until Paul turns it off, granting an inky black alibi. Packed in as they are, legs tangle and hips kiss. Will finds himself next to Serge, exactly where he wants to be. Somewhere in the distance, fireworks glitter the sky.

CHAPTER 8

A FEW DAYS AFTER the Fourth of July, Joe is back behind the register at Delphi's, feeling better in his yellow vest, but better than shit doesn't mean much. The hours drag, except when customers keep him occupied. A local seeks a jigsaw, a contractor needs help repairing a drill, a Duffel asks about fencing because a wild turkey ran into his. Otherwise, the day stutters and stalls, giving him ample time to marinate in his shame for having used again at home, for fucking up the picnic for his family, for being a fuckup in general.

It was confirmed in the way Will looked at him that morning, with such pity and disdain, how he just walked away when Joe told him to go back to college, like Joe wasn't even worth a response. Then Troy picked him up and they played video games until late, the massacres on-screen less violent than the self-punishment in Joe's head. He was supposed to go to work yesterday but woke past noon on Troy's bedroom floor, his body feeling as pulped as the pixelated ones from their games. Troy covered his shift, which he's done a few times already this summer, because Troy understands. He was there, too, on the Swinton dock in May, and he knows that Joe is stuck there.

Matt's lakeside home had been their default clubhouse since middle school, when Matt's grandfather died and left it to the Swintons. It wasn't big or special, just two small stories wrapped in warping yellow clapboard under an old shingled roof—what Joe once heard his mom call a "teardown"—but it was the favorite of their friends, owing to its perch on Shelby Lake and especially its basement, which was cut into the hillside and followed the footprint of the entire house. That room featured low wooden beams, water-stained walls, brown carpet, and two squishy green sofas; cozy in winter and airy in summer, when the sliding glass doors were left open.

The lake that early May night had been a radiant blue-black in the moonlight. A handful of Joe's friends were huddled around a small portable firepit on the dock, bottles of beer and bourbon at their feet. Callie was newly single, and Matt had prepared Joe to make a move.

"Don't let her talk about him," Matt advised, referring to her ex. "If she comes to you to process or even complain, she won't come back for the good stuff."

"But if I listen to her, won't that make us closer?"

"For the wrong reasons! You don't want to turn into her fag best friend, do you? Focus on being the rebound. You gotta put passion behind the wheel, Joey, or you'll get nowhere. Trust me."

And Joe did because Matt's track record backed it up: a string of relationships, if they earned that label, with Griffin's most desirables, at least while they were in school, before the post-graduation slump. But at his peak, Matt, with his buzzed head, unusually wide nose, and eyes that squinted shut when he smiled, was envied by the guys, pined after by the girls, and cherished by the teachers for being an entertaining and surprisingly decent student. He and Joe had been best friends since sixth grade, and since then Matt had been goading him to loosen up.

"Your tight ass needs to relax," he said when they entered high school. "Try some poppers, Joey, but not so much you let something in the back door, okay?"

That explosive laugh, that blast of confidence. Where did it come from? And how could it contain so much cockiness, criticism, and care all at once? In Matt's howl, Joe also heard a challenge to defy the strict abstinence with which he'd been raised.

When Joe finally lost his virginity their freshman year, Matt gave him a bottle of whiskey and said, "Congrats on becoming a heterosexual." Matt continued to coach Joe in matters of mating with the same unrelenting encouragement he brought to coaching his Little League teams. Heading into that May night with Callie, Matt had called it "the big game" and said Joe was "at bat."

It got off to an auspicious start. Matt had just slipped away to his bedroom with his latest fling, some sad, skinny pixie from another town. Julie was on the dock, laughing with Troy on one side of the firepit, and Joe was on the other side, finally alone, or at least semi-privately face-to-face, with Callie. Her delicate head, slightly hooked nose, and sharp chin were all inclined toward him, that geometric face loosely framed by the folds of a blanket, flickering black and yellow from the popping flames. Her large eyes appeared to welcome his adoration.

Both the proximity to her and the pills he'd inhaled before she arrived made it seem as if the fire were crackling in his brain. They passed a joint back and forth, a promising act of secondhand touch. They were talking about his father. And when she spoke, Callie's words took shape in the frozen air, fused with her exhaled smoke, and together danced away in a cloud.

"So your dad."

"What about him?"

"Don't play dumb."

"I am dumb."

She laughed. Her voice was deeper than her small body suggested, and her laugh was deeper still. He loved how it contradicted her physical fragility, both an expression of joy and a warning against misjudging her. "Shut up, Riley," she said. "Is he going to win this thing or what?"

He was hypnotized by the cloud formed from her breath. "Maybe. Unfortunately."

"Why is that unfortunate?"

Joe shrugged and pulled the strings on the hood of his sweatshirt, pinching it around his face. "Just can't really see it. Been watching him pour beers all my life, hard to imagine him in a suit, in Washington, talking about serious shit."

"I can see it. He's a smart, serious guy. Like you, sometimes. It'd be cool if he won."

That was the first time Joe thought of his father winning the race as a potential plus rather than a social liability or a personal loss. If Callie thought it cool, maybe he could come around to that viewpoint as well. In the past few months, the campaign had dominated all conversation in the Riley house, filling the rooms with a mildly unpleasant stench, the way a small undetectable expired item in the fridge contaminates the rest of the groceries.

That noxious smell had recently begun to manifest as a rotten internal feeling as it dawned on Joe that, should Chip win, those comforting chicken dinners and his father's patient, steady presence—an antidote to his mother's prying, puritanical intensity—would abandon him for the nation's capital. Of course, so, too, would the silent, disappointed stares and occasional exasperated outbursts of Bud Light Riley. Joe wouldn't miss those. But he hadn't really considered the total impact of his father's potential absence, what the subtraction of his crucial counterbalance would do to the Rileys' precarious equilibrium.

"I guess it would be kinda cool," he finally said to Callie. They eased into silence but kept smiling at each other in the manner of two people trying to determine whether their smiles asked the same question and gave the same answer.

CALLIE IS HERE now, waiting for him at Delphi's at the end of his shift, wearing her ice cream parlor uniform of white button-down shirt and red-and-white-striped vest.

"Goat cheese and cherries," she says, holding out a container to him. "Thought you might need a sugar boost today."

But she's all the boost he needs, and her presence instantly calms him. "Don't they have any regular flavors?" When he smiles at her, his cheeks quiver from lack of practice.

"Duffels don't do regular flavors," she says. "You want vanilla? Get a milkshake at Nana's. This is what I brought you."

In the parking lot, he finishes the strangely tangy ice cream. This time, when she proposes that they head to Rainbow Rock for sunset, he agrees.

It's a short drive up and around the soft curves of Mount Heron (though "Mount" is generous), then a short walk along a well-trodden trail to an outcrop hovering over the Munsee River Valley, with its quilt of farms bordered by the silver string of the river, blue hills beyond, and a brass-tack sun pinned just above the horizon. About a dozen people are already there with cold beers to their lips, having come from jobs at AJ's Supermarket or Mikey's Sporting Goods or, if they're ambitious and itching to leave Griffin, then maybe the Artisan, the egregiously refined new boutique hotel in town.

The sun's farewell spectacle, plus the soothing brew and familiar company, bring Joe a rare peace. Troy wanders over and stands beside him. "Doing all right, Joey?"

With Callie at his side, now under his arm, yes, he is. For the first time since May, he can see a way back to happiness. Then Troy's sister, Aimee, joins them.

"Hey, Joey, saw your little bro the other day." She's dragging on a cigarette, and it's as though the smoke has piled up around her eyes in thick black lines. "Me and him been working for Carly this summer. Saw him swap numbers with the Banks guy at his fundraiser a few weeks back. So, either going undercover for your dad or, like, *literally* going under covers with the enemy."

The valley seems to echo with snickering. Pressure builds in Joe's head and chest, as it always does when Will is demeaned in front of him. Always has. Since they were kids, Joe understood that his younger brother's shy and contemplative ways made him an easy mark for anyone who sought to establish schoolyard dominance. And since Matt was one of those alphas, Joe found himself an abettor to the teasing, though only in private. In public, he played Will's defender, shielding him from any outright bullying or physical harm. But among his friends, when Will wasn't around, Joe tolerated the mean jokes and ugly insinuations. Sometimes he instigated them.

Ironically, the resulting guilt made him a better brother at home, where he was always available for a board game or a shared project like the glow-in-the-dark galaxy over Will's bed or, later, sharing a secret beer behind the bar when Will started working at the Buck, which was also a convenient excuse to see Maren. Joe adapted to his uneasy role of being both his brother's protector and his offender. But after Joe graduated from high school—after he and Matt turned darkly inward and Will announced that he was what Joe always suspected and feared he was—whatever inscrutable bond keeps unalike brothers together had frayed. Joe never told Matt about Will. He knew he'd have to defend his brother and wasn't sure he would.

So now, when Will is again disparaged in front of him, Joe sinks into a familiar self-loathing silence. His body trembles, but then Callie's hand is on his back, acting as a release valve.

"Fuck off, Aimee," Troy says, to which she shrugs, stamps out her cigarette, and heads to the cooler for another beer, having said what she came to say.

"Let's get out of here," Callie whispers. "I'm hungry, anyway."

At Nana's, she finishes her burger, while half of Joe's sits untouched in its basket.

"What happened on the Fourth?" she finally asks. "I was looking forward to the picnic."

He pushes away his basket, slumps in the red vinyl booth, and says to the window, "Who cares."

"Did you use?"

"Yup," he says, no point pretending. He grins at his reflection, amused by his honesty.

"Shit, Joe. You think this is funny?"

"Nope."

"I thought after Matt... I thought we were done with all that. Aren't you scared?"

He should be, but he's not. If anything, he's nostalgic for the Lab, which is where he can most easily locate Matt in his memories, even if he understands, in some stubborn awareness, that that's where the problems started. But that's where Matt is, so he keeps trying to go back.

THE SUMMER BETWEEN eighth and ninth grades, that transitional limbo when unworldly middle schoolers strive to become disenchanted freshmen, was when the big Swinton basement became Griffin High's most notorious den. Because Matt was popular, the gatherings there were large, frequent, socially significant, and daring. His own audacity encouraged boldness in others, and the basement became a safe space to experiment—romantically, sexually, eventually chemically. Matt began referring to it as his "laboratory," and soon everyone called it the Lab. There, relationships commenced and concluded (it was where Callie and Dean debuted their coupledom senior year, and tearily split this past New Year's Eve), friendships were forged and fractured, truces among warring cliques were brokered, and a running tally of libidinous "firsts" grew.

Alcohol juiced the gatherings in the early years, but then the kids with ADHD began bringing their meds to share, having learned (or been taught by older siblings) that they facilitated a night of drinking minus the blackout. Others swiped bottles from their parents. Athletes injured in soccer games or wrestling matches, Matt and Joe among them, began contributing their own prescribed painkillers. Adderall, Oxycodone, Vicodin, Percocet; pro-focus, anti-anxiety; sleep aids, study aids; crushed and snorted; 10 mg in pure white, 20 mg in soft pink, 40 mg in mustard yellow, 60 mg in angry red, 80 mg in mossy green (aka the Green Goblin). An exhilarating journey over the rainbow; a Lab-made experiment in chemical camaraderie.

At first, use was social and sporadic, and the effect was a thrilling, fearless clarity. Joe felt empowered by the drugs. They breached his bulwark of inhibition and gifted him a shield of self-assurance. He craved the mellow rush of relinquishing control and the shared euphoria that became part of his bond with Matt, making their already close friendship feel even closer and truer. The pills brightened their mundane days with saturated light, like when Joe's mom widened the kitchen windows and added colorful tiles above the sink.

At the start of their senior year, aware that college wasn't in their future, Joe and Matt began to seek more extended escapes. They spent more and more time searching for and acquiring drugs. They became stingy with their stash. The communal revelry that had defined the Lab evaporated. Half the regulars were scared off by the harder stuff; the other half doubled down on their commitment to excess, drifting off into their own cocoons. By the end of the year, the thrill of collective abandon gave way to more personalized, increasingly desperate pursuits of diminishing highs. The spirit of the Lab, so welcoming in its first few years, flickered and dimmed. Several people overdosed and were revived. Someone's older sister overdosed and was not.

After graduation, the days and years lost the natural structure of school, which had dictated and moderated their usage, concentrating it on weekends and school breaks. And with it, they lost the public performance of being students, which had been its own check. As much as Joe liked Delphi's, as much as work gave its own shape to his days, and as much as Matt found similar distraction at his various contractor gigs, neither provided the kind of social participation that, in retrospect, had been a an important, if imperfect, guardrail to their cravings.

Even as they drifted away from their former classmates, Matt and Joe still tried to convince them to swipe pills from family members and, when that source dried up, recruited friends of friends and vague acquaintances for the task. Someone with a recently pulled wisdom tooth or a local Iraq war vet—people with legitimate prescriptions but in need of cash. After that, they resorted to buying or bartering with various dealers. Corrupt doctors, unscrupulous coworkers, shady figures camped out at Washington Manor, the town's low-income housing complex. Eventually Joe connected with an unlikely regular dealer, someone with their own reasons and needs.

Joe's savings from Delphi's quickly ran out, as did Matt's construction earnings. So they'd grab a twenty here and there from their parents' wallets. They'd volunteer to get groceries and toss a fifty-dollar gift card into the mix. A few times, Joe even siphoned off damaged tools from Delphi's that were headed back to the manufacturer and sold them online, until Amir started asking questions. One Sunday while Matt's parents were at church, he and Joe drove to a pawnshop a few towns away with a pair of Matt's mother's earrings; they sold their Christmas gifts by New Year's.

Each time Joe felt disgusted. And each time it felt as necessary and justifiable as stealing bread for a starving child.

The missing valuables and the boys' uncharacteristically aggressive behavior led Matt's parents to remove the bathroom locks. Joe suspected that his parents went through his dresser. Matt began wearing gym shorts under his jeans, keeping his drugs in the mesh pockets in case his parents searched the denim ones. Joe thought this was stupid until one day last fall, his mom saw a bulge in his sweatpants pocket and asked what it was.

"Nothing," he said. (It was a bottle of pills he'd taken from Matt's mother.)

"Let me see," she said.

"Hell no!"

"Don't talk to me like that. Show me."

"Fuck off."

"How dare—" Diane reached for his pocket and Joe swiped at her, their wrists connecting in an excruciating smack. Diane cried out, held her wrist, and looked at Joe in horror. He flung his arms around her, sobbed an apology, and ran out the door.

BUT THAT COOL May night on the dock, Joe was feeling good again, buoyed by Callie's smile and Julie and Troy's nearby laughter. Though he hadn't said it out loud, he believed that if he could be with Callie, he wouldn't need all the other substances. She'd be enough to keep him afloat. The promising warmth of their intimacy that night made Joe feel certain he could kick the habit this summer. And when Joe got clean, Matt would as well, and then they'd be able to leave this mess behind.

Joe really did want to leave it all behind. His use (not addiction, can't touch that word) had become an exhausting cycle of lies, theft, and self-delusion in service of attainment and ingestion, followed by a few brief, blissful hours of satiation and oblivion, then the long, chilling vacuum filled with scraping pain, at which point all peripheral thoughts blurred into a single demanding priority: Make the pain stop.

The cycle repeated.

In between, though, were pockets of grace, like the sudden smooth seconds of weightlessness during an otherwise turbulent flight. That night was one such moment, when Joe glimpsed, as if through a heavy mist, the outline of what might be a path toward recovery, and that outline resembled Callie.

Matt and his pixie had been gone for maybe half an hour when they heard a scream. It came from the second-story balcony. No words, just wailing. Seconds later, the pixie was in the backyard, stumbling toward the dock. They rushed to her. A chair fell into the lake and was swallowed.

"Okay, calm down," Joe said. "What—"

Julie cut in. "Where's Matt?"

The pixie gasped, her fragile face painted blue by the moon. Joe watched it turn bluer. "Talk to us!"

She choked, coughed. "He's . . ."

"Bedroom?"

She nodded frantically.

Joe and Julie struggled up the muddy slope to the house, then through the back door and up the stairs to Matt's bedroom, his cluttered cave, a shrine to sports. Matt sat on the floor, against his bed, shirtless, his back curled elegantly forward, his shaved head hanging, eyes squinted shut, a needle jabbed into the thick carpet beside him.

Joe turned to Julie. He was calm. "Where's your Narcan?"

The resignation in her face will always haunt him. She shook her head slowly and stared at her slumped brother with agonizing remorse. She collapsed next to him, slapping him, yelling, apologizing.

Joe called 911. The medics arrived within ten minutes and plugged Matt's unusually wide nose with the applicator. First one nostril, then the other, then both again, delivering the molecules that would neutralize the overdose and yank him back to life.

After a few minutes, though, one of the medics shook his head and said, "Shit."

Then they took Matt away in a stretcher, lifeless.

But Joe is still there.

AUGUST

CHAPTER 9

LATE SUMMER IS AN excellent filter through which to show a home. Even Griffin's most unimpressive residential offerings look better against a solid blue backdrop, lit by a high, benevolent sun, and tightly hugged by dense flora. But vegetation can be deceptive.

"Don't buy a home until you've seen it in winter," Diane warns her clients, doing her due diligence. Come November, that celebratory burst of hydrangeas morphs into a tangled knot of twigs, and that leafy protective wall of willow at the lawn's edge transforms into a porous web that permits the glare of oncoming headlights and reveals a frighteningly intimate view of the neighbors. So, a note of caution: "Make sure you love it year-round." Her clients nod with enlightenment but are usually too impatient to take her advice.

On this mid-August Saturday afternoon, she stands a few blocks north of Granger in front of a unique property framed by thick hedges of neatly groomed boxwood, prancing yellow potentilla, and pom-poms of lilac. The brick factory that will bloom soon into a high-end hotel sits just around the corner, and across the street are the townhomes that Diane sold in June, where Maren is living for the next two weeks until renovations begin, after which she will move to a friend's couch until Diane can find her next temporary residence.

In front of Diane is a peculiar new seasonal flower giving her side-eye. It's a Chip Riley sign, planted in the strip of lawn between sidewalk and street. Normally finding his name around Griffin would deliver bubbles of pride, but today it reminds her that she is not with him at the county fair, one of his favorite municipal events. The Rileys attended annually as a family until the boys were in high school, and Chip and Diane have continued to visit each year since. Chip had assumed she'd join him there today. Surely she could skip a weekend of house showings to support her husband during such a crucial time in such a significant year?

But she could not. A friend of Serge and Luke's has come to town this weekend, house-hunting with urgent intent and a serious budget. For the family's sake—"For Chip's sake!" she argued—she could not afford to say no. And she shouldn't be made to feel guilty for it, either. Not that anyone has implied as much, but she can't stop silently justifying and defending herself against unspoken, possibly imagined accusations. Diane turns away from the prosecutorial sign and studies the dramatic facade of the home she is about to show, a stunning three-thousand-square-foot 1869 Gothic Revival with vaulted ceilings and tall, skinny stained-glass windows.

It is a church. Or, rather, an ex-church. An *excommunicated* church. There are, in fact, plenty of superfluous such churches in the Munsee River Region, all eager for transfiguration. Lutheran in the Victorian style; Episcopal in the Romanesque style, etc. These born-again architectural proselytes are all the rage among the Duffels, who seem to delight in the sacrilege of living in former houses of worship. Diane loathes the trend. She must remind herself that the churches are already lost, converted to the religion of real estate. If they're to be sold, it might as well be by someone like her, someone with reverence for their past lives who will pray for their souls and ask God to keep the spirit alive in them, which she does.

A few minutes later, Serge's friend jogs up to her in a collegiate T-shirt, with shaggy golden hair to match his golden-retriever likability, and hugs her by way of introduction.

"Diane? Davey! It's *such* a pleasure to meet you."

Because Davey is Serge's friend, she already assumed that he is of Serge's kind, and the expressiveness of his hands and voice seem to confirm it. As he chatters about his stay in Griffin so far, Diane again marvels at the demographics of her clientele, all so polite and handsome, or at least looking like the best version of themselves. She recognizes how much more comfortable she has become with them, less fretful of a verbal misstep that might offend, less wary of how these transactions reflect on her own faith. As a result, she's more willing than in the past to ask about their personal lives, which is how she comes to learn that Davey has recently split from a boyfriend of eight years and is looking for renewal.

"And why Griffin?" she asks.

"Serge can't shut up about it, for one. And I'm in need of a slower pace. My ex was the butterfly, always soliciting invitations. Every weekend was a parade of cocktail hours and dinner parties."

"Mmm." Diane wonders whether to envy or pity Davey for such a plight.

"The way Serge describes it, Griffin sounds pretty low-key and casual, right?"

"Right," Diane says, though she questions Davey's definition of "low-key." And she doesn't consider Serge's large, immaculate home or this church "casual." The discrepancy between Davey's modest stated aims and the grandeur of the building before them amazes her.

"And I figured, hey, maybe I'll meet someone a little more down-to-earth here," Davey says, scratching behind his ear. "Someone who appreciates a more laidback lifestyle, who doesn't need half a dozen social engagements to call it a successful weekend, you know?"

"Well, you should meet—" She stops herself from suggesting he ought to meet her son. It's the first time she has mentally placed Will in a relationship with one of these men, and the image that flashes before her is scandalously explicit: Will and this golden-retriever man snuggling on a couch. She turns away from the picture in her mind. "Well, I hope you meet someone," she says, and abruptly moves toward the entrance. "Let's take a look!"

Heading up the front steps, she tucks her rhinestone cross necklace into her blouse, lest it somehow influence Davey's experience of the space.

Inside, he gawks at the rainbow painted by the stained-glass windows on the hardwood floors, coos at the pews repurposed for dining benches, and giggles at the pulpit resurrected as a bar. She pretends not to hear when he makes a joke about having sex in the choir loft-cum-bedroom. Did he even consider that such a comment might upset her? Perhaps if she hadn't hidden her necklace. But better that he feel comfortable.

At the end of the tour, he announces, "It's kind of camp, right? I love it."

Having heard this term from clients, Diane understands what he means and knows it's not mean-spirited. Nonetheless, she can't help but feel saddened that this place, where a man of God once preached Scripture, has fallen from such grace, even if it eventually falls into the paws of this very sweet fellow. To demonstrate her amenability, she smiles and directs his attention to the outdated kitchen, which she suggests could use a rethink, perhaps go in a more rustic direction.

When they return to the sidewalk, Davey pauses at Chip's sign and gives it a funny look of familiarity, as if the name already means something to him, though she can't imagine how.

"That's our congressional race," she says. She would love to claim her husband but will not risk contaminating her business with politics, particularly given the very few degrees of separation between this client and her husband's opponent, and especially given Davey's clear impiety. Davey might wonder about her last name, but the coincidence escapes him.

"His opponent is Serge's friend, right?"

"Oh, gosh! I don't know," Diane says with a little laugh, as if politics are just so silly.

Then Davey scrunches his nose and drops his voice. "Are there a lot of them around here?"

"Who?"

"Them." He gestures to the sign. "That party."

"It's, uh, pretty evenly split, I think."

"Hmm." He thinks a moment, then looks at her with a glint in his eyes. "Well, if I end up taking this place, that's less of them and one more of us!"

"Ah!" she says, and gives him a neutral "Wouldn't that be something" shrug. Her mind snags on his presumption. "More of *us*"? She's confused, then insulted, then flattered, then confused for feeling flattered. Maybe her act and costume are too convincing. She shouldn't hide her necklace.

Silence hangs. In her discomfort, Diane defaults again to gossip and volunteers to Davey that the next house they'll see on their daylong itinerary is a foreclosure, the victim of its owner's gambling habit.

As she slides into her red sedan, she looks back at the church's stained-glass windows. She's reminded of retired Pastor George and is struck by the fact that what he predicted, what she'd feared and fought against with the anti-marriage campaign, has indeed come to pass. Same-sex marriage is now just a mundane reality, which makes homosexuality itself seem almost mundane, which is why she's selling homes—and churches—to the Pauls and Stans, the Serges and Lukes, the Daveys. It all seemed so benign at first. Then Paul bought his home to run against her husband, and Davey may buy this place to help Paul succeed. It turns out that gay marriage *was* a Trojan horse to political power after all—and these men don't even seem to realize it! She scoffs at the thought until it dawns on her that she helped open the gate.

THAT NIGHT, CHIP is cordial when she asks about the fair.

"Oh, you know," he says.

"Again, I'm sorry I couldn't make it."

"Really, Di, it's fine. Gabby and Will were there, we stayed on top of things."

"The showing went well, I think."

"That's wonderful, honey."

The words are sweet, but his tone is flat and robotic. It's one of his go-to lines, pulled from a short list of preset options that he deploys like a Magic 8 Ball when he's annoyed or overwhelmed or simply distracted, which all seem to be the case these days:

"That's wonderful, honey."

"Geez, Di, I don't know."

"Gosh, that's a toughie."

But after his dismissal of her day, Chip becomes thoughtful and says, almost to himself, "Speaking of Will, that kid's carrying his load on the campaign. Didn't expect it, to be honest."

"Don't you think he's acting kind of distant?"

"He's always been distant. But he's been showing up at headquarters and events, especially lately, and he was a big help today. We're lucky to have him."

Usually the rare occurrence of her husband praising their son would fill Diane with joy, but she's stuck on Chip's "we," which refers to the campaign and does not include her.

"In fact," Chip continues, "I was wondering . . ." He looks at the ground, cups the back of his neck, places a fist on his hip. His pondering pose. "Well," he says to the advisory board of his feet, "Gabby could use another pair of full-time hands . . . Couldn't pay, but he'll understand . . . And he'd be saving on room and board . . . That kind of experience and responsibility . . ." He looks at Diane for the tiebreaking vote. "Deputy campaign manager. What do you think? How many other college kids can say they helped run a congressional campaign?"

In Will's promotion, Diane senses a silent indictment of her own lack of involvement, a devaluing of her significant in-kind financial contribution. It takes her a moment to locate charitable words. "I'm sure he'll be honored," she says.

The next morning, alone again at First Presbyterian, Diane can't get comfortable. The pews are as hard as usual, but instead of being reassuring in their solidity, they seem to resist her presence. Her body is as unsettled as her mind, which throbs from a poor night's sleep. She feels guilt for abandoning Chip this weekend, anger at feeling that way just for doing her job, and a strange new jealousy toward her son. If Will accepts Chip's offer to work full-time on the campaign, he will remain at home throughout the fall, which means her own commitment to the campaign will continue to be judged against his.

She stews in this scenario for several minutes. Then her gaze drifts over to Raina Swinton, wearing an emerald cardigan set, sitting alone. Diane has heard that Derek isn't taking Matt's loss well and is now frequenting the Lucky Buck almost daily. She is hit with a wave of remorse, splashed by self-disgust. While Raina has been sitting there in unfathomable grief, Diane has allowed herself to wallow in pettiness, turning her self-pity into ammunition against her husband and son.

She closes her eyes, takes a breath, and fingers the rhinestones of her cross. This is why she returns each Sunday. This is why Jesus keeps calling her back. To rediscover gratitude and reacquaint herself with grace.

The possibility of Will remaining at home for the next several months now looks like an obvious blessing in the form of an extra pair of eyes on Joe. Because there's no pretending anymore, Joe is fading. As in getting noticeably thinner, his face wiped of expression except for the occasional frightened or furious scowl. But also fading as in skipping family meals, coming home later and later, disappearing during the days. He says he's at Delphi's, but she can't believe him, not when his boss, Amir, keeps calling, exasperated and concerned. Not when a gold bracelet from her mother has gone missing, and several twenties from her wallet, which might explain Joe's evasiveness.

She thinks again of her chat with Raina under the church maples last fall. Did Matt behave like this before that tragic night? Would things with Joe be different now if Diane hadn't been so dismissive, so willfully blind, then?

She finally finds the courage to approach after worship. "How are you doing, Raina?" She places a hand on Raina's arm.

Raina looks at it. "I'm okay, Diane. How's Joe?"

Her directness renders Diane momentarily mute. "He's fine."

"He didn't look so good when I saw him the other day at Delphi's."

Diane bristles in defense as she hears her own observations spoken aloud. "He has bad days."

"So do I." Silence spreads between them until Raina takes a breath and says, "I have to say, I'm surprised at you, Diane. And Chip."

"What have we . . . ?"

"It's what you haven't. I heard that Chip declined to speak at a Munsee Recovery meeting. There's barely anything on his platform about drugs, just something small at the bottom, like he doesn't . . ." Her voice goes scratchy. "Like he doesn't know the cost."

Diane grabs for a response. "That's not . . . Raina, you know Chip cares deeply about this. You must know that. But I'll speak to him. I promise."

Raina nods and begins to turn away but pauses and turns back. "Joe didn't look good, Diane. I know what I'm talking about."

Diane speeds home, her car seeming to take its cue from her racing heart. She rushes inside and calls to Chip but finds him on the phone with a member of the Griffin Town Council.

"I know he's a stubborn bastard, Rich, but he's been my best friend for more than thirty years, so I don't want to hear about this being our last resort!" He's practically frothing, working his way into Bud Light Riley. "What I want is a goddamn solution!"

When he's off the phone, she learns from Chip that Gerry has rejected another offer on his land and that the town council is now considering a vote next month to authorize the use of eminent domain on part of his property for Griffin's new sewer system. She knows that the council is bound by deadlines tied to state funding, that they have successfully negotiated compensation with five other property owners whose land is needed for the project, and that Gerry is the last holdout.

"I can't vote against him, Di, but I can't be the one that holds up this project."

"You've made him a very reasonable offer, and he's being very unreasonable in return."

That is as much as she'll allow herself to say. The sewer system is needed for the brick factory project to proceed, and the promise of that development has been the basis of her sales pitch for the surrounding properties, which she has not shared with her husband. She has been careful to avoid advocating too aggressively for anything related to the brick factory, fearing that Chip might ask her to stop doing business in the area to avoid the perception of a conflict of interest. She quietly curses Gerry for standing in its way.

Chip shakes his head. "This is a nightmare."

She defrosts three frozen dinners because Chip is too busy and tired these days to cook. Will isn't home, as usual lately, but she knocks on Joe's door in hopes that today might be a good day. A few minutes later, he emerges, stooped and sallow-eyed, and sits at the table. He is mostly mute, but Diane can endure the silence as long as he's here.

Shortly after they finish, a car jostles down the driveway, and Joe heads to the front door.

"Where do you think you're going?" Chip yells after him.

"Why the fuck do you care?"

"Hey! How dare—!"

Joe slams the door behind him, sending shivers through the house.

Chip smacks the table and mumbles, "If that kid gets himself arrested in the middle of my fucking campaign . . ."

Later, Diane begins to bring up her encounter with Raina, but Chip is on the couch, curved over his laptop, bathed in electrical blue, writing to his fellow council members, reviewing plans, contracts, and the laws of eminent domain. He doesn't want to hear it.

"He's slipping," she says.

Chip doesn't look up: "Gosh, that's a toughie." One of his Magic 8 Ball answers.

Then it's after midnight and Chip is in bed with his computer while Diane pretends to read the latest *National Holiday* as she silently berates her husband for his apathy while also praying to God for the safe return of their son, and imagining the phone call or knock on the door that will mock her prayers and destroy her. Finally she says, "I think the whirlpool is sucking him in. Like it did Matt."

"He's grieving," Chip says, still looking at his screen.

"I'm worried that his grieving might become destructive. Or already has."

"I don't know, Di." It sounds callous, but then Chip looks up. She sees the alarm in his eyes and realizes that perhaps these fixed responses mask his fear as well. Perhaps staying up on his computer is his way of keeping vigil. "What do we do?" he asks.

"I've found places that can help."

"Expensive places, I bet."

"How can you—"

"Think about money? That's all I think about. I spend my days begging for ten dollars from complete strangers. I'm trying my damnedest not to use family finances, like I promised, but . . ."

"So we shouldn't waste them on Joe in case *you* need them later?"

"Come on, Di. That's not . . . We don't even know if he needs a . . . if he needs to go anywhere. Besides, if it got out that I couldn't fix these issues in my own family? When I'm trying to convince people I can fix the whole district's problems?"

"So just ignore it, then?"

"You wanted to keep him out of any potential spotlight, remember? This might only make things harder for him. Let's just keep monitoring it, okay?"

"Is that what we're doing right now?"

"Only three months until the election, Di. Then we'll see."

Can she hold her breath for three more months?

Half an hour later: the crunch of dirt, an engine's purr, the clunk of a car door, and more crunching as the engine fades in retreat. Then the click of the front latch, a cautious stumble through the hallway, the thud of Joe's door. With an exhausted sigh, Chip closes his computer, and Diane turns off the bedside lamp.

CHAPTER 10

WHILE PAUL VISITS A senior living facility in New Plymouth, a former factory town forty miles south, Stan settles into the breakfast nook at home with his second espresso and *The Griffin Gazette*. He's tempted to ignore the local paper and turn instead to the distant business news, art reviews, style trends, and travelogues of the big-city paper, which last week featured another giddy guide to the Munsee River Region. Hiking trails, swimming holes, breweries with cleverly named IPAs, and festivals in all varietals of music, food, design, theater (the latter courtesy of Serge).

But he knows he must open the *Gazette* and face Celia Rhodes eventually. It's just that every time he reads one of her sobering stories, it's like a lightbulb around the Munsee marquee in his mind sputters dark, rendering the region less illuminated and yet somehow more clear.

For example: her rebuttal to the city paper's Munsee guide, in which she reminded her readers that the charming stone bridges periodically crossing the region's parkway were intentionally built at a height that precluded buses, and thus public transportation, and thus poor people, and thus, primarily, nonwhite people. Hence, all of Griffin's current appeal is actually built on a history of exclusion, perpetuated today by prohibitive home prices, retail rents, and craft cocktails each the price of a fast-food family dinner. Such disheartening reporting doesn't even account for the increasing sharpness of her campaign coverage. So Stan has developed a guardedness around her byline, even as he cautiously seeks it out and has come to respect it.

But today he unfurls the *Gazette* with particular apprehension, and yes, here is her latest: "Congressional Candidate Confronts Inconsistency in Energy Policy, Investments."

It's not a surprise, of course; they've all been holding their breath. After the Independence Day Picnic, she followed up with questions, then more questions, then gave Paul an opportunity to comment on the story's findings, which are efficiently summarized in the headline. The best response the Banks campaign could offer was that (in Paul's carefully scripted words) "the investments are managed by a third party as part of a broader fund that we do not have direct control over," which has led to an "unfortunate impression" and "an inaccurate representation of my values and commitment to the environment through energy innovation."

Or, as Stan now interprets the dry quotes: "You got me."

He smacks the paper on the table, harder than intended, and a painful warmth spreads through his palm. He rereads the article, and the sting in his hand spreads to his head. This was avoidable. Paul should have anticipated this. Or Jeremy, or the finance girl, whatever her name is. Stan will have to attend the staff meeting today, which means cutting short his morning ritual. He looks out onto the birch grove. The cluster of thin white trunks seems stifling in its tall density, like a barred fence around an embassy.

The staff meeting is as awkward as Stan anticipated. His attendance has the effect of a principal's surprise classroom drop-in or a CEO's impromptu warehouse visit, heightening the stakes while insisting that business continue as usual. Under Stan's scrutiny—head tilted down so his bald pate becomes a spotlight, or eyes pelting the speaker with skepticism—the young, smart, expensive staff loses its sureness. It doesn't help that he publicly chastises Jeremy for not foreseeing the conflict of interest, then snaps at Paul when Paul comes to Jeremy's defense, then grills the finance director over the sorry state of donations.

Their lackluster fundraising is also why Stan insisted, several days ago at home, that Paul postpone a visit to a meeting of the Munsee

Recovery support group so he can attend *Fodder*'s launch tonight as a guest of honor instead.

"But we haven't addressed drugs," Paul argued. "I barely mention it on the website. I was waiting until after this meeting to draft something more substantive. *Fodder* will be fine without me."

Stan hadn't expected pushback. "Yes, *Fodder* will be fine," he told Paul. "But you won't be fine without *Fodder*. That event puts you in front of two hundred potential donors, and every minute you're there financially supports this campaign exponentially more than a minute with a bunch of addicts."

Paul glared at him. "A bunch of addicts? Are you serious?"

"No, are *you* serious, Paul? About this race? About my money?"

Paul froze, eyes big before narrowing into vexation.

Stan took a breath. "Sorry." He returned to his clipped business tone. "When Celia's article comes out, any day now, you need to be living and breathing tractors and soil, okay? Combat this energy thing by doubling down on agriculture. Be the farmer's best friend."

"I understand my responsibility to fundraising." Paul crossed his arms in an unfamiliar stance of impatience. "And to you," he added with a note of scorn. "But how can I develop a policy response if I don't sit down and talk with the people affected?"

"How about your policy response is 'Don't do drugs'?"

"Why are you being so insensitive?"

"Maybe because none of those people are going to vote for you anyway, Paul, if they vote at all. And because none of them gave a shit when it was our epidemic." Stan turned away, steadied himself on the bar, poured himself another drink. "Jeremy will reschedule the visit. There will be plenty more opportunities before the election. Not like anyone's going to recover before then."

When Stan turned back, he encountered a look he'd never seen from Paul, something approaching disgust. It unsettled Stan, this new hostility, because it required a degree of self-assurance that Paul hadn't possessed previously—it had always been Stan's job to provide it.

Stan almost apologized. But doing so would be to admit his callousness, so stubborn pride reasserted itself. “Oh, stop,” he said, hiding behind his tumbler. “I’m just being pragmatic. You need to prioritize your finances, Paul, otherwise the rest of it doesn’t matter.”

AT CHERRY HILL Farm, Dalton checks out the day’s last customer and scribbles in a notepad as Eric watches, inhaling the store’s now familiar fragrance of sweat, leather, and straw. He’s struck, as always, by Dalton’s size, the great mass that has been formed by hard work, that has earned its strength from necessity, unlike, say, Alex’s tight physique, which has been sculpted like a trophy for the sole purpose of being admired. Dalton’s body, in contrast, is indifferent to aesthetics.

When the customer leaves, Eric approaches the counter with two bottles of raw milk.

“Sorry, we’re closed,” Dalton says, looking down.

“Fine, I’ll leave.”

“Fine. Leave me stranded, then.”

“Oh, I’m not here for you,” Eric teases. “I’m here for this milk.”

“You’re a dick,” Dalton says, but his lips flicker upward.

Dalton rings Eric up and adds more scribbles to the page. When he’s completed his calculations, he finally looks up, and his swampy eyes clear. Eric smiles, though he knows it won’t be reciprocated yet. Inside the shop, even when it’s empty, Dalton maintains a facade of unrecognition. He takes his time closing up. Eric offers to help, but Dalton scoffs.

“Don’t need your help,” he says, not angry or defensive, just stating.

“I know, but it’ll make things go quicker.”

“If you’re in a rush, you don’t have to wait.”

“I just thought—”

“It’s cool.”

“But I’m your ride.”

“No shit.”

Since their meetings have become more regular, Eric has been picking Dalton up from the farm and dropping him off at the end of the evening. The truck died, Dalton explained, so his dad needs the van. Eric hasn’t inquired since, but it seems like a long time for a truck to be out of commission.

Dalton locks the barn door and slips into Eric's car with a quick glance around, as if suspicious of what the cows might think. When they're safely on the main road, Dalton places a hand on Eric's knee.

Back at the cottage, they head to the bedroom, undress, and meet on the mattress. Their desire hasn't faded, but the novelty has, which makes Eric wonder whether this thing with Dalton has exceeded the parameters of his and Alex's arrangement. But he justifies it by noting that Labor Day is only a few weeks away, and then he will return to the city and return fully to Alex. So whatever this has become, however consistent it appears in the moment, it will soon reach its expiration date, as every bottle of milk quickly does.

They shower and relocate to the kitchen. Dalton has brought ground venison from the farm and stands at the stove in his boxers, forming patties with near-comical care. Eric opens a bottle of wine and pours two glasses before recalling Dalton's sobriety. He pours one of them into the sink, then leans against the refrigerator with the other.

"Sorry," he says. "Sure you don't mind?"

"Why would I mind?" Dalton pours oil onto the hot pan.

"Just . . . you know, if it's tempting. Or inconsiderate."

"Neither." The oil pops. "Why are you always watching me?"

"I don't know. I can't help it."

"It's weird."

"I know. I'm sorry."

"I don't mind."

As the burgers bubble in the skillet, Eric chops vegetables for a salad, sets the table, and lights a candle. He and Alex rarely eat at the table, preferring to dine by the flickering light of the TV, whereas he and Dalton eat only at the table because it's the sole safe table in Griffin available to them.

"Well, isn't this fucking romantic," Dalton says when they're seated. The comment seems to indict Eric, even as he suspects that Alex would somehow be okay with this situation. Disappointed by the secrecy, perhaps, but not devastated by the affair itself. He might even support it as a necessary antic of Eric's solo summer. Alex has always been the more open between them, emotionally and experientially, which Eric credits for his own ability to embrace their relationship's newly porous borders. And for that expansion of thinking, he's appreciative. In fact, in this moment, sitting across from Dalton with a candle between them, Eric loves Alex as much as he ever has, albeit differently, with more distance but also more depth.

After dinner, Eric opens his laptop to finish some work while Dalton lies on the couch with one wide hand behind his head and the other, impressively, holding open Alex's dog-eared copy of *Middlemarch*. Within a few minutes, though, Dalton gets impatient with the florid language and begins rummaging through flyers, receipts, and magazines that have accumulated on the entry table

He discovers the Chip Riley flyer that Will dropped off over a month ago and waves it at Eric. "Wouldn't have pegged you as a supporter."

"I'm not. That was for the old owner."

"Right. Should've figured. You'll vote for the faggot 'cause you're a faggot, even though that guy knows shit about this place."

The animosity is sudden and hot, and Eric is startled by the epithet, which Dalton spits rather than sings ironically, as Eric's friends do. He's also surprised that Dalton has an opinion on the race.

"So you think I should vote for that guy?" Eric gestures to Chip's wide smile and decides to withhold how well he knows Paul.

"You'd never let yourself. Even if no one ever knew, you'd feel like a traitor to your kind. But if you vote for the other one, you'd be a traitor to this town, and to me. So, either way."

"But aren't you also my kind?"

Dalton looks at him with the same expression of distaste he wore when he first encountered Eric at the farm store. "No," he says, as though that were obvious.

"What's my kind, then?"

"Fancy fags."

"What's that supposed to mean?"

"Pretty self-explanatory, don't you think?"

The epithet stings again, but its qualifier stings more. He and Alex may like nice things, and know rich people, but "fancy"? That implies wealth, which they don't have. Not when they buy secondhand furniture, stay in second-tier accommodations, fly coach. Not when they have financially stretched for this tiny second home—in farm country, no less, not even on water!—which they must renovate themselves with a modest budget.

"I guess," Eric says, "but that's a little unfair, don't you think? Lumping us all together, assuming we're all the same, that it's just about whoever's most like us."

"Isn't it exactly about that?"

Eric takes a moment to dig up a response, but before he can, Dalton claps abruptly and says, "Welp, getting late. Gotta be fresh for the cows. Ready to take me home?"

Dalton is up early each morning for the first feeding and never stays past midnight or the point when things get too personal. "Afraid you'll turn into a pumpkin?" Eric joked one night as Dalton fled, to which Dalton replied, without a smile, "I'm never not a pumpkin."

Eric has two options now: continue to push back and extend the argument in hopes of better understanding Dalton (or at least better defending himself); or chalk this exchange up to yet another of the many little disparities that both feed and foil their relationship and trust that by their next encounter, all will be mutually ignored.

Eric reluctantly gets his keys. When they're halfway back to the farm, he asks, "Can I join you?"

"Where?"

"Tomorrow morning, with the cows."

Dalton furrows his brow. "No."

"Why not?"

"'Cause I don't want you to meet my dad."

"Why not?"

"Seriously? Because he's an asshole. Because he hates fags and doesn't know his son's one, so I sure as hell am not going to introduce him to my boyfriend."

In the car's darkness, Eric stifles a smile at being referred to that way. And despite his instant rejection, the question seems to soften Dalton. Again, his hand finds Eric's knee. When they pull in front of the farm store, he jumps out of the car and disappears into the dark. He never lets Eric drive him all the way to the house.

A few days later, Dalton tells Eric that his dad is going out of town to visit Dalton's grandmother a few states away. He'll be alone with the cows, a big task for one person. "So if you still want to, like, role-play a farmer, be my guest," he says. "Come tomorrow at five, and don't wear a polo."

"In the evening?"

"In the morning, dick."

ON FOUR AND a half hours of sleep, Eric pulls into the small parking lot in front of the rust-colored barn, which is a black mass against a waking sky. Dalton leans against a wall and, without a word, hands Eric a thermos of coffee and a pair of mud boots, then leads him to another barn where the cows are housed. They stack a trolley with milking machines, buckets, and iodine and wheel it into the milking barn. Then they lead fifty magnificent, sleepy beasts into the stalls. Classic black-and-white-spotted Holsteins, big Brown Swiss, docile reddish Guernseys, and a few Jerseys with their sweet doe eyes. Heads are loosely locked into place under chalk signs bearing their names: Ruby. Apollo. Henrietta. Sprinkles. Dalton pets their noses, pats their hinds, and touches his forehead to the brow of a large fawn-colored cow called Maple before guiding her to her designated stall.

As the cows munch hay, Dalton soaks a rag in iodine, wipes their teats, and attaches the pumps of a silver pulsator. The machine shudders to life with insistent clicks, and a rhythmic whooshing soon fills the barn as milk runs from udder to plastic tube to metal pipe, feeding giant containers in the sterilized adjacent room. Dalton demonstrates, Eric imitates. He watches Dalton move among the animals with peaceful purpose, envying his ease and assurance.

Afterward, as the cows chew the remaining feed and calmly relieve themselves with impressive force, Dalton pours two cups of the fresh milk, which is warm and frothy. Then he begins cleaning the pens and shoveling manure. Eric grabs a shovel to help. He feels Dalton watching him. He glances back, expecting to see amusement or a hint of scorn but finds instead an expression of intense tenderness. They both look away quickly.

They then trudge up the small hill to the house, a dingy white square with a row of dormer windows over a creaky covered porch. Dalton hesitates at the door, as if considering whether to let Eric in, which makes Eric appreciate how intimate this invitation must be. Inside, it is sparsely furnished in a palette of mismatched wood. The living room is neat from neglect; the kitchen is its cluttered opposite. Seated at a breakfast nook are stacks of mail, a few scattered books, rows of receipts, and a calculator awaiting input.

Dalton clears the table, then prepares a breakfast of extraordinary orange globe eggs and bacon with crispy-soft biscuits that Dalton's dad baked before he left. They have said very little all morning, but after the meal, Dalton starts speaking earnestly, as if a cabinet has been unlocked, its contents tumbling out. Eric suspects the cabinet's key is related to the way Dalton looked at him earlier.

"It's pointless, you know," Dalton says.

"What is?"

"All this, what we just did. We might as well have let the milk run into the gutter."

"I don't understand."

With his head, Dalton indicates the receipts. "Equipment, feed, fuel. Fucking property taxes. Can't keep up. Do you know how much a gallon of milk costs?"

"I don't."

"How the fuck don't you know that?"

"I usually don't drink milk."

"You buy milk from me every week."

"I don't pay attention to the price."

"Of course you don't." Dalton glares at him. "About four dollars. And I mean the good stuff. How much do you think we get from those dollars?"

"I really don't know."

"When it's sold at a supermarket, we get less than a buck. Sixty cents if we're lucky. Which means we lose money every day, on every cow. We could've just jerked off all morning, which would've been way more fun, and me and my dad would be just as well off, or just as screwed. Same thing, really." He squishes a corner of his biscuit with his thumb. "That's why I started the farm store. For the Duffels. Charge more, keep more. Put the milk in a glass bottle, now you've got yourself a premium product. Turn it into cheese or, if you're lazy, yogurt, and now it's what your kind calls 'artisanal.' Dad thought it was a stupid idea, too much extra work, which, he's right. We still sell most of the milk to a big producer, but the store's helped some, especially when I brought in meat from other farms, and since that magazine wrote about us."

"I had no idea." Eric reaches for something encouraging. "Your dad must be proud."

"Fuck off. Dad's never been proud of me. Sure as hell not now." Dalton examines the biscuit's buttery indention. "He's starting to lose it." His voice goes flat, as though he squished that too.

"Why do you think so?"

Dalton shrugs at his plate. "Used to yell at me all the time. Call me lazy and clumsy and stupid. Just teasing, kinda. I got used to it, never took it personally. Other times he'd be decent."

He looks at Eric as if seeking permission to continue, so Eric nods.

"But in the last year, all that stopped. It's like he's twenty years older and just, I don't know, defeated. Used to talk about fishing, hunting, used to laugh. Now it's like he's lost." The biscuit's flat as a saucer. "He said to me the other day, 'What would you do if I got rid of the cows?' I mean, what the fuck? He's never talked like that. My great-grandfather started this farm, it's more a part of this family than I am."

"That can't be true."

"Sometimes I'm not sure."

"Well, what *would* you do? If there was no farm."

Dalton leans back, examines the demolished dough, and stays silent.

"Do you even like being a dairy farmer?"

Dalton is quiet for another few seconds, eyes downcast. Eventually he says, "I like the routine. Especially the mornings. Just me, Dad, and the cows. Not talking, just doing. It's always the same, but in a good way."

Dalton's description stirs something in Eric. That's what he was missing, he realizes. Routine. A sense of quiet rhythm. That's what he's found here in Griffin. He used to relish the city's unpredictability, the promising question mark of each hectic day, until that endless expectation became exhausting. This summer he has experienced the serenity of a regular, unremarkable routine, the pleasure of empty hours.

While Eric indulges these peaceful thoughts, Dalton remains in turmoil. He shakes his head sharply and says, "Dad never visits Grandma. She and him don't have a good relationship. She's a bitch. So either she's sick or he's sick or . . ." He leans forward and tears the dough into pieces.

Eric says, "He's lucky to have a son like you."

Dalton laughs, an angry, hollow laugh. "Oh, fuck, man, what a stupid thing to say! But you wouldn't know better. And I can't blame you if I didn't tell you." His swampy eyes fill to the reedy shores of his prominent brow. "I'm drowning, man. And I'm pulling him down with me."

"What do you mean? Drowning how?"

Dalton looks at Eric for several long seconds before standing and clearing the plates. When he's at the sink, turned away, he says, "I got a DUI this summer. My second this year."

"Are you serious?"

"Of course I'm fucking serious. That's why you've been picking me up. I lost my fucking license." He turns on the faucet and starts rinsing. The water muffles but doesn't obscure his words. "I mean, I still drive sometimes when I have to. Like when I first came over. But I'm trying not to risk it too often."

"Two in a year? You were drunk?"

"Wasn't alcohol."

Eric waits, but Dalton doesn't explain, so he asks, "What was it, then?"

Dalton reaches for the pan that cooked the golden eggs. After a bit of scrubbing, he says, "They found powder. Just a baggie, but I should've gone to jail, except Dad's friends with the town supervisor and knows the police and judges and stuff, so he helped get me off with just the suspended license and mandatory recovery meetings."

"What kind of powder? Like cocaine?"

Dalton laughs his hollow laugh. "You think I can afford coke? You *are* a fancy fag." He turns off the faucet, so what he says next seems to echo through the kitchen. "Heroin, mostly, though it started with pills, which started with a stupid tractor accident a few years ago. So, yeah, if you want to leave, feel free."

"I don't want to leave."

"Okay." Dalton grabs a dish towel and begins drying the egg pan with great concentration. "Good," he says, and turns away, but not before Eric sees his face flood with relief.

CHAPTER 11

A GREAT WHITE TENT sits in front of a big red barn strung with round yellow lights. Underneath it, rows of long tables are adorned in wildflowers and rustic place settings as a bluegrass band plays frisky rhythms on a small stage. Like all professionally produced publicity events, the *Fodder* fundraiser feels like immersive theater, each attendee a performer costumed in some expression of "country chic." Paul and at least a dozen others play it safe and wear gingham, while Stan looks like an Ivy League cowboy in crisp dark jeans and a western-style cashmere-silk shirt with pearl buttons. While getting dressed, Stan laughed at the absurdity of their new life; at a charity event in the city last year, they walked a red carpet in tuxedos.

He watches Linda Goodwin, *Fodder*'s enterprising founder, nervously eye the growling sky, which looks like a thick gray stew. A strong gust spreads her black bangs with their flashy gray streak into a fan above her head. She smooths them down and hurries over to Stan and Paul, kissing them on both cheeks. There are so many people she wants to introduce them to! She slides her arm into Paul's—the gesture of possession used by many a host—and leads him to clumps of balding men in blazers and women with gauzy shawls draped over bony shoulders. Stan slips away.

He spots his friends huddled near the bar, looking like a fraternity of swanky wranglers, all holding pink drinks with bobbing blueberries. With them is a handsome stranger with shaggy golden hair, a weekend guest whose name he's already forgotten but who apparently is looking to buy in the area and join their growing gay commune. Nearby, he also sees Leon pretending to examine auction items while stealing looks at the wranglers and their cocktails. Stan smiles with pity and approaches.

"A spa package? Sure, why not! You deserve it. What's the bidding at so far?"

Leon looks up, startled then relieved. "Three hundred. Though really, what good could a facial possibly do me at my age, with this face?"

"It'd be for a good cause, at least."

"Is it, though?"

"Well."

They laugh. "Are you here on official business?" Leon asks. "Is Paul participating? Or just, you know, supporting a 'good cause'?"

"Both. Paul bestows a bit of political clout on the endeavor, ostensibly connects the magazine's mission to his agricultural agenda, and meanwhile gets to hobnob with a favorable crowd on someone else's dime."

"He has an agricultural agenda? Doesn't strike me as the type."

"It surprises me, too, sometimes."

"How's the campaign coming along, anyway? I hear he's closing the gap."

"Yes." A pause. "Miraculously."

"You're surprised?"

Stan shouldn't share so much, but it feels good to vent, and Leon's air of irreverence encourages his own. Besides, Leon is safely separate from the campaign and from Stan's frivolous friends crowding the bar, none of whom would be here, he's sure, without the promise of those beverages. In any case, in the middle of this white-tent, yellow-light, pink-drink, bluegrass circus, Leon appears to Stan like a grounded, needed confidant, someone who can be trusted with a small confession.

"To be frank, I am a bit surprised, yes," Stan says. "It's not that Paul's not working hard. He is. Harder than I've ever seen him. And he's had some strong moments, it's just . . . I think he's a bit overwhelmed, actually. With the operation, I mean. So many people telling him so many different things, mostly how to spend money, and he doesn't have the experience to evaluate it all. He gets paralyzed, and then he spends and spends because that looks and feels like *doing*. So yes, it's all working, but between us, he'll bankrupt me before the polls close."

"Bankrupt! Really?" Leon laughs heartily, relieved at the trusting return of Stan's candor.

"Of course not, I wouldn't allow it. But I've already spent nearly twice what I originally intended to spend, and I've just learned the campaign is strapped for more—and it's only fucking August!" Stan washes the admission down with the rest of his cocktail and mumbles into the empty glass, "Honestly, by the terms of our prenup, it'd be cheaper to divorce him."

"Oh, come now! You can't see it that way. He's learning." Leon savors his new role as counselor. "Think of it as sending him to a good college for electioneering."

"At the campaign's current cost, that'd be a ten-year degree."

"I can't speak to the price of an elite education these days, but I'm sure he's a quick study."

"He is, but it's also a matter of message. He's got a pretty good grasp of the issues, and people seem to respond well to him." Stan thinks again with regret about their argument over the Munsee Recovery meeting. "I know I'm hardly an unbiased source, but his compassion is genuine. It's just . . . his opponent is so established and well-liked . . ."

"Riley."

"That's right." A pause. "Do you know him?"

"No, of course not." Leon hesitates. "Not personally." He wants to offer Stan something that will solidify this intimacy without connecting him to the Buck. "Though, actually, I just learned something surprising about him, completely by chance, that you might find interesting."

WILL CAUTIOUSLY APPROACHES the swanky wranglers with a tray of little green sculptures made from something grown on the property. He stands expectantly before them, but the men swarm the edible art without noticing him.

He swallows. "Hey, guys." For an excruciating second, their eyes scan and analyze his face, searching for a name.

"Will," Eric says, apparently the only one to remember. "Nice to see you."

"Ah, yes. Will," Serge says. "What an unexpected pleasure! You seem to be everywhere these days." Others smile vacantly, some still struggling to place him.

"You remember everyone?" Eric says, feeling responsible for Will's comfort. He recounts everyone's names, though weeks after Paul's pool party, Will can correctly identify each of them, except for a new addition called Davey. Handshakes are not possible given the food he's balancing, but the men bob their heads in greeting.

"Shame to see you back in clothes," says Alex with a wink. Everyone laughs except Eric, who thinks the comment distasteful. Will relishes it because it affirms that, despite the current indicators of his inequality—his tray, his all-black uniform—he now shares a sensual history with them, however recent and brief. He is relieved when they widen the circle and pull him into the conversation, which concerns a contemporary circus troupe performing at Serge's festival.

"Truly amazing," Serge says. "You guys have to come see it. You, too, Will." Will beams, and Serge continues. "I'd have stayed to watch the show again tonight, but it felt more important to be here to support our community, you know?"

The men nod, humbly acknowledging the philanthropic gesture of their presence. Eric swallows a laugh, but a smirk escapes. He can only imagine what Dalton would say if . . . He stops when he sees Alex staring at him.

Then a discordant female voice. "My apologies, gentlemen," Carly says. "I know he's enticing, but I have to borrow Will for a few minutes." She beckons him with a hooked finger. When they're at a safe distance, walking quickly toward the catering tent, she snaps, "Can you stop flirting for one fucking second and get the apps out?" Will rushes to assist the other staff.

After the appetizers are served, Linda Goodwin replaces the bluegrass band on the small stage, grips the mic, and embarks on her own well-practiced stump speech.

"Tonight we honor the agricultural vitality of America with the launch of *Fodder,* a print and digital platform that champions the farmer and celebrates the farming lifestyle." Someone whoops, which earns a raspberry-lipped smile from Linda. A rumble of thunder wipes it away.

"With probing and deeply emotional stories," she continues, glancing to the sky and speaking faster, "presented with the highest design and production values, we will reclaim the dignity of the American farmer and help the next generation thrive!" She pauses for applause, which arrives on cue, and which she accepts with a triumphant head toss. "Whether you're just visiting for the weekend, or you spend the summer here as a part-time resident, or you're like me and took the full-time plunge, we're all agricultural ambassadors here. Each of you has an important role to play, and you're playing it tonight." A wave of goodwill and self-satisfaction sweeps through the wildflower-strewn tables.

When Will arrived earlier, he flipped through the fat first issue of *Fodder,* a copy of which is placed on each seat. Inside, the heavy matte paper features photos of sultry agriculturalists in unsullied clothes, plump bread loaves, jugs of creamy fresh milk, articles about the hemp boom and heritage chickens. The cover showcases a beautiful couple imitating *American Gothic* with a red apple impaled on the pitchfork. *Fodder* has an attractive package, Will concedes, but a perplexing message. It exalts local farmers but ignores the issues that frustrate them, like subsidies, big-ag monopolies, factory farms, and America's self-defeating dietary priorities. If this crowd, and this pet project, were really interested in the plight of regional food producers, they could support the coalition of independent growers, cattle farmers, and meat processors advocating for better state and federal policy.

But Will has been to the coalition's pancake breakfast fundraisers with Gerry and his father, who's a board member, and the *Fodder* party is far more impressive from a culinary perspective, a design perspective, a see-and-be-seen perspective. It's an expertly presented performance of compassion, Will concedes. And one that won't make a damn difference to anyone in Griffin.

As Linda speaks, Will hears a tap overhead. Then another as raindrops hit the thick plastic tent. Hopefully a passing sprinkle. Linda hears them, too, and wraps up by introducing Paul, who bounds to the stage. To Will's surprise, Paul launches into a detailed critique of the Farm Bill and proposes adjustments to it that would address the Twenty-sixth District's unique needs, then highlights the work of a social justice farming collective and concludes with an impassioned call for a more equitable food system that is both more specific and more heartfelt than Linda's speech was. She stands behind him with tight raspberry lips, her slow flat-handed clap seeming to admit this.

Meanwhile, the metronome of raindrops gains speed. Carly dispatches her team to begin serving the family-style dinner, and Will soon finds himself with a trough of local trout at the table where Stan, Paul, and Linda are seated.

"I'm not a political person," she's saying to them, before dropping her voice to add, "but of course I'm on your team." When Will sets down the fish, nobody looks up. She continues: "I'm determined to keep *Fodder* out of the partisan muck, it's the only way to be taken seriously these days. My only goal is to promote Munsee food and farmers. I even invited Riley tonight. It's true! Never heard back, but I get it. Not exactly his crowd, is it?" She delivers the question like a punch line, and the three of them chuckle as Will quickly retreats.

The downpour arrives. There's an uncovered gap of about twenty feet between the event tent and the catering tent, and each trip back and forth rinses Will with a quick shower. Umbrellas are handed out, and he attempts to balance his tray with one hand while shielding it with the other. The trout remains unspoiled, but Will does not. His black button-down sucks at his skin, and his hair flattens against his forehead. With water sliding down his nose, he drops off another tray and is turning away when:

"Why, thank you, Mr. Martindale," Leon says.

His faux name, spoken in that deliberate way, is as welcome as a lightning strike. His impulse is to ignore Leon—given the clamor and rain, he might get away with pretending he hadn't heard—but something about

Leon's demeanor at the pool party a few weeks ago, his air of animus, alerts Will to the danger of dismissal.

Will turns to him and says, "Sure. My pleasure." He glances around the table of unfamiliar faces and realizes that Leon has been seated alone. The swanky wranglers are a few tables over.

"I have to tell you," Leon says, raising his cocktail to Will, "this beverage is no match for your concoction at the Buck. I would much prefer one of those right about now."

Will wipes his face. "Tonight I'm just the fish guy."

"And not exactly out of water at the moment, are you? Well, I hope you'll make me one of those delights soon. I haven't seen you there lately."

"I've been busy." Will brushes back watery strands of hair. "Catering gigs and . . . juggling other stuff."

"I see." Leon inspects the dripping kid and decides he's tired of this evasiveness. "You know what I learned recently that I was not aware of? Chip Riley owns the Lucky Buck! Isn't that remarkable?"

Will's wet skin goes cold. "Yeah. I know."

"Of course you do. I just found it so interesting that you work for him *and* have become so friendly with Banks. Very bipartisan of you!"

Will shrugs, short and violent. He doesn't trust his voice.

"It's just, your boss is your friend's opponent," Leon continues. "An odd predicament, no? Do they know you work there? I mean, his party isn't exactly a friend of the gays. I imagine that must be strange for you."

Will's sticky shirt feels tight and suffocating. "It's just a fucking job."

Leon is startled by the intensity of the response and fears a repeat of their last encounter at the Buck. "No need to get defensive, William. A job is a job. I respect that. I was just curious that you didn't bring up the connection at the pool party. It would have made quite a splash, so to speak. Anyway, I apologize. I feel I'm always putting my foot in my mouth with you. Allow me to make amends. A drink after this? Someplace dry?"

"I have to stay and clean up."

"I'll wait."

"It could take a while. And I got a ride with Carly."

"I can take you home. I don't mind."

"No. Thank you."

Leon stiffens at the hard finality of the rejection.

"Will!" Carly stomps toward them through newly formed puddles, and Will is grateful for the forthcoming chastisement. She smiles angrily at Leon and says, "Please excuse him." Then, sharply to Will, "Get moving." He slinks away in relief, but his neck prickles, sensing Leon's cold stare following him.

The storm settles directly over the fundraiser. The sky flashes white, followed by a series of roars. For the next hour, Will avoids Leon and makes a show of working extra diligently. He collects the ravaged troughs and platters, distributes desserts, darts between tents, and dispenses with the umbrella, which only slowed him down. His shoes sink into mud, his pants squeak with each step. He sees Paul and Stan duck into their car and drive off. He never got a chance to say hello.

Someone taps his shoulder, and he turns, his soggy hair spraying Serge's face. "Ah, now you look more like the Will I remember from the pool," Serge says, his voice lazy with drink. "After-party at our place?"

"I'm a bit . . ." He looks down at his sopping clothes. "And I don't have a car. My boss drove me."

"Hmm. I'm sure you can leave a bit early with us. Someone will take you home." Serge grips Will's shoulder. "And we'll get you out of these wet clothes in no time." His smile goes roguish; Will's legs go liquid.

Will approaches Carly about a premature departure. "At the request of your illustrious clients," he says with a little aristocratic bow, hoping the humor will soften her. He indicates Serge and the other wranglers, some of whom do employ her services.

"You've got to be kidding me," she says.

"I worked the Banks event," he says. "Counting tonight, I've worked *two* Banks events for you."

"I suspect that's more to your benefit than mine," she says. "Sorry. This storm's made a mess of everything. I need you tonight. You can play with your new friends some other time." She looks back at the men. "I guess fraternizing with Banks's crew doesn't worry you anymore, does it? Now can you please finish busing?" She leaves him dripping on the slimy ground.

But the prospect of cleaning up after Linda Goodwin and her self-aggrandizing party while soaked like a sponge is suddenly untenable. Will sees now that continuing to work for Carly is actually a step back from the prospects dangled in front of him at Paul's pool party. With her, he remains in Griffin at ground level, granted only glimpses of a life beyond. But those men are his ticket out. For the first time, he is being invited to join them as a guest rather than as hired help. In a month, he'll go back to school anyway, back to working at the rec center. There are only so many opportunities left to solidify his relationship with these men, to plant seeds for next summer and beyond. A warm tingle of defiance returns.

The storm has subsided, leaving behind ribbons of mist. Will contemplates his dilemma: spend the remainder of this summer under someone else's thumb—Carly's, his father's—or finally claim it for himself? He is so stirred by the gravity of this question that he sets aside other considerations, such as whether he can financially afford to walk away from this job. And does this mean he's walking away from his father's campaign as well? The weight of these thoughts presses on him. He feels himself sink into the saturated ground. To extract himself will require a concerted exertion of strength and resolve.

He fails to pry his foot loose. He tries again. Finally he frees himself and begins walking. His shoes are squishy, his back damp from rain, from sweat, from his thrilling audacity. He marches up to Serge.

"Let's go," he says.

A DOZEN MEN pack into three SUVs, some drunk, others just loose and lively from an evening of noble toasts. Will is in the back of Serge and Luke's car (Luke drives; Serge is sloshed), seated between Alex and Eric. The cars pull out of the parking lot as Leon watches from a distance with festering fury. The caravan proceeds along dark, narrow roads steaming from the recent rain. Headlights sweep across homes slumbering in the haze, ghostly barns, and foggy black oceans that turn out to be meadows dotted with startled deer. At a sharp turn, Alex slides into Will and stays there, keeping knees in touch, allowing a free pinkie to rest on Will's thigh.

Ahead, the first car abruptly swerves off the road and stops on a grassy turnout.

"Shit," Luke says, pulling off after them. "Did they hit something?" The car behind them follows suit. The inhabitants of the first car spill out, laughing.

Luke rolls down his window. "You guys okay?"

Nate stumbles over. "Score one for us!" he says with a maniacal grin. He slaps the roof, sending metallic reverberations through the car. At the edge of the light beams, Davey regards something on the ground.

"What the hell happened?" Serge says.

Nate's large torso shakes with glee in the window's frame, and he slaps the roof three more times. Behind them, riders in the third car totter into the headlights to inspect the object of amusement. Will's heart somersaults as Davey holds up a Chip Riley sign.

"They dared me to hit it!" Nate shouts, and is promptly shushed. He continues in a raspy whisper that is not much quieter. "And y'all know I can't turn down a dare."

Davey yells, "Tell them the game!"

Nate shoves his face back into the window and says, in the blunt way inebriated people attempt to turn serious, "So, we meet at the house in a half hour. The car that collects the most Riley signs gets top-shelf booze, and everyone else has to drink beer. Got it?"

Luke looks at Serge, who smiles and shrugs, while Alex laughs his consent. Eric sends Will a sympathetic look, then says to Nate, "What are we, in college?"

"Well, darling, technically no, though I did entertain a visitor from campus just the other night." Nate's eyes fix on Will. "Actually, one of us here *is* in college! Mind if we borrow your age for the night, Will? Just for the sake of a little juvenile fun."

Will doesn't have time to process the sneaky way that Nate's sassiness, which Will enjoyed poolside, has taken a brutish turn. Never mind

Serge's tacit endorsement and Alex's cackling approval. But how else can he answer?

"Whatever," he says as his stomach tumbles again. He made his choice.

The cars return to the road and disperse. Luke heads down a residential street, and within minutes, they find one of Chip's signs on an untamed lawn in front of a ramshackle home.

"Figures," Serge mutters.

Luke flips off the headlights and idles. They sit in silent anticipation, bodies rumbling with the engine, unsure what to do.

Abruptly, Will unbuckles his seat belt and climbs out over Eric. He feels as if he's climbed out of his head, too, like it's been hacked by some insurgent impulse. He observes himself walking to the sign, grabbing its thin metal rods, and uprooting it with an angry yank fueled by all the fear, frustration, and hurt he's collected and bottled up over the past year. Seconds later, he's back in the car, back in his body, breathing heavier than the physical exertion warrants. He regains control of his brain and watches as clumps of mud fall from the sign's stakes onto his already spoiled shoes.

Serge turns and pats Will's knee. "Well done!" he says. "Oh, shit! Forgot you're still soaked. Let's get this boy to the house!"

But first there are more signs to collect. Will sits silent and shivering as the pile of his father's name grows in the trunk. The warmth of his earlier defiance has cooled to icy indignity, becoming a calculated question: how to redeem this night and make his shame worthwhile?

Their car does not win the contest, so after Will has changed into Luke's T-shirt and sweatpants, he submerges his agitation in bottle after bottle of a bitter summer ale until his bladder begs for mercy. On his way to the bathroom, he encounters Eric in the narrow hallway. They're face-to-face but can't look directly at each other.

Eric touches his forearm. "Hey. I'm sorry," he says. "I know he's a family friend."

They hear footsteps, so Will slips past him and into the bathroom. He sits on the toilet, relieving his bladder, woozy head in shaky hands. To accept Eric's sympathy means acknowledging his own actions—

walking off a job, vandalizing his father. But that wasn't him. That was Will Martindale, a rash and reckless character who surprises, excites, and slightly spooks him, and who owes nothing to Chip Riley. As long as he remains in that character, he can delay his guilt.

Will takes a breath, makes a fist, and punches his other palm. He slaps his face with cold water and flings open the door to find Davey waiting with a hungry grin. But Davey isn't the reason Will is here, the reason for his sacrifice. Davey won't redeem this night. Will stumbles past the man with the shaggy golden hair to find the man with the stiff silver coif. He locates Serge, who tells him that Eric has volunteered to take him home.

"I want to stay," Will says. He places his palm on Serge's chest in a way that requires no interpretation.

When the last person leaves, Will participates in his first threesome, a concept that has always intrigued and intimidated him. But it proves to be the perfect reward for this regrettable evening. Serge and Luke are, by a matter of decades, the oldest men Will has been with, and he finds he much prefers their relaxed and confident doting to the aggressive groping of the baseball player with the Cheshire grin at college. Twisted in Serge's and Luke's limbs, Will feels sophisticated and justified in doing what he needed to do to get to this moment. He is then shown to one of the guest bedrooms and given a stack of fresh towels.

He wakes the next morning thinking he's in the nicest hotel room he's ever stayed in, hungover with shame but still roused by last night's dalliance. He pushes aside thoughts of Carly and his father and thinks again of the dynamic between Serge and Luke, which is what most stirred him: their clear affection for each other as they shared in a new seduction, indulging in both partnership and promiscuity. He notices the thoughtful touches of hospitality around him—a bedside water bottle, a mini mouthwash next to the sink—and considers that this gorgeous hotel of a home may be just as much a part of his domestic dreams as the men who inhabit it.

In the kitchen, Serge shovels eggs into his mouth while scrolling on his phone, already dressed in slacks and a button-down. When Will enters, he stands to offer coffee and ruffles Will's hair as he hands over a mug.

"Sorry I have to run," he says. "Got to get back to the festival in time for the matinee. Luke will take you home when he gets up."

"No problem," Will says as his vision of a morning romp evaporates. He drinks his coffee at the glossy island counter and watches Serge gather a coat and a duffel bag. The coffee is richer and smoother than any he's tasted before, which he realizes could be said of Serge as well.

At the front door, Serge turns back. "My day off is Tuesday. Talk then?"

Will smiles. God help him, he has no regrets.

CHAPTER 12

THE NEXT TIME ERIC picks Dalton up from the farm store, on a warm Wednesday evening, they go to the cottage, get off, make a quick dinner, then drive to the high school in Vernon, nearly an hour away. They trace a path through the maze of corridors, past stacks of metal lockers and bulletin boards, and into the small library, where a dozen people sit in colorful plastic chairs in a clearing within a forest of bookshelves.

The meeting of the Munsee Recovery support group begins. A short, plump woman named Susan with spiky white hair and a delicate porcelain face entreats everyone to help themselves to pizza, packaged cookies, and instant coffee on the folding table behind them. She then initiates a round of voluntary sharing, which comprises the next hour. Among the volunteers: a young Latino man in the matching hat and sweats of a hockey team chokes through fear of his mother's relapse; a matronly-looking white woman in prim attire tearfully admits to her own slip in sobriety; a frail older man with sagging chalky skin relays a recent visit to his daughter in jail, sharing his relief that at least there, she's safe. Eric waits for Dalton to speak, assuming that's the reason they are here tonight, but he doesn't.

Then Susan dons the reading glasses that have been resting on her chest by way of a beaded chain and solemnly introduces a guest speaker. His brief bio: army vet, disgraced lawyer, recovering addict, treatment program founder, now head of the state's opioid prevention task force. A thick, stern man with a white crewcut and a strong but softening pink jaw looks stoically forward as Susan recites his life's failures and achievements to a group of strangers. Among them is a woman who Eric guesses to be around his age, early forties, in black jeans and a loose black T-shirt. She has been eyeing Dalton behind the drapery of her copper hair since they entered. She catches his eye, and they nod to each other.

The crewcut man straddles a chair and speaks in a loud, cocksure voice, sharing his story of near-self-destruction with a clinical detachment that suggests he's told it a hundred times before or that it's the only possible way to get through it without reliving it, probably a bit of both.

"Drugs are your subconscious solution to a problem you don't know you have," he says evenly. "That's why you use, or at least why you started."

He pauses to let the insight linger, scanning the room to ensure each person absorbs it. Then he recounts the problem he was unaware of: suppressed PTSD from a tour in Iraq during the Gulf War that resurfaced in the wake of 9/11 and the subsequent invasion. He began drinking more, popping pills, socializing less. His life began to buckle and shrink. He retreated, was fired from his firm, found heroin. As his body adapted, he kept using not for the high but for the numbness. "I didn't care about feeling good," he says without emotional ornamentation. "I just wanted to stop feeling bad."

During the recounting of this story, Eric watches Dalton, who's hunched forward, elbows on knees, hands alternately drooping over shins, clasping his neck, cradling his head. Sometimes he looks up at the speaker, sometimes down at the floor.

"Addiction is a disease of isolation," the speaker says, now pacing his small carpeted stage as if giving a corporate talk. "The solution is connection."

Is Eric part of Dalton's solution? He realizes, with a small jolt, that he would like to be.

When the man finishes speaking, Susan thanks him and again makes a pitch for the food in back. The pizza must be cold by now, but Dalton gets a slice. When he does, the woman in black follows him to the table and touches his arm. He flinches, which makes her recoil and return to her seat, flustered. While Eric considers this strange interaction, Susan says something to the group that makes him turn abruptly toward her, something about HIV, which is not a term he hears often these days, and certainly didn't expect to hear tonight. The sound of that acronym pierces him, each letter its own puncture wound.

". . . when my cousin got sick. And half his friends. It was the stigma they were fighting." Susan removes her glasses. Her porcelain face assumes a marble toughness as her voice heats up. "And it's the stigma we're fighting, too, right? The shame. The looks, even from your own family, that say, 'It's your fault. You can change. Why should I help you?'" She takes a deep breath. "My cousin didn't accept the stigma. He and his people demanded help. They demanded action. The parades, the marches . . . They were *visible,* not stuck in a church basement since 1935 or"—she opens her palms—"a high school library. They refused to be anonymous." She says all this in a single exhale, giving the last line all her remaining air: "We need a movement like that!"

Her words crash against Eric like waves against a rocky cliff, violent and beautiful. He's been sitting here, feeling piously apart from the group, but now he is implicated, now his pain has been added to the collection in the room. He knows that stigma. He knows that shame.

He has known it for fourteen years, since that exhilarating, reckless summer on that slim crescent coast. Eric, then twenty-nine, worked at one of the harbor hotels, checking in guests, tending bar, cleaning rooms done up in nautical drag with anchors stitched on pillows, whales swimming across wallpaper, framed posters of sailor knots. Loops, hitches, bends. The Double Butterfly, Triple Crown, Slippery Eight. How many of those rooms did he later visit at the invitation of their occupants? Singles and couples and small groups, a carousel of carousals, fueled by powders and pills that sent pillows to sea and left posters askew. He'd never felt more coveted, never more accepted, his sails never more open to the sharp winds of sex. The guests came for a weekend or a week, and during their brief stays, he would experience the complete wash cycle of a romance, from drenched entangling to wringing final spin. He dreaded and cherished their departures, the wordless returning of keys, a final stolen touch, the breathless declarations of lust and appreciation stowed in their duffels. He missed each of them madly for hours, until the next tempest checked in.

That fall, after a routine checkup and subsequent tests, Eric learned the cost of his voyage. In the alley in back of the clinic, he crouched behind a dumpster and broke. For the next year, he raged and mourned, privately. Why must the price of pleasure be so high? Why are only some asked to pay?

Eventually he found, if not peace or even acceptance, then at least acquiescence. He submitted to his fate and began his medical regimen. He was frequently reminded how lucky he was to be diagnosed in this century rather than the last. He reported regularly to his doctor and responsibly disclosed his status to his sexual partners, which, in the pre-prophylaxis days, scared many of them off; several delivered their rejections with stinging cruelty. Then Eric, age thirty-three, met Alex.

After their first few dates, already enamored of the short, muscular man with flashy style and disarming candor, Eric asked Alex why he was unafraid to date a positive guy. Alex rolled his eyes and said, "I came out to Chinese missionary parents. I'm not afraid of anything."

"No, but really."

"Really? Because it's nice to know you've experienced prejudice, too, and that you're also stuck with it. I couldn't be with a guy who didn't understand the exhaustion of that."

Eric fell for Alex because Alex made him feel coveted again, despite his virulent seaside mistake. Together, they fancied themselves both wise to the world's unfairness while still appreciative of its delights, a stealthy team of discerning outsiders.

So Alex knows, of course. As do their friends. As does Dalton, who, when Eric revealed his status, had said, "At least you can't relapse," which didn't make sense at the time but does now.

Eric has never told his family. Why should he add to their worry? That has been his attitude for fourteen years. Here in this library, though, surrounded by Dalton and his fellow addicts, Eric realizes that rather than bravely fight stigma, as Susan just described, he succumbed to it, unwittingly returning to the closet of secrets he thought he'd already escaped. The crashing waves of her words yank him underwater and toss him back into the suffocating loneliness he felt behind that alley dumpster so many years ago.

Then Dalton's wide, warm hand is on his knee, a stunningly public display of care. Eric wonders if Dalton has heard this speech before, if he already made the connection between their diseases. Maybe it's why he returned to Eric after their first tryst, why he asked Eric here tonight, to show him their related burdens and silently suggest that they might share the weight.

Then Dalton snatches back his hand as if he'd forgotten they're not alone. But the lingering warmth is a comfort to Eric, expressing something new and real. Eric looks straight ahead, eyes damp, breathing hard. Is Dalton offering to be Eric's solution as well?

Susan introduces another speaker, a local sheriff's deputy, to share a regional update on overdoses. The deputy walks to the front, takes a wide stance, places hands on her holster, and rattles off stats. The numbers are startlingly high. Ambulance calls to homes, to schools, to gas stations. Rescues. Arrests. Deaths. Hearing the deputy recite them distracts Eric from himself. The stats are a guardrail that keeps him from falling over the cliff he's balanced on. They also appear to serve this purpose for Dalton, who nods along rhythmically, counting himself among them like a sinner at church who sees himself in the sermon.

Eric looks at Dalton in awe and thinks that this kid could be, probably should be, passed out in a friend's bathtub or a public restroom, maybe between quixotic stints in rehab, maybe behind bars. But somehow he's here, fingers tented over that handsome, smashed nose, facing his affliction in a way that Eric has never really been able to face his own.

The sheriff's deputy winds down her presentation. "It's an election year, you know, so it's an opportunity. They only talk about this, only promise resources, when there's a high-profile reason. The conversation's cyclical, and emotion equals action, so . . ." She nods with pursed lips as if to say, "Do with that what you will."

The room collectively nods, and the event is over. Susan insists that people eat more pizza. Eric feels empty, so he takes a cold slice. On his way out, needing tangible proof of this evening, he grabs flyers from a table filled with pamphlets, business cards for substance abuse hotlines, and purple buttons that say "Ally" in cursive font. That color, that word, look very out of context here, as though they accidentally wandered in from another support group that would also have something to say to Eric.

Outside the high school, Dalton lights a cigarette and offers it to Eric, who accepts. The woman in black approaches. "Hey, D," she says, and lights up as well.

"Hey," Dalton mumbles, hands buried in back pockets.

She scrutinizes Eric, glances at Dalton, and understands that introductions are up to her. "Maren," she says, extending a thin arm inked with thorny vines.

"Eric."

Dalton looks down and provides no additional information.

"Good to see you here," Maren says to him.

"Uh-huh."

"I heard about the little run-in."

Dalton takes back the cigarette from Eric. "From who?"

"Your dad mentioned and I—"

"So he's still blabbering about my problems to the whole fucking world?"

"I think he was just trying to find a way to share his own problems."

"You mean me."

"Not just you." She taps away ash. "I'm worried about him. He's drinking a lot . . ."

"What's new?"

"He sounds lonely."

"Good thing he's got you." His words float in dense smoke.

She looks away. There's a long silence. Neither of them acknowledges Eric.

"I'm sorry," she says at last. It sounds heavy and deep, covering more ground than just Dalton's dad.

Dalton accepts this with a nod. "You good?"

She shrugs. "Housing's a bitch. Just got kicked out of my last place, which was temporary anyway. Sleeping on a friend's couch till I save some cash for the next cubbyhole, though even the shit cubbyholes are out of reach these days."

"Saving cash, huh?" Dalton's voice is sharp. "More shifts?"

Maren looks away. "And some side stuff. Just temporary, like I said, but give me a call if . . ."

"Right. Well, good luck." He stamps out the cigarette, turns, and walks briskly to the car. Maren gives Eric a raised brow before he follows.

Halfway back to the farm, as their headlights capture lone driveways, patches of thick forest, and parcels of anxious deer, Dalton says, "She was my dealer."

"That woman?"

"After my doctor stopped prescribing, my buddy introduced us. She was working with another doctor in Glenellen, shady guy. Anyway, we had a relationship for about a year."

"A dealer-client relationship?"

"Well, yeah, it started that way, but then I couldn't afford much, so she said not to worry, she was happy to share with close friends. And the way she said it, I knew what she meant. It was clear she was interested in me, and I mean, I wasn't into her, obviously, but I also had no money. I'd been with girls before so . . . it just kind of worked out for a bit."

"Then what happened?"

"We were pulled over. They didn't find anything, but it was there, they just missed it. It freaked her out, so she stopped selling, at least for a while. And without the drugs, nothing to keep the relationship going, so." He looks out the window, into the blackness. "Guess she's back at it, though. Probably at the meeting to score clients." He's quiet for a moment, then adds, "Users aren't the only ones trapped."

They're silent the rest of the way. In front of the barn, Eric says, "Let me take you to the house."

"I'll walk."

"You don't have to insist on being alone."

Dalton looks down, shakes his head, and releases a defeated laugh. "Okay. You going to be with me?"

ON FRIDAY, ERIC heads to the train station to pick up Alex, who's arriving on the 6:17 with their guests for the weekend, Brian and Stephen, two rowdy city friends contemplating a home in the Munsee area. Eric is already exhausted by the expectations of entertaining but determined to offer a warm welcome. Except the 6:17 pulls in at 7:03, and everyone is irritated.

"Fucking late again," Alex says as he heaves his duffel into the trunk. "I swear this place is becoming a third-world country."

The preprogrammed itinerary commences at Bramble & Berry, where they meet Nate and his guests, two indistinguishably muscly men with pug faces who spend most of the night debating a divisive new musical. Back at the house, Alex shows Brian and Stephen to the guest room, which was restored earlier to a state of quasi-completion—not yet painted but furnished with a bed and dresser. While they unpack, Eric prepares nightcaps and Alex tidies up the living room. He sees his copy of *Middlemarch* open on the coffee table.

"Should I be worried?" he asks, holding it up to Eric before returning it to the bookshelf.

"About what?"

"Eric, come on. You haven't read a book since college. Whoever he is, he has good taste. But fuck buddies don't usually stick around long enough to read thousand-page novels. So you want to tell me what's going on?"

Alex could have laced those words with poison, but he says them with what sounds like real care, which has always been one of Alex's best traits, his ability to choose concern over condemnation. One of Eric's vainest and most pointless traits is his difficulty accepting such grace.

"Nothing. Really," he says. "It's nobody, a local kid. He was just curious."

Alex nods, unconvinced, and goes to check on the guests, leaving Eric to berate himself, less for the lie than for disparaging Dalton.

On Saturday they head into town for an afternoon of shopping on Granger, and Eric finds that Griffin looks very different to him now. He keeps thinking of the deputy's cold recitation of the sobering data. That's here? Among these farm-to-table restaurants and artisan candle boutiques and art galleries? His surprise is pathetically naive, he knows. He's well aware that social ills surround him in the city, too, just as stark and dreadful. He has, after all, spent the summer designing flyers and websites for organizations addressing them. But long ago he made a bargain there that allowed him to accept the city's poverty and pain as part of the unavoidable balance of life in a chaotic urban center. There is something different, something especially sour, about the discovery of despair in what is supposed to be his retreat, like encountering rot in their cottage attic, which he and Alex have barely examined and plan to ignore. Why poke around in decayed corners when there's nothing you can, or intend to, do about them?

But he can't seem to shake the shadow cast over Griffin by the Munsee Recovery meeting, perhaps because that shadow takes the shape of a specific someone with a beautiful smashed nose and a strong, bony brow; someone not of his kind but who has become unexpectedly important to him.

On Sunday they take Nate's boat out on Shelby Lake. A few drinks in, Alex sits next to Eric and says, "At least pretend, for fuck's sake."

Eric thought he'd been hiding his melancholy well. "Sorry, it's just . . ." He looks around. "Just all this. Always trying to amuse ourselves. To what end?"

"What are you talking about?"

"Nothing."

"Look, whatever this is"—Alex wipes the air in front of Eric with his palm—"put it away and try to be a good host for two more fucking hours, okay? This is embarrassing."

Eric tries. He joins a circle of men sipping rosé. He laughs and drinks along. But he also keeps thinking of the school library, keeps hearing the porcelain-faced woman say, "We need a movement like that!" as she looked right at him, or so he now imagines. He watches his friends sunning on the bow of the boat and splashing in the water, some veterans of that very movement, others merely its blind, blissful beneficiaries. He thinks of Dalton, whose only possible retreat is a second pill, not a second home. Eric's friends have burned through more joy in an afternoon than many people get in a year, and he wishes he could bottle up some of the excess and share it.

Sunday evening, Eric deposits Alex and their guests at the train station, waves goodbye, then heads to Cherry Hill Farm to pick up Dalton.

Monday and Tuesday are fantastically unproductive. All the projects on Eric's screen look like impossible puzzles. He keeps thinking of Dalton's hand on his knee, which he now interprets as both offer and plea. He puts aside his work and turns to the flyers he grabbed on his way out of the meeting. He visits their websites, which leads to more websites and page after page of sobering, often tragic stories. Each could have been Dalton. Each could still be Dalton. Eric tenses with a sudden instinct to protect.

On Wednesday evening, because of a notice he came across in his research, he finds himself driving an hour west, over the river, to Clarksdale. As he exits the vicinity of Griffin, leaving behind the storybook strip of Granger Street and the industrial drag of Kinghill Road, he considers how small the radius of his life has been here, consisting almost entirely of trips to town or a friend's nearby home, as long as that friend lives less than thirty minutes away. The landscape expands around him in fields of green and gold displaying corn at its tasseled highest and snails of baled hay, interrupted by weathered old barns, the occasional gas station, and periodic roadside farm stands promoting their produce and pies—these days, chiefly peach. The sky above mimics the seasonal fruit in darkening swirls of orange and pink.

He pulls up to an unassuming town hall with a small circular patch of grass and a flagpole. In the main room, fluorescent lights bounce off a linoleum floor onto rows of folding chairs and a table with more flyers, brochures, and a hot-water boiler for tea and coffee, nearly identical to the setup of last week's meeting in the library. Clarksdale's wild-whiskered mayor introduces the same task-force man from that meeting, with his thick neck and white crewcut. The man gives Eric a nod of recognition and repeats some of last week's mantras ("Addiction is a disease of isolation," etc.) before moving on to the science of opioids, the savage assault that is dope sickness, the savior that is naloxone, and a demonstration of how to shoot it, via the little rocketlike applicator, into the victim's nose to inject the reversal chemicals.

Along with eight others at the training, Eric, the only one in a polo shirt, repeats after the instructor, "Peel. Place. Press."

An hour later, he departs with a party favor in the form of a small blue bag containing a naloxone applicator, plastic gloves, a breathing barrier mask for mouth-to-mouth resuscitation, and some info cards. He tosses it into the glove compartment and drives back to his empty home feeling somehow more helpless than before, like a tourist to a troubled country returning with a purely symbolic souvenir, soon to be forgotten.

SEPTEMBER

CHAPTER 13

THE SUMMER SLIPS AWAY as summers do, in the same way the Munsee River flows forward, its impressive speed evident only when observing the brisk journey of a floating stick that's upstream, now downstream. The days remain warm and richly saturated with color while the evenings assume a pleasant chill, putting sweaters on standby.

To mark the conclusion of his extraordinary summer, it's fitting that Will is back in Paul's pool, in another tight circle. He balances a cup of rosé on the water's rippling surface like a pro, wearing the turquoise Speedo Paul gave him on the Fourth of July two months ago, though he feels years more worldly, at home in both circle and swimsuit. He is less guarded and shy, no longer approaching each gathering like an audition for the next.

Much of the past month since the *Fodder* event has been spent in water. Lakes, pools, the swimming hole in Vernon; a loop of revelry and relaxation, the most satisfying summer of his life. Each second has felt fully alive, yet within each waged a war of opposing emotions: gratitude and doubt; joy and a persistent dread that it will end soon. Which it will after this weekend, when the calendar calls these men back to their full-time city lives. But at least he approaches that milestone with a sense of accomplishment. He finally feels secure in his position here, a regular rather than a visitor. He credits Serge, now standing to his right, their toes wrestling underwater, for greatly assisting his integration (while also building his confidence in bed).

Just last weekend, Will joined Luke at Serge's festival for the season finale, an avant-garde dance-theater work that was one of the most peculiar and captivating things he's ever seen. There, Serge reiterated the offer of a summer internship, and for the first time in his life, Will is bullish about his future. He visualizes it through imagined artsy snapshots of that respectable job spliced with social scenes from the past few weeks: hikes to Laurel Falls, outings on Nate's boat, and all the extravagant meals in between, particularly those at Bramble & Berry.

Since it opened two years ago across from the Lucky Buck, that establishment's big glass wall had beckoned and warned Will like a lighthouse. None of these men knew the excitement and apprehension with which he finally entered the place, nor his shock at experiencing vegetables so inventively transformed and steaks so brazenly spiced. All of a sudden, his father's game of chicken dress-up appeared artless and absurd. But when the bill arrived, his vision blurred with the reminder that he was still a visitor in a foreign land and had miscalculated the exchange rate.

What he consumed in under two hours at Bramble & Berry cost more than he earned in a shift at the Buck. And it appeared that, despite allowing himself only a single beer, he would be subsidizing his companions' many rounds of cocktails and their cultivated taste in wine. Credit cards clattered onto the table; no one glanced at the total. Will mimicked their dispassion, blindly throwing down his debit card and stoically signing for his share. Later, when he finally looked at his receipt, he felt like the victim of a petty theft. But he returned again and again, seeing it as an investment in his professional prospects, just as his mom invests in her appearance and shops at Poppy's Pantry, thinking it's a secret.

From the seasonal bookend of Labor Day, that outlay feels justified as he deems his assimilation a success. He's become an assumed participant in weekend gatherings and excursions. He contributes jokes that begin with "Remember when," even if the reference point is confined to this summer. Despite some angst over his general refinement, his ever present financial insecurity, and that small matter of his forged identity, Will Martindale (née Riley) has absorbed the customs of this country and learned to capitalize on his areas of contribution. He assists with food prep, makes a sweep to collect platters and utensils, does the dishes, replenishes the rosé. In short, he is still a caterer, but not for Carly; still a bartender, but not for the Buck.

His skills have earned him a place in this pool, where today's banter turns to the hectic fall, which, for everyone around him, comprises a robust city-centric itinerary of weddings that require costumes, galas that require bow ties, and a procession of highly anticipated cultural premieres. One of these men, though, will return to Griffin regularly to check up on a major renovation project.

"Davey, when do you close on the church?" Luke asks.

"Next week," says the affable man on Will's left, whose hand has brushed up against Will's enough times to imply intention.

"Are you doing any work on it?"

"Oh, God, yes. Redoing the floors and master bath and ripping out the hideous kitchen. That's to start. Eventually I'd like to turn the altar area into a gym space."

"Sacrilege!" Serge mockingly clutches his chest. "Does Diane know your plans?"

"Not all of them." Davey smirks. "But she gave her blessing to gutting the kitchen, so all kosher there. She suggested going rustic, but Alex has talked me out of it."

"I mean, it's not a *barn*," Alex says. "Rustic is over. Too on the nose."

The water instantly feels like an ice bath as Will's mother inserts herself into his new life. Apparently she has been here all along. He's struck dumb and feels utterly naive to finally acknowledge that these men are the very "um, couples" to whom she has been selling homes for years—and that he has spent the summer fucking and frolicking with them. The rosé he's just tossed into his mouth clogs his throat. He coughs violently.

"You okay?" Nate asks, and Serge places a hand on Will's back.

"Fine . . ." Cough. "Yeah, fine."

"Easy there!" Serge says. Will waves away the attention and the irrational fear that his reaction might somehow be traced to his mother's name. Has she mentioned him to her clients? Might they somehow connect the dots to his father? How did he not consider all this sooner? He takes another sip to soothe his throat. The wine's pleasant sting inspires a redeeming thought: If she's selling homes to these men—Paul Banks's friends!—and profiting off them, is Will's socializing with them really any worse? He begins to rationalize his way to calm, until . . .

"Hey, Will," Nate says. "When do you go back to school? Haven't classes started by now?"

The one question he hoped to avoid.

"I'm actually not going back this semester," he says with unconvincing nonchalance.

A hush blankets the pool, as if he has announced an unfortunate medical diagnosis. Eric, who's been noticeably subdued lately, stands alone in the shallow end and stares at Will behind mirrored aviators.

"Is everything okay?" Luke asks, as though he can only imagine a family illness or mental breakdown as a reason to pause college.

"Yeah, of course," Will stammers. "I just . . . I needed to make some more money."

Looks of pity pelt him, all conveying support while betraying complete unfamiliarity with such a scenario, except for Alex, who nods with recognition.

In fact, Will is not returning to school because he has agreed to serve as his father's deputy campaign manager.

He hesitated when offered. He was eager to go back to college, eager to move closer to graduation and into life beyond, eager to demonstrate his new carnal confidence to the baseball player with the Cheshire grin. Besides, to remain in Griffin without access to the fine dwellings and vivid diversions of his new friends means to remain in the colorless Griffin he has outgrown.

But in the end, he saw the offer as an olive branch his father hadn't even known he was extending, affording Will the chance to atone for the theft of the campaign signs and for this entire summer of defection. So Will accepted with matching solemnity.

It's unpaid, Chip made clear, which means Will must keep shifts at the Buck. But his father promised that the experience would "pay off down the road." Whatever road his father envisions, though, is not the same road that Serge's theater internship would send him down, and it's Serge's path that animates him most. If, at the start of summer, Will was merely enamored of these men, he is now inspired and persuaded by them. The goal is no longer to simply penetrate their world—the goal is to remain.

The pool licks his ribs, and the men look at him with concern over his postponed education while Will thinks of phone banks, fundraisers, and endless canvassing.

"I wish I'd taken a semester off at some point," Luke says, wiping away the awkwardness. "But in any case, we'll see you when we come back on weekends, right?" Whether Luke means it or is just being polite, Will grabs on to this life jacket of kindness.

"And now you can come to my birthday party," Alex adds.

Will knows that Alex turns forty at the end of October because he bemoans this fact with great frequency. To celebrate, he'll host a formal dinner at one of Munsee's famous mansions, the former summer home of a prominent nineteenth-century industrial family. Will hoped for an invitation but didn't expect one. He and Alex haven't developed a personal rapport, in part because he didn't want to encourage Alex's flirting, in part because Will is abetting Eric in keeping a secret from Alex. Thus, distance from the couple seemed prudent. But now Alex is extending a lifeline to stay connected to these men in the long months between now and next summer. The party is close to Election Day, and though he'll only become more enmeshed in his father's campaign in the meantime, Will can't bear to fall off their radar. He can't risk being forgotten.

"Thank you." He tries to downplay the breathless gratitude in his voice. "I'd love to."

Eric trains his mirrored lenses on his husband. He knows that Alex has extra seats for the dinner, since a few of their friends have sent regrets. It's considerate to invite Will—charitable, really—but the invitation leaves Eric irritated, excessively so, which makes no sense until he realizes it's because Will isn't Dalton. Because although those two are of the same kind—locals to Griffin, outsiders to this group—Will has been embraced, while Dalton will never be in this pool or seated around a decadent dining room table, and he doesn't even want to be. Eric will see Will again soon at Alex's party, and probably next summer, and perhaps for years to come.

But a few days ago, engine idling at Cherry Hill Farm, Eric said goodbye to Dalton for the foreseeable future. Tomorrow Eric and Alex will return to the city for a busy fall of work and social obligations. They've rented out their cottage for much of the popular apple-picking season to offset the mortgage, so Eric doesn't know when he'll be in Griffin next, or rather, in Griffin alone. It was harder than he expected to tell this to Dalton.

"I'll be back, on and off," he said, the words sounding pathetic as they formed.

"Well, I'll be here, on and on," Dalton said dryly to the dashboard. The door was already open, and he had one foot on the gravel.

Eric put a hand on Dalton's nearest knee. "I'll see you soon." It was meant to be reassuring but came across more like an apology.

Dalton looked at Eric's hand as if it were a wasp, something unwanted that couldn't be swiped away easily. "It's fine," he said.

"I promise," Eric insisted.

Dalton looked at him with a sad smile and said again, in the defeated tone of an absolution, "It's fine." Then he slid out of the car and shut the door before Eric could respond.

The gloom produced by that farewell overwhelms him now. Eric is unable to hide it, which is why Alex is next to him, leaning in, exasperated. "What the fuck is going on with you?"

"Nothing."

"Do you want to go?"

"We just got here."

"Oh, *I'm* staying. I'm asking if *you* want to go. You don't seem to want to be here, or anywhere these days. You're doing your detached thing again, acting like this is all beneath you. So no need to indulge us. You have my permission to leave."

Eric should apologize again, explain himself, reassure Alex that it will all be okay, that he's just confused. But when he looks at his husband, he sees only his own sad face reflected in Alex's dark sunglasses.

"Okay, I'll leave."

"I'll let you know when I'm ready to be picked up." Alex exits the pool and goes to the bar.

As Eric heads inside to gather his things, he brushes past Stan coming out. Stan is in a sour mood, irked to be hosting yet another one of these inane gatherings. He indulged it in July, but now the election is two months away. Each day matters, yet Paul planned this impromptu party without consulting him. Stan held his tongue, choosing not to pick another fight until Paul asks him to run out for more ice.

"Ice? *That's* what you're asking of me, Paul? We are weeks away from your first political race. You're behind but within the margin of error, and what you're most concerned about is whether your boyfriends have cold wine to drink? Are you shitting me?"

"Babe, calm down. We literally had nothing scheduled this afternoon. I went to two events this morning, and I'll go to five tomorrow, and every goddamn day until the election. But God forbid I should take a few hours to recharge and remind myself that this place is actually our home, too. Never mind. I'll get the fucking ice myself."

As Paul storms out, Leon arrives. He is pleased to have been invited back, grateful for a second chance to ingratiate himself with Stan's friends, determined to leave them with a favorable impression by summer's end. He finds Stan at the bar with Alex.

"Everyone seems to be rushing off! Have I missed all the fun?" Leon chuckles, then turns to Alex. "Your husband looked very eager to escape. Had enough already?"

"I've had enough of *him*, that's for sure." Alex refills his cup and returns to the pool. Stan and Leon exchange amused looks, pour themselves drinks, and follow.

"Hello, gentlemen," Leon says with excessive aplomb. He is committed to inoffensive cheeriness until he sees Will and again feels the rush of humiliation from being left behind at the *Fodder* event weeks ago. "Oh, there's William," he says with contempt. He kicks off his sandals, sits on the pool's lip, dunks his feet, and flutters them menacingly in Will's direction.

Will is unsettled by the angry little ripples racing toward him, their wet animosity. He looks around for sympathetic witnesses, but no one seems to have noticed.

Stan sits beside Leon and submerges his legs as well, then asks the group with a resigned sigh, "So, what are we discussing?"

"Alex's little Gilded Age soiree," Nate says.

Everyone laughs, including Alex, though his smile is tight and short. Stan contributes a knowing chuckle; he is partially subsidizing the event as a birthday gift.

Leon is horrified to realize that he alone seems unaware of this event. And the exclusion feels like an official verdict confirming that he has made no inroads into this group, which means he faces a lonely frigid winter and a soggy spring ahead. Who knows whether these men will even remember him come next summer?

"A big birthday requires a big celebration," Stan says with magnanimous authority. "I'm already thinking about my sixtieth."

Leon seeks any foothold for participation, however small. "Good for you!" he says. "You deserve a blowout."

"We'll see how things turn out with the election."

"Oh, don't be so cautious! Whatever happens, Paul owes you, after all you've done for him this year. That is, as you said, if he doesn't bankrupt you first. Mhah!"

In the stagnant silence that follows, Leon immediately feels the weight of his error. He has violated the group's unspoken rule against acknowledging its own wealth, but worse, he has violated the trust of his only ally among them. To apologize feels too shameful an admission, so Leon grins maniacally, silently begging Stan to accept it in jest and forgive him.

"Well," Stan says, doing neither.

The conversation claws its way back to levity, and Leon continues to laugh and kick his legs in the cool water. But now it feels like desperate treading, which is how he has felt since coming to Griffin, how he felt in the city, and, if he's honest, how he's felt most of his life. How quickly he has been misunderstood once again; how exhausting it is to keep trying, and failing.

Someone proposes more rosé, and it becomes a collective mission. The group exits the pool, leaving Leon dangling on the ledge. He watches them fill their cups and giggle over something he is sure relates to him.

Meanwhile, Stan has disappeared. (Stan is upstairs with his magazine again. He didn't want to be around when Paul returns.)

The message to Leon is clear, and it scorches. No matter his efforts, these men extend him no benefit of the doubt. They have decided he is not one of them. He heads indoors to gather his belongings, passing Paul carrying a large bag of ice.

Paul ignores the fleeing, angry old man, determined to salvage the day. Facing his friends on the back patio, he swipes off his shirt, wiggles out of his shorts, and yanks down his underwear, eliciting raucous applause and piercing whistles from the pool.

"Naked, now!" he shouts, prompting another wave of cheers.

All summer, Will has watched greedily as the men around him defiantly discarded their swimsuits, their bodies gleaming with dignity. If such exposure felt impossible a few months ago, it feels imperative now. Emboldened by Serge's proximity, Alex's invitation, and Leon's departure, Will slips off his turquoise Speedo. There is now no barrier between his body, this merciful liquid, and the liberated fraternity that he has officially joined.

LEON CAN'T BEAR to return to his small apartment, which would feel all the more claustrophobic thanks to the mocking presence of that Louis XVI mahogany console, so rashly purchased in a moment of hope, when he thought a piece of furniture could forecast the future. Instead, he finds himself back at the Buck, a place that is both comfort and defeat. It is not where he would prefer to be, but the calm familiarity of the scene soothes his disappointment. The hummingbird sisters sink shots as Gerald drains a beer at the bar in front of a college football game. Then he's beside Leon.

"Hey, Lenny. Been a while."

"Hello, Gerald. And it's Leon."

"Well, it's Gerry for me. Don't deny someone's nickname. And don't refuse your own, Lenny. It's a gift, which is rare coming from me."

"Please, no name games today, Gerald."

"Geez. What's eating you now?"

"The usual. Regret and indignation." Leon laughs bitterly. "Sorry, I'm not good company today."

"Company is company. I'll take what I can get. Cows are lousy talkers, and Chip's busy running around the entire goddamn district, taking away my land."

"So the council went through with it? Exercised eminent domain? I'm sorry, Gerald."

"Well, not yet. But there's a hearing next week to authorize it."

"And you're going, I presume? To fight it?"

"Hadn't planned to. No point. They have the votes, Chip can't stop 'em, and I don't think he even wants to. Bastard won't call me back and never comes in here anymore, so can't beg him directly, either. All the others made a deal, I'm the only dipshit left. They'll take my land in the end, nothing I can do about it."

Gerald's tone of injustice and defeat sounds raw and familiar, intensifying Leon's own feelings of futility. He puts a hand on Gerald's shoulder and says: "For God's sake, then, go to the meeting and state your case! They have to face you there. Make them feel like the thieves they are. It may not change anything, but at least you'll be heard. Show those fuckers you won't be ignored."

THAT SAME WEEKEND, before she returns to school, Callie drags Joe to a big Labor Day party at Troy and Aimee's house, which has replaced the Swinton basement as the gathering spot of choice among their friends.

They've attended a few get-togethers here throughout the summer, and each time Joe was haunted by Matt's absence. To escape the ghostly void, he got drunk and found whomever he needed to find for whatever substance was available to smoke, swallow, or snort to dull himself. He had no desire to return today, but Callie argued it would be good for them to be around friends, which he interprets to mean that she is losing patience with him.

All summer, her apologetic smile pacified him, but by August, the shared grief that knit them together had begun to loosen and untwine.

They continued to go to Rainbow Rock, but the moment the sun faded over the distant mountains, a tide of despair would rise within him. A few weeks ago, Callie said, "I can't stay in your sadness anymore."

"You're not sad?"

"I am. All the time. But I want to try not to be."

Joe wanted to try, too. "Maybe you can help me."

She nodded and rubbed his arm, and he did try. They sat in the red and chrome booths at Nana's Diner and drank milkshakes like 1950s teens, but Joe kept feeling the phantom weight of Matt's arms spread across the faux leather seats and refused to go back. They walked along the riverbanks and talked of the future until it became clear that only Callie could imagine one. Then they watched movies because there was nothing more to say. Their kisses began to feel calculated and purposeful, like they were meant to console or persuade rather than excite. Back in June, when summer stretched ahead, her presence had inflated him with hope, but now that summer is almost over, it only reminds him that he will soon be left behind.

He can't find her at Troy and Aimee's house, which is a crowded, dim, inadequate replica of the Lab, somehow devoid of both intimacy and room to breathe. The music is loud, so voices are louder. Joe huddles in a corner, hiding behind a floor lamp. Aimee finds him anyway.

"Riley, what the fuck is up with your little bro?"

Joe shrugs, but the question vexes him because he's seen Will so infrequently this summer that in moments of semiconsciousness, he has wondered whether he still has a brother.

Aimee continues, "Left me fucking high and dry a few weeks ago. Or, actually, high and fucking drenched."

"Don't know what you're talking about," Joe mumbles, looking past her. "Don't care."

"Well, let me tell you, then." She points the long neck of her beer at him. The lamp doubles the shadows around her eyes, already dark from makeup, heightening the menace. "He walked out in the middle of an event. Just walked away with a bunch of Duffels like he was a goddamn guest while the rest of us had to keep working. At first I thought Carly let him, 'cause the gays are her best clients and Will was, like, one of her most popular dishes." Her laugh is a callous wheeze. Joe senses others turning toward them, tuning in.

"So when they're all, 'Can we take Will home with us?' like he's some kind of doggie bag, she can't say no. It's good business to say yes." Aimee retracts the accusatory beer to take a sip, refueling for the next lap. "I mean, there's a name for that, but I'm not gonna say it." Snickers bloom into laughter. "But then Carly told me she *hadn't* allowed it. That he'd just gone. Fucking quit! Like he's better than us, one of *them* now. How fucked up is that?"

Joe burns as though the lamp above him has become a heater. The airing of his brother's sexuality and public promiscuity produces hot shame and cold confusion. The Will that Aimee describes is a Will that Joe doesn't know, a Will living a vibrant other life that doesn't include him. And with this realization comes a half-formed fear: If Will is at college or invested in their father's campaign, he is tied to Griffin, tied to their family, and the distance between the brothers might be bridged eventually. But if what Aimee says is true—if Will has fallen in with these Duffels, if he chooses them and follows them to the city—the distance between them will only grow. A flicker of despair forms in his chest, and he douses it with anger.

"I don't give a shit about Will," he says.

He steps through the lamp's scalding spotlight, across the room's seemingly vast expanse, then out the back door to the dark porch, where one of his classmates, a Lab regular back in the day, calms him with the chemicals he seeks. Injection is the only option, which is agonizing, because all he can see is the needle stuck at an angle in the carpet next to Matt. But once the drugs are inside him, Joe becomes safely cocooned in a private chamber of fog. From behind that haze and through the kitchen window, he watches Callie reenter their old lives, laughing with her girlfriends, smiling at less troubled guys. He knows that he cannot follow her.

CHAPTER 14

TWO WEEKS LATER, DIANE joins a handful of volunteers for a Saturday phone banking session at Chip's headquarters. It's her second shift since Davey bought the church, earning her a sizable commission and Paul Banks a vote. She tries not to think too much about the inverse relationship between her success and Chip's, or their bank account and her sense of sanctity, or the fact that a charming golden retriever of a man is now seeking companionship in close proximity to her son while entertaining blasphemous ideas of what to do in a choir loft.

She is here because the election is imminent, and she feels like a student waking to the reality of an impending exam. She tells herself that this abrupt sense of obligation has nothing to do with Will's promotion and the hint of jealousy she tasted as a result. No, this is simply about being there for her husband at a crucial moment. She'll make calls today and canvass tomorrow after worship. She intends to maintain this schedule until Election Day. (Conveniently, house showings drop off after summer anyway, so she can afford to be a more engaged spouse.)

Heading into the fall sprint, Chip has regained a comfortable lead in the polls, thanks in part to the fallout from Celia's article about the Griffin Investment Group and from the small swell of volunteers who have appeared with sudden civic fervor, inspired by the same urgency that compelled Diane. Chip's campaign feels livelier and more efficient these days, an operation clicked into place. Beginning this month, events double their pace, and fundraising goals hit daunting heights as financial filing deadlines rush closer, causing solicitation emails to adopt hysterical decibels of desperation and ethically questionable degrees of hyperbole.

Gabrielle oversees it all with commanding proficiency. No longer a novice, she has somehow become a political professional in the past six months. In a blur of big-patterned blouses, trailed by devil-may-care brown curls (and now by her deputy, Will), she directs the small staff acquired over the summer to tackle the day's overwhelming menu of tasks, then prepares volunteers to begin making calls. She escorts Diane to a chair in a less loud corner, hands her a script that treats the voter like a distracted kindergartner, then abandons her to orient others. Diane certainly didn't expect special treatment for being the candidate's wife, but neither did she expect to be quite so unsung.

After fifteen minutes, she learns that she hates phone banking. The rude intrusion, the threat of confrontation, the numbing boredom of wrong number after wrong number, the pointlessness now that everyone screens their calls. When she does reach someone, she finds herself slipping into the singsong voice and crisp language of a midcentury secretary. "Well, we *so* appreciate your support, sir." "Oh my! Let's remain civil, shall we, ma'am?" It's as if creating a fictional version of herself makes it easier to sell a fictional version of her husband.

An hour later, Chip returns from a Rotary Club breakfast in Cranston, a hamlet to the west best known for its annual blueberry festival. Diane is mid-ring on a call, about to hang up, when someone actually answers and she must launch into her script. Chip waves and disappears into his office, joined by Gabrielle.

As the voter on the line chatters about his distrust of government, Diane stares at the closed door. Shouldn't she be in there, too, strategizing like an adviser rather than making calls like a nameless volunteer? Is it that they don't think she'll add value? Or more likely that she's displayed so little interest for so long that they haven't thought to include her. The call finally ends, Diane marks the voter as "undecided," and a few minutes later, Chip and Gabrielle emerge from the office shoulder to shoulder, laughing. Is Gabrielle wearing makeup? Diane is pretty sure she didn't when Chip hired her in February.

Then an eruption from the other side of the office. "Well, fuck!" yells Terry, who remains an eager, exasperating team player. He holds up his phone. "You guys, check this shit out. It's Banks's newest perfume commercial."

Despite Gabrielle's objections that the premiere of an opponent's attack ad should not be screened for volunteers, everyone gathers around him. Chip grimaces, bracing himself for another polished product to come from the Banks campaign. Diane is heartened when he looks to her for reassurance, and she goes to stand by his side.

When Terry plays the ad, it's immediately clear that it is unlike the previous ones. No sweeping rural landscapes and soaring music and potpourri of identities. Instead, an angry pixelated face fills the screen, frozen in grainy close-up and creviced with age, eyelids sloping downward in defeat but irises dark and alive with resentment. Above them, bushy white brows like snowdrifts. A gruff voiceover asks, "How well do you know Chip Riley?"

"Oh, God," Diane whispers when she recognizes Gerald McAfee's face.

Chip grabs her hand. "Jesus Christ," he groans.

"No way," Will says.

Gabrielle shoots them a confused, worried look.

Gerry's face unfreezes, and the frame widens to reveal last week's crowded Town Hall meeting. He's standing behind a microphone placed in the aisle, shouting: "How dare you, Riley! That land's been in my family for three generations! And I intended to make it four! But this town . . ." He stabs a finger at Chip. "You! You think you have a goddamn right?"

The clip comes from the local public access livestream. It cuts to Chip sitting behind a table on a raised platform with four other members of the Griffin Town Council. Diane knows how much that meeting tortured Chip, but his expression on camera is composed and could be read as dismissive. The camera returns to Gerry, who yells: "What kind of town does this? What kind of man does this to his *friend*?"

The image freezes on Chip's inscrutable face and stamps it with the word "Traitor," which makes Diane gasp. Again the gravelly voiceover:

"Chip Riley is no friend of the farmer. If he won't defend us at home, how can we trust him to have our back in Washington?" Then the small sponsorship tag, "Paid for by the Griffin Congressional Committee."

The cramped Riley headquarters sits in excruciating silence. The volunteers look to Chip, but he's stunned into stillness.

"Well," Diane says, anointing herself his surrogate before Gabrielle can, though Gabrielle looks as dumbly horrified as everyone else, Will included. "That was ridiculous! A complete mischaracterization of that... *situation.*" She laughs as though it's a prank. "I mean, *really.*" She wishes she had more to say, but her mind is unable to refresh.

No one looks at her. A volunteer asks, "What's the Griffin Congressional Committee?"

"The goddamn financial mercenary of the Banks campaign," Chip mutters, voice boiling.

Diane senses Bud Light Riley ready to explode. She's reaching for something—anything—to douse or distract from the tension when Terry yells: "Fuck the carpetbugger! That's a low blow, but I guess a low blow is what he's good at, am I right?"

Gabrielle begins to object, but another volunteer, an older woman with crispy yellow hair and a tobacco-scratched voice, gives a husky guffaw and says, "Carpetbugger, ha! That's a good one, T."

Terry beams, his wit finally rewarded. Another volunteer can't help but laugh, giving permission to others and allowing Chip to add his own forced chuckle. He says with almost convincing nonchalance, "All right, everyone, enough of this nonsense. Let's get back to it!" He claps twice, as if to chase away what they've all just seen, then retreats to the office. Diane follows, closing the door before Gabrielle and Will can join them.

Chip sits at his desk, hunched over his computer, and watches the ad again. Diane observes the adolescent roundness of his spine, how his beard almost touches his chest, how his protruding stomach makes him look like a Laughing Buddha. The image produces in her a protective pity and the thought that this might be the opportunity she's seeking to reassert herself as primary comforter and counsel.

"What you did was necessary," she says. "It's what was required for this town to move forward. Everyone knows that. You're helping a lot of people, Charles. People who probably won't vote for you because they're told you don't care about them. But you're helping them anyway. And you're doing what's right for Griffin, and trying to do right by Gerry, even if he won't let you. For Banks to exploit it the way he has . . . I get that this is how things are done in this game, but it's not right."

"That meeting was a nightmare." he says. "But it happened. I did that to Gerry. What do I do now?"

From her vantage point, Diane peers down on Chip's soft, circular shape. He looks up at her with frank, fearful openness. All along, she's been afraid that politics would make him unrecognizably strong; she never considered that the experience could render him unrecognizably vulnerable.

"Tell the story from your side. Stand up for yourself! Go after Banks, for goodness' sake!"

"Well, I can yap to the *Gazette* for days, but that's not going to hit the people who will see this ad, the reach he's able to purchase. Our TV budget's already eaten up by the October ad buy, and I'm not anticipating winning the lottery or getting a boost from the national committee any time soon."

"No, you're not going to win the lottery," Diane says quietly. She rubs the rhinestones on her necklace and thinks of Davey's church. "But I had a very good summer."

He squints at her and inhales. His eyes sparkle with hope but he says, responsibly, "Are you . . . We said we wouldn't spend our own money. And Joe . . . who knows if we'll need . . ."

"We haven't needed it yet. Like you said, maybe we won't. He's been calmer lately, don't you think? Maybe he just needed to be back to his routine. Maybe he just needed time?"

Chip lets her questions linger. He nods, starts to speak, stops, starts again. "You said you wanted to redo the bathroom. I couldn't ask . . ."

"The bathroom's fine. It still works."

JOE OFTEN WAKES in the middle of the night, his mind panicked and his body pained, then he tumbles back into a steep unconsciousness that may or may not release him in time to open Delphi's. When he does emerge from his stupor, his father is already off courting voters, and his mother is off courting buyers. His brother may be at campaign headquarters or may still be asleep because Will came home late a lot this summer, if he came home at all. And now, thanks to Aimee's intel, Joe knows where Will's been.

Joe eats cereal by himself and bikes to Delphi's if his body allows, if it doesn't refuse his efforts. Troy has resumed computer science classes at the community college, so now it's just Joe and Amir and the other full-time, year-round staff, gruff but affable older men and women who kindly leave him alone. The customers only care whether he can solve their minor problems, and their indifference is a gift. Delphi's is still the place where he feels safest, where he is useful and not pitied, where the hours retain some semblance of shape. Meanwhile, everything outside Delphi's has pooled into one big gray puddle to avoid. Especially his family.

After the incident with the Independence Day Picnic, his parents stopped including him in campaign-related activities, which was a relief and a bruise. He's become a liability, best left alone in hopes that he'll disappear, which he's happy to do and has essentially done. His self-estrangement from his family would hurt, or hurt more, if not for the numbing substances that obliterate his capacity to care.

The campaign exacerbates it all, a suffocating presence in their small home. Pamphlets featuring his father's mocking smile crowd the dining room table; lawn signs shouting his father's name are piled on the sofa. At infrequent family dinners (at his parents' insistence), Joe might as well be a spectator watching a game on TV that is both boring and complex. His parents and brother ignore him as they strategize with animated hands and challenge one another in judicious, agitated tones. In this shared project, Joe sees an improvement in the relationship between his father and brother, for which he is glad and jealous.

But the family meals have also grown contentious, illuminating new fissures. Tonight his mother harps about some ad that apparently has to do with Gerry McAfee.

"Charles, I gave you—*we* gave the campaign that money to fight back, not hide behind some . . . some Hallmark card. How can you ignore those ugly accusations?"

"Gabby thinks if we directly address it, it'll give it more oxygen. She says we should combat the *impression* but not repeat the ad's claims. Otherwise, we'll just spread it to more people."

"Oh!" Diane throws up her hands. "Well, if *Gabby* says, then—"

"No!" His father slaps the table, and the dishes rattle. "I'm sorry, Di, but you do *not* get to show up at this late stage and criticize her. She's been nothing but a blessing to me."

Diane looks away. Will and Joe instinctively look at each other with enlarged eyes. They've rarely seen their parents argue or witnessed their father's ire directed at their mother. This brief moment of brotherly connection is almost comforting, but then Will turns to their mother and says, "I'm also inclined to agree with Gabby."

The direct challenge is startling, but Will has lately directed a new coldness toward their mother which seems to contain an inexplicable superiority. Then again, since becoming deputy campaign manager, he has adopted a strange zeal around the campaign, which makes their father proud and their mother suspicious, and feels at odds with Aimee's crude Labor Day disclosure. If Joe were at all engaged, if he felt in any way invested in this conversation or this campaign, he might call out his brother's hypocrisy. But his current state allows only for distant observation.

Will's dismissive comment—as well as his alliance with Gabrielle and traitorous use of her nickname—gives Diane a new target, and she aims with the wild desperation of the wounded. "Well, sweetie, your *inclination* is weak and naive," she says. "We have to hit back. You should *want* to hit back."

Will laughs. "And this is Christian grace now?"

Diane gapes at him. "What do you know about faith?"

"I know that it can change its mind whenever convenient."

Her face freezes and threatens to crack.

"Okay, okay, enough!" Chip says. He holds out his palms, a referee forestalling a brawl. "Who wants ice cream?"

Ice cream makes Joe think of Callie in her candy-cane costume, the half-melted half-pints she used to bring him. He'd take whatever she offered him now, even goat cheese and cherries, for a minute of her presence.

Diane glares at Will. "Whose side are you on?"

Will hesitates, and the smugness leaves his voice. "Dad's."

"You sure about that?"

Will's eyes flip between their parents. "Of course," he says.

After a few long seconds, Chip goes to the kitchen. Joe hears the clink of ice cream dishes being stacked and the clang of metal spoons. That isolating, soulless sound is almost too much for him. A dish breaks.

"Godammit!" his father yells, which propels Diane from the table. She shuts the door to the kitchen, leaving Joe and Will to contemplate their plates.

"Mom's right," Joe says to the chicken bones in front of him.

"What?"

"I know about you and Banks."

Joe still doesn't look up, so he can only imagine an expression that matches the fear and anger in his brother's voice when Will says, "I don't know what you heard, but it's bullshit."

"You're a traitor."

"I'm the only one who's been helping Dad this summer."

"By fucking his opponent?"

In the vicious silence that follows, they hear their parents murmuring in the kitchen. Joe finally looks up and sees his brother's quivering face, his mouth twisted in rage.

"*You're* the fucking traitor!" Will says. He gets up and shoves his chair forward. It screeches on the floor and knocks into the table. "Nothing but a burden to this family. Fucking deadweight." He bolts from the room, leaving Joe alone at the table. A second later, a door slams.

Joe sits impassive for several minutes until he finds himself, somehow, collapsed on his bed, a well-known despair bubbling up, while he also feels a pulling down, the tug of a whirlpool. He lies there for an hour, trying to resist it, staring up at his own faded glow-in-the-dark constellation, a sibling galaxy to the one in Will's bedroom. Then he sends a text, gets a reply, and, when he's sure everyone has retreated for the night, leaves the house, grabbing his dad's car keys and a couple of twenties from his mom's purse. They'll hear the car, they'll know he's gone somewhere, but he doesn't care. They're used to it now.

Ten minutes later, he pulls into the familiar parking lot. An earlier light rain makes the asphalt shimmer, reflecting and smearing the bar's neon signs, one of which announces that the Lucky Buck is closed. But within a minute, a door opens and a short, slim figure trots over, the black jeans, black T-shirt, and dark copper hair blending into the black, shiny ground. It is the woman he's desired from the moment she came into his home, the woman who has captivated him with her lovely, troubled eyes; the woman who supplies him.

Joe rolls down the window and rests his arm on the ledge. Maren places her hands tenderly on his balled-up fist, just as she did the night before the Independence Day Picnic, when she came for dinner. He'd quietly asked for something to ease the anxiety of a public event, then walked her to her car to receive a small plastic bag. He had meant to take only a fraction that night but couldn't help himself, ruining the picnic for his family.

They smile sadly at each other in the parking lot. Perhaps she's thinking of that earlier exchange as well, or any of the half dozen since. He unfurls his palm, and she swaps the bills for another little bag. As usual, the brush of her hand delivers its own high.

"Say hi to Mom and Dad for me," she says.

A FEW DAYS later, Maren stands behind the Buck's bar, thorny inked arms folded with impatience, waiting for Leon to order. "One of those green G and Ts, please," he says automatically before realizing that he still associates the drink with Will, which now bestows a bitter beforetaste. She has already started to prepare it, though.

As she minces herbs, Leon scans the space and is somewhat heartened by the dependable presence of the other Buck regulars: the hummingbird sisters, the liquor store lesbian, the young bespectacled Black woman and the genial, dimpled man she's usually with. The Buck has become as comfortable to him in the past few months as his own apartment, but at least here he doesn't have to look at that ridiculous old console. He means to resell it but can't in Griffin. To do so here would be to loudly advertise his failure.

After Maren presents Leon with the unwanted cocktail, a scruffy man in a plaid shirt takes the seat next to him and says, "You like that thing?"

"I don't see how that's any of your business."

"Sorry, pal. Guess we haven't met. I'm Chip Riley, I own this place, so it literally is my business." He offers his hand. "Didn't mean to offend."

Leon eyes it cautiously, then accepts. "Chip Riley the politician?"

After they shake, Chip raises his palms in protest. "No need to sling insults. But yeah. You registered to vote?"

"Not here." Why the lie? Leon can't say. Perhaps a reflex to maintain impartiality.

"Guess no reason for us to talk, then."

Leon raises his brows.

"Kidding, pal. Just kidding." Chip readjusts himself, turning more fully toward Leon. "Always got time to talk to my patrons."

"Even these days? Just a month until the election. Shouldn't you be out hustling?"

"Oh, I am. Pounded pavement all day today in Dover, then heading to some stuff tonight around here. But I found a happy hour–sized hole in my schedule and figured I'd make sure folks here remember me. In all honesty, I was hoping to run into a friend I've been avoiding, except I'm thinking he might be avoiding *me*."

The disclosure seems too personal until Leon considers perhaps it's because he's not seen as a voter that Chip feels he can speak freely. It's as though Leon's solitude, the very thing that tortures him, is also the thing that invites unexpected intimacies—from Gerald, Stan, and now Chip. "What'd he do to you?" Leon asks.

"More like what I did to him. You can see for yourself on the damn TV.

But I don't think he's avoiding me out of anger. More from embarrassment that the whole stinking mess got so public."

"I see." Leon takes a sip of his drink and tastes remorse. After his last conversation with Gerald, when he'd urged the man to confront Chip, Leon had called Stan to apologize for his comments on Labor Day and share what he'd learned about the pending eminent domain issue. Stan didn't answer, but in a voicemail, Leon told him to pay attention to the upcoming town council meeting, that something useful might come of it. Leon still hasn't heard from Stan. Some good that intel did him.

But he didn't consider the impact of his ploy on the poor old bigot, whom he's become strangely fond of. "I'm sure your friend will come around," he says, but he wants to move away from this topic. "So you think everyone else here has forgotten you?"

"Not really. More like I don't want to forget *them*. When I'm back, it's like watching a rerun of an earlier episode of my life. This was my whole world, everything between these walls. Same cast of characters, same dialogue. I always knew what to say. Now I'm meeting so many people, always improvising. Just feels good to be back in a familiar scene."

"A reunion special."

"Right! That's good. What was your name again?"

"Leon."

"Nice to know you, Leon. How's the drink?"

"So-so. But your interest in it is confounding."

"It's just that my son came up with it, and I have to admit, I thought it was kind of silly. We don't generally do cocktails here. But I've got to hand it to him, folks seem to like it, judging by the amount of gin showing up on my invoices. Just never saw anyone actually order one until now."

Leon cocks his head. "Your son came up with this?"

"Yup. Freckled face working here all summer. Kinda spacey, but he's a good kid."

Leon looks at Chip for a few suspended moments. "William?"

"Yeah. Will. You met?"

"Mmm. A few times. But you're Chip Riley, yes? And he's Will Martindale, no?"

"Martindale? No, no, that's our street. He's Riley, same as me. Son, employee, and now, actually, my deputy campaign manager. Which, never would've thought."

"Is that right?" Leon works to control his voice. "Extraordinary."

"Why's that?"

"No reason."

"Well, look, I'm glad you're enjoying that drink. Maren, sweetie? Get this fellow here another one, on the house."

"Oh, you don't—"

"My pleasure. Now I gotta get back to the grind. Nice meeting you, Leon."

"Likewise." Leon's about to tell Chip to give his regards to Will but decides against it. He's still dazzled by the discovery. "Good luck with the election."

Leon fishes a cucumber disc out of his drink and chews in amazement. Chip Riley's son! Of course! Pulse gaining speed, he considers that he may have stumbled upon a new line of credit that will allow him to climb out of his social bankruptcy. He takes an elated, celebratory sip. Then someone else fills the space that Chip just vacated.

"Diet Cokes for me and the pastor."

Leon swivels toward the peculiar order and sees the young bespectacled Black woman.

"A pastor in the pub?" he says with cheerful faux concern. "Congregating with us sinners? How blessed are we!"

Celia looks suspicious and says nothing.

"Oh, don't mind me," he says. "I'm just tickled to learn that a man of God is among us and that he, too, is watching his calories. Where is the gentleman, if I may ask?"

Celia's hand becomes a gun that she aims at Reggie, sitting in a back booth, tapping at his phone.

"Ah. I would not have guessed. And since appearances are clearly deceiving me today, might I ask if you're also a woman of the cloth?"

Celia giggles, looking younger than Leon initially thought in the dim light. "I'm a woman of words," she says.

"But not *the* Word?"

She giggles again. "Not that word. Many words."

"Many words about what?"

"About whatever. School board meetings. Cattle auctions. Crime sprees. Real estate trends. Drugs. Restaurant openings. Politics. Should I continue?"

"General interest, then."

Her firearm finger sets its sights on Leon and reverberates in the affirmative.

"So you must know the fellow who was just in, the one running for Congress."

"Of course. Known him for years. And I'm covering the campaigns. I could give you their stump speeches right now, if you want to hear them."

Leon laughs. "That's all right. But I'm curious, what do you make of it? Of the candidates?"

"Opinion's the one thing I don't write. Can't stand commentary or criticism."

"Some say they're art forms."

"Which means they're performances. I don't perform. I *in*form. Which, God knows, this town needs more of."

"Touché. That's very clever. Which makes me even more desperate to know your thoughts on our friend Chip and his young challenger."

"Sorry." She pulls an imaginary zipper across her lips.

"Oh, come on! I just moved here. And I'm not even registered. I've got no skin in the game. Just trying to understand this town better. It seems a tad confused about itself. Off the record, I swear."

Her eyes inspect his for any hints of insincerity. They remain doubtful.

"Obviously you think highly of Riley," Leon prods. "Or you wouldn't be in here."

"As I said, I've known Chip for years. He's the kind of guy you want in the job, even if he has blind spots. Big ones. We don't see the world the same way, but I'm glad he's in it."

"And the other? Does he see the world your way?"

She shrugs. "Probably more so."

"So it's a question of which matters more, the person or the policies? The classic conundrum! I don't envy you the choice."

Maren places the drinks before Celia and asks her, "On the tab?"

"On *my* tab," Leon insists.

"Oh, thanks," Celia says.

"My pleasure. A tithe. For your astute insights."

Celia laughs and turns to leave.

"Excuse me," Leon says. "What was your name again?"

"Celia Rhodes."

"And where can I read your writing, Celia?"

"The Griffin Gazette."

"Wonderful. I'll look for it."

Celia returns to Reggie, and Leon observes them for a minute.

"Another one?" Maren asks, collecting his empty tumbler.

"No, thank you."

"Compliments of Mr. Riley."

"Well, in that case."

CHAPTER 15

AFTER ERIC'S UNSTRUCTURED SUMMER in Griffin, the city's fall schedule feels as strict and stifling as a school semester. Always someplace to be, some deadline to hit. Plus the homework of maintaining his social life, and days that begin earlier than he'd prefer.

In Griffin, he came to dispense with alarms and let the sun nudge him into consciousness. But here in the city, he must deploy blackout shades to block neon lights, then rely on electronic bells to slap him awake. In Griffin, he ate oatmeal on the porch, listening to the insistent trill of black-capped chickadees and white-breasted nuthatches. Here, he downs a protein shake.

There, he read *The Griffin Gazette,* getting to know his neighbors through their accomplishments, arguments, milestones, and misdemeanors. He became an avid reader of the police report, with its almost charming chronicle of every DUI, robbery, and domestic dispute in the area. Rather than worry him, as such a list would do in the city, these minor crimes seemed to give Griffin a mischievous character—at least until his visit to the Munsee Recovery meeting, after which he stopped romanticizing lawbreaking. Now he scans headlines in the city paper, feeling caught once again in the sadistic cyclone of national politics. He sits at the kitchen counter with his laptop and thinks of his former forest view while staring at the brick wall across the alley.

Most nights, he has obligations: a dinner scheduled weeks ago, a show that's been on the calendar for months, a prefab fundraiser serving the same recycled cut of industrial beef. Once, he loved it all. Alex still does, and it's not easy to share a life that stimulates one person and suffocates another.

The weekend ahead promises more of the same, beginning with a loud birthday party, followed the next morning by a brunch across town with acquaintances who have been stuck in the same conversational loop for as long as Eric's known them. Where did you travel this summer? Where are you traveling this fall? Winter? Spring? Alex insists that he enjoys their company, possibly because they run in the kind of high-end circles that could generate high-profile interior design work, but Eric has reached his limit. He tries to go off script.

"So what was the *worst* part of your summer? What's been your most disappointing trip?"

But this is met with good-natured laughs and dismissed as a joke, when all he wanted to do was penetrate the slick surface.

He is losing interest in facades, increasingly impatient with his participation in a privileged life, though that seems to be what the city requires of him, or at least the slice of the city that he has carved out for himself. In Griffin, alone in his small cottage, and in Dalton's company, he found a simpler, more satisfying existence. But back here, in his expensive, bustling comfort, he must face his excesses.

On Saturday, there's a gathering for a big gay dance party. Eric used to adore vast halls vibrating with uninhibited camaraderie, but now he just sees aging men on artificial highs ogling their replacements. At the door, on the precipice of another bacchanal, Eric decides to head home. Alex shakes his head and follows their friends into the club, and the next morning, they fight about Eric's growing detachment. They don't shout, they never do. Alex asks questions, Eric tries to explain himself, fails, and shuts down.

"It's just . . . Never mind. I don't know what I'm trying to say."

"You do, Eric. But you don't want to say it."

"I feel . . . I feel like I can't catch my breath."

"Okay, but you've never felt this way before. What's changed?"

What's changed is that Eric has been shown another option. It has made him ask whether his routine here, always racing at city-speed, is in fact the one that fits him best, and whether Alex, with his constant pursuit of status, his reverence for luxury, the energy he absorbs from a crowded calendar and a crowded room, could ever be content to live full-time in the stillness of their small house in the woods.

"Maybe . . ." Eric inhales for courage. "Maybe I just need a break from all this."

"All this? You mean our lives? The life we've been living together for the past decade? And just after you had a three-month break from"—Alex waves his arms wildly—"all this?"

The ferocity of the movement signals that Alex has lost patience, which is the reaction that Eric dreads. Just as Alex feels acutely the insecurity of their social standing and tracks it by minute measurement, so, too, does Eric carefully calibrate his relationship with his husband, irrationally fearful that once out of balance, it may never find equilibrium again. He knows, or has been told in therapy, this stems from the shame and unworthiness that infected him, along with the virus, that summer long ago. And it now manifests in an almost oppressive gratitude toward the man who rescued him, and whose love and approval he still covets—even if that man's presence, in this city, is becoming equally insufferable.

"What if I went back to the cottage? Just for a week or two? I can paint the guest bedroom, since we didn't get to it this summer. And help Paul with the campaign."

"And finish reading *Middlemarch*?"

"It's not . . . That's not why I want to go. Look, since we've been back, there have been times when I've felt like the summer didn't happen, or that it's a distant memory or something from a movie. Sometimes I can't even remember parts of our house, like which side of the hallway our bedroom is on. I know that's crazy. But I do remember how calm I felt, which I hadn't felt in forever. I think I have to go back to remind myself that I can still find it there."

"We're going back in two weeks, before the next renters arrive, and again for my birthday at the end of October."

"But that's just for weekends. And you've already committed us to dinners and brunches and a gallery tour. Which is fine, really. But . . .

This is what we wanted, right? A place that's always there for us when we need it?"

"Yes, but the operative words are 'us' and 'we.'"

"This is still about us."

Alex looks at him with a skeptical expression but sympathy in his eyes. He shakes his head, and again his arms fly up, part exasperation, part resignation.

The following morning, Eric leaves the city. As he drives past the suburbs and onto the wooded parkway, he experiences a small spasm of guilt that is soon soothed by a swell of relief. This is his first fall drive to the cottage. He can track the season's transition in the trees, the magnificent collective ombre from late-summer green in the city to brilliant autumnal tones as he approaches Griffin. Driving down his dirt driveway under a canopy of color, ascending the steps on this cool, cloudy day, Eric has the feeling of returning to himself.

He goes to Poppy's Pantry to stock up for the week and leaves with an overly abundant selection of prepared foods. He contacts Stan to arrange a few volunteer shifts for Paul's campaign, despite his ambivalence toward Paul's candidacy. It justifies his escape from the city and feels like a gesture of commitment, a kind of letter of intent, toward his new home. When calling voters, he is instructed to introduce himself as "your neighbor," which at first sounds false but eventually sounds, if not quite accurate, then at least momentarily true and perhaps plausible in the future.

But during these calls, he can't forget the challenge that Dalton posed to him: You'd never let yourself vote for Riley. You'd feel like a traitor to your kind. But if you vote for Banks, he said, *you're a traitor to me.*

And because Eric does feel like he's betraying Dalton, he doesn't visit Cherry Hill Farm or inform Dalton that he's back in town. He didn't lie to Alex. This week isn't about returning to the mysterious local who reads Victorian classics and keeps their refrigerator full of raw milk. This is about time, and space, and making more room for himself.

As promised, it's also about home improvements. They made good progress over the summer—the bathroom off the kitchen is an oasis of new tile inhabited by the ducklike brushed nickel faucet. Eric had found it unexpectedly satisfying to watch the project progress to completion. Now Alex has tasked him with collecting paint samples for the guest bedroom as well as a few items for his upcoming fortieth-birthday party. So, a few days after Eric has resettled in Griffin, he returns to Delphi's Hardware.

ON THE LAST Friday in September, Joe stares at faux fireplaces, artificial lawns, and patches of decking from behind the register at Delphi's, feeling like a gutted house, a facade of a person, as the cruel demands of his anatomy reassert themselves after last night's abasement. He's ashamed to have used at home, down the hall from his sleeping parents, ashamed to know he'll do so again as soon as he gets the chance. The shame swirls in his head and becomes a sharp vortex.

But he couldn't help it. Last night, he felt like every bone in his body was cracking, releasing toxins directly into his blood. He squirmed and writhed and smothered his face with a pillow to stifle his cries. Sweating, shaking, he found the green sweatpants, fished out the newest little plastic bag with the white dust that Maren warned was stronger than what he was used to. Quickly, quietly, he inhaled. His armpits and crotch dampened; he shivered; his head pulsed until those savvy chemicals embraced him and his body found its balance. He entered his private chambers, the blank room in his mind where nothing penetrates, where his body is free of need. No thoughts or feelings to contend with, just a cancellation.

He woke late, humiliated and angry with himself for not being able to muscle through the urge, determined to seek help as soon as his father's campaign is over. He was due at Delphi's in half an hour, but that was impossible given his cruel headache. He would call in sick, as he does increasingly, knowing Amir would suspect the real sickness, sigh, and say, "Gotta take care of yourself, Joey. Better be here tomorrow." But as the phone rang, a small internal tapping told him that what he needed most was to go in, be helpful, solve someone else's problem today. He hung up, took his dad's truck (Chip had gone to headquarters with Will), and now stands dazed behind the counter, hollow but glad to be here.

Except the remnants of last night's binge and its vengeful hangover make his nerves scream. He'll have to placate them soon, give in to the nonnegotiable demands of his cells. But not here. It can't be here, the one place where he feels a modicum of competence and control. He will wait, he always tries to wait, until it's unbearable, hoping *this* time it doesn't reach that point, *this* time he can ride the surge of discomfort safely to shore and break the cycle.

He hears Delphi's automatic doors open and feels a cloud of unseasonably warm air puff into the store. He has seen this customer before; he recognizes the trimmed ginger beard and tortoiseshell glasses. He can't recall the name but knows that he knew it once and knows he should greet this man with familiarity. His body does not want to move, and his mind does not want to force it to, but a habitual, mechanical force overrides them.

"Hi," Joe says, already out of breath. "Good to see you," he wants to say but can't.

"Hi, Joe," the man says, frowning.

"Help?" Joe asks.

"Um, yes. Please."

The customer seeks paint—"A handsome gray," he says—so Joe slowly leads him to the paint section, where he examines swatches for Midnight Train, Foggy Valley, and Summer Storm before settling on a misty slate called Gothic Castle. Joe looks at the dreary palette over the man's shoulder, seeing himself in each of the options.

"Dark," he says, possibly out loud. The man stares at him. "I can have it mixed for you," Joe offers like a plea.

"Thank you." Then the man says, "Actually, I'm looking for place card holders as well. For a party. Do you have an 'Events' section?"

Joe coerces his body to the small "Entertaining" aisle, just a few shelves crammed with disposable paper and plasticware. Normally Joe would leave the customer alone, but proximity feels safer. The man selects a bag of small metal rings perched on round bases. "These'll work," he says.

At the counter, Joe goes to ring the man up but stares at the screen for several seconds. "Sorry. Name?"

"Eric." The man frowns. "Eric Larimer."

Joe pulls up the account and sees the list of previous purchases: power sander, tiles, more paint (Desert Dunes), cabinet hardware, a faucet. He adds to it Gothic Castle and the card holders. Eric thanks Joe, collects his purchases, and then hesitates, as though there's something else he wants to say. Joe looks at him expectantly, but Eric only offers a worried half smile. After Eric leaves, another puff of warmth rolls over Joe.

Eric's departure has the effect of a bathtub plug pulled. The air begins to drain, and Joe feels a spiraling tug that is almost pleasant. He replays the interaction in his mind, reaching to recapture the concern in Eric's eyes. He rereads the list of Eric's purchases still displayed on the computer. Power sander. Tiles. Desert Dunes. Knobs. Faucet. He imagines a house with smooth wood floors, updated shower, sand-colored walls. A home improved, which is the opposite of Joe's home, a home deteriorating, because of him. He has let his family down. He will continue to let them down. He cannot envision a future in which he will ever make them proud again.

His cravings return with angry force. His nerves and muscles curse him, insult him, threaten him. They will destroy him, they say, unless he abides them. They demand poison, but poison is preferable to what they will unleash if he doesn't oblige. He is in the whirlpool now, whipping around a sinking axis of despair, a centripetal force pushing him toward the vortex. Extracting himself means defying the laws of physics.

Then Amir is beside him. "Joey, you good?"

"Just gotta eat, I think."

"Take an early lunch."

Wet and trembly, Joe moves toward the white pickup truck at the far end of the parking lot. The vehicle undulates in the heat rising off the asphalt, a refuge in the distance.

"Desert Dunes," he says to himself. Desert Dunes. It becomes a mantra.

He falls into the driver's seat. He starts the truck and conjures cool air.

A brown paper bag rattles beside him on the passenger seat. In it: a sandwich, an apple, and a bag of potato chips, which his father left for him on the kitchen counter, as he's done for as long as Joe can remember. He dumps his lunch and smooths the bag on his lap. From the glove compartment, he extracts another small bag, the solution to his other hunger. He spills its white contents onto the brown paper.

One breath, two breaths. Salvation enters him.

He leans back. Already he can feel his body cease its rebellion. The murkiness morphs into something kinder, gentler. A foggy valley.

Suddenly a gun goes off within, initiating a race.

His heart leaps like it's clearing hurdles. A hundred yards! Two hundred yards! The race doesn't stop.

His heart keeps leaping, leaping, leaping. He's hurdling a mile, hurdling a marathon.

He feels apart from himself. He watches another Joe take increasingly shallow gulps of air.

His heart sprints toward a finish line that he senses is the last and only real endpoint, a realization that relieves rather than frightens him. As his body pushes to breaking, his mind cozies up into its private chambers, where everything is reassuringly blank.

Outside, a shadow appears. A soft knocking. A blast of warm air that engulfs him. He feels his body being shaken. The shadow retreats, and Joe relaxes back into blankness.

A minute later—an hour?—the shadow returns and draws near as if to consume him.

Another warm blast, this time as if directly into his brain.

His heart stops leaping.

The race is over.

OCTOBER

CHAPTER 16

ON THE SECOND WEDNESDAY of October, Chip charges through the halls of Griffin High, a single-story maze of interlocking brick boxes that hasn't changed much since he and Diane were students. He was never in a rush back then, just roving around with the other football players like a herd of happy cattle migrating from one grazing spot to the next. And Diane had watched, invisibly, as the splendid beasts passed. It's almost comical that she's now chasing Chip down these same halls, a quarter century later, as Gabrielle shuffle-runs behind them like a lost new student late for class.

Meanwhile, Paul's crew hits a dead end at the locker rooms, and Stan must ask a janitor for directions to the gym, where a small stage sits in the center of the basketball court. The bleachers have been pulled out to accommodate the audience, which exudes the sports fan's rabidity, the theatergoer's attentive skepticism, the teenager's dull air of obligation. The stage glows under a few studio lights, populated with a couple of tripods and cameras—a modest effort for a local news broadcast. From a distance, the tangled strands of black electrical cords make the setup look like an abstract oasis covered in vines.

For several days last week, it was unclear whether Chip would participate in tonight's debate, whether it would take place at all, whether the race itself would be disrupted by Joe's overdose.

In the immediate aftermath, Diane blamed the campaign for bringing this misfortune into their home. All her initial apprehension about Joe returned in a storm of guilt, regret, and anger at her husband, the damn politician. She went so far as to suggest that a pause might be prudent. But when Joe was discharged two days later, she watched Chip's fear and sadness harden into a protective shield of obstinacy. The race became his self-prescribed pain relief. He insisted that the debate go on.

Now she stands stoically beside him and touches his elbow. "You'll be great," she says, which comes out sounding as canned and hollow as his Magic 8 Ball phrases. She tries again: "I'm so proud of you." It isn't better, but he takes her hand and squeezes it.

Paul and Stan enter from the opposite side. Except for a brief glimpse at the Memorial Day Parade, it's been nearly eighteen months since Diane last encountered the Bankses in person at their house closing. She remembers them as easy clients, curious and personable. She appreciated Stan in particular, his elegant assuredness and the occasional, unexpected wry quip. Afterward, when they sent her a gift basket to express their thanks and pleasure in being her neighbors, she allowed herself to imagine a forthcoming dinner invitation to their grand new home, a taste of Griffin's glamorous side, which she sells but never experiences.

Now, as they and their entourage move briskly and besuited toward the debate organizers, Paul and Stan appear to Diane like what they clearly always were: calculating political entrepreneurs, setting up their operations by investing in the necessary real estate.

A few minutes later, Chip and Paul are invited onto the stage. They meet in the middle, under a drooping banner of a cartoon jaguar, and shake hands for the first time. Or rather, their palms collide, a clash of the fleshy webspace between thumb and index finger meant to investigate intent and weakness. Their eyes sparkle with rancor, recognition, and respect. They are two comrades who understand each other's ambition and exhaustion better than anyone else. But primarily, according to national expectation, they are enemies, envoys, embodiments of all the grievances and prejudices of their respective tribes, not just in this room but across this country. They meet here tonight not only as aspiring regional representatives but as gladiators in the bloody arena of national politics. Or so that's how people seem to want it.

Observing the adversaries, Diane despises Paul's slickness (but admires the sheen of his dark blue suit and immovable hair), while Stan distrusts Chip's forced grin (but is struck by how disarmingly brawny he is up close in a plaid shirt and tan corduroy blazer). In seconds, the confrontation is over. Diane moves toward the bleachers to find her seat but finds Stan in the aisle first.

"Diane, hi!" he says with a nervous smile. When they last interacted, they hugged goodbye. Should they hug now? He extends his hand.

"Stanley!" she says, as if she didn't expect to see him here. "How . . . How's the house? Have you done anything to it?"

"We haven't touched it, really. We've been . . ." He laughs. "You know."

She smiles, then imagines what they must look like together, and her smile slides away. "Anyway, I'd better . . ."

"Of course. It was nice seeing you, Diane. And, well, good luck, I suppose."

They part, leaving Diane feeling unmoored. She spots Maren and pushes through a crowded row to sit next to the closest person here to family, though Maren doesn't meet her eyes. When Diane is settled and the awkwardness of seeing Stan subsides, she is overcome by déjà vu. Here she is at another big municipal event where she should be next to her sons and filled with nothing but pride for her husband. Instead, she is alone and distraught and forced to fake her enthusiasm, while Stan Banks looks effortlessly at ease.

Despite the surrounding commotion, she's still in that bleak hospital room where they kept vigil over a web of wires and tubes swaddling her elder son. Now Joe is home, thank Jesus, and Will is keeping watch again. But she can't bear this cruel repetition. When she looks up, Chip is staring at her, his eyes vacant. He looks miserable, especially next to Paul's exaggerated cheeriness. She can't allow him to drown in despair. She straightens up and straps on an encouraging smile. He imitates her, readjusting his posture and adopting a more engaged expression, pretending to be fully present.

Stan settles amid Paul's section, composed mostly of some boisterous cheerleaders from the campaign staff, and sees an unexpected supporter a few rows away. Leon is staring at him. Stan hasn't spoken to him since the

Labor Day gathering over three weeks ago, when Leon made that gauche and insulting comment about their finances. It's not that he was terribly offended, merely finished. Stan has done what he can for Leon. He tried to bring the man into his social group, but it's not a match.

He did, however, appreciate that Leon brought Gerald McAfee's town council appearance to his attention; the resulting ad was effective. Stan realizes now that he forgot to respond to Leon's messages. The campaign has been all-engrossing, and he just hadn't found the time or energy to stroke Leon's fragile ego. But seeing him at the debate, Stan is chastised for his rudeness. Leon's attendance softens him—there's nothing more sincere than showing up. In fact, Leon appears to be the only one of their Griffin friends in the audience tonight. It's midfall and midweek, after all. Everyone else is consumed by, and consuming, the city's spoils.

Leon sees Stan's sustained attention and dares to lift a hand, less a greeting than a request for amity. Stan raises his hand and grants it. Leon exhales with relief. His presence is one of the few things he has left to offer. That and the intelligence he has gathered. First Gerald and now the extraordinary insight into the true identity of Will Martindale. This time, though, he must tell Stan in person. He needs to see Stan's gratitude, to personally receive his thanks. He will do so as soon as the debate concludes.

CHIP AND PAUL take their seats behind a folding table that faces Celia Rhodes, the evening's moderator, in her own costume of eager professionalism: starched white button-down, black slacks, thick rectangular glasses. Her face is an unnerving mask of determination.

A signal from a camera operator prods her to tap a mic, emitting a muffled scratch that calls the audience to attention. Celia waits for silence, challenging the crowd with a scowl, as though to warn them that they'd better not disappoint her. Satisfied, she smiles and introduces herself and the candidates, reading their bios from note cards, delivering words that sound reverential but which she infuses with an undertone of suspicion, or so Diane detects.

Celia explains the evening's structure—opening statements, a facilitated exchange, questions from the audience—and invites Paul to begin. He nods gravely and stands slowly, as though to give the audience time to take him in. In his introduction, he presents himself as a feisty, forward-thinking professional who would be the region's most dynamic advocate for change.

"I may be the newest resident on this stage," he says, in a clever gambit to preempt the expected criticism, "but that comes with new ideas, a new perspective, and new opportunities." He smiles throughout his speech, passionately pounds out points as required, gestures in just the right way to energize his words.

When it's Chip's turn, he begins to counter this impression with aw-shucks humility and his long local résumé but finds he hasn't solved the problem of his hands. He cups them in a ball, releases them to flop at his sides, clasps them behind his back, flails comically—a physical manifestation of his mental distraction. Diane is dismayed by his lack of verbal buoyancy. His sentences plunge as though attached to a fishing sinker. Paul, meanwhile, has picked the perfect face to wear as Chip speaks, one that suggests he's considering, then rejecting, his opponent's views. Rather than rise to Paul's exuberance, Chip hunkers into himself. His body caves, his voice sputters.

Celia then chips away at their favorable self-portraits. She challenges Paul on his political inexperience, forcing him to address his energy investments once again, which he does with a tired laugh, as if it's an old joke.

"I didn't intend that to be funny, Mr. Banks," she says, which wipes away his grin.

"No, of course not. It's just . . . I thought I had put this to rest, this misunderstanding."

"I'd appreciate it if you could clear up the *misunderstanding* one more time."

He does, or at least gives the impression of doing so. Though the words he speaks don't ultimately provide clarity on the conflict between his profitable portfolio and his aspirational policies, the tone and speed of his response, and the artful deployment of several wonky multisyllabic terms, convey confidence and assurance. To Stan's delighted ears, the performance is that of a politician significantly improved from six months ago.

Celia shuffles her note cards and turns to Chip to probe some of his more unpopular actions as Griffin town supervisor, including the Gerald McAfee affair.

"Anything you would like to say to Ger—to Mr. McAfee now?"

"How dare she," Maren says with little effort to lower her voice. "Traitor."

That's right, Diane thinks, feeling the flicker of indignation. Why is Celia giving fuel to this story? A Buck patron for years! Where are her loyalties?

A few rows away, Leon, a Buck patron for mere months, feels another pinch of regret for spurring Gerald to take his grievance public. He scours the crowd again but still doesn't see Gerald.

Onstage, Chip nods. "This situation pains me greatly. Celia, you know Gerry's been my friend forever, and I don't intend for that to change. That ad was a cheap shot, it got the whole situation wrong, and—"

Paul jumps in. "How was it wrong? Those were his words, not mine!"

"Mr. Banks, please. I'm asking the questions here, though that is also my question, Mr. Riley. What do you think was misrepresented?"

Diane shifts in her seat. Even at a distance, Celia looks and sounds older and more formidable, no longer the curious, giggling junior reporter whom Chip's known for years. Now she's a surprisingly blunt, incisive woman with an intimidating aura of civic mission that appears to supersede personal affection.

"I wish Gerry didn't have to make the sacrifice we're asking of him. I wish he didn't think of it as a sacrifice, that I could make it clear to him, to everyone, there's no other way to bring this vital utility to our town, that it's for the public good, and that he's being more than fairly compensated." The words are compassionate, but Chip's tone is not. In battling his discomfort, he comes across as impatient and irritated. "What my opponent misses or, I should say, willfully ignores, is how many people this project benefits, how necessary it is for the folks in our area who've been left behind by our fast growth. But since he doesn't know this place well enough to know who's getting helped, he focuses on the one guy getting hurt."

Chip leans back and crosses his arms as if to signal an end to the conversation. Paul leans forward, ready to pounce, waiting for Celia to give him permission.

She eyes him warily, as if put off by his hunger, not quite ready to drive the debate directly onto the disputed property of poor Gerry. She hesitates, then flips to her next card and segues into an unrelated topic. In shutting off the valve of eminent domain, leaving Chip with the last arm-crossed word, she grants him a small point. Diane exhales in relief, revising her previous concern, while Stan scoffs at Celia's caution and her perceived favoritism.

For the next half hour, Celia facilitates predictable exchanges on farm relief, environmental protections, guns, and education. Then she says, "Affordable housing is an ongoing obstacle to both growth and stability throughout the Twenty-sixth District. Mr. Riley, what have you done, and what do you plan to do, about that?"

"Sure," Chip says. "Well, that's a serious problem with no easy solutions. It's not like we can just build more apartments everywhere. It's about keeping home prices in check, keeping short-term rentals in check, making sure the people raising those prices and renting those homes contribute more to *this* region instead of wherever they come from." He turns pointedly to Paul.

Celia receives the baton. "Mr. Banks, as someone who, until recently, didn't live in the district and who resides in what has been reported as a very *unaffordable* house for most of the district's residents, I'm curious about your plan."

Stan glowers on behalf of his husband, whose only viable reaction is to nod thoughtfully and ignore the barb.

"Look," Paul says, both elbows on the table, a position of frankness, "I get the optics. But I'm here because I believe our district is special. When you live in a special place, people want to be part of it, and I don't think it's smart to discourage that. Especially when they're fixing up old homes, opening new businesses, hiring locals, transforming whole parts of town for the better—"

"That's gentrification!" Chip throws up his hands. "You bemoan it in the city and celebrate it in the country."

"Chip— Mr. Riley, please." Celia holds up a palm. "It's not your turn."

"Sorry," he says, then can't help himself. "Face it, Paul, *you're* the problem."

The gym's chemistry shifts. The audience is newly alert, a willing conduit for this electricity. Diane and Stan feel the static in their necks.

"Excuse me?" Paul twists toward him.

"Mr. Banks, let's get back on track," Celia says.

Chip presses. "I said, 'You're the problem,' Paul."

"Well, you're the problem, too."

"Ha! How in the hell do you figure that?"

"Gentlemen," Celia pleads.

Paul ignores her. "The brick factory. You approved its transformation into a luxury hotel, and already the values of the surrounding homes have skyrocketed."

"That project has generated dozens of local jobs and will be a magnet for dozens more."

"Sure, which generates profits for your family."

"Gentlemen!"

"What in God's name are you talking about?"

"Your wife's selling half the homes around there!"

Diane's heart collides into her chest.

Chip blanches, and his voice plummets. "You leave my wife out of this."

Paul holds his breath as he seems to make a calculation. Then he expels it: "How can I, when she sold us our house, too?"

Diane closes her eyes. Leon's mouth falls, and around him the audience thrums with arousal. Chip slumps in his chair. Stan gapes in scandalized delight. Paul has picked an effective time and place to detonate that bomb.

When Diane reawakens to the scene, Chip is not looking at her. He won't look at her, though it feels as if everyone else is, especially Maren, whose stare feels particularly hard.

"Okay, okay," Celia attempts to call her courtroom back to order, though she no longer sounds desperate. There's a fresh gleam in her eyes as it appears, to Stan's amusement, that she's just realized a rowdy colloquy is perhaps more to the debate's benefit than a polite, snoozy exchange, largely because it promotes her role from mere moderator to ringmaster. "I want to remind you both that we're holding a structured debate here with a protocol and predetermined time for responses. Please abide by them. This only works when you both play by the rules. That said, I want to pick up on what Mr. Banks mentioned. It seems to me it *is* relevant that Mr. Riley's family might personally profit from his policies, and I want to give him an opportunity to address that."

Stan absolves Celia for his earlier charge of favoritism as Diane curses the young journalist. She has always suspected that Celia's chummy patronage at the Buck was strategically intended to neutralize her clear political predisposition against Chip. He apparently never thought that, though, because he now looks at Celia like a lover betrayed. Diane almost turns to Maren to commiserate but, in light of the topic at hand, can't face the person she has helped make homeless.

Chip struggles to modulate his voice. "I would never, and have never, allowed *anyone* to sway me toward a decision I didn't think was right or best for this community. My long record of service backs that up." He should stop there, but Diane can hear that he's working himself up, looking to land a punch. "I don't care who sold Paul his house. My wife and I have lived in our same home for more than twenty years. For my opponent, and people like him, to waltz into town, buy big fancy houses, and accuse *me* of intentionally driving up home prices is just insulting. But that's what you get with a *carpetbugger*."

Somewhere within the crowd's confused murmuring, Terry's bawdy laughter cuts through.

Stan's eyes bulge. Paul sits up and says: "Wait, what?"

"Shit," Diane whispers. She spots Gabrielle standing off to the side of the bleachers, head down, hands balled into fists. Chip leans back in his chair, crosses his arms at his chest again, and sets his mouth in a straight line. Only the alarm in his eyes, when they find Diane, reveals a shameful recognition that he has absorbed and regurgitated Terry's toxins.

Celia appears caught off guard. She twists toward Chip with a look that is equal parts doubt, disappointment, and distaste. She makes a note on her cards, frowns, then nods to herself.

"I'm sorry, Mr. Riley, I need to address your comment. You seemed to indicate Mr. Banks's identity . . ."

"No, Celia, that's not—"

". . . which brings up a past issue I think is necessary to revisit for context and clarity. I wasn't aware of your wife's . . . professional relationship with Mr. Banks." It sounds tawdry phrased that way, Diane thinks, as though she's being accused of adultery. "But a few years ago, *The Griffin Gazette* reported on the tension surrounding the state's legalization of same-sex marriage."

Chip closes his eyes and takes a long, deep breath before opening them. His face is blank and impassable. Diane shivers. Paul on the stage and Stan in the bleachers exchange mystified looks as to why this issue is being broached. Leon leans forward.

"In one of our articles, a spokesperson from an anti-same-sex-marriage campaign was quoted voicing her adamant opposition to the effort—"

"Celia," Chip says softly. "This isn't necessary."

She looks at him, then continues. "That person was Diane Riley, your wife, and in light of your earlier comment, I'd like to know if you agreed with her then and if you still do."

Paul's stunned face speaks for the crowd. Stan feels as if he's been slapped. His face actually tingles. But why has this revelation hit him so viscerally? It's the deception, the hypocrisy of being quietly condemned while simultaneously flattered for financial gain. That's what stings. He looks at Diane a few rows over, expecting to see defiance, readying himself for outrage. But a hand covers her mouth; her eyes are stricken. He feels a trickle of pity instead.

Diane feels only the crowd's hot scrutiny. If she weren't sitting in the center of the row, if every person in this space weren't so damn quiet and riveted, if she weren't herself immobilized by humiliation, she would flee. But a small consolation: Thank God her sons aren't here to hear this.

Onstage, Chip says sharply, "That issue has been decided, and I respect it."

"That doesn't answer my question, Mr. Riley."

"You pointed it out yourself, Celia. Mr. Banks and his husband live in a big, beautiful, and again, very expensive home that my wife helped them purchase. That *does* answer your question."

"And what about your son?"

Another perplexed hum buzzes through the audience. What does Chip's son have to do with anything? Diane, still reeling, nearly faints. Stan and Paul look at each other, baffled by yet another inexplicable swerve. Leon smirks in anticipation of Will's exposure, disappointed only that he won't have the pleasure of informing Stan himself.

Chip's expression remains fixed, but his eyes narrow harshly. "My son is not important."

"Mr. Riley, I'm not sure—"

Bud Light Riley cracks. "Godammit, Celia! Enough with this bullshit! Can we just get back to the *actual* stuff that affects the *actual* lives of the folks in this district?"

The entire auditorium holds its breath as it awaits instruction on how to respond.

To Diane's great relief, a strong smattering of applause convinces Celia to move on. When Celia informs the audience that they are entering the Q&A portion of the debate, her subdued tone suggests that she has decided to abandon her flirtation with provocation.

Paul leans back with the relaxed grin of someone on the cusp of impending victory. His team shares a smug smile; Stan's eyes shine with pride. At this point, Chip can only hope to salvage the evening by somehow securing a draw. Diane's hands are clasped in her lap in prayer.

A slim Black woman asks a question about taxes, and an emotional brown man asks one about health care. Then a double-wide white man stands and reads so quietly from an index card that Celia must ask him to start over and speak louder.

"As you are both aware," he says, finding a staccato strength that must come from some deep well of pain, "this district is the highest in the state for per capita drug overdoses, and among the highest in the nation. What factors do you see contributing to this, and how will you combat them?"

Celia serves the question to Paul first. "Mr. Banks?"

"Yes, thank you." He stands and buttons his jacket as though to acknowledge the topic's gravity. "You're right, sir. The drug crisis *is* a national tragedy, claiming more of our neighbors every day. Maybe some of you here have been personally affected by it. Some of us on this stage have as well . . ."

Perhaps Paul means it as a gesture of solidarity. Perhaps it's just the politician's habitual way of claiming personal connection to manufacture sympathy. But to Diane, it feels like Paul has pointed directly at her and Chip, like he has indicted Joe.

Stan has a different thought: Paul is speaking again in the generic terms and platitudes that he defaults to when he hasn't grasped a topic. Paul never made it to a Munsee Recovery meeting, and Stan recognizes that as a mistake.

"We need to help people make better choices," Paul says twice, and his nervous smirk of ignorance appears. Stan notices the local crowd shifting uncomfortably as they realize they know this issue better than Paul does.

When it's Chip's turn, he rises slowly. His body emanates existential exhaustion, as though Paul's perceived insinuation of Joe has flung Chip back into that hospital room and sucked the anger out of him. So rather than respond emotionally, he gives a dry recitation of statistics, as if numbers are the only safe space to tread. Diane feels the audience shift again with boredom.

Whether Chip notices this as well, or whether he stumbles instead upon some internal insight, something makes him stop. He stares at the table for several seconds, his chest heaving. Diane rocks forward, ready to run down and comfort him if that's what he needs. But then he raps twice on the table and looks up, his expression hard.

"I could go on and on, but you already know the facts. You see the facts all around you, passed out in a gas station bathroom, or through a coworker's tears. Well, I know the facts because I saw them laid out in front of me last week, tangled up in hospital sheets, in the shape of my son." His mouth trembles. He leans on the table, swallows, raps on it again.

"My opponent here fundamentally misunderstands addiction. He'd like you to believe that the victims are at fault, that they've made a bad choice, that they could just make a better one. Well, let me tell you something, Mr. Banks"—he turns to Paul—"you can choose your addiction as much as you can choose your sexuality, and neither should condemn anyone to apathy or death."

Paul recoils. Stan burns, though he's not sure whether from offense or from feeling somehow chastised. Chip's words conjure a different hospital ward, decades ago. Stan can almost feel Asher's damp hand again.

Diane nods and keeps nodding. Beside her, she feels Maren shrivel, as if this exchange has opened a spigot that is draining her. Diane takes her hand, which is shaking. Maren flinches.

Chips continues. "But that's what you get with someone who doesn't understand a place or its people, the kind of people at my pub every day who come just to see a friendly face and share the burden of life. I'd welcome my opponent there, too. I really would." He turns to Paul, who has not managed to find the right face for this speech. "First round's on me. Actually, all rounds on me if you care to stop by and meet some real folks to discuss how many jobs they've had and lost in the past ten years, how the decimation of farming is leading them to despair, how many friends and neighbors they've sacrificed to the plague of drugs in our community, the fear that their own children . . ."

Chip's voice catches. Maren emits a small cry, releases Diane's hand, struggles out of the row, down the bleachers, and out of the gym.

Chip watches her leave with dazed concern, then swallows and climbs back to anger.

"But my opponent doesn't care about all that. He's only interested in himself, his status, his personal goals. And he wants to use *you* to attain them. He thinks he can buy a seat in Congress by buying a house in Griffin. The question is, will we let him?"

CHAPTER 17

ON SATURDAY NIGHT, A parade of cars proceeds down a gravel driveway that opens into a generous circle, at the center of which stands a somber stone angel. From the cars emerge stylish loafers, slim trousers in shades of autumn, and coats of wool and tweed in handsome browns, grays, and navies. Attendants in puffy black jackets replace the drivers and speed away as guests are ushered into the foyer of the grand nineteenth-century manor that Alex has chosen for his fortieth-birthday party, an hour south of Griffin on Munsee's banks.

Alex greets his friends from the elevated perch of a marble landing in the entrance hall, a somewhat silly position of ownership because all are aware of the manor's primary profession as a wedding venue. But Alex, like many a bride before him, will pretend for the night that he's a member of an old aristocratic family who, a century ago, populated the region with their summer palaces.

Will wears his insecurity along with his church slacks and Chip's tan corduroy coat, since he doesn't have his own. Three months ago, at Paul's Fourth of July pool party, he learned to undress in the style of these men. (The turquoise Speedo stuffed in his underwear drawer remains a symbol of that education.) But *dressing* in their style is much harder. In his too-large coat, he feels more exposed, somehow, than when he finally cast his swimsuit aside on Labor Day.

His sartorial anxiety, however, is just a diversion from the wallop of the debate. When he learned of what transpired, he felt like he'd been stabbed by a three-tine pitchfork. The first prong was Celia's seditious insertion of him into the conversation. The second was his mother's unearthed homophobia and hypocritical home sales (not news to him, but now public). The final spike was his father's piercing phrase, "My son is not important." If Will had heard those words in person, he might never have healed from them. As it is, he hasn't returned to headquarters or spoken to his parents since.

Despite the message Will hoped to send with his absence, Gabrielle recruited him in service of damage control, demanding that he sign off on a statement of continued support for Chip, which she wrote but attributed to him. She circulated it to any news outlet that caught wind of the Rileys' humiliation, which included a few national political websites and even the city paper, which has taken a sudden interest in the unexpectedly close contest featuring prominent "power gays" of the urban moneyed class.

Why did Will agree to the statement? Because he wants to believe that Chip spoke out of fluster, not malice. Because he isn't ready to give up on his father. But seeing the statement in print and online, claiming his name while ignoring his hurt, made him feel like an offering and his identity, an alibi. The statement ostensibly came from William Riley, of course, not Will Martindale. So it didn't out him, at least not in the way he most fears being outed now.

Along the driveway, he notices a cluster of maples to one side, the leaves muted and mature, crisp and sparse, preparing for hibernation, which sounds so soothing. But for as long as he's granted, Will intends to cling to these men like the stubborn leaves, then cling to the promise of them through the barren winter until he can return come spring. He buttons his coat and enters the manor with the alertness of an undercover agent, a feeling he thought he'd retired in July.

The guests gather in a drafty, opulent parlor of crimson rugs and curvy mahogany furniture covered in shiny green silk. Will is greeted by a waiter about his age, heavyset with round glasses and frizzy brown hair, proffering champagne. Will accepts the drink and notices the waiter's glossy black shirt and slacks—Carly's uniform. He scans the room and there she is, in the far doorway, arms folded. It's the first time he's seen her since he abandoned her two months ago at the *Fodder* event. He raises his glass and his brows in an innocent, pleading way, as though asking for forgiveness. She frowns, looks at her watch, and is gone. He rinses his guilt with a thousand tiny bubbles.

After refilling his glass, Will heads to a cluster of men in one corner posing with their crystal coupes and erupting in the very specific kind of overly boisterous laughter reserved for drinking sparkling wine in flamboyant homes. As he approaches, he sees Stan at its center, and next to him Leon, who flashes Will a fearsome grin.

Leon wasn't meant to be here, but a few days ago, Stan found him in the swarming high school gym after the debate and said, "It was good of you to come."

"I support you and Paul in the ways that I can, with the currency that I have," Leon replied. He hadn't received the credit he deserved for directing Stan to Gerald McAfee's Town Hall appearance (never mind the regret he feels about it now), and he was determined not to let his intel regarding Will Martindale be similarly squandered. "Speaking of which, there's something I must share with you—"

"I need to find Paul." Stan turned away, scanning the crowd. "But before I forget, are you free Saturday?"

"I believe so."

"Alex's little event, if you care to attend."

"He wouldn't mind?"

"I'm underwriting half of it, and Paul now has a campaign conflict. You can be my date."

Leon received the invitation as a gesture of appreciation for his in-kind contribution. "In that case, thank you. I look forward to it. But quickly, the thing I wanted to tell you—"

"There's Paul. We'll talk Saturday." And Stan was gone.

Now Leon hovers by Stan, looking for the right moment to connect the dots between Chip Riley's anonymous gay son and the young freckled object of obsession in their midst. Merely holding this information grants him the confidence of relevancy. And rather than tampering with Leon's intention, Will's arrival has inflamed it further by reminding Leon how effortlessly this kid has insinuated himself with these men while Leon has labored again and again to earn his place. The audacity of Will appearing incognito at an intimate dinner for one of Paul's friends, just after his father disparaged them all . . . Unconscionable! Unacceptable.

But now is not the time for exposure. Stan is in an uncharacteristically gabby mood, fueled by champagne and residual adrenaline from the debate, which he's currently discussing for the benefit of those who couldn't attend, meaning all of them.

"I know I'm biased, but I've got to say, Paul did a fabulous job," he declares as his glass is topped off by the roving waiter.

"I can confirm it," Leon says, eager to remind everyone that only he among them was present.

"Though Riley did himself no favors," Stan says.

"It was an embarrassment," Leon adds. "Not just a bad performance but quite disgraceful." He spins this comment at Will like a curveball.

Will's fair skin has been on a low simmer since arriving; now the burner under his face flares, turning his cheeks pink. He considers leaving the circle, leaving the party even, except to do so will look too conspicuous.

"And disparaging, too!" Leon continues. "I always felt the homophobia just below the surface here." He shakes his head as if he's been warning them for years and they must now accept the regretful truth.

"Is it, though?" Nate says. "Homophobic, I mean. That word Riley used, I'd never heard it before, and frankly, I can't decide what to make of it. And Diane, well, very disappointing. It's hard to reconcile. But maybe she's changed her views since then."

Stan is equally conflicted. Leaving the debate, he and Diane passed each other again, and her look held nothing but remorse. Stan hadn't decided how he felt, so he turned away when she started to speak. Days later, he still doesn't know, but he's sure that outrage is the most beneficial response for the campaign, so he adopts it. He glares at Nate's compassion. "If *we* say it's homophobic, then it is." His eyes twinkle with the power inherent in claiming offense.

Nate shrugs. "It was funny, though, that word. You have to admit.

I know it was meant to be derisive, but am I the only one here taking pleasure in it? Aren't we all 'carpetbuggers,' then? Interloping fairies? It makes me feel so much more tactical and notorious than I'd ever imagined myself!"

Stan frowns, then raises his empty glass and jiggles it at the waiter for more before continuing. "But when Riley said that word, he also made clear what this is really about. The arrival of the gay plague. Which, a generation ago, was the thing that killed us but now, apparently, *is* us. Yesterday we're dying in droves while they ignore us, *blame us* in fact, and today we're responsible for this town's identity crisis and the half-century-long deterioration of rural America? I mean, *really*. I spent my twenties trying to save my brother and my friends. Now all I want is to lie by my pool in peace with the ones who are left. I mean, give a girl a fucking break!"

The men, amused by Stan's rare display of cheek and personal candor, declare their assent with nods, snaps, and little lifts of their coupes. Will joins in this collective gesture of approval until he sees Leon scrutinizing him. He buries his face in bubbles.

A bell rings, and two heavy wooden doors part to reveal the dining room. As the group seeps toward it, Will feels a hand on his elbow, stubble on his ear, and hot breath on his face. "I'm glad to see you find 'carpetbugger' amusing," Leon whispers. "I had wondered if Will Martindale's sympathies might lie elsewhere. Maybe closer to home."

Will faces him, sweat beading on his nose, and Leon laughs. "Oh dear, you look absolutely stricken! But don't worry, Mr. Riley, your secret's safe with me." He continues past Will and enters the large room where twenty-two elaborate place settings, an army of silverware, and a garrison of goblets occupy a single long table covered in white lace, bouquets of tumbling ivy and roses, and towering candelabras twisting above it all.

The men circle the table in search of name cards, and Will, trembling, takes his seat across from Stan, who is next to Leon. Serge is on Will's left, and Eric is at the head of their end of the table, opposite Alex by about eighteen feet plus a gauntlet of dancing flames and flora. Once settled, Will and Eric finally acknowledge each other. Will smiles meekly at him, shaking his head to indicate he's fine. But Eric fixes him with a worried stare, one that contains a new tragic intimacy forged during their last encounter, two weeks ago, at the hospital.

WILL HAD BEEN at Serge's that afternoon, drink in hand, feeling blithe and cosmopolitan, when he saw three missed calls from his mother. By the time he arrived at the hospital, his buzz was an aching throb. He found his parents wrapped around each other, staring down at the outline of Joe. Will didn't know yet whether there was still a person within. The older brother who so intimidated Will with his sullen silences, volatile outbursts, mocking comments, and unreadable eyes was now a question mark wrapped in white. Will went straight to the bed, knelt, and took Joe's damp hand. He couldn't remember the last time they'd spoken to each other. Weeks, at least, though they hadn't said anything kind to each other in years. Joe's weak pulse was an accusation.

It was only when Will turned back to his parents that he noticed the figure in the corner. It took a moment to make sense of the face.

"Will," his father said. "This is Eric."

Will squinted to conceal his shock, and Eric mimicked this tactic, looking from Chip to Will and back. Then his eyes grew with new understanding.

"He . . . found Joe . . . and . . ." Chip barely managed the sentence. "Thank God."

After administering the naloxone in Delphi's parking lot, Eric had followed the ambulance here and eventually was introduced by a doctor to Chip and Diane as the man who had saved Joe's life, a title too heavy for Eric to comprehend. After a doubtful moment, Eric had recognized the name and face, even without Chip's brochure smile, even with those ravaged eyes. The man whom his friends had, for months, relentlessly derided fell onto Eric's chest and sobbed his gratitude.

Eric was jolted anew by Will's appearance, though in the next instant it seemed almost natural they should meet in this place, as if all their encounters throughout the summer—Paul's fundraiser, Eric's front porch, the *Fodder* dinner, the many pool parties—had been the stepping stones to this moment.

Under the fluorescent lights, against white walls, beside the computer tracking Joe's heartbeat, Will was struck by how ordinary Eric looked in this room, how lost. Until that moment, he'd always associated Eric's bright polos with the colorful brushstrokes of lakes and lawns. Until now, Eric had been a tranquil, peripheral figure in the idyllic scenes that comprised Will's enchanted summer, scenes so untouched by worry they seemed to preclude even the possibility of tragedy. But Eric's pale, agitated presence in the stark, sterile hospital had punctured that illusion.

Will said, "Thank you, Eric."

Eric nodded and said, "I'd better go."

He moved toward the door, but Chip rushed to intercept him, gripping his shoulders. Chip kept his mouth shut as though afraid of what sound might escape. Diane swayed in place. She raised clasped hands to tearstained lips, then held her hands out to Eric in a gesture of blessing. Eric bowed his head, awkwardly, and fled. As Chip turned into Diane's arms, Eric paused to look back through the horizontal slats of plastic blinds that cut the Rileys into ribbons, as he and Will shared another moment of bewilderment.

ALEX STANDS AT the head of the table, holding a glass of platinum fizz.

"If I can have your attention for just a moment," he says. He waits for the chatter to subside, taking in the portrait of splendor and friendship before him. "I want to thank you all for helping me celebrate this milestone, which you know I've been dreading." Polite chuckles and a measured pause. "I'm a little overwhelmed, actually. When we got our place here, I thought of it as a vacation cottage. A weekend escape. I didn't imagine this." His champagne flute floats in a semicircle around the room. "I never thought our house would come with such a caring, generous community. I grew up the poor, gay kid of immigrant parents, and I've never felt such warmth and acceptance. If you included that in a property's value, the price of our house has already doubled." Big smiles all around. "Of course, for some of you, that's the cost of your grounds maintenance." Good-spirited laughter, especially from the wealthier attendees. "But the point is, you all add immeasurable value to our lives here."

Among the appreciative murmurs and light applause, Will finds that Alex's sentiment resonates. He, too, never could have imagined being included in such a scene. And while Griffin is Will's only home, not some pleasant surprise included in the purchase of a fantasy, these men have shown his town to have the capacity for more openness, more sensuality, more inspiration than he ever thought possible. They have increased its value for him as well.

Alex faces his husband across the table's cluttered expanse. "Even though Eric and I still spend the majority of our time in the city, you all have made this place our true home." It's a nice note to end on, but then he adds, with a wry laugh, "Well, I guess I should say *I'm* still mostly in the city. I suspect Eric's leading a double life up here." The room rewards this with scandalized snickering. Eric manages a good-humored expression as he lifts his glass to Alex, whose smirk seems to say, "You deserved that."

Alex continues, "But even if life occasionally takes us down separate paths, what's important is that Eric and I are building a home here together, and I look forward to sharing it with him, and with you all, for many years to come."

Eric's body fills so swiftly with gratitude that it catches him off guard. The rarity of hearing Alex's affection spoken so publicly, and Alex's ability to acknowledge their current distance while expressing confidence in their future, hits Eric with unexpected force. It's enough to crack the shell of discontent that has formed around him over the past several years. And those cracks allow him to glimpse the reserves of love and appreciation he still carries for his husband.

Eric raises his glass and, all around him, glasses raise in response. The champagne's acute acidity sears Will's throat in a way that implores him to remember this moment. Bouquets of salad appear, white wine enters the correct chalice, Serge's leg lays against his, the room splits into disparate conversations.

Leon catches his breath. Many years ago, early in his relationship with Peter, he celebrated his own fortieth birthday in similar fashion, with similar sentiments and the suggestion of a long-shared future. Then a beautiful young boy arrived to rob him of it. With a new beverage to mark the evening's progression, Leon swallows his sorrow and proposes a toast among the five men comprising their end of the table: "To your husband on his birthday," he says to Eric. Then to Stan: "To your husband on his impending victory."

Glass taps glass, eyes lock eyes, Leon winks at Will as if flicking a dart.

"That's very sweet," Stan says, "but I think victory is still a bit optimistic."

"After that debate, I'd say he's in good shape," Leon says.

"He's shrunk a double-digit lead to almost a margin of error," Serge adds with a small gesture to Stan, as though to credit him for the achievement.

"Serves Riley right," Leon continues. "He was really on a tear about how we city people are coming here and destroying the region, like an invasive species. But an invasion of what? Good taste? Money? God forbid!"

"But what's truly astonishing is Diane," Stan says. "Selling us a home after fighting to deny us the security of inheriting it should one of us die. I can't wrap my head around it."

"I can't believe I didn't make the connection sooner," Serge admits. "And I just referred Davey to her! But you must have realized all along and never said a word."

"Paul and I agreed not to make it a thing. But now, this hypocrisy, I can't ignore it."

Hypocrisy! Yes, Leon thinks, this is his cue. It's time for beautiful boys to learn that deception has consequences.

"Speaking of which," Leon says. "You all heard that Riley has a gay son? Astonishing!"

If not for the room's golden gleam, Will's blanched face might have attracted attention. His vision blurs as he feels Leon tightening his squeeze. Can he flee before the entrées? What difference would it make? If he is to be exposed, if all this is to be snatched from him—these friends and luxuries, his promising prospects—it will happen whether he's here to witness it or not.

Eric looks equally ashen and says softly to Leon, "Please don't." He says it as much for Alex's sake as for Will's.

Leon raises a brow at Eric, wondering what he knows, and says loudly, "Don't what?"

Serge is rubbing Will's knee under the table when he says, with grotesque irony, "How awful for that kid! To grow up with such bigotry."

Leon maintains his volume. "Though actually, the kid works for the campaign. William, a nineteen-year-old college student, that's what the paper said. He defended Riley's debate comments." He sips his wine and stares at Will.

Will stiffens. All evening, all summer, it seems, Leon has been playing with him, waiting to pin him down. Will doesn't understand this animosity. But whatever the reason, he knows he's trapped. Exposure is inevitable. He understands, finally, the impossibility of his charade. His body slackens in defeat.

But resignation can also be a stimulant. At the moment of submission, Will discovers a well of resolve. He just had to sink low enough to find it. Face furiously flushed and body prickly with a courage that's been brewing for nearly six months, he twists himself taller.

"He's a good father."

A baffled hush falls over their cluster, as though a pocket of sound has been sucked from the room. In the void, Will hears his pummeling heart.

"Excuse me?" Stan says, as though choosing, for the moment, not to comprehend.

"Chip Riley is a good father."

"Why would you say that, Will?" Stan asks with crisp impatience.

"Because he's *my* father. And Diane is my mother."

Stan's expression remains rigid, though his eyes vibrate with something resembling wonder. Coldness spreads on Will's knee where Serge has withdrawn his hand.

"Wait . . . You're Chip Riley's son?" Serge's voice is incredulous and loud enough to halt the independent conversation transpiring next to them. Within a few seconds, the entire room has quietly reoriented toward Serge.

"Chip Riley's son!" Leon repeats for the benefit of those just tuning in, desperate to get credit for the revelation. "But if I'm not mistaken, your name's Martindale, isn't it? Will Martindale?"

Eric snaps, "Shut up, Leon."

But Leon is intoxicated with the redemption that is within reach. His voice echoes against the richly papered walls. "So you've infiltrated the enemy camp! All summer you've been *spying* on Paul . . ."

"That's not true," Will says. "I never meant—"

"Except you kept lying! About your name. About where you work."

Serge jumps in. "Where he works? He worked for the catering company."

"He works for his father. For the campaign. And at the Lucky Buck!"

Stan looks at Will. "You work for the campaign?" His expression is less hostile than Will expects.

Will nods.

"And at the Lucky Buck?"

He nods again.

Stan turns to Leon. "How did you know that?"

"Because I saw him there."

"You patronize that place?" Stan processes the data. "You've known all this, held on to it, and chose to out him here, at Alex's party?"

Leon's face morphs from rage to pathetic awareness. "I tried to tell . . . It's the hypocrisy! Like you said. He still supports his father. He deceived us!"

"Well, apparently he's not the only one."

The exposé ends abruptly as the waiters enter to remove the salads. Finding the room in stunned silence, they expedite the gathering of plates. Among the clattering of porcelain, Leon is crushed, Stan is subdued, Will is numb.

The collective gaze shifts from accuser to accused. A calm comes over Will, the kind that accompanies the acceptance of an ending.

He lays his napkin on the table and pushes back his chair. He looks at Serge, who is looking straight ahead, and says a silent goodbye to his unlikely silver lover, goodbye to next summer at the festival, goodbye to whatever future might have followed. Then he gives Eric a small nod of thanks. He thinks it right to apologize to Alex, so he walks the length of the long table, under the scrutiny of so many pairs of eyes—some puzzled, some angry, some forgiving. He stands in front of Alex and says, "I'm sorry." Alex shrugs, perhaps in acceptance, perhaps in denial or dismissal. Will turns and retraces his steps. He exits peacefully.

IN THE FOYER, Will's fortitude dissolves. He struggles for air. Outside, he finds the valet engaged with a phone. He waits and, for a while, doesn't mind not being noticed, until the scene of his departure starts to replay itself and his breaths become short and sharp again. He thrusts his ticket in front of the valet, spurring him to trot off and, a minute later, return with the battered gray sedan.

Inside his car, Will hesitates. Driving away from this mansion will be to depart the promised land he was just allowed into. But what can he do? His tourist visa has been revoked, and he is being extradited to his country of origin. His eyes teem with failure and from the loss of all the beauty left behind.

As he is about to drive away, the passenger door opens, and someone is beside him.

"Pull over there." Eric indicates a patch of gravel in front of a small side house that might once have been servants' quarters. Will obeys. He puts the car in park but leaves the engine on. He is, after all, in the middle of an escape.

Eric turns to him. "Look. What Leon said . . ."

"He wasn't wrong."

"But it was wrong of him to do it like that."

"And wrong of me to lie to you all."

A pause. "You didn't lie. Not *exactly*."

"Now they all think I'm a spy."

"They don't." Another pause. "Well, maybe."

Will takes a breath. "Maybe I *was* spying, but not for my dad. For myself. I felt I'd somehow gotten access to some secret place where I was shown a better version of my life, where I finally felt comfortable with myself. I just wanted to stay as long as possible."

"It's really not so secret. Or so special."

"Only someone on the inside would say that."

"Yeah, well, only someone on the inside would also see how exhausting it can be. I mean, look at this." Eric gestures to the estate. "All this to impress and entertain. Pretending we can afford it."

Will speaks to the steering wheel. "Can't you? I mean, you threw this fancy party."

"We had help."

"So what? That just means someone cares. I'd give anything to fill a room with people who cared about me. You guys are so lucky and don't even seem to know it."

Eric is quiet for a moment. "It's just . . . I keep wondering what it all must look like from the outside. All this . . . fanciness, as you said . . . what people must think of it. Of us."

"They're envious."

"Or disgusted. But maybe disgust and envy aren't so far apart. Alex and I are probably the poorest of our friends, but I'm still surprised by how oblivious I can be, how hard it is to remember that not everyone lives like we do. Or wants to."

"That's not a very oblivious thing to say."

Eric nods and tries to accept this generosity.

Will says, "You didn't tell them about me. About my connection to the campaign, and my family, even after you knew. You could have."

"Wasn't my place. It just seemed like something you wanted to keep separate. And I know my friends. I love them. But sometimes I wonder if they aren't as closed-minded as they accuse everyone else of being. Anyway, you didn't out me, either, after you came to my door."

"I just . . . I didn't want to assume."

They both look ahead. The headlights make gauzy cones of mist.

"How is he? Your brother?" Eric asks.

Will continues to look forward, eyes straining. He blinks once, twice. His breath stutters. Finally he says, "I don't know. My parents took him to a rehab center this morning. I'm not sure for how long." He pauses. "They wanted to contact you. I heard them ask the hospital for your information."

"Why don't you just give . . . Oh. They don't know we know each other?"

Will shakes his head. "Guess I have to tell them now, don't I?" He relives the disgrace, the free fall of this night, mere minutes old. "Fuck." His head, heavy from the thought, drops on the wheel with a thud. He savors the smack. Then something snags in his mind. He sits back up. "With Joe, where did you get . . . And how did you know how to . . . ?" But his eyes are brimming, and another word might make them breach.

Eric is quiet, then says, "I'm both proud and not so proud of the answer. Short version is, someone I met this summer showed me a different side of this place, and I guess I chose to see it. I know that's vague, but that's the best way I can describe it right now."

Will thinks of that canvassing visit. The blue van, the familiar silhouette. Dalton? Has it gone on all this time? He wants to interrogate Eric, to understand the connection, but the effort to form any more questions feels so daunting and pointless. And then so, too, does every effort of the past six months—the lies, the hiding, the foolish hopes. His eyes overflow with fast, hot currents.

He bows his head, and Eric's arms are around him, his beard scratching Will's skin, catching Will's tears. Will looks up into Eric's milk-chocolate eyes, and for a moment, it feels like they might kiss, not in passion but in search of some solace the other might provide, a token of thanks. A farewell.

But both pull away in unspoken agreement that a kiss will not achieve this purpose, that it is unnecessary because they have already provided each other some delicate comfort.

At that moment, Will's headlights catch a figure exiting the manor. Leon stands outside the entrance, looking longingly back until his car arrives. He shouts something at the grand home that they can't make out. Then he slams his car door and speeds away.

There seems to be nothing more to say. Eric squeezes Will's shoulder, then exits the still-humming car and returns to the party, to his husband, to his friends, to the place where Will is no longer welcome. Eric's rough beard has left Will's face pricked and raw.

Driving home, as Will takes the dark curves at high speed, he must wipe his eyes every few seconds. His headlights sweep across shorn cornfields, brush over darkened porches, and flash through thick woods, the view splotched and distorted by tears.

Suddenly his lights land on the big brown body of a deer, grazing just off the road. It looks up, more curious than startled. The lights illuminate its eyes, rendering them blank, reflective mirrors. The deer tenses, ready to dart. But in what direction? Off into the trees or straight into the road to greet Will? He's been driving these roads for years and is accustomed to indecisive animals. If this deer decides to jump in front of him, there's nothing to do but brace. He almost welcomes it. He's been used by his family, rejected by his friends, ashamed of his own deception. He is ready to accept his punishment.

But the deer decides she'd rather not move, and Will's car swings safely around the bend, his heart hammering with relief and disappointment.

CHAPTER 18

FIRST PRESBYTERIAN IS THE last and only place Diane wants to be this morning. It's the Sunday after the debate, her first time back at church since Joe's overdose and since checking him into the treatment facility. She needs to sit with her soul, be in conversation with God, hear Reggie's soothing words. But she can't bear the stares of her fellow congregants, their squinty judgment, the radiation of their pity.

Or perhaps they are welcoming her with compassion, perhaps their smiles are genuine, perhaps they're unaware of her pain. Who can ever correctly interpret another person? The surrounding worshippers might as well be mirrors, since the judgment and pity are all hers.

Reggie muses on Jeremiah's denunciation of corrupt kings and priests. It's both too abstract and too close to home this morning, so Diane turns instead to the three maples outside, their remaining ruby and gold leaves quivering against gray sky, until she considers that those faded colors are signs of imminent death. She thinks of Will's childhood assessment of this transition—God at work—and reminds herself that God is at work in all areas of her life, however terrifying, humiliating, and generally unbearable His work has been over the past two weeks.

This is exactly what she feared all along as Chip steadily progressed in local prominence: this scrutiny, even if only imagined, that defines her by *his* actions and inactions, robbing her of her hard-earned self-achievement. Should he win, this will become her new reality. She is tempted, when called to prayer, to ask God for Chip's defeat.

When worship concludes, she keeps her gaze down and heads toward the exit, adrift in these thoughts. Raina Swinton, wearing a teal cardigan set, steps into her path.

"So *now* you understand, Diane? *Now* you and Chip are facing what's right in front of you, when it's hooked up to a monitor? Now that you've determined it's politically advantageous?"

"Raina! No, that's not . . ." Diane is stung by this uncharitable reading but wonders if there's truth in it. She takes a step back and fingers her cross. "That's absolutely not . . . Chip's devastated. We're both devastated. We didn't know if Joe would make it."

"But he did. And Diane, I truly am relieved. I prayed for him. You must know that I asked Jesus to spare him."

"Thank you, Raina."

Raina sucks air in stutters, and her words become watery. "But I'm mad, too, because you got a second chance, and I didn't. And Chip up there . . . talking about what he's gonna do *if* elected, when neither of you did anything before? When I warned you!" She covers her eyes with her palm. Diane takes a risk and grabs Raina's other hand, which Raina allows, though there's no reciprocal squeeze.

"Raina, I'm—"

"No!" Raina wipes the air in front of her, swatting away her sorrow. "I don't want an apology, if that's what you're offering. I want Chip to do *something*, win or lose. Give me that." She retreats to the waiting arms of her husband, who ushers her out.

Diane stands in the aisle for another minute. Several people quickly pass who otherwise would have greeted her. They're embarrassed for her, she decides. Or that's just her projecting again. More plausibly, the hunch of her shoulders, the misery on her face, repels them.

Back in her car, she sees several missed calls from Chip and a text message imploring her to come to *The Griffin Gazette* offices right away.

THE PAPER'S HEADQUARTERS, a three-room suite on the backside of the Lucky Buck's parking lot, is underfurnished and covered in notepads, stacks of yellowing newsprint, thickets of discarded electrical wires, and piles of outdated technology. When Diane arrives, she finds Chip and Celia in stilted small talk. The *Gazette*'s two remaining editors pop in to say hello, but nothing in these polite exchanges would suggest to an observer that Chip has been friendly with them for over a decade, that he used to share monthly beers with *Gazette* journalists and editors when the team consisted of more than a dozen people.

Those staff happy hours were where Chip and Celia first developed their rapport, when he relied on her reporting to justify items in the town budget, or to alert him to issues under his radar, while she in turn relied on his on- and off-record insights and access to sources. There was a strong feeling of unofficial partnership in their shared commitment to Griffin and the broader Munsee region, an assumed alliance in their resistance to the Duffel makeover. At least until the campaign. Now it seems that any semblance of remaining affection was drained by the debate.

"Shall we get to it?" Celia says briskly when Diane is seated.

"Just waiting on Will," Chip says.

"Will's coming?" Celia looks concerned.

"You said it was something to do with him and the campaign, so I felt he should be here."

"I'm not sure—" Celia begins as Will enters.

"Hey, Celia," he says cautiously. He's surprised to find his mother present.

Celia shifts squeakily in her rolling chair. "Well, here you are. I wish I didn't have to do this, but . . ." She explains that she was finalizing a story this morning when the link arrived with the subject line "Banks secret video." She almost deleted it as spam, but the specificity of its reference to Paul begged her to look. And then, well, "I'm sorry, but it's the only way."

She presses play on her laptop and rolls out of the way so the Rileys can watch.

Shaky, grainy security camera footage, seemingly filmed by a phone, reveals a large swimming pool—the Bankses' pool, which Diane knows well because she remembers pointing out to them that few rural pools boast such sweeping views. That pool and those views are framed on-screen from an elevated perspective, a slight fishbowl effect curving its edges. The time stamp informs them that it is Labor Day, late afternoon. Some men lounge on the pool's edge while another small group clusters in the water.

Dread pricks at Will's pores. He knows this scene. He can see the back of his head in that cluster. And he knows what happens next. In one corner of the screen, Paul emerges from the house and, within seconds, has swiped off his shirt, unbuttoned his shorts, and yanked down his underwear.

"Oh my God!" Chips yelps.

"Why are we seeing this?" Diane asks in the same squeal that emerges when the family watches horror films and she senses impending violence. "Is that Serge? And Davey?"

Celia doesn't answer. Chip shoots his wife a scathing look.

There's no sound, but they can see Paul has said something that rouses the other men to shed swimsuits, including Will, though he is still facing away from the camera. The Will who is watching quickly fast-forwards through the surveillance footage in his mind to recall how things progressed. Not long after they discarded suits, they moved to the hot tub. He now sees the cluster in the pool break apart and head toward the pool's steps. In seconds, he will be standing naked on the deck in full view of Celia and his parents.

How has this moment—the moment when he felt most free and brave in his life—so quickly and savagely been turned against him, transformed into such extraordinary punishment?

Will's on-screen avatar turns toward the camera. Given angle and distance, you could claim that it's not possible to accurately identify a face. But Diane has no doubts. She knows that face intimately. She has watched, with joy and incomprehension, as it has transformed over nearly two decades into something both unmistakably itself and increasingly unknown. It is the face of the son beside her, freckled and drained of all color.

"Jesus Christ!" she shrieks with the force of a cork shot from a magnum. The phrase is a reflex, not meant blasphemously, but she immediately wonders whether she has taken the Lord's name in vain. No, she decides, it is justified. She had called out to Him in genuine anguish. She cannot accept Will in this scene, she cannot accept him as one of those men. Seeing him there, in the middle of this debauchery, not only confirms his sexuality, it forces her to confront the terrible truth that sexuality is not only an orientation, it is an action. As the grainy figure of her son approaches the pool steps on-screen, she fears it is too late to turn away.

Will lunges forward and slaps shut Celia's laptop.

"What the hell did you do that for?" Chip barks.

"You don't need to see any more of it," Will pleads.

"What do you mean? You've seen this already?"

"I'm in it, Dad! I'm fucking *in* it."

Chip leans back slowly. The Rileys seethe, still and silent, for nearly a minute until Chip turns to Celia, his voice scarily soft. "What are you planning to do with—"

"This is *blackmail*!" Diane spits the word.

"Di, please."

Since shutting the screen, Will has had his eyes closed. Still self-blinded, he clears his throat and says, "Who sent it?"

"We don't know," Celia says. "The email address was generic, and there was only a short message saying this would be of interest for our election coverage." She turns to Chip. "One of my editors is of the mind that there's nothing here, ultimately, but the other thinks that after the debate"—she spins her hands to encompass all the regrettable things said there—"the revelation of an explicit, um, *friendship* between Paul and Will is actually not a small or irrelevant thing."

"For God's sake, Celia, this is . . . this is sabotage!" Chip pounds her desk, causing a mug of pencils and pens to jump and clang its concurrence. "It doesn't hurt just me and Paul, it poisons the whole race, drags the entire district through the mud. We'll be a national laughingstock! The *Gazette* wouldn't allow that, right? You least of all. If I know you, which maybe I don't."

Celia sighs. "I can't promise anything, but I don't disagree."

Silence again encases the Rileys. Will should say something. Explain. Apologize. Defend himself! Once again, gumption evades his grasp. His mouth doesn't work, but his body does. He's now moving toward the exit, down the stairs, into the parking lot, and jogging to his car when he hears behind him, "William!"

He turns to find his father advancing across the asphalt.

"Are you running away?" Chip shouts. "You drop a bomb like that, then just up and go? Like you did before college? Detonate and retreat and just leave us there with that . . . that *scene* that might ruin the thing I've worked hardest for my whole life? Because my son—my *son!*—who I thought was loyal, was deceiving me this whole time?"

Will attempts to speak but can't.

"What?" Chip yells. "What are you saying?"

Will's head shakes violently of its own volition.

"No? No *what*? Speak, goddammit!"

Will tries. Words form but get lost in a choking sob. The pathetic sound stokes Chip's fire.

"You make calls for me! You knock on doors for me! But behind my back, you're laughing at me. Mocking me! And now I have to watch my son humiliate me in the most *disgraceful* way. With them!"

Will's head swivels faster side to side, flinging tears. "They didn't know," he finally gasps.

"Know what?"

"That you're my fucking dad!"

Chip's face twists. His voice takes on a new acerbity. "Is the fact that I'm your father shameful for you, Will? I had no idea that I had become such a liability in your life."

"I didn't mean—"

"Don't you dare say that! Of course you meant. You did *exactly* what you meant. Running around with the goddamn Duffels, suddenly too good for us. Pretending to support me while playing up in their castles, looking down on us." The pressure builds inside Bud Light Riley. "I get it, why you were so upset about the debate. Acting as offended as Paul. Because you're part of his world now. Or at least they let you *think* you are. And that makes you just a goddamn—" He catches himself, and by not selecting a word, he allows Will to imagine them all.

But Chip's loss of control stirs Will to regain his own. "I didn't pretend anything," he says, his breathing steadier. "I didn't *pretend* to support you. I *actually* supported you. I'm the only one in this family who really has. But I knew this place would never accept them, the way Mom never accepted me."

Chip steps back as if Will has taken a swing at him. "Hey, wait a second. Give your mother some credit, okay? I know you don't think she tries to understand your . . . that she doesn't get you, but she tries. She struggles, but she tries."

"I haven't seen any struggle."

"Doesn't mean it's not there. I've seen her change. I've seen this town change, too. Maybe a few years ago there was more misunderstanding, more discomfort."

Will thinks of his mother's marriage campaign meetings, the fresh-baked cookies that accompanied the ugly, accusing posters. "Oh, I remember," he says. "The discomfort was *very* clear." True, she now sells homes to husbands, he grants her that. But the self-interest behind it complicates a more generous reading of her motives. In his present bitterness, Will refuses to see it in any other light.

"Don't take the wrong message from this," Chip says. "It's got nothing to do with them being gay. People distrust them because they're bringing their politics here, and for a lot of folks, that's sin enough. They're resented because they're rich, or at least rich by comparison, and not subtle about it. And Paul's a pretty blatant example of that obliviousness. He represents something that makes people feel like they've done something wrong, like they *are* something wrong. And they don't like being made to feel that way by a kid who's got it all, and flaunts it, and thinks he deserves to represent them because . . . well, just because he thinks he deserves it."

Will is silent for a few moments. "They don't look down on you or mock you," he says. "They just want to be left alone. Who are they hurting, anyway?"

"But who are they helping?" Chip snaps. "I don't give a good goddamn about them being here. But they have no right to influence the direction of a place they use as a weekend getaway when the rest of us have to live real lives here. Gerry. And your brother." He swallows and coughs. "What do they care about people like them?"

"My friend saved Joe."

Chip frowns. He's about to speak, but Will sees it register: the hospital. Eric. Chip puts a hand to his head. "Jesus Christ," he says.

Will begins backing away. "You don't have to worry, though. I won't be seeing them anymore. You're not the only one who feels betrayed. Turns out I'm not important to them, either."

He gets in his car and drives off, leaving his father behind.

DESPITE CHIP'S NEW national profile, most Lucky Buck patrons remain as disinterested in the political circus around them as the Brothers mounted on the pub's walls. Some are vaguely aware of the ripples generated by the debate and the increased interest in their district that, refreshingly, has nothing to do with its precious culinary scene. While a few regulars hustle on behalf of Chip in the campaign's remaining days, the majority continue to do what they do here regularly. As soon as Leon takes his regular seat, Gerald is beside him.

"Lenny! Been a while. Mare, a fancy green drink for this stranger."

"Oh, God, no. Please not that one." Leon brushes away the air in front of him, rejecting the repellent beverage. "Just a whiskey on the rocks, thanks."

Maren looks at Leon blankly, unamused by his dramatics. "Okay," she says, then turns to Gerald. "On you?"

"How about on the house? It's my birthday! In a month, for real this time."

"Sorry, Ger."

"'Course you are, everyone's always sorry. On my tab, then. What the hell? Doesn't matter anymore, anyhow."

"When did your bar tab ever matter?" Maren mumbles.

Leon says to Gerald, "What have I done to deserve this generosity?"

"You're sitting here talking to me, Lenny. That's more than most folks these days, including that one." Gerald ticks his head toward Maren.

"Cows ignoring you again, too?"

"Ungrateful shits. And my fuckup kid, also an ungrateful shit. And Chip." Gerald shakes his head.

"What about Chip?"

"Wants nothing to do with me. The town council meeting, the commercial, the goddamn debate."

If his whiskey were in front of him, Leon would drain it in one guilty gulp. He gets Maren's attention. "Can we start with a couple of shots over here? Vodka. On me."

"What'd I do to deserve *that*?" Gerald says.

Leon sighs. "For whatever reason, Gerry, you seem to like me."

Gerry looks down with a small triumphant smile. "'Course I do. Why wouldn't I?"

Maren delivers the shooters, which Lenny and Gerry tap and swig.

"The council meeting," Leon says. "You had every right. And the commercial wasn't your fault. Chip knows that."

"I don't think he blames me. But he holds me responsible, know what I mean?"

"Just the madness of the campaign. The spiteful game of politics. You had nothing to do with it. He gets that."

"I s'pose. Problem is, the madness isn't going away if he wins. But he will. Go away, I mean. Off to Washington. Moving on from this town, from the Buck. I can feel it. I know he'll win. He's gotta beat that fa—uh, sorry, the other guy."

"I'm starting to hope he does."

"That right? Even though you're one of them?"

"I don't think they see it that way."

Maren sets the whiskey in front of Leon. He stares at it for a moment, thinking again of Alex's party, the stuffy room and the stares that turned on him after Will exited with a dignity that surprised and punished him. Leon knew immediately that he had miscalculated again. His attack, intended as a show of allegiance to Stan, a corrective to the unfairness of Will's deception, had backfired. Around the room, he saw disgust on every face. Then Stan leaned in and said, "Probably best you leave as well. For Alex's sake."

Leon sat dumbfounded, then thrust back his chair and made a conspicuous exit. On the front steps, waiting for the valet to return with his car, he stared at the closed doors of the grand home and knew there was no way back inside. When his car pulled up and there was nothing left to do but depart, the full weight of his rejection crushed him.

"Fuck your fraternity!" he shouted to the house. Then he fled.

"Well, fuck 'em, right?" Gerry says, as though he watched the replay of the party in Leon's mind. "You're one of us now! Mare, darling, another round, will you? And take one for yourself. You deserve it, putting up with me all these years, a real angel."

"Don't call me that," she says with unexpected intensity.

"Sorry, damn!" Gerry lifts his glass to Leon. "Fuck 'em who think they're better than us!"

Leon laughs because he has tried to do just that. They drove him to it, Will and the Bankses. The kid ignored and replaced him; Paul excluded and disdained him; Stan blamed and banished him. It is exactly what he had feared and expected. As in his previous life, Leon Rogers was easy to dispose of.

"Fuck 'em," he says, and throws back his second shot. The spirit scalds his throat and sutures his regret for sending Celia the video.

"Thatta boy," Gerry says, and throws an arm over Leon's defeated shoulders.

Leon is surprised when the arm remains, surprised at the delicate comfort it brings. Both men fall silent, lost in their respective disappointments, almost unaware of the touch between them and its brief, alleviating power.

Then Gerry's arm falls away. "Christ," he says.

Chip and Diane enter the Buck and scan the space. Chip stops when he sees Gerry. The old friends stare at each other for several seconds. Then Gerry raises a hand and Chip imitates the gesture. He starts to approach until Diane grabs his arm. Chip hesitates, then follows her to a booth in the back.

Leon stares at Diane with interest. There she is: Chip's wife, Will's mother, unlikely Realtor of choice among Paul's circle, apparent homophobe.

He tried to identify her at the debate but didn't manage. She's flashier and more imposing than Leon pictured. He can see where Will gets his slender freckled nose and restless eyes. But she looks more distraught than the scheming, priggish woman in his mind. Her words are inaudible, though her hands speak distress, flailing at Chip until she drops her head into them. Chip calls Maren over, and she quickly delivers a glass of white wine and a Scotch.

Leon suspects he knows the cause of this commotion and, of course, who is responsible: a big, hairy weapon of self-destruction, that's who. But when he sent the clip to Celia, he never once envisioned, or desired, to observe the effect of his ruse on the family. He finds that it gives him no pleasure. He turns away from the debrief. But Gerry is drawn to it. He's out of his chair, heading toward them with determination.

Maren calls after him, "Ger, I wouldn't." But he doesn't look back.

In the booth, Chip and Diane sense someone approaching and turn toward the hostile interference. As soon as he's in front of them, though, Gerry deflates, as if simply facing his friend again has drained him of anger.

"Chippy," he says, gripping his trucker cap in both hands. He blinks and sways and seems uncertain for a second before breaking into a bashful, childlike smile. "Heya, Diane. Been a while. How you doing?" His words are slow and slanted.

"Gerry. Hi."

"Sorry to interrupt. Just, I've been waiting for Chippy here. Was hoping to talk to him."

"Now's not a good time, okay, Gerry?" Chip's tone is weary, impatient.

"Right, right. Gotcha." Gerry rotates his hat as if turning a steering wheel. He looks at Diane, and his face brightens. "You must be so proud of him! Our Chippy's such an important guy now. Makin' all of us proud. Isn't that right?"

"Gerald," Diane says, crisp and flustered. "We're in the middle of a bit of a crisis, okay?"

"Oh! My bad, my bad. Didn't realize . . ." He goes quiet and his forehead wrinkles. He begins to turn away but then reverses and says to Chip, as if posing a challenge, "So when we going hunting? Shotgun season's been open a few weeks already. The window's closing."

"Got to get through the race, Gerry."

"Of course! Gotta finish the race, gotta finish the race. You're going to win, Chippy. I'm sure of it. Nobody can stand that little carpetbugger you're up against."

Both Chip and Diane tense. "Don't use that word," Chip says.

"But you—"

"It was a mistake."

"Huh. Well, when you beat the bastard, we'll go hunting, yeah?" He points to the wall-mounted bucks. "Gotta find these guys another brother, right?"

"We'll talk, Gerry," Chip says.

Gerry blinks again, now in disbelief. His affability vanishes, his anger breaks the surface. "'We'll talk'? What the fuck does that mean, 'we'll talk'?"

"Gerald, please," Diane says. "Not now."

"Not now?" Gerry breathes heavily. "So when? Next time Chippy *happens* to come in and I *happen* to be here and he *happens* to decide not to ignore me?"

"Gerry, for God's sake, calm down!" Chip says, and there's heat to his words.

"I'm calm, man, I'm calm." Gerry holds his hands up and takes two messy steps backward. "Sorry to interrupt." He takes two more steps back, points his hat at Chip, and says to Diane, "Important guy, your husband. Goin' to Washington. We'll miss him, won't we? Question is, will he miss us?"

"Nice to see you, Gerald," Diane says, cold and conclusive.

Gerry stares sadly at her then at Chip, who's looking down. "Well, all right, then," he says, and turns around. He takes a few steps, then twists back. "Take care, Chippy. Know I'll always be rootin' for you."

NOVEMBER

CHAPTER 19

STAN ALMOST CAN'T REMEMBER what life was like before the campaign hitched a ride on his every thought. But that may also be because the promise of this race has floated abstractly in his mind for years, long before he and Paul moved to Griffin, before they'd even heard of the Twenty-sixth District and its political potential. If Paul hadn't run here this year, he'd have run somewhere else, sometime soon. But it feels fortuitous that it should be here and now, when circumstances have conspired in their favor, as if the Munsee River summoned them. Only eighteen months after their first visit, Paul is on the verge of representing their adopted home.

In the campaign's final weeks, Stan attempted to recruit his friends to remain in Griffin after Alex's birthday to help with the sprint to Election Day. He promoted it as a kind of service vacation, a political Habitat for Humanity where a week of moderate labor produces a year's worth of self-satisfaction. Only Serge and Eric accepted his offer.

Stan is grateful for their commitment but disappointed and unsurprised that so few others in his Griffin circle have supported Paul's campaign with their time and talent. At this critical moment, most are back in the city, where their real lives continue to unfold. At Paul's pleading, they have all reluctantly written one final check. But other than offering him financial support (and pouring money into their homes), none of them seem to consider Griffin worth a more meaningful investment. That's the trouble with second homes, Stan realizes: You just want to be in them, not look beyond them. He understands this without judgment.

Empathy takes energy, and his friends draw their energy from the city. They come to Griffin to relax, but politics is not relaxing, and comfort doesn't motivate, it placates. Just because they've bought the right to vote here doesn't mean they must spend their empathy here.

A shame, though, that Paul wasn't more effective in mobilizing them. And a shame that none of them saw the value in donating a single weekend to the cause of American democracy, which they profess to care so deeply about, and the state of which they will surely bemoan later, despite having passed on the chance to shape it more substantively.

But there's no time to dwell on people's hierarchy of values. In this frantic final stretch, Stan feels like he's on a runaway shopping cart hurtling downhill, gaining exponential speed, with no mechanism for braking. It's thrilling except for the unpredictable yet inevitable speed bumps, one of which came in the form of that poolside security footage, which they hit at full velocity. Stan felt airborne, disoriented, aware of fast-approaching asphalt.

Celia summoned them to the *Gazette*'s offices a few days ago to screen the clip, like it was some exclusive film. Paul railed against Will, assuming him the double agent, while Stan sat fuming in silence.

Back home, Paul continued his rant. "Think about it! He just appeared one day and then was *everywhere*! All summer! Looking for the perfect opportunity to entrap me. He leaked it, I'm sure he did."

"He's on there, too. He's as exposed as you are. He has just as much to lose."

"Lose? What does he have to lose?"

"It's equally humiliating for his family."

"You're defending him?"

"I am, actually. Because you know who's responsible for this situation? You, Paul."

"Me? How did I—"

"Your goddamn shamelessness!" Stan's roar brought the air to a standstill. "You couldn't keep your clothes on for one fucking summer? Couldn't get through your first election without a goddamn orgy! The years of planning . . . All the people who trusted you . . . All the—God!—all the money I've spent. And how close we are to the end! Yet you insist on having your fun. Hosting your parties. Filling this house with men and . . ." He waved his hands above his head, chasing away sex. "And to get caught on camera. Our own camera!" Stan laughed wildly. "It's a joke. A fucking cliché. The promiscuity! The debauchery! It's exactly what they think of us, what they've *always* thought of us, and what they will always think of us, because we—because you!—keep proving them right!"

Stan turned away, breathing heavily, and looked out the large glass walls onto the pool, which had been shut down a few weeks ago for winter. Now modestly covered, it pleaded innocence.

"There's nothing wrong with that video," Paul said behind him.

"Don't be ridiculous. If it got out . . . *when* it gets out . . ."

"There's nothing to apologize for. Nobody in that clip—or after that clip, for that matter—did anything they weren't allowed to do."

"But it doesn't matter!" Stan whipped around. "Don't you get that? It's not about your enlightened enjoyment. It's about *their* discomfort." He gestured to the window, indicating the world beyond. "It's their *perception* that matters. And perception is prejudiced, so you will lose."

He wanted to throw something to punctuate this judgment. A twisty glass sculpture on a nearby credenza looked like a good candidate. But it would be unnecessarily costly, and Stan has spent enough money on this race as it is.

So he hurled the following instead: "It would be the end of everything I've worked for."

Paul looked at Stan in a curious way, with an expression that the younger man had never directed at the older one before. Stan recognized it as disappointment, and it cut him.

"That *you've* worked for?" Paul said with unnerving calm. "Alone? I see."

Then he left the room, leaving Stan frozen in regret, a knot of apprehension forming in his throat. A frightening thought struck him: In his effort to pull Paul through this campaign, has he pushed Paul away instead? Regardless of outcome, what if, at any point, Paul determines that the political path isn't for him, and therefore, Stan isn't, either?

Stan turned back to the window, shaken. The sun had set, and in the dusk, the covered pool began to blend into the patio. He was reminded how, just a few months ago, that now-hidden water contained laughter. Around it bodies baked in heat and joy. Stan reached back further to summers long past, to similar sweltering communions on wooden decks, ritualistic immersions under a large American flag. The oasis that Asher had led him to. Once, he'd participated in that joy. He had accepted all its expressions and considered it the most important and radical thing in the world. At his window overlooking Griffin, he wondered, when did I become afraid of it? When did I become so ashamed?

He had buried that vital, carefree version of himself when he buried Asher. And decades later, it was Paul who helped him begin to unearth it again. With terrifying clarity, Stan suddenly saw how recklessly he has risked his marriage, and his happiness, for this shot at power. If Paul were to lose this race, might Stan lose *him*?

The following day, Celia called to inform them that the *Gazette* would not run the story. "We're not in the business of embarrassing our district on behalf of an anonymous disgruntled resident," she said.

"Thank you," Stan said.

"It's not a favor. This is a decision based on journalistic ethics and our civic responsibility."

"Either way, thank you."

As Stan hung up, it struck him that whoever sent the video—and he's pretty sure he knows who the culprit is—still managed to cause extraordinary damage between him and Paul and, he imagined, among the Rileys as well. Otherwise, why not just post it online? Almost as if the goal had been to sow distrust and instigate confrontation—or to simply share hurt. Perhaps that had been the intention all along.

A WEEK BEFORE the election, Will visits Joe at the treatment facility. He should have come sooner, but Joe didn't respond to his text messages. So Will waited. Joe always had a way of making Will feel forever the unwanted younger brother. Or that's Will's excuse for keeping his distance, a convenient cover for his cowardice.

The truth is, the image of Joe looking so weak and unresponsive in that hospital bed has haunted him since. He couldn't bear to see Joe again in that state, so he sought refuge in the bubble of Duffel distractions that allowed him to defer despair, until it burst at Alex's dinner. Then his guilt came flooding in, filling him with an overwhelming need to see Joe.

He arrives unannounced, unsure what he'll find and whether he'll be welcome. The grounds comprise a series of brick bungalows with covered walkways between them and well-maintained landscaping, which Will takes as an endorsement for the quality of care. He finds Joe in his room, on the bed, a pale white face wedged into the corner of a white wall, arms hugging denim knees, ropes of hair obscuring tired eyes.

"Finally," Joe says, which feels to Will like a dart to his chest.

"I meant to come sooner."

"Bullshit."

"You were ignoring me."

"You were waiting for an invitation?" Joe looks away. "Why didn't you come with them?"

"They're not so happy with me right now."

"I know, I heard all about your affair with Banks . . ."

"I never—"

"Don't care, but anyway, thanks."

"For what?"

"For taking some of the heat off me. Making it so I'm not the only fuckup in the family. I appreciate it."

"I've gotten good at letting people down."

"Something we have in common, then. Maybe we're brothers after all."

Will recognizes the attempt at humor but can't find the strength to smile. Something heavy hangs on his face, forcing a frown. "I know I've let you down, too."

Joe eyes him cautiously. "What do you mean?"

"Because I wasn't there—"

"Nope. Don't know what you're about to say, but no. Wasn't that. There's nothing . . . I mean, I didn't mean to . . . you know. It was an accident."

"Wouldn't have made a difference, though, if you'd actually . . ." Will trails off.

"Makes a big difference to me. That I wasn't . . . on purpose."

The air becomes humid in the thickness of their embarrassment. They have never spoken this openly with each other before. Even at their closest, when sharing secret beers behind the Lucky Buck bar, they conveyed affection through a teasing joke, a knowing glance, a knock to the shoulder, but never with the actual articulation of feelings and fears. The speed and honesty of this exchange spooks them into silence.

Will reaches for an off-ramp and notices the room's stately oak furniture, its generous size. "It's nicer than I imagined," he says, looking around.

"It's not a fucking hospital," Joe says with a smirk of relief.

"I know. I saw you in the fucking hospital," Will says, trying to match Joe's flippant tone in hopes that it conceals, but also conveys, his concern. "But this looks expensive."

"Insurance covers some, but they splurged. Said they thought I'd take it more seriously if I knew how much it cost."

"Are you?"

Joe looks away. "I'd take it seriously anyway."

"Can they even afford it? With the campaign and all?"

"Apparently Mom can. Heard her say to Dad thank God for her Duffel clients. And that they'll redo the bathroom another time."

"I hope you feel guilty."

"Actually she didn't say 'clients,' she said 'Will's Duffel boyfriends.'"

"Fuck you."

Joe releases a satisfied huff. Then his face turns solemn. He makes several attempts to speak. Eventually he says, "I've never . . ." He starts again. "I've always been cool with you. You know that, right?"

Will doesn't trust his voice, so he nods.

"I just didn't know how . . . And then Matt . . ."

"Thanks." Will attempts to save them both from this excruciating testimony. They stare at each other, mystified, until Joe nods and redirects.

"So this campaign circus is almost over, huh? Can't say I'm bummed to have missed it."

"Can't say it missed you, either."

Joe smiles, grateful to return to teasing. "Another week till Dad's a full-time hotshot, right? Till he wins his ticket to Washington and replaces us with a second family of a hundred thousand adopted constituents?"

"It's a toss-up now."

"Really? Your boyfriend has a shot?"

Will laughs. "You really are an asshole."

"And you really are a traitor."

But Joe doesn't sound like he's joking, and Will doesn't know whether to defend himself or accept the charge, so he remains silent and red. Despite all the ground covered this afternoon to reach each other, there is still so much frozen distance between them. Joe goes on, his voice jagged and unstable.

"You're a traitor like me. And selfish like me. I failed them, too. But way worse. What's most shitty is that I'll keep doing it, keep wasting their money here. No wonder Dad's running away to . . ." He looks at his hands clasped between his knees and shakes his head. "Doesn't matter. I know how this works. I can't solve this. Matt couldn't. Nobody can." He takes a shaky breath and looks up at Will with wet, wild eyes. "I'm a lost cause, and they know it." He turns away. "But they'll forgive you, and you have to forgive them, too, okay? You have to go back. We can't both bail on them."

Will blinks away the rising tide behind his own eyes and nods.

"And while you're at it." Joe focuses on his knotted fingers. "Don't bail on me, either, okay?"

For the next hour, Joe shows Will around the facility. They play foosball in the game room and drink sodas in one of the many seating areas that appear at regular intervals, as in an airport lounge. They don't talk much more, but in their proximity, the glacier between them begins to thaw further, enough so that Will is able to say, "You're going to stop using, right?"

"Of course!" Joe's answer is too fast, too emphatic, almost a punch line. "That's the truth. And a total lie. One of them will be right. Like you said, it's a toss-up."

From there, Will drives straight to headquarters, because if he doesn't, he might never go back. Gabrielle shoves a bunch of papers at him and says, "If you ever want to work on another campaign, don't even think about asking for a recommendation."

"Where's my dad?"

"Should be on his way to the local TV station soon. Headed there shortly myself."

"Why?"

"Final debate, God help us. Let's see if he's learned any lessons from the last one."

CHIP SLOUCHES IN front of the bathroom mirror, trimming his beard. The snipped hairs disappear into his furry belly, which hangs over his towel. Every half minute, he emits a melancholy sigh.

"Enough!" Diane says. "I can't take any more of your moping. What is it?"

He turns around, looks at her with defeated eyes. "Maybe I should pull out?"

"Of the debate? The race? Don't be ridiculous."

"I don't know if I'm cut out for this."

"What are you talking about?"

"This role I'm supposed to play." He sighs again. "To run a town, you've got to be practical, get stuff done, compromise so the trash gets picked up. But now I'm supposed to be an ideologue? A national spokesman? Sorry, not interested. Not good at it."

"And this is news to you?"

"All the things folks seemed to like about me on the local level, they're now suspicious of because they assume I'm more loyal to some broader cultural agenda than to my own hometown. Half the district automatically distrusts me because of the party letter next to my name, whatever that happens to mean to them. And on top of that, our son's ashamed of me, and my best friend . . . Christ! Gerry sounded like he's gone off the deep end."

"Gerry's been going off the deep end as long as I've known him. He wouldn't be himself otherwise. As for Will, I don't know what to think about him right now. Never imagined he'd be so deceptive. And careless! Flaunting his . . . It's . . . I won't say what it is."

"To be fair, Di, he didn't choose to advertise that . . . whatever that scene was."

"But just *being* there. With *them*. In that way! It's not right."

"That sounds a lot like the Diane from several years ago I'm now forced to defend."

"You don't have to defend me, Charles. I stand by my faith."

Chip begins to speak, then retracts his lips into a tight grimace. She knows this look of dismay.

"What?"

"It's just . . . You know I'm not a fan of those guys, for many reasons. But I thought maybe in some way they were helping you with the Will stuff. I thought if you accepted your clients, maybe it'd be easier for you to accept our son."

She stiffens, feels her jaw tighten, her neck strain. He sounds more thoughtful than judgmental, but she hears only accusation in his words. "I acknowledge Will's desires. But it's the secrecy! That's what kills me. How many lies has he told us this summer? He risked your entire campaign! How can you be so forgiving?"

"I've forgiven you, haven't I?"

She goes cold, then hot. "Excuse me?"

"You've been just as involved with those men, haven't you? Not in *that* way, of course, and not behind my back, but still. The brick factory thing? And selling Paul his house, for God's sake! Before you knew better, but it's no less embarrassing having it broadcast in front of all our neighbors."

She stares at him for several long seconds as her internal temperature builds. She speaks with stilted control. "My work supports this family, Charles. It has supported you and this campaign, if you ever cared to acknowledge that. I'm sorry that it occasionally conflicts with your goals. But I will not apologize for it or be made to feel guilty."

Chip's mouth parts briefly before he reseals it. A moment later, it carefully parts again. "I'm not asking you to apologize. Or feel guilty."

She waits.

"God knows I'm aware how much you contribute to this family and how grateful I am." He exhales. "But sometimes it feels so . . . removed. *You* feel removed."

"I've been trying to keep it separate, for your sake."

"Or yours."

"Yes, and mine." She puts her hand on his shoulder. "Because I love my work."

As she states this simple truth, she considers the many polite, appreciative men she has helped in the past few years who have allowed her a degree of professional success and self-pride she never imagined possible. In return, she realizes, they have unknowingly offered her a path to salvation for her fervent attempt to deny her son the same domestic contentment she happily sells them. After the anti-marriage campaign, she didn't know how to both defend her faith and evolve within it, but she understands now that the surprising trajectory of her work has been a part of that process. Perhaps when she opened the gate to the Trojan horse of these house-hunting husbands, she also smuggled in the seed of her own redemption. Perhaps it will soon grow into the apology she has never been able to articulate.

She takes a deep breath. "And I accept my son," she says.

Chip looks up at her. He lifts her hand from his shoulder and kisses it. Then he turns to the mirror, runs his hand a few times over his head, and lifts his face to examine the state of his nostrils. Chip always becomes preoccupied by his appearance when he's nervous. Diane smiles and finds herself relieved to return to matters of politics.

"Washington will be lucky to have you, Charles. And I'm willing to lend you to the people for however long they want you, as long as you stay you. And as long as this family can stay together."

"Our family will always come first," he says, a bit too quickly. A conflicted silence follows before he continues. "We were so careful with the boys, not to make them policy symbols. If I'd have known what this campaign . . . if there was the smallest chance that Joe . . . I swear I never would have . . ."

"You couldn't have known. We can only thank Jesus for sparing him, and us. Now we have to stay vigilant." She smooths his damp, thinning hair and removes a fallen eyelash. "You've run a good campaign, Charles. I wish I'd been a bigger part of it. Or, in light of the debate, maybe a smaller part."

"Come on, Di, don't . . ."

"It's okay. I've been wanting to say that for a while. I know it's no secret that I didn't want you to run. For selfish reasons, but also because this process seems to bring out the worst in people. I was scared that it would do the same to you. I should have had more faith." She laughs. "You'd think that with all my faith in Jesus, I could find some for my own family. But Jesus is easy to love. Faith in people is much harder."

She pivots him back to the mirror. "Now, finish your grooming, mister. And no more moping. Just a few days left, and you don't win a close race leaning back. So, chest forward, Charles."

WHEN CHIP AND Diane arrive at the television studio, Paul and Stan are lingering outside the greenroom, conversing with Jeremy. They stop as their rivals approach. The candidates and their spouses regard each other for the first time since the school gym, and since the scandalous video.

Nobody looks very happy. Diane blinks at Stan and he blinks back. She now sees Paul as the pied piper who seduced Will into the realm of her prodigal clients, and Stan thinks of Chip as the Machiavel who probably didn't plant his son as a spy but could have.

"Almost across the finish line," Paul says, simply because something has to be said.

"Almost," Chip says, and sticks out his hand. Their palms click into place. Diane knows it's an automatic gesture, a formality, but she's awed by Chip's ability to keep doing it, even with someone he despises.

The candidates sit behind a polished curved desk in front of a screen that will soon display election-related graphics. Chip looks anxiously at Diane, and Paul focuses on the camera, even though it's off. The moderator, with his smooth black hair and rumbling baritone, goes over the debate's format like he's imitating a sports announcer.

At this point, Will slips into the studio and stands next to his mother, who looks at him with surprise. He scans the room and finds Stan looking at him, too. It's the first time they've seen each other since Alex's birthday dinner, and neither can decide how to acknowledge the other, so they just continue staring, searching for signs of mercy.

The moderator goes live. After introductions, he invites the candidates to give opening statements, beginning with Paul, who delivers a rendition of his previous opening statement, though modified to include a more sensitive reference to drug users (careful not to implicate any of the Rileys) and a plea for a more tolerant district (careful to implicate all of the Rileys).

When it's Chip's turn, Paul rearranges his face into that effective expression of curious skepticism. Diane holds her breath. She has read Chip's opening remarks, which he rewrote with Gabrielle to showcase his pragmatism, and they're fine, but the question is whether he can erase the angry, erratic impression he gave at the last debate and replace it with calm conviction. As she waits for him to begin, she notices that he's looking intently at her.

No, not quite. He's looking next to her, at Will. Chip squints into the studio lights and nods, as if agreeing with himself about a decision he's just made.

"Actually, I want to say something else first. About the last debate."

Diane looks at Gabrielle, who's a few feet away, and finds her looking back with trepidation. The campaign manager shakes her head, as in "I have no idea what he's doing," then shrugs with helpless open palms. Diane fingers her cross necklace and turns back to her husband, who begins:

"Okay, here's the thing I want to say about that. It got more personal than I expected. Some people in my life, the most important people in my life, were brought into the conversation in ways that I didn't think were fair. I got flustered and frustrated and said some things I regret. That night, I didn't call upon the grace that my wife constantly teaches me. I didn't show my son Will the loyalty he's shown me. I didn't convey the compassion for my friend Gerry that I actually feel. And regarding an unfortunate word I chose for my opponent, well, I forgot in that moment that Banks, though Lord knows I think he's the wrong man for this job, he's my neighbor. And if there's one thing I want for this district, it's for that to still mean something."

The studio is quiet, either waiting for Chip to say more or letting what he said settle. If this debate were taking place in an auditorium, the audience's reaction would indicate how his statement has been received. As it is, the TV crew just looks placidly on. The only clues as to the impact of his words are Stan's slack jaw, Diane's wet eyes, and the silly smirk Paul wears when he doesn't know what to say.

Will's chest surges with a mix of emotions. Relief, disbelief, and a stunned realization that his defense of his father's goodness at Alex's birthday, which felt at the time more a testimony of faith than fact, has been justified. A reflection of his father's character, sure, but maybe also the earned dividend for Will's small recurring deposits to the enterprise that is his family.

Chip looks around, as if unsure what he's said and unsure whether to proceed. The moderator nods him forward. "Okay," Chip says. "I'll leave it there."

CHAPTER 20

EARLY THE NEXT MORNING, Dalton rises at five a.m. to milk the cows with his father, as he has for the past fifteen years, since he was twelve. They usually meet in the kitchen for a silent coffee, having long ago dispensed with even a bleary "good morning." Their relationship no longer accommodates ritual politeness, and mornings haven't been good for a while. But even with the stubborn friction between them, Dalton takes some comfort in knowing that they can still meet in the quiet of the morning milking. In the rhythm of that routine, against the thrum of pumps and the crinkle of cows munching hay, they're granted an hour's daily truce.

His father is not in the kitchen. This isn't unusual, especially as of late. Sometimes his father gets up early and heads down to start the milking on his own. More recently and more frequently, he's been sleeping in or, rather, stuck in a sedated snooze.

So Dalton brews a pot of coffee because none's been made. He waits a bit longer. He checks his father's bedroom and sees a clumsily made bed, the sheets carelessly covering the mattress, the pillows askew but uncharacteristically more or less in place. This is odd. His father hasn't made the bed in months. But his father often acts odd, and Dalton thinks little of it.

He trudges down to the barn alone, crunching gravel and twigs and the season's first snow, which fell during the night, heralding a coming storm. The icy glaze crackles and melts instantly underfoot. He stops and listens as a startled animal scrambles away in the darkness.

He comes to the rust-colored barn, which stands in proud silhouette against a still-star-dusted sky. The first thing he notices is the closed door, then the strips of light that frame its edges. This, too, is strange. Usually when his father gets started without him, he leaves the door open so the white light spills out. It's probably just laziness, but Dalton likes to think of it as a welcome mat conceding a residual connection between them.

Approaching the door, he sees a piece of paper fluttering in the chilled breeze. He grips the handle and pulls as he reads:

"Don't enter. Call the police. I'm sorry for everything but it's better this way. You're free now."

The door has already begun its outward swing, the momentum flinging it wide as if by the door's own will, and Dalton is too confused to stop it.

Inside, yellow hay is dyed red where the toppled cows lie motionless against one another. Ruby. Apollo. Henrietta. Sprinkles. And his beloved Maple, now a large, motionless fawn-colored mound. Some eyes are open, some closed, some shocked, some peaceful. Blood no longer dribbles from the bullet wounds in their heads; the streams have already soaked the straw.

And in a dark corner of the barn, shotgun in hand, his father, Gerald McAfee, shares their fate.

CHAPTER 21

THE PEWS FILL WITH men and women who have come straight from the first milking. The musty scent of hay, the essence of dead grass, permeates the church as though they have all joined Gerald McAfee at the scene of his crime. His fellow farmers and drinkers mumble that they can't believe it, but they say so without conviction. They can very much believe it. However horrific his method, Gerry isn't the first around here to permanently walk away from his debts.

The hardest part for Diane is watching Chip approach the funeral like a campaign event—a defensive maneuver, but so unfair to him. Last night, she rubbed his back as his head bounced softly on his chest in soundless sobs. But now he dons a mask of stoicism, too aware of the attention paid him, understanding too well that the looks of sympathy also hold questions about how his municipal dispute with Gerry seeped into the race. His passive acceptance of condolences is an excruciating exhibition of self-restraint.

Will and Joe are here. Both her sons finally by her side. But why is this the thing that grants Diane the public family portrait she has long sought? Why is sadness often the most reliable means of congregating?

All the Buck regulars are here, too. Jittery, numb, unsure how Gerry would want them to mourn, unsure what the place will be like without his constant joking, needling, complaining. They've lost members of the Buck family before, to accidents, overdoses, cancer, relocation. They know an absence reconfigures a place in unpredictable ways.

Celia and the liquor store lesbian are next to the hummingbird sisters, who scoot over to make room for Leon when he arrives. When seated, he realizes that the statue on the other side of him is Maren, staring ahead, eyes red and wide, battling an interior storm. Sensing his presence, she turns to him. He offers her a grimace of sympathy and she collapses forward, coppery curls falling like chains around her face.

Three rows forward, Joe and Will sit between their parents. It's the first time the Rileys have been to church together in years, and though the occasion is heartrending, Diane finds solace in returning to this configuration, the familial sandwich that once contained all the joy she could ever hope to hold. She looks at them in wonder. The boys wedged between her and Chip are impenetrable, intimidating creatures. She thanks God for whatever tenuous thread keeps them tied to her.

Dalton is on her other side in a too-small suit. She tries not to stare at his roughly carved face but is repeatedly drawn to the petrified pain in his eyes. She knows the son resented his father and the father resented his son, or that's how it seemed. But she was witness to their antagonism for decades and also saw their hidden need, even if both men were too afraid to recognize it.

She is furious at Gerry for leaving Dalton with such unrequited rage. What's the boy supposed to do with it now? She puts an arm around his wide back and keeps it there throughout the service, which is a good service, an appropriate commemoration. Reggie does a fine job capturing Gerry's buried kindness while acknowledging the very unkind ways he could be with people. When Reggie leads them in the final prayer, Dalton's shoulders shake.

Merciful God, we confess that we have sinned against you
in thought, word, and deed,
by what we have done,
and by what we have left undone.
We have not loved you with our whole heart and soul
and mind and strength.
We have not loved our neighbors as ourselves.

THE SMALL RECEPTION at the Lucky Buck afterward carries hushed murmurs of disbelief, sporadic blasts of silence, an eruption of forced laughter, the occasional clink of glass. The regulars are huddled around the bar, with Leon among them, pacifying themselves with stories of Gerry's grumpy antics, flushing down their grief with shots of brown liquid. Will has taken his usual place behind the bar, assisting Maren, pouring out pints for himself and Joe.

Chip and Diane have sequestered themselves in a cracked-leather booth with Dalton, hoping to avoid the line of condolences, but one after the other, guests slide in to repeat the same canned phrases of sympathy that hold real hurt.

After a few suffocating minutes, Diane excuses herself and heads out back. On the small landing next to the trash cans, she looks over the black asphalt to the forlorn dumpsters on the far end of the parking lot. She struggles for breath, then takes in a rush of cold, sharp air that punctures the protective barrier around the unbearable accumulation of the past year: Joe's overdose, Will's disclosure and subsequent deception, the public scrutiny of Chip's campaign, Gerry's death. It's too much, all this. She shivers and can't stop shivering, then finds herself convulsing as the wet weight within erupts into laughing sobs.

"Mom?"

She wipes her eyes and turns to find Will in the doorway, just a few feet away, but he looks as distant as ever. It's been over a year since she took him to college and felt him slip away. But somehow, he's still here. She studies him—his tall, lanky frame in a posture of newfound sureness—then opens her arms slightly, a gesture of weariness and regret, as well as a small opening.

He hesitates, then comes and encircles her. Her hands grip his shoulder blades as they used to, and she lays her cheek against his chest, her tears seeping into his shirt. After a moment, she feels the blessed heft of his head resting on hers.

AS FRESH SNOWFLAKES fall slanted in an insistent wind, Dalton drives directly from the Buck to Eric's cottage.

From behind parted curtains, Eric watches him hesitate at the wheel of the faded blue van, as if back in the same trance, engaged in the same internal battle, as when he first drove up half a year ago. It's been nearly two months since they last saw each other. They haven't texted much, so Eric was surprised to see Dalton's name appear on his phone as he was dressing for the annual AIDS advocacy gala in the city.

"My father fucking shot himself," Dalton wrote.

Eric untied his tie and called the parking garage for his car, intending to leave immediately and stay with Dalton for as long as he was wanted, ready to explain it all to Alex. But Dalton threatened to cut ties completely if Eric showed up at the farm or the memorial service.

"I don't want you here. Don't make yourself part of this."

So Eric attended the gala. He smiled in his tuxedo and bid on auction items and drank cabernet, all while arguing with Dalton in his head, begging to be part of this. The next day, having heard nothing more from Dalton, he told Alex that he needed a post-gala break and would be spending the week in Griffin, that he wanted to be there for the election.

"Okay," Alex said. He didn't question Eric's motive but added, "I forgot to send in my absentee ballot. Can you drop it off for me?"

Now, when Eric opens the door, Dalton sways. His swampy brown eyes have drained to mud, and his impressive wingspan is tucked away behind him, his shoulders forming a frown. Eric fiercely enfolds him, which Dalton resists at first, actually struggles against Eric's embrace, before allowing himself to be led inside.

Dalton heads straight to the living room, grabs a tumbler from the bar cart, and pours himself a whiskey. He swallows and pours another.

He looks up abruptly, as if something outside has beckoned him. He drifts over to the sliding glass door that faces the small backyard and the dense columns of trees beyond. He presses his head against the pane, his strong brow meeting its own reflection to forge a hardened bone bridge.

Eric observes him, unsure where he is meant to be or what he is meant to do.

A doe approaches the edge of the yard. Dalton straightens, and this abrupt movement attunes her to the presence of a nearby observer. When she darts off, Dalton finishes his second drink and slides the door open. He's on the small back deck, then down the steps and onto the lawn, which is brittle with accumulating snow.

Eric follows, and soon they are stomping through damp white woods toward the river, which they hear before they see. By the time Eric catches up, Dalton is squatting on the banks, answering the river's wet howls with his own. The fast, voracious flow consoles him, as does Eric's arm, as the last of the daylight gilds the water's turbulent surface.

ELECTION DAY

ELECTION DAY ARRIVES, BRIGHT and brisk. Paul wakes with optimism.

"I'm going to win," he says with a sleepy grin. "I know it."

Paul's childlike certainty amuses Stan, and he smiles in return. But it spooks him because he is unsure of the consequences—for him, for them—if the prediction proves false. "You will," he says. He hesitates, then takes Paul's hand. "But if you don't, it's okay. We'll be okay."

Paul frowns at this curious display of affection. Then he seems to grasp the anxiety beneath Stan's comment. He looks at his husband with his new, calm clarity. "Of course we will," he says, and kisses their clasped hands.

They drive into Griffin to cast their votes at Town Hall, a one-story redbrick box with a white gable, white columns, and a short turret clock. The building looks to Stan like the blueprint of democracy, embodying some American ideal of reverence and humility. A large flag ripples on a pole out front, and not for the first time this morning, Stan thinks of Asher.

It's more crowded inside than they expected, including a photographer from the *Gazette*. Given the demographic distribution of the Twenty-sixth District, many of those voting here are registered partisans of Paul, so he's greeted warmly. Seeing him surrounded by such enthusiasm, Stan allows himself a dose of his husband's certainty. He breathes achievement. Paul has acquitted himself (mostly) admirably in his first campaign. It's a promising start.

But alone in the booth, cut off from the political pageantry, faced only with the solemn ballot before him, Stan shudders in a gust of apprehension. Is Paul ready to win? What happens if he doesn't?

He has asked and suppressed these questions for over a year. Standing in Town Hall reminds Stan that he hasn't just invested significant money in this race, he has placed a bet on this community. If Paul loses, will they stay? Or might the next opportunity require another move, another home, another mad cycle of expensive ambition? The questions suddenly feel far from theoretical. If Paul pulls this off, it will be something of a miracle.

Then a reassuring thought. If Asher were here, he'd say: "It is already a miracle."

Stan exhales his doubts and fills in the bubble next to his husband's name. Despite all of his connections, all of his resources, this is the last and only thing he can do for Paul now.

When Stan emerges, he spots Leon. They grant each other a polite nod before Stan turns away. There isn't anything to say, really. Twice rebuffed, Leon retreats behind folded cardboard walls, resigned to the fact that this may be his only election in Griffin. He's already contemplating another fresh start. Next time, in the next place, he'll try again, he'll be better.

In the meantime, he considers the options before him. On the one hand, there's the candidate who aligns with his worldview, who will vote the right way on the issues he prioritizes, who is of his kind, though only in the most superficial way. On the other hand, there's the candidate who seems decent, for whatever that's worth, and who is probably the right guy to represent this place. It's not an easy choice.

He dawdles, deliberates, and chooses Chip. He chooses Chip because Gerry can't. And because he never really liked Paul anyway.

Not long after Leon departs, Eric drops off Alex's ballot and sees Paul posing with voters. Stan strolls over. "You know you can mail those," he says with a jovial wink.

"Alex forgot . . ."

"Of course he did."

". . . and I was already coming up."

"What for?"

Eric looks away. "Something I needed to take care of."

Then Paul is upon them. "Can you believe it?" he says, as if he's already won.

"Congratulations!" Eric says, though he didn't vote for him.

Paul hugs him fiercely, eager to share his happiness and, Eric suspects, eager to be photographed in an impromptu moment of impending triumph.

THE RILEYS ARRIVE at First Presbyterian to cast their votes, and Diane takes in the patriotic brightness of the scene. Red door and white chapel against a brazen blue backdrop that feels irresponsibly cheerful, indifferent to their pain.

Chip and Joe brush past a reporter, but she and Will remain outside for another minute, taking solace in the barbed breeze. After the small storm, the trees wear sparkling snow jewelry while the ground is a mottled patchwork of ice and brown. She follows her son's gaze to the graveyard maples, where God has stripped the trees of their chromatic beauty, leaving a message of mortality in their bare branches and the bodies buried at their roots. Inside, that message sharpens when the two of them pass through the sanctuary where, two days earlier, Gerry's memorial took place.

In the basement, a short line has formed in front of a card table where Pastor Reggie checks names off the rolls with a large thermos of coffee at his side. He arrived at five a.m. along with the other volunteers, two from each party, with folders and pouches filled with ballots and security tabs and checklists. So many checklists! All to be verified and signed at the beginning and end of this long, mundane, momentous day, all part of the small, tedious effort of doing democracy.

Reggie stands to hug the family and hands them their ballots.

Shielded behind a booth, Diane stares at her husband's name, feeling injustice on his behalf. The culmination of this intense marathon, which should grant him a moment of proud repose, has been spoiled by a private sadness that makes it all seem so insignificant. But the earnest ritual of voting, and the formality of the ballot, reminds her of the enormity of this endeavor. Chip is part of a 435-piece puzzle, meaning she is, too, along with hundreds of other political spouses like her, all feeling as ambitious, ambivalent, and overwhelmed as she does.

Diane carefully fills in the bubble next to Chip's name. She tries to imbue this act with meaning, to make it a gesture of faith, an apology to Gerry, a vow to her sons. It feels senseless until she slides the ink-dotted sheet into the scanner and experiences the satisfaction of registering a cosmic complaint.

Nearby, Will examines the candidates on the ballot, who seem to symbolize not a person, or even a political entity, but each a different part of himself: the upbringing that shaped him, and the blurry, alluring future that will determine who he becomes. He tries to release all obligation and expectation. He simply looks at the names in front of him. Both are intimately familiar and simultaneously foreign. Which of them best represents him now?

The confusion is fleeting, and the question is moot because he realizes that only one of them has earned his respect: the good, imperfect father who is doing his best and always has. He makes a mark next to Chip Riley.

Joe has no such struggle, at least not right now. The struggle came earlier, through bloody inner brawls during sleepless nights, and through the tortuous months leading to this moment as he realized he was drowning, reaching for his family, and unable to speak his need for them. Will's recent rehab visit only highlighted Will's impending departure—back to college, then maybe to the world of the Duffels. Joe cannot bear to send his father away to Washington as well. It's selfish, he knows, but selfish is what he has become.

Sorry, Dad. I need you here.

He picks up the pen and votes for Paul Banks.

THAT EVENING IN Griffin, under a blackberry sky, the double-branched streetlamps along Granger illuminate the honey locust trees reaching to the river. The Bankses enter the classy mellow yellow of Bramble & Berry to the cheers of staff and supporters, while across the street, the Rileys arrive at the Lucky Buck, loudly lit, crowded, and rowdy.

At each venue, food is served, drinks are poured, and attendees giggle in nervous anticipation as they float in that cathartic limbo between the closing of the polls and the first inklings of outcomes, the collective held breath during which the nation's sails go slack pending news of the wind that will determine its next direction. In their respective locations, exhausted and expectant, the Rileys and the Bankses await the results.

MEANWHILE, A PUFFY figure in a padded jacket with a wool beanie and foggy tortoiseshell glasses pauses on the corner between these two establishments, untouched by the electric tension within.

As he waits for the traffic light, Eric studies the framed gaiety of Paul's party within Bramble & Berry's big glass wall. He should be there, celebrating with his friend, but in light of his vote, it would feel disingenuous. He experiences another prick of guilt and lets it pass.

In the end, he looked at the ballot through Dalton's eyes and agreed that Paul hasn't yet earned the job. He doesn't regret campaigning for Paul, though, which he did out of a genuine sense of fellowship. But he does feel like a traitor, as Dalton warned he would, albeit a thrillingly independent one.

He turns to the Lucky Buck, which he has always been aware of but somehow never really seen. He knows the Rileys are hosting their own party in there, and if he didn't already have a destination, he might have dropped in.

When the light changes, Eric continues down Granger to the chrome curves of Nana's Diner, where Dalton is smoking against the entrance ramp's metal railing. When Dalton sees Eric coming, he flicks his cigarette into the street and heads inside.

Once Eric enters the restaurant, it takes him a moment to identify Dalton's wide back in the farthest booth, facing away from the door.

There are half a dozen other customers sprinkled around, all indifferent to the day's political significance and its looming consequences.

"You hiding from me?" Eric jokes, sliding in opposite Dalton.

"If I was, you found me." Dalton holds Eric's gaze.

To Eric, the day's significance is that he and Dalton are out in Griffin together for the first time, and that Dalton proposed it. Eric looks at the smashed nose and proud brow across from him and suppresses a smile.

"What?" Dalton asks.

Eric opens the large laminated menu. There are so many options.

"Just all this," he says.

ACKNOWLEDGMENTS

THE GREATEST AND MOST unexpected reward in writing this book has been experiencing a solitary project become a collective endeavor through the ideas, insights, and general encouragement of my incredible community of cheerleaders and collaborators.

Primary among them are three vital partners. To my magnificent agents at CAA, Andrianna deLone and Tia Ikemoto: Thank you for your unshakable faith in me and this book, from the beginning and throughout. It has fortified me when my own faith wavered. To editor extraordinaire Jade Hui: I couldn't have asked for a more astute reader, a more savvy producer, or a more spirited champion. It was a true honor and joy to work with you, and I'm forever grateful.

My deep appreciation to Peter Borland and Hannah Frankel for embracing me and this book and carrying us across the finish line. And I'm in awe of the passion, professionalism, and commitment of the entire Atria team at Simon & Schuster in matters of copyediting, design, marketing, and everything in between. Special thanks to Debbie Norflus and Dayna Johnson for such enthusiastic promotion, as well as Joseph Papa for additional guidance and support.

The journey to this point began over a decade ago when the Dorot Foundation, and the inspiring guidance of Neil Harris, gave me the time, freedom, and permission to explore writing, which led me to the Shaindy Rudoff Creative Writing Program at Bar-Ilan University. All my professors and fellow students there shaped and sharpened me, with special thanks to Evan Fallenberg, for his mentorship and ongoing support, and to Katie Green, for her shrewd critiques, warmth, and continued friendship.

The bridge between that education and this book is Nicola Orlando, who envisioned a writerly future for me before I could see it for myself and whose stamp of approval on the first, chaotic draft of what became *Town & Country* is a big reason why I even attempted a second one.

After the half-dozen drafts that followed, a roster of trusted friends from various eras of my life graciously agreed to read the evolving manuscript and each made important contributions. Some have already been mentioned, and additional thanks go to Nikki Rubin, Riley Pearce and Lucas Stratton, Daniel K. Isaac, and Chris Rovzar and Cub Barrett.

Ed Kuester and Miguel Ferreyra de Bone were also valued early readers and are treasured neighbors (along with Kris and Ian!) in our beloved Pinkbelt. And to my entire Hudson Valley crew: Thank you for the rich and cherished camaraderie that inspired this story.

To all friends and family who at any point inquired about my progress, offered reassuring words, read the manuscript, shared in the many frustrations, and celebrated the small triumphs: Your interest, enthusiasm, and optimism were integral ingredients in the final product. Special thanks to Erik Piepenburg and Brian Bannon for the regular check-ins, and to Grant Ginder and Charles Tolbert for the professional wisdom and advice.

For crucial knowledge and priceless perspectives on rural life, politics, and socioeconomic dynamics, I'm indebted to Rachel and Steffen Schneider of the Institute for Mindful Agriculture, Emily Bronson of the Berkshire Taconic Community Foundation, and former US Representative Chris Gibson.

My Paragraph Writing Group helped me dissect and troubleshoot many chapters-in-progress over several years. Many thanks to the consistent participants during that time: Maureen Traverse, K.A. Keener, Pamela Holcomb, Deanna Richards, Donasia Sykes, and an extra shoutout to Vanessa Walters for help navigating the publishing puzzle.

I'm still pinching myself to have earned the early endorsement of two literary heroes, Colum McCann and Andrew Sean Greer, who I now also hold up as epitomes of generosity.

My sense of community was formed early through deep relationships with my nearby, close-knit, fun-loving relatives. To the Rotenbergs, the Goldsteins, the Gross-Schaefers, and the Alperts: You have all made an indelible impact on my life, and thus this book. Your reliable presence then and now brings me such joy, gratification, and comfort.

It's been such a blessing to acquire another loving clan in the Mack family. To John and Christy, John C. and Lucia, and Jenna (also a key early reader), as well as Ria Mills: Thank you for your immediate and complete embrace, your enduring support of this undertaking, and for all the good times along the way.

To the world's best brothers, Robbie and Alan, whose teasing keeps me humble, whose respect I've always strived to deserve, and whose shenanigans always make me eager for the next visit home: You guys mean the world to me. And thank you for bringing your amazing spouses, Cal and Kelsey—as well as your beautiful children, Ava, Rhys, and Roman—into our lives.

Stephen Mack—my husband, best friend, first editor, ace brainstormer, fiercest advocate, most trusted advisor, brilliant photographer, and endless source of strength, calm, and laughter. This book is yours as much as it's mine, which I say with immense pride and gratitude. I've loved sharing this adventure with you, and I love sharing this life with you.

My thanks begin and end with Jim and Denise Schaefer, the greatest parents one could ever hope for, the models of integrity and decency that fuel this story. You made clear from the start that all roads through life were available and valid, and your unconditional love gave me the courage and confidence to follow some very unlikely and uncertain roads. Thank you for your trust and belief—it's what allowed me to believe in myself. Somehow, all those roads converged to produce this book, which is my gift of appreciation to you.

BOOK CLUB FAVORITES

READER'S GUIDE

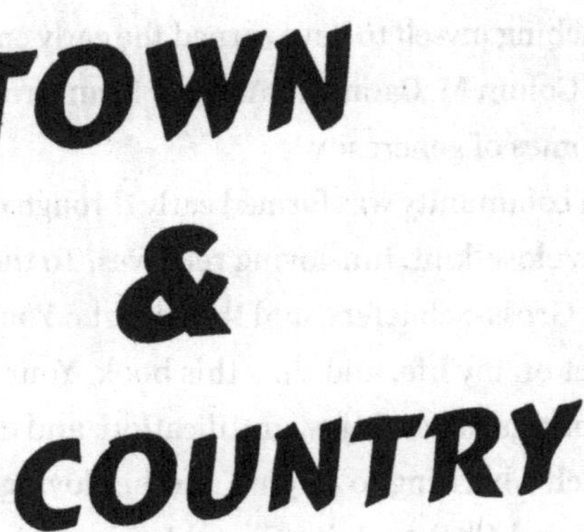

READING GROUP GUIDE

This reading group guide for Town & Country *by Brian Schaefer includes discussion questions intended to help your reading group find new and interesting topics for consideration. We hope that they will enrich your conversation and increase your enjoyment of the book.*

TOPICS & QUESTIONS FOR DISCUSSION

CLASS DIVIDE IN GRIFFIN

From the Memorial Day parade at the beginning of the novel, it's clear that Griffin has become a town with a strong economic divide between locals and affluent second-home owners, or "Duffels." How does this divide illustrate the obstacles faced by its inhabitants and inform the story's central tensions? What towns, cities, or regions near you does this fictional place remind you of?

SHARED DISILLUSIONMENT

Seemingly all the characters in *Town & Country* grapple with dissatisfaction or disconnection from their lives in some way. For example: Will's feelings of alienation after returning home after a year away at college, and lonely Leon's struggle to start fresh in this town where he knows no one after the end of his marriage. How does this through line reflect the needs and challenges of finding community, regardless of where one lives?

MARITAL STRAIN AND BREAKDOWN

As the congressional race heats up, Diane and Chip's marriage is strained by political ambitions and their shifting roles within their own family. Simultaneously, the pressure of the campaign takes its toll on Stan and Paul's marriage. What most intrigued you about the changing dynamics of these relationships, and did you find them reflective of broader societal issues?

THE ROLE OF POLITICS

Chip is far from perfect as a father, a friend, a congressional candidate, and more. Yet, in certain ways, he emerges as the moral center of the book. How did you weigh his conflicting motivations against one another, and what did you make of the novel's portrayal of the intersection of personal ambition and public service? What role does public service play in your life?

CHARACTER MOTIVATIONS AND GROWTH

Diane's internal struggle between her faith, changing familial dynamics, and desire for personal gain is a central theme in *Town & Country*, as is Eric Larimer's growing discomfort and questioning of his lifestyle and the priorities of his and his husband Alex's social circle. How did you initially judge their respective values, and did your perception of these characters change as the story unfolded?

IDENTITY AND BELONGING

As Will explores his identity and struggles with his sense of loyalty, which fuels much of the rising action of the novel, the election forces him to pick a side. What does his struggle reveal about the competing influences that shape a person? Must they always be in conflict? What are some opposing forces in your own life?

COMMUNITY VERSUS INDIVIDUALISM

The narrative explores tension between communal values and personal desires, a frequent topic in discussions of American ideals and individualism. How do the various characters balance those opposing forces, and how does that balance express itself differently for Duffels and for full-time residents of Griffin?

UNEXPECTED EVOLUTIONS

At the beginning of the book, characters seem almost stereotypically defined by where they primarily reside: Duffels live lavishly with little concern for their rural neighbors, while townsfolk resist change and outsiders. How did these perceptions morph as the story unfolded? Which character or characters surprised or moved you most in their journey?

THE ENDING

The author leaves the ending of the novel up in the air. Did you find the ambiguity satisfying or disappointing? Who do you think wins the congressional race, and is that different from who you wanted to win? What does the ending reveal about the nuances of local politics compared to national politics?

BONUS TOPIC

Imagine Griffin a decade from now. How do you think the town will continue to evolve? Which characters do you think will remain residents, and which will find homes elsewhere? What do you hope for Griffin and its inhabitants?